"A decadently delightful love story that refuses the form." —*Publishers Weekly*

"An unforgettable love story."

—*Booklist* (starred review)

"Deliciously romantic and poetic." —*Fresh Fiction*

THE GOOD, THE BAD, AND THE DUKE

"Sparkling . . . a richly engaging romance with a heroine we should all resolve to be more like."
—*Entertainment Weekly*

"Utterly delightful in every possible way." —*Bookriot*

"Effervesces with lighthearted romance . . . sweet and sultry in equal measures." —*Publishers Weekly*

"[An] emotionally rich, exquisitely wrought tale that superbly celebrates the redemptive power of love."
—*Booklist*

THE LUCK OF THE BRIDE

"Sparkling dialogue, a dash of deliciously tart humor, and just enough soul-searing sensuality to keep romance fans sighing happily in satisfaction." —*Booklist*

"Brimming with family, hope, and tender sensuality, this shrewdly plotted, gently paced romance is especially satisfying." —*Library Journal*

"A lovely, sweet, and touching love story."
—*RT Book Reviews*

THE BRIDE WHO GOT LUCKY

"Rising star MacGregor once again demonstrates her remarkable gift for effortlessly elegant writing, richly nuanced characterization, and lushly sensual love scenes."
—*Booklist* (starred review)

"A heady mix of action, wit, and sexual tension. Readers will eagerly turn the pages to see how this intense story concludes." —*Publishers Weekly*

"Deliciously provocative in historical detail . . . there is everything in this novel and more. *The Bride Who Got Lucky* is absolutely brilliant!"
—*Romance Junkies* (5 stars)

THE BAD LUCK BRIDE

"With its beautifully defined, exceptionally appealing protagonists, intriguing secondary characters, and graceful writing deftly leavened with wry wit, this classic romantic story line becomes something marvelously fresh and new, thus making MacGregor's stellar debut a must-read for any fan of Regency historicals."
—*Booklist* (starred review)

"An impressive debut . . . plenty of sizzle."
—*Kirkus Reviews*

"This charming tale features a refreshing array of happy families, solid relationships . . . The book's promise of a delicious story is well realized, building anticipation for future installments." —*Publishers Weekly*

"Well-paced, powerfully plotted debut where love and revenge vie for center stage. Here is a romance that reminds readers that love is complicated, healing, and captivating. MacGregor's characters are carefully drawn, their emotions realistic and their passions palpable. Watch for MacGregor to make her mark on the genre."

—*RT Book Reviews*

"Delightful! Janna MacGregor bewitched me with her captivating characters and a romance that sizzles off the page. I'm already a huge fan!"

—*New York Times* bestselling author Eloisa James

WILD, WILD RAKE

JANNA MACGREGOR

St. Martin's Paperbacks

This is a work of fiction. All of the characters, organizations, and events portrayed in this novel are either products of the author's imagination or are used fictitiously.

WILD, WILD RAKE.

Copyright © 2020 by Janna MacGregor.

Published in the United States by St. Martin's Paperbacks, an imprint of St. Martin's Publishing Group.

All rights reserved.

For information, address St. Martin's Publishing Group, 120 Broadway, New York, NY 10271.

www.stmartins.com

ISBN: 978-1-250-29601-6

Our books may be purchased in bulk for promotional, educational, or business use. Please contact your local bookseller or the Macmillan Corporate and Premium Sales Department at 1-800-221-7945, ext. 5442, or by email at MacmillanSpecialMarkets@macmillan.com.

Printed in the United States of America

St. Martin's Paperbacks edition / February 2020

10 9 8 7 6 5 4 3 2 1

For those who ever felt they didn't fit in or
weren't welcomed
but forged ahead and created their own place
in the world

Acknowledgments

M y dear reader, you make this the best job in the world. You deserve a bow.

Alexandra Sehulster, an editor extraordinaire, I'm fortunate to be able to work with you. Thank you for helping me craft these characters into such special and loving couples. Devin wouldn't be nearly as naughty without you.

Corinne DeMaagd, you were there from the very beginning, and with infinite patience taught me so much. Holly Ingraham, thank you for your pivotal role in making my dream come true. Marissa Sangiacomo, Meghan Harrington, Mara Delgado Sanchez, and everyone at St. Martin's Press, you are spectacular at making certain each Cavensham Heiress made a proper debut into the world.

Kim Rozzell List, you are incomparable in all you do and a pure genius. When you said you'd help me that first day, you turned *The Bad Luck Bride* into the luckiest bride. I can never say thank you enough!

Finally, I couldn't write a word without the love, laughs, and encouragement I receive from Greg, the author of my romantic life.

Do not allow a sorceress to live.

Exodus 22:18

Yet like a phoenix, she'll rise from the ashes.

Source unknown

Prologue

London, autumn 1805
Harold's Emporium and Haberdashery—a boutique
that caters to exquisite tastes and the highest caliber
of clientele

S end the bill to my husband."
    If the Marquess of Warwyk fell dead of an apoplexy
fit when he received the twenty-pound bill of sale, then
the Marchioness of Warwyk, *his dutiful wife*, would
consider it money well spent.

The fine fabric of the pristine christening gown trick-
led around Avalon's fingers like silken water. Instinctively, she pressed a hand against her still-flat stomach.
Only the finest garment in all of England would suit the
future Marquess of Warwyk when he made his official
appearance in five months.

Whether her baby was a boy or girl made little difference to Avalon, even if her husband, Richard Pearce,
the Marquess of Warwyk, had drunkenly decreed last
night that she'd better perform her duty and provide an
heir. When he'd murmured with an annoying hiccup
that bedding her was like holding a block of ice, she'd
walked out of the room without a glance.

Perhaps she needed to pray harder for a son. An heir
would keep the filthy rotter out of her bed forever.

"My lady, the lace netting over the gown comes directly from the Highlands. A crofter's daughter creates it only for me. No other shop could offer the workmanship that you see on this exquisite gown." The shopkeeper carefully straightened the lace train that had been dyed to match the white silk. "Many have tried to discover her location, but they'll never find her. She only sells her lace to me."

"It's beautiful." Avalon nodded. Though twenty pounds represented an outrageous amount for a tiny garment that would only be worn once, she considered it an investment. Hopefully, future generations of Warwyks would wear it and remember her kindly when they brought the gown out of storage when their own children were christened.

She couldn't wish for anything more. Her husband had made it his life's work to berate her to anyone who would listen. But a woman had to retaliate her horrid treatment in creative ways. Outrageous bills for clothing fit Avalon's needs quite nicely.

The bell over the shop door rang, and Mr. Harold, the shopkeeper, looked up to greet his newest customer. His face suddenly matched the stark white of the christening gown. Avalon glanced in the newcomer's direction.

A beautiful woman with blond hair entered the store by herself. Spots of rain darkened the forest-green velvet of her spencer. Her cheeks bloomed with a pink blush, no doubt from the exertion of a brisk walk. By the shape of her clothing, she appeared to be late in her pregnancy.

"If you'll wait outside, I'll finish with Lady Warwyk"—Mr. Harold scrunched his nose and swept his hand in the air as if brushing away something offensive—"then assist you."

The woman nodded.

Before she could exit, Avalon held up her hand.

"Please don't leave on my account. It's raining buckets outside." She turned her attention to the shopkeeper. "Would you have it delivered later today?"

"Of course, my lady," he said. He glanced quickly at the woman and shook his head. He pasted a smile on his face and addressed Avalon, "Since it's raining a little harder now, may I escort you to my sitting room in the back? I have a lovely tea you could enjoy until your footman arrives with an umbrella."

"That's very kind, but I don't mind waiting here. Go ahead and help your other customer."

Mr. Harold nodded his head, then ducked behind a curtain into another room.

The woman took a step forward, then stopped as if debating whether to approach or not. Her blue eyes wary. Avalon smiled in encouragement, and the woman reluctantly closed the distance between them.

"Mr. Harold is renowned for his christening gowns," Avalon said. "Are you looking for one?"

Slowly, as if afraid Avalon would bite, she crept closer and shook her head. "No, my lady. I'm picking up a peignoir for my lying-in. My . . . the baby's father had it made for me." When she reached Avalon's side, she studied the christening gown on the counter. "It's lovely." She slowly released a breath, then turned her attention to Avalon. "Is it for you?"

Before she could answer, the shopkeeper returned with the most exquisite negligé Avalon had ever laid eyes on. The iridescent pale coral silk shimmered in the light. The gown and light robe were so sheer that you could practically see through the material, guaranteeing that every inch of the woman's body would be displayed for her husband's delight.

Suddenly Avalon's heartbeat hitched. What must it be like to have a husband who valued you so much that he'd spend a fortune on nightclothes? The ensemble before her would make any woman feel beautiful—even after giving birth. The lucky woman had found a kind and caring husband.

Avalon snuffed the brief bout of envy.

Fate, in the form of her parents, had decreed that Avalon's only purpose in life was to secure a marriage that would be beneficial to all the parties involved—except Avalon. She'd wanted to marry her third cousin, Lord William Cavensham, but her parents had forbidden the match. When she'd tried to sway their thinking, her parents had commanded in unison that "a bargain had been struck." Then her father had further instructed that if she didn't marry the man they'd chosen for her, she could find someplace else to reside. Her mother had gone so far as to threaten she'd keep Avalon's young sister from socializing with her.

At the words, Avalon had seen her dreams for a happy marriage disappear like wisps of smoke. But now that she was pregnant, life offered her another chance for love, and she wouldn't waste it. Her baby would receive all her devotion, attention, and care. She was finished with trying to win her husband's affections.

Avalon leaned close to the stranger so they wouldn't be overheard. "The christening gown is for me. I'm expecting, too." She lowered her voice. "Your husband must care for you deeply. That peignoir is extraordinary."

With a slight nod, the charming woman blushed as Mr. Harold wrapped the exquisite garments carefully in paper. When he handed it to her, he nodded curtly as if dismissing her. Avalon frowned at the man's gruff manner. No matter where the woman came from or who she was married to, she didn't deserve the censure apparent in the man's manner.

Summoning the resolve to counter the man's rudeness, Avalon boldly asked, "May I offer you a ride so you're not drenched from this downpour? It wouldn't be good for you or the baby if you became chilled."

The woman smiled, and her eyes brightened. "I thank you for your concern and gracious offer, but I have a carriage coming."

The door opened again, and a Warwyk footman entered with the requisite umbrella. He stopped in his path as his gaze darted between the other woman and Avalon.

"I'm ready, John," Avalon said. For an irrational moment, she wanted to hug the woman before her. Since she'd married the Warwyk ogre, she had few friends. "Good luck to you and your baby."

"And to you, my lady," the woman answered. "You're very kind."

Avalon nodded without taking her leave of the shopkeeper. She exited the establishment with the footman holding the umbrella over her head. A coach-and-four slowly drew behind her own smaller carriage. Streaks of rain magnified the luster of the black lacquer paint on the luxurious coach. The mystery woman's husband must be rich.

As Avalon's carriage lumbered carefully through the rain, a pang of regret hit her. She'd failed to ask for the woman's name and if she might call upon her. She nestled deeper into the velvet squab, then leaned her head back against the cushion. The pleated red satin roof didn't hold her attention as her thoughts drifted back to the woman. Perhaps they'd become friends, and Avalon would have someone intimate, a friend she could confide all her worries and concerns to.

There was only one way to rectify the situation. She'd

send a note to the shopkeeper asking for the woman's name.

Four months later
London—Warwyk House

Avalon took another sip of the tea and focused on the lovely gold and white furnishings in the salon. Not seeing the room during the months she'd lived outside of London at Warwyk Hall did little to change her opinion of the ostentatious decorations. Elegant but crass at the same time, it was Avalon's least favorite room in her husband's London home, Warwyk House. She'd never call it her home. Not after she'd discovered that her husband had lived with his mistress here before he and Avalon had married.

Tired of being sequestered at her husband's ancestral home at his command for months on end, Avalon had traveled to the city today. She wanted to be closer to her little sister who lived in town with their parents. At the age of seven, Sophia was growing up way too fast, and Avalon wanted to be there for her. So Avalon waited for her husband to arrive so they could at least come to an understanding. Avalon had written to Richard several times during her sojourn to Warwyk Hall without a response or a resulting visit even though she was a mere thirty minutes by coach northwest of London.

But here she sat—alone and waiting to make her plea.

Though the servants hadn't said anything directly when she'd arrived, it was clear Richard hadn't come home last night. No doubt he'd spent the night with his longtime mistress, the Covent Garden Rose. It made little difference at this point. Avalon had a sham marriage, and nothing would change it.

The silence in the salon grew deafening. Deciding to retire to her room until Richard arrived, Avalon pushed herself to her feet. Two things happened at once. Avalon's baby kicked with such force against her ribs that she gasped in pain, and the mystery woman from Mr. Harold's shop walked into the salon.

The mystery woman stopped abruptly, then slowly blinked her eyes—twice.

Avalon matched her blink for blink. The absolute wonder that she'd conjured the woman from thin air broke something light and free within her chest.

"Lady Warwyk?" the woman asked politely. "Is Lord Warwyk expecting you?"

The lightness in her chest sunk immediately. How did the woman know her husband? Why was she here?

They stared at each other again.

"You had your baby," Avalon murmured. The slim woman before had been beautiful when she was pregnant, but now she was radiant.

Suddenly, several giggling young women who appeared just shy of twenty entered the salon followed by her husband, holding a baby.

With not a single brown hair out of place and his clothes immaculate, Warwyk looked like the devil himself had come calling. At his entrance, he examined her from the top of her head to the tips of her toes. "What are you doing here? I didn't summon you."

Immediately, her newfound spirit dampened as she waited for his repugnant comments and jeers to spill her way.

"How opportune that you're here." Richard's matter-of-fact voice echoed around the room.

Every hair on Avalon's arms stood as if ready to run from the blistering diatribe that would soon erupt from her husband.

"I'd like to introduce you to the love of my life, Miss Mary Bolen, the woman I *wanted to marry* before your parents forced me to choose another." Richard turned his gaze to Mary and the baby he was holding. "This is our baby, Richard Bolen, the son who should be my heir," her husband drawled as he cradled the infant close to his body as if shielding it from Avalon. He hugged Mary tightly with his other arm, then loudly whispered, "At least one good thing resulted from the marriage."

In exchange for marrying her, her father had given Richard the property he'd wagered and lost at a hunting party. Avalon knew the litany by heart. She should say the words and rob her husband of his endless delight at belittling her.

"At least I received Bumble Green for her." He tugged Mary closer as he glanced Avalon's way but continued to discuss her as if she weren't even there. "I dare say she rumbles along like an elephant. Not at all elegant like you, my love."

The sarcasm in his voice rolled in waves around the room. Avalon's breath hitched, and only when the baby kicked again did she gasp for air. It wasn't her husband's mockery that made her want to escape and hide.

It was Mary, her husband's mistress—the Covent Garden Rose, the very person Avalon thought might be a friend—who stood before her, clearly embarrassed, if her red cheeks were any indication.

"My lord, that's enough," Mary chided in a honeyed voice.

It took every ounce of strength Avalon possessed not to fall to her knees. Suddenly, a high-pitched peal of laughter rang around the room. She'd always known that fate could be unkind. But cruel? It had delivered Mary straight to Avalon, not as a friend, but as her husband's paramour. The infernal noise continued until Avalon realized it was *her own* maniacal laughter filling the salon while all of her hopes for a true friend melted into a pool of bloody mockery.

Clearly uneasy, Richard and his guests stared at her. He handed the baby to one of the young women.

When her laughter finally quieted, Avalon rested her hand on her stomach in a show that she claimed the baby for herself. "Warwyk, you're too late," Avalon taunted. "*Your* Mary and I are old acquaintances." She turned to Mary and with her most pleasant voice, said, "You knew who I was at Mr. Harold's. I wish you would have introduced yourself. It would have made all of our lives so much easier." Avalon glanced at the others in the room. "Who are these distinguished guests, I wonder?"

For a long moment, no one spoke. Finally, Mary broke the silence. "They're my girls, my lady. They work for me at the White Dove."

Richard pulled her tighter against him. "Avalon, Mary is moving in."

"Richard," Mary said firmly. "That's not decided."

Ignoring Mary, Avalon's husband sharpened his gaze. "She'll be your lady's maid."

"*Richard*," Mary warned.

"You're right, as usual." He chuckled. "Avalon, Mary doesn't want to be your lady's maid so you should leave immediately for Warwyk Hall."

Suddenly, the out-of-sync cogs of thought realigned in Avalon's mind. The bastard had hurled the ultimate insult at her. The White Dove was a popular pub within the financial district, but everyone knew it was a bawdy house with expensive prostitutes who served only the wealthiest men as they were the only ones who could afford the "birds of love."

She lowered her voice. "You brought a madam and her whores into my home? Now you want me to leave?"

"Now see here." Richard's icy voice grew razor sharp as he came to stand before her. "This is my home, and I say who is welcome and who lives here. My Mary is a brilliant woman who runs a well-respected business. Only the finest gentlemen are allowed access—"

"Finest gentlemen?'" she challenged. "Why are you allowed access then?"

"You black-hearted bitch," he seethed. Suddenly, he raised his hand as if to strike her.

"Do not touch me." Avalon closed her eyes as she wrapped her hands around her middle to protect the baby. Having never been physically hit by another, it was the only thing she could think of to do. A rush of air blew past, and she braced for the blow.

"*Stop it.*" Mary's voice ricocheted around the room.

When Avalon opened her eyes, Mary stood between her and Richard. He slowly lowered his hand with a look of contriteness at his lover's chastisement.

"She's your wife. Carrying your baby, your possible heir. She deserves respect," Mary said decisively, reminding the beast he should act civilized. She turned to Avalon. "Are you all right?"

Stunned, she blinked at Mary's question. Before she could recover and answer, two men, tall, with hair as black as ravens, entered the room.

Avalon put her hand on the nearest chair to steady herself. It was just her luck that Richard's best friend, Gavin Farris, the Earl of Larkton, and his younger brother, Mr. Devan Farris, had joined their macabre play. Larkton typically ignored her, but Devan Farris was a true menace.

He was one of Lord William Cavensham's best friends, and Devan hated her for jilting Lord William.

The two men's eyes grew wide as they surveyed the scene before them. The tension grew unpalatable between all of them as no one spoke a word.

Finally, Richard lifted one arrogant brow. "Welcome, gentlemen. You're just in time to see me throw out Lady . . . what do you call her?" His gaze landed on Devan Farris.

"Don't, Warwyk," Devan said. He tilted his head as if baffled, before his eyes widened in understanding. He turned to his brother. "You brought me here for these women?"

Devan's brother didn't answer.

"Aha, I remember. You call her Lady Warlock," Richard cawed like a crow. "*Warlock* means a creature who's hostile toward men. A perfect description, Farris. She is a witch with a cold personality to match."

Everyone's gaze rested on hers.

"Leave now," Richard growled.

Heat hotter than Satan's hell scalded Avalon's cheeks. For a moment, she grew faint and she locked her fingers around the chair, determined not to fall. She took a deep breath, then slowly released it, summoning every piece of pride she could muster while her heart lay shattered. She would not let them see how much Warwyk had hurt her.

Without another word, she quit the room. Once she was outside, she collapsed against the hallway wall while her mind grappled with what had happened. Footsteps grew louder.

"Lady Warwyk?" Devan Farris called.

The gentle lilt in his voice irritated her. "Leave me be," she snapped.

Ignoring her command, he took a step closer and

held out his hand. "May I help you or escort you somewhere?"

The regret in his warm green eyes made her cringe
inside. How embarrassing to be seen reeling from
Warwyk's disdain. He might think she cared.

"I think you've helped me enough for one day." Avalon pushed away from the wall, then headed toward the
family quarters. Two steps later, she stopped. With as
much grace as she could muster, Avalon turned slowly
so she wouldn't lose her balance. She regarded him as
if he were a rotten piece of cabbage. "Aren't you supposed to be celibate while you're in seminary school?
What *exactly* do they teach you at Oxford besides cruel
name-calling?"

Without waiting for his reply, she continued on her
way. She could feel his gaze on her back. In response,
she lifted her head a little higher. Under no circumstances would she show Devan Farris or the others any
weakness.

When she reached the marchioness apartments,
she directed her loyal lady's maid, Henrietta Calvert,
to pack all her belongings for a return trip to Warwyk
Hall, the ancestral seat. Avalon decided then and there
to move into her own town house as soon as her baby
was born, one that she would demand that her husband
gift her in celebration of the baby's birth.

Along with the town house, Richard would also
shower her with endless new gowns, accompaniments,
furs, and expensive parures of rubies and sapphires. He
might as well add a set of emeralds to the bunch. They'd
match Avalon's green eyes. Plus, her husband would
commission a fine black lacquer coach and purchase
four white horses to pull it—much like he'd done for
Mary Bolen.

And her husband would also order the most extravagant negligées for Avalon from Mr. Harold.

Every woman in town would be envious of Avalon's newfound good fortune. She'd keep the gifts as insurance. She'd never be financially or, more importantly, emotionally vulnerable or susceptible to her husband's cruelty or her parents' outlandish demands again.

And Richard would pay all of that and more. For there was one thing of value that tied Avalon to Warwyk. It was something that Richard desperately wanted—an heir.

He'd better pray for a boy as hard as Avalon would, for there was one thing for certain in their marriage.

He'd never touch her again.

A friend loveth for all times, and a brother is born for adversity.

King Solomon

Chapter One

October, ten years later
The London home of the Earl of Larkton

Don't dawdle, Devan." The Earl of Larkton stood without ceremony and waved his youngest brother inside his massive study. "You're late, and we've matters to discuss. There's no sense in both of us having the entire day ruined. In order to salvage what we can of the remaining hours of daylight, I suggest you enter so we can finish this as quickly as possible."

"Always the hospitable host. You haven't lost your touch at charming your fellow man, *Larrrkton*." Devan delivered his most insincere smile, then sauntered into the room as if it were his study and not his eldest brother's domain.

"Will you quit calling me that?" his brother huffed. "When you mock me, you sound like a chirring grasshopper."

"What, *Larrrkton*? Perhaps you'd prefer 'Lord *Larrrkton*,' or perhaps 'my Lord *Larrrkton*'?"

"God save me," Larkton mumbled under his breath.

"Earl of *Larrrkton*, then."

"You are the bloodiest aggravating bastard of a brother a man could have."

Devan counted the seconds. One. Two. Three.

"After all I've done for you, this is how you treat me."

It was like clockwork. Three seconds after the usual "*bloodiest* aggravating bastard of a brother" comment, the dull but mandatory "how you treat me" always followed.

London at large could set their clocks and time pieces to Devan's brother's exclamations.

Mr. Devan Farris, the most dutiful vicar in the whole of London if he did say so himself—wait—in all of Great Britain—made himself at home, then reclined in the well-worn leather chair in front of the desk belonging to his brother, Gavin Farris, the Earl of Larkton.

"This is for you," Gavin said as he handed a leaded crystal glass to Devan.

He took a sip of the excellent brandy, then sighed his contentment. "Where are the others?"

"Your brothers, Hearne and Niall, have taken Elizabeth out shopping." Larkton eased himself into his desk chair and surveyed Devan from head to foot. "Your sister wanted you to take her. She says she enjoys your company when you escort her. Apparently, she likes your tastes in gowns."

"High praise from Elizabeth," Devan acknowledged. "I have a much better sense of fashion than anyone else in the family." Too bad that all his talent was wasted since he was a member of the clergy, and they were expected to wear black.

"Spare me," his brother muttered. "I've news for you."

Devan took another sip, knowing that Larkton waited for him to show a least a hint of interest, but Devan wouldn't give him the satisfaction of knowing that his curiosity was piqued.

Larkton drummed his fingers on the desk, then picked up his brandy and downed the rest of it. His face twisted into a scowl that no doubt resulted from the liquid burning his throat. "I've a new assignment for you."

"New assignment?" That made Devan sit up and take notice. "Why?"

Larkton opened up the top desk drawer, then threw a copy of *The Midnight Cryer* to the edge of his desk. "Read it."

Expecting to find a scathing article about himself seducing a milkmaid in the wilds of Northumberland where he was currently assigned to a parish, Devan scanned the rest of the articles, until one small tidbit caught his eye.

LADY CANDLEWICK IS INCREASING HER FLOCK OF LITTLE LOST DOVES WHO'VE DECIDED TO FLY THE COOP.

Devan wanted to roll his eyes at the name of Candlewick. Everyone within London who was anyone called Lady Avalon Warwyk *Lady Warlock* behind her back. He should know. He was the one who'd penned the name. At first, he'd called her that when she'd cruelly jilted his best friend, Will Cavensham. But it had turned into a name of honor after that day when he'd seen her face the humiliation of her husband's ridicule. Avalon Warwyk had shown a strength of character the likes he'd never seen before.

"Since there isn't a single scintillating article describing my exploits with the beauties of Northumberland, I wonder why you want me to read this one?" Devan released a feigned sigh of boredom, then took another sip of the brandy.

With nostrils flared, Gavin lifted a single black eyebrow. Such a look had caused numerous ladies to swoon around him. Tall, but not as athletic as Devan, Larkton could intimidate many a man with just such a look. However, Devan held an inch or two height advantage, which allowed him to look down at the earl. When they were younger, Devan could always best his oldest brother in a game of fisticuffs. He had little doubt he could do the same now.

Unfortunately, Larkton hadn't given him reason yet to challenge him.

More's the pity.

Thankfully, the afternoon was still young, and knowing his brother the way he did, Devan was certain—at the very least—an exchange of harsh words between them would occur within the hour. Though they cared deeply for one another as brothers, there was always a hint of Gavin's self-assured arrogance that resulted from his status as first born swirling around them.

"Did you see the story about Lady Avalon Warwyk?" he asked.

"Lady Warlock, you mean?"

Devan's brother nodded. "Lady Warlock—Warwyk I mean, recently settled two more prostitutes into her home village of Thistledown. I want to know why and where she's getting the money."

"Why do you care?" Devan challenged.

"You know why I damn well care."

The sound that emerged from Gavin's chest resembled a growl, like a dog ready to attack. Devan exhaled silently. That was the sign that he'd pushed Larkton too far too fast. Though his brother was only five years older than Devan's thirty-one years, Gavin became more like an old man every day. He angered more easily than ever before. Devan would have to talk to his brothers and sister. Hopefully, the pressure of restoring the earldom to profit wasn't taking too much of a toll on him.

"I'm the Marquess of Warwyk's guardian, and the

conservator of his estate. It's my responsibility to ensure that the boy grows up ready to take over the marquisate. If there's anything to take over and she isn't spending it all on rehabilitating prostitutes." Gavin leaned back in his chair and stared at the ceiling for a moment, clearly lost in his thoughts. Eventually, he returned his attention to Devan. "I should have never agreed to serve as guardian and conservator when Richard asked me. This is all too much work, but that's why you're here. I need your help."

Devan still leaned casually against the back of his chair, but his senses grew acute, waiting for his oldest brother to explain. Gavin never asked for anyone's help, particularly Devan's. In his position as a vicar, he knew enough to wait. People seeking help from a clergyman would usually spill their guts within fifteen minutes. It'd taken Gavin twenty, as he was normally tight-lipped about private matters.

"Richard was nothing but an arse, but an entertaining one. He kept a bevy of beautiful women surrounding him at all times. With such easy influence and wealth, I'm afraid to admit, he swayed me as a young man." He rested his elbows on the desk.

Devan didn't answer but he could empathize. When he'd been at university, he'd become friends with young peers who hadn't inherited their titles yet, but they were as rich as King Crocsus. While he, the fourth son of the Earl of Larkton, had no wealth to call his own.

But there was one huge difference.

His friends were good people. They never excluded him from their revelries and didn't seem to mind that he was practically penniless. But more importantly, if he needed anything from any of them, they'd have helped him with no questions asked.

And they would never treat their wives the way the Marquess of Warwyk had treated his.

Gavin hadn't been so discerning in his choice of friends, it appeared.

"Be that as it may, I've accepted the responsibility," Gavin admitted.

"What can I do to help?"

Devan's offer was met with a look of surprise from his older brother. "That was much easier than I care to admit."

"I haven't agreed to anything," Devan answered.

"You will, because of the money I'm going to offer you," Gavin said.

"You have my undivided attention."

The look on his brother's face appeared comical rather than his typical sardonic visage. Devan just smiled serenely, then waited for his brother to continue.

"I need you to find out where she's getting her money for the buildings she's investing in. Rumor has it that she's opening a home for former prostitutes alongside a nursery or foundling home of some type. If she's somehow circumventing the Warwyk solicitors and dipping into the cash reserves, I want to know immediately."

"Come now, Gavin. That's preposterous. The estate bookkeepers would know when and if money was being spent."

"Only if she doesn't have them on her private payroll," Gavin said. "You're familiar with her reputation. Money runs through her fingers like water. Richard was forever complaining about her spending habits." He ran a hand down his face. "Thousands of pounds she spent. I have to make certain she's not doing the same thing again." He straightened, then stared at Devan. "Why prostitutes? You'd think she'd hate them after Richard's liaison with Mary Bolen."

"Who knows? She's always struck me as a woman with a keen sense of convictions. She doesn't make any decision lightly, from what I've witnessed." Over the years, Devan had watched her at events. A cool attitude and a subdued, strong bearing were her hallmarks. "She's not the type to blame Mary Bolen for her husband's vile behavior." Devan took another sip of brandy, then looked around the room.

His brother hadn't changed a single thing in the room during the last twenty years. It was almost like a memorial to their father, who'd been a loving parent and a dutiful husband to their late mother. They'd been deeply in love and Devan had found himself blessed to be a part of such a family, even though his oldest brother had the uncanny ability to rile a *turnip* with his meddling and arrogant attitude.

"Perhaps it's Lady Warlock's chosen charity, one she feels strongly about," Devan added.

It was unfathomable that he was defending her. Particularly after she'd jilted one of his best friends, Will Cavensham, to marry Richard Warwyk. But Devan had enough life experience to know that not everything was as it seemed in such circumstances. He had little doubt that William was now ecstatic that Avalon had jilted him all those years ago to marry the wealthy Richard Warwyk. It had left Will free to marry the love of his life, Lady Theodora Fanruig, a Scottish countess in her own right.

"Try to see what you can find out for me?" Gavin asked. "That's your parish assignment. You're the new vicar in Thistledown. You'll fill the post at the start of the new year."

Devan stood abruptly. "I don't want another assignment. I'm perfectly happy with my little parish in Northumberland. I consider it my home. You can't just move me around like a chess piece on a board."

"If you're not satisfied with my help, then why didn't you marry one of the heiresses I've introduced you to?"

Gavin asked. "You could be living a life of luxury in town instead of the wilds of Northumberland."

Why was he surprised that Gavin would choose now to bring up the parade of women he insisted Devan meet for the purpose of marriage? All of them were fair of face and came with massive fortunes as an inducement, but not a single one had interested him. It didn't help matters that Larkton never accepted his reason for refusing each and every one of them.

Though Devan's reputation was that he was a consummate flirt who adored the ladies, the truth was much simpler. He'd not settle for some type of an arranged marriage with an heiress he didn't feel any affection for. He wanted to fall in love just like his parents had. But his well-cultivated reputation had a slight benefit in keeping his brother from *constantly* prying into his business—though Gavin had started to become annoying with his list of eligible heiresses.

"If you think your list of ladies is so titillating, then why don't you marry one?" he taunted. "I understand Miss Barbara Overfield is still looking for a match."

"Calm yourself, little brother. Let's not fight over your lack of interest in marriage. But you should know that I've added a little something to whet your appetite. For extra money, you'll tutor Lady Warlock's son, Thane. According to his last instructor, the young lord's Latin is atrocious. I want the boy out of her clutches and ready to attend Eton by the beginning of next year's school term. The Marquess of Warwyk needs to become his own man and not coddled by his mother."

"I'm tired of you manipulating my life." Devan didn't hide the anger in his voice. "Every time I settle into a new parish, you ask the bishop to have me reassigned."

"One of the benefits of being friends with Bishop Marlowe." Larkton continued, "Come now, I'm trying to help you in your career. Each new assignment is at a larger parish. It brings more money and more prestige. Marlowe has even suggested making you a rector. If you continue your climb within the church, you might find yourself a bishop someday. Besides, this is the first time I can recall asking you for anything in return. If you agree to this last assignment, I won't ask you to move again. I'll let you pick where you'll go next if you want to move. You have my word."

Devan examined Larkton. His brother nodded as if acknowledging Devan's unease at agreeing to such an assignment. But Devan wasn't going to make it easy for him. He enjoyed his parish in Northumberland. The people were warm, friendly, and giving of their hearts. The position had allowed him to visit Will and Thea after their marriage several times, and Devan valued that friendship immensely.

To give up his friends and community for Lady Warlock seemed harsh, but perhaps he could have fun with her. A little excitement in his life would make the winter pass by quicker.

"How much does the position pay, and what amount are you offering for tutoring?" Before Gavin could answer, Devan added his own demand to the offer. "You tell her you're sending me to spy on her. Roniden, you have enough resources to find out what she's doing without my help. But the young lord is another matter. It's admirable that you're looking out for Lord Warwyk's future. Since he's under your protection, you owe it to him that he receives the necessary training and education. I'll gladly help you with him but not Lady Warlock."

Gavin sat back down and shook his head. "You can't dictate the terms of the assignment."

He finished his drink, then stood to leave. "I just did," Devan answered.

*A time to love, and a time to hate: a time of war,
and a time of peace.*

Ecclesiastes 3:8

Chapter Two

January, three months later
Warwyk Hall, about ten miles outside of London

Avalon read the first line in the letter from her son's
guardian, Gavin Farris, the Earl of Larkton. By all
appearances the words resembled something innocuous,
purely designed to lull a person into thinking it contained real concern with a touch of whimsical affection.

*My dearest lady, I do hope this finds you and
your intrepid son well.*

"Avalon, did you hear the news?" Seventeen, on the
cusp of eighteen years of age, Avalon's sister, Lady Sophia
Cavensham, looked up from her embroidery and smiled.
Her gaze darted to her friend Miss Penelope Rowley, the
one and only niece of the wealthiest gentry landowner in
the shire. Though she was two years older than Sophia,
Penelope had become somewhat of a fixture at Warwyk
Hall over the last six months since she'd moved to her
aunt and uncle's home. The two women were insepa-
rable.

Penelope let out a dramatic sigh then collapsed in
a swoon across the pink-and-gold brocade sofa. In the
process, she kneed the table, upsetting the delicate pink
china cup and saucer. "Oww."

Avalon tried to ignore their chatter. The Earl of Lark-ton's correspondence had increased in frequency over the last several months. The weekly letters were turning into biweekly posts. Each one wanted more and more control over the Warwyk estate and more decision-making control over her ten-year-old son, Thane Pearce, the Marquess of Warwyk. She doubled her concentration on the letter as she read the entire first paragraph.

*The purpose of my correspondence is to
inform you that I've appointed a new vicar for
the village of Thistledown. The man comes with
impeccable standing and experience. In addition,
his educational training is second to none. He's a
protégé of Lord Bishop Marlowe.*

"He's extraordinary." Sophia's dreamlike whisper floated through the air like a dandelion seed.

"He's . . . simply exquisite." Penelope's voice joined Sophia's in a chorus of dazzled fascination.

*My dear Marchioness, it's my pleasure to
announce that my brother—*

Avalon swallowed the sudden onrush of bile that marched up her throat. *It couldn't be. Fate was not that hateful.*

"Mr. Devan—" Sophia sighed.

"Farris." Penelope finished the sentence and slowly drew her hand against her forehead as if saying his name caused her to faint.

"No. Not him." Avalon murmured the words aloud. The sanctimonious prig had arrived to make her life a living hell. Avalon grimaced to keep from casting her accounts. Now she was just exaggerating like the girls.

She wasn't really physically sick, but the news could make a person ill. "When did *he* arrive in the village?"

Clueless as to how the news affected her older sister, Sophia scooted to the edge of the crimson-and-white-striped club chair that sat adjacent to Avalon's matching one. "Two days ago. Penelope and I just happened to be walking in front of the vicarage when we saw the Earl of Larkton's coach arrive. The new vicar followed behind on horseback."

Penelope nodded vigorously as if Sophia's story needed affirmation.

Avalon wanted to roll her eyes. The two women "never just happen" to do anything. They orchestrated and connived everything from shopping to men. God save anyone who crossed their paths. If one of the girls took a shine to any of the *ton*'s marriageable men, then London's finest would soon understand what it meant to be hunted.

As the girls continued their chatter, Avalon devoted her full attention to the rest of the letter. Better to finish the horrid task, then take a long walk through her gardens. Though it was January and bitterly cold outside, a brisk hour of exercise would help Avalon clear some of her unease at the news that Mr. Devan Farris had invaded her village.

> *I've considered your request that the young marquess continue his studies at home, but at the age of ten, his interests would best be served by attending Eton sooner rather than later. That's where boys turn into men. Your suggestion that he attend Harrow won't do. His father had insisted that I promise he attend Eton. However, since his Latin skills are somewhat lacking, I've decided to hire my brother, Mr. Farris, to tutor him in the subject.*

Her blood simmered at the words. The earl's declaration was nothing more than gilding the lily. Everyone within fifty miles of London knew that Devan Farris sought to marry an heiress. Until he found one, the fortune-hunting vicar thought to use her son's marquisate to pay double for his services. Since her son's estate paid for the vicar's wages, Mr. Farris would receive another wage from the coffers for tutoring lessons.

But what really brought her blood to boil was that the smug vicar would be nosing into her business, and that wouldn't do at all. She and only she ruled the parish with a fair and impartial hand. No one, including Devan Farris, would upset her world.

> *I've instructed my brother to send a note when he arrives so he may call on the young marquess and evaluate the boy's abilities for himself. If there are any other subjects where the young lordship is lacking, then Mr. Farris may tutor him in those also.*
>
> *My brother is quite gifted in numbers also. Perhaps you could allow him to review the estate books. It never hurts to have someone else examine the expenditures. Anything I can do to lighten your responsibilities is my pleasure.*

Avalon gritted her teeth. Devan Farris reviewing her books was nothing more than a spy expedition. Larkton thought she'd not see through such a thinly veiled scheme.

> *I know we share a difference of opinion on your son's educational requirements, but madam, as a man, I believe that my knowledge and insight are far superior to yours. Since I'm his only male*

legal guardian and the conservator of his estate, my wishes tip the scales, so to speak. I hope that you'll come to see the wisdom in my decision. I'm hopeful that Mr. Farris will help in that regard also.

Yours,
Larkton

Her long-dead husband, Richard, had haunted her for the last nine years by appointing his friend Larkton as guardian and conservator of the marquisate. Avalon had been forced to continuously steer the earl to her way of thinking. She'd handled him like a piece of china—delicately but purposefully.

Devan Farris was another matter. The man was one of the few in the male species who could rattle her. The sympathy in his eyes that day Richard had humiliated her still bothered her. Then when he'd followed her out into the corridor? She shuddered at the memory. It was one of the last times she'd ever shown she'd been hurt by her husband's actions, and Devan Farris had seen her weakness. Now he was here to poke his nose in her business.

There was only one thing to do. Avalon would write a polite declination of Mr. Farris's tutorial services, then she'd continue to argue that her son still wasn't ready to attend Eton. Really, she hoped he'd never be ready. Avalon had seen the effect of these schools on young men. It turned them from sweet, caring boys into selfish, rakish bullies. That's what had happened to Richard. If she'd needed more proof, then Warwyk Hall had provided it. The loyal staff had been quite open that he'd become a different person after he'd finished his studies. He'd returned a cruel brute of a man.

Thane would not fall victim to such temptation.

Sophia interrupted Avalon's musings. "Naturally, we introduced ourselves to the new vicar." She took a sip of tea, then leaned back against her chair. "You should invite him to dinner as a welcome."

She'd rather invite a Scottish wildcat to dinner. At least the conversation would be more interesting than what Mr. Farris could offer.

"As the Marchioness of Warwyk, it's your responsibility to welcome him into our community," Sophia continued.

"May I come to dinner when you invite him?" Penelope purred.

Sophia stifled a giggle, then nodded. "I've heard he's a wild rake."

Avalon shot her a look. "Sophia Maria Cavensham."

Sophia straightened in her chair at the chastisement. "How rude of me. I apologize. I meant he's a devout rake."

Penelope leaned forward in her chair and lowered her voice. "My uncle said that the Earl of Larkton and the bishop sent Mr. Farris here to deal with the 'ladies' since he's a man of the world." She shrugged. "Seems the church wants to discover why so many have settled here."

"Is that what you think?" Sophia asked Avalon.

"No," she answered. "Perhaps the church wants to find out more about the dormitories and the other structures we're building so the women have a place to live and work. They undoubtedly want to know how we're accomplishing such a feat."

"So where does the money come from?" Penelope asked.

"The Ladies Auxiliary earns money, and I've supplemented with some of my own," Avalon said.

"I've never understood why so many have settled

here in Thistledown." Penelope's brow crinkled into neat rows.

The answer was simple: Avalon had purposely invited them here. Some of the women had no place to go when fate had turned its back on them. Avalon had seen enough in her time on earth, and truthfully her experience with her parents and her short marriage to Warwyk, to understand their plight to a certain extent. She hadn't experienced the horrors of prostitution or poverty or even the violence they must have had to face. But she couldn't sit idly by when she had the resources to help. So, she'd made it her business to provide a refuge for them to seek shelter when they wanted out of prostitution.

"Our village is prosperous because of the marquisate," Avalon said. "We're the wealthiest community this close to London. It only makes sense that the women would try to settle here and start a business. It's our Christian duty to help them."

When the last two women she'd invited had arrived a month ago, they'd kept to themselves except when they had business with Avalon. As the Marchioness of Warwyk, she had instructed her steward to open an empty cottage the Warwyk marquisate owned in the village for the women to let. It was a perfect place for the women to live. The small rent they paid went into the Warwyk coffers. Of course, Avalon had given clear instructions to the steward not to share the information with the marquisate's conservator, the Earl of Larkton, or his representatives. This was Avalon's business.

Her carefully crafted community would not be destroyed by Thistledown's new vicar. A tiger never changed its stripes, and Mr. Farris was renowned for causing havoc whenever he came in contact with her. She only had to think up a plan for convincing the vicar to leave. Perhaps she'd offer him money to take a position elsewhere. Of course, she could have her personal solicitor handle the transaction, but Avalon had little doubt she'd be successful in eradicating the Vicar of Vermin, the King of Pests, from her village. She'd learned everything she needed to know about men from her husband, Richard. When he'd humiliated her that day, she'd vowed never to allow any man to have any say in how she lived her life.

Yet, after ten years, the humiliation of the confrontation with her husband still stung and caused her cheeks to heat. It was inconceivable that at the age of twenty-eight, he still had an effect on her. It had been nine years since he'd died from a fever, and she'd never missed him a day. A true match made in hell. It wasn't a very Christian thought, but it was the truth.

If it hadn't been for Mary Bolen, Avalon might have suffered real pain that day. The thought that he might have struck her and injured her baby or, God forbid, worse sent chills skating down her back. Though she and Mary came from different worlds, Avalon would always think of Mary kindly even if she was her husband's lover. Mary had been the only person who'd ever stood up for Avalon.

When Richard had turned to Mary Bolen for companionship that fateful day, Avalon had turned to Warwyk Hall, the ancestral seat. She'd spent her lonely days cultivating a community that epitomized warmth and welcome. How ironic that she wanted to remove the vicar from their friendly and hospitable community. But this was no ordinary man. He was sent to spy on her. Under no circumstances would Avalon allow such a surly, corrupt soul as Devan Farris to invade her perfect home and village, which led to only one conclusion.

Avalon would visit the new vicar and make him an offer his greedy soul would joyfully accept.

"My lady, perhaps the vicar is counseling one of the members of his flock and can't be disturbed." Avalon's lady's maid, Henrietta Calvert, twisted her fingers together in a knot. Four years older than Avalon, the petite woman had been a comfort over the years. "I've heard it's a pleasure to look at him," Henri added. "Handsome as the devil, some say."

"Hush, Henri," Avalon lightly admonished. "Remember Lucifer was the most handsome of all angels until he was cast out of heaven. Then he became a monster."

Henri nodded, and Avalon smiled in reassurance.

She couldn't lose Henri to the insidious charms of the vexatious vicar. Her maid had been with her since Avalon's introduction into society. Loyal didn't begin to describe Henri's devotion, and Avalon felt the same about Henri. She'd have never survived the last month of her pregnancy if it hadn't been for Henri. After the midwife had ordered complete bed rest, Henri had stayed by her side night and day.

"I won't be dissuaded in my work by a new young vicar, and neither will you." Avalon's toe tapped in a sharp pattern against the wooden floor of the vicarage entry. It was beyond the pale for Mr. Farris to keep her waiting for fifteen minutes, but perhaps her maid was correct. Perhaps someone in their community needed guidance.

Mentally, Avalon went through those who currently needed a little extra attention.

There was one family in Thistledown that Avalon constantly worried about. They'd suffered tremendously over the last several months. Mrs. Annie Dozier, one of the prostitutes who had first settled in the village, had given up her occupation as a light skirt to start a new life. Six months pregnant at the time, she'd had nowhere to go. So Avalon had taken her in.

James Dozier, one of the Warwyk tenants, had immediately become smitten with Annie and had married her immediately. It had been a match made in heaven. Though Byrnn wasn't James's son, he'd treated the boy as his own. But fate wasn't kind to the couple. James died five months ago from a head injury after falling off their barn while he'd repaired the roof. James Dozier could only be described as strong and rugged, but after lingering for several days, he'd succumbed to death, leaving Annie pregnant once again and their son, one-year-old Byrnn, alone. Annie and Byrnn had struggled mightily to make ends meet this winter.

Avalon had taken to visiting weekly with a basket containing enough food to last the week. It was a small thing, but Avalon enjoyed her weekly visit with the two. Holding the squirming Byrnn in her arms, Avalon thought of all the times she'd held and cuddled with Thane, the only good thing to have come from her marriage.

"Lady Warwyk, Mr. Farris will see you now," Mrs. McVey, the vicarage's longtime housekeeper, announced. She held a tray in her hands with freshly baked cinnamon and current buns along with a fresh pot of tea.

"Thank you." Avalon stood, then followed the housekeeper to the vicar's study. She really didn't need the escort as she'd visited the elderly vicar, Mr. Knightley, literally hundreds of times over the last ten years as they'd worked on various projects together. A devout and fair man, he'd proven to Avalon that a few men were worth their weight in gold. Mr. Knightley had wholeheartedly accepted Avalon and her need to help these women. When he'd retired and moved to his daughter's home in Brighton, it'd been a loss for their community.

The study door stood open, and Mrs. McVey entered with the tray.

Avalon stopped in the hallway and turned to Henri. "Ask for a cup of tea from Mrs. McVey. Keep her in the kitchen for as long as you can."

Henri's eyes narrowed in understanding. "You don't have to ask twice, my lady. I'll keep her entertained for as long as necessary. All I have to do is ask about her nephew in Perth." Henri shook her head and smiled. "She'll not let me get a word in edgewise for at least an hour."

"I'm hoping I won't need that long," Avalon whispered, ensuring that they weren't overheard. With the offer she planned to make, she had little doubt that Mr. Farris would agree to anything she said. It should only take ten minutes to have him eating out of her hand.

She inched her chin up, then proceeded into the vicar's study, summoning forth every ounce of courage and persuasive ability she possessed. As Mrs. McVey fussed with the tea tray on a small table between two chairs, the black-haired, green-eyed devil looked up from the papers on his desk, then captured her gaze.

For several moments, they appraised one another like one combatant does with another before an epic battle. Well, he didn't have to worry about her just yet. She'd not unsheathe her weapons unless absolutely necessary. If he played nice, then she'd play nice too.

Slowly, with a deliberate insouciance and an impertinent smile to match, Mr. Farris walked around his desk to greet her. "What a delightful treat to have tea with a member of my new flock today. How did I get so *lucky*? Lady . . ."

She tightened her stomach as if preparing for a blow.

". . . Warwyk."

Over the years they'd met at various social engagements. It was an understatement to say they were never pleasant. He'd always privately called her Lady Warlock after she'd jilted his best friend, William Cavensham. Too many times to count, she'd wanted to inform him why she'd been forced to jilt William. But really, would he understand? Or just think her complacent in her deceased parents' scheme for wealth and prestige?

Both of her parents had succumbed to an illness several years ago, but her mother's words still gnawed through her thoughts when she thought of her marriage to Richard. *"Climb the ladder of the peerage until you find the highest-ranking unmarried lord, marry him, then beget an heir and a spare. After you satisfy that sole duty, then you're free to do whatever you want."*

She released the breath she hadn't realized she'd been holding.

As if the vicar knew that he'd unsettled her, he graced her with a smile that would have charmed Lucifer and his minions if they had been in attendance. Such a grin emphasized his full lower lip. Because the fierce winter wind was relentless in its pounding of flesh, the majority of people suffered from cracked and chapped lips. His looked perfect. An intense urge made her want to reach out and touch his lips with her fingers to see if they were as soft as they appeared.

Instead, she licked her lower lip to gauge the condition of her own.

"Hungry?"

She shook her head once. "No."

The gleam in his green eyes seemed to suggest he wasn't talking about biscuits or scones. His eyes were one of his most striking features. Large and seemingly endless in their green depths, they reminded her of a lush forest inviting one to rest and forget one's worries. His features could only be described as angelic. His straight nose fit the shape of his face. Dimples graced both sides of his mouth when he smiled.

He looked like a royal prince with his bearing.

Much like the Prince of Darkness.

This was pure madness that had possessed her. Why was she mooning over his eyes? She doubled her determination to see this through. She had a mission, and nothing would deter her from it.

Somehow, she'd forgotten how tall he was. He'd reached her side and currently stood towering over her. He took her hand in his and slightly bowed over it. Though she wore gloves, the heat from his hand seeped through the kidskin leather. As if scorched, she yanked her hand from his.

What was the matter with her? He was the enemy.

Six months ago, they'd met at the wedding breakfast party for William and his lovely bride, Lady Theodora Eanruig. Avalon had relished being invited to the breakfast as it meant that all was forgiven between her and William. Though he was her third cousin, since their great-grandfathers were brothers, he'd been a suitor for her hand when she was seventeen, until her parents had squashed that dream like a rotten potato.

But the breakfast hadn't been without its problems. Mr. Farris had sat next to her and teased her throughout the meal and accompanying toasts from family members. When he'd called her the despicable nickname of Lady Warlock, she'd been tempted to toss her glass of champagne in his face. She'd gone as far as picking it up.

But when she'd seen the love on William's and Theodora's faces, she had forced herself to take a sip, then set it down. How uncouth to upset their special day because of the vicar's rudeness.

"Thank you for tea, Mrs. McVey," Mr. Farris said without taking his gaze from Avalon.

As if nailed to the floor, Avalon didn't move. He'd have to retreat first.

"Where are my manners? Lady Warwyk, please forgive me. Do come in." He waved a hand to the two chairs that sat in front of a cozy fire. Between them, an old but sturdy Chippendale table held the tea service. Two hot steaming cups of tea sat side by side on the tray. He picked up one, then raised one brow in question.

"No sugar, just cream, please." By now, the gallop of her heartbeat had slowed to a barely controlled canter. His hand dominated the saucer and teacup. Seemingly unaware of the turmoil playing havoc with Avalon, he handed the cup to her.

"Something to eat?" he asked.

She shook her head instead of answering.

He didn't serve himself. Instead, he turned slightly in his chair and regarded her. That was her cue to start the conversation. Carefully, she sat the teacup on the table and met his gaze.

"Let's not make this any more uncomfortable than it currently is." Avalon pasted a slight smile on her lips. "I received a letter from your brother today, along with some unsettling news."

"I see. How may I assist you?"

He didn't blink or smile. The seriousness of his countenance caused her to momentarily consider fleeing the study. But that wouldn't serve anyone's interests.

"I'll come right to the point. I don't approve of you as the new parish vicar."

His eyes blazed for a moment, but she'd not back down.

"Let me explain. The Warwyk marquisate has invested heavily in building the parish and community. Your renowned talent for helping troubled parishes would be wasted here. Personally, I'm committed to the care and safekeeping of these people and have done so for the last ten years. This is an idyllic place with bright prospects for all the residents. Frankly, we just don't need someone like you here."

His eyes softened and he nodded his head, giving her hope that convincing him to do her bidding wouldn't be difficult. "I can understand how unsettling this must be for you."

The empathy in his voice emboldened her. "Even the church must see your time should be devoted to another parish, one that needs firm guidance." She released a pent-up breath. "We've a lovely women's auxiliary group which meets weekly to find ways of helping those who need a hand. We're a close community who pride ourselves on helping those who have fallen on hard times."

He nodded again, and a slight grin creased his lips. His green eyes had darkened in color.

"Pride is a dangerous trait, my lady." The words sounded harmless, but she heard the threat in his mellifluous baritone. It was a warning shot to take heed. She stiffened her spine just as the vicar stood and then walked to the fireplace. With his back turned, he fed another log into the fire, then adjusted the burning ones with a poker.

While he tended the fire, her gaze traveled the length of his breeches as she studied his long and muscular legs. The remarkable definition in his calves resulted from hard physical work and not just walking from one parishioner's home to another. What could he possibly work on that would cause his muscles to be so defined?

His legs fascinated her, and her fingers itched to touch them.

Her palms grew wet while her pulse pounded at the sight of his body. It was simply sinful on her part to ogle him. Long ago, she'd put aside her cravings for the physical touch of a man. Now those cravings roared to life at the most inopportune time. She was practically salivating over the new vicar's haunches—she closed her eyes—their soon-to-be *former vicar*—that's all she had to remember.

Normally, she'd always thought of the vicar's study as a comfy and cozy place whenever she'd visited Mr. Knightley. However, with Mr. Farris in the room, it had shrunk in space, and everything within it set her on edge.

He set her on edge.

"Are you warm enough, Lady Warwyk?" He had turned from tending the fire and stood staring at her. Slowly, that devilish smile of his spread across his full lips. He taunted her as if he knew exactly what she was thinking.

She schooled her unease as best as she could. "Indeed. I'm not cold."

"I never thought you were," he practically purred like a large cat playing with its prey.

She would not let him unsettle her any further. "Mr. Farris, we're God-fearing people in this village. We've enough trials and tribulations to handle on a daily basis. Your placement in the community is simply a poor match. I'm sure you understand."

"I do," he soothed.

When he walked back to his chair, she couldn't help but notice the exquisite cut of his morning coat. It fit him like a glove, and the buttons reflected the firelight as if gleaming in approval of him.

Avalon took a sip of her tea in a desperate attempt to regain her bearings. No matter how handsome Mr. Farris was, she couldn't let her thoughts drift anymore. "I'm a fair person, and I won't let you go away empty-handed. I'll give you a cash settlement to leave and provide a stipend until you acquire another parish better suited to you."

Mr. Farris's brow drew into neat lines. "But I've been appointed to lead this parish. Only my brother and the bishop can change my appointment."

"I'll write the bishop and explain the circumstances. I have little doubt you'll be assigned a new parish within the month. Since I'm in a generous mood, I'll pay your stipend for two years. You could use the money and hire a curate to take your place until you're ready. Perhaps you could travel or"—she waved her hand in the air—"something."

"Or something?" Resting his arm on the back of the chair, he studied the fire.

Eventually, a tenuous but somewhat peaceable quiet enveloped the room, occasionally interrupted by the crack of a log breaking in the fire. Avalon allowed herself to relax. The vicar had never made it a secret that he wanted to marry an heiress, which meant he was motivated by money.

"My offer is generous. As soon as you accept, I'll contact my solicitor and have the papers drawn up."

He turned to her and flashed a brilliant smile. One that bespoke his ready acceptance. Avalon smiled in return.

"Your generosity knows no bounds, my lady." He leaned toward her as if to speak with her intimately.

She matched his movements, anxious for his agreement. When their gazes caught, he studied her with such an intensity that she believed he could see every fear, hope, and want she possessed. Something tugged deep inside her chest, and she tried to ignore it, but the pull became more powerful, more resolute. Perhaps it represented the constant loneliness that shadowed her every day of her adult life.

But she feared it was more. This man might have the power to peel a layer from her very essence, one that she'd carefully cultivated to protect herself. Never again would she allow herself to be manipulated in the name of other people's wants and desires. She'd fight Devan Farris with every power she possessed. He'd never discover her secrets. The quicker he left their village, the better it was for all, including her.

He nodded once, and she allowed herself to relax for the first time this morning.

It was done.

"How could I refuse?" He smiled.

Such a simple act emphasized his angular cheekbones and the perfect set of those wide green eyes. Sophia and Penelope had declared him handsome. Unfortunately, Avalon completely agreed.

"Excellent. Until you're reassigned, I'll allow you to tutor my son. That'll add additional monies to your savings." She relaxed slightly and smiled. "I'm so happy that we've come to a mutually beneficial resolution."

"I thought it was for the benefit of the village." He tilted his head slightly.

"Of course," she said hastily. "That's what I meant."

"My lady." His voice deepened. "I am truly sorry, but I must decline your generous offer."

Shaking her head slightly, Avalon must not have heard him correctly. He couldn't be turning her down. She was offering him the world. Or at least, a nice salary that not many in the church would ever hope to earn. "You mean the tutoring? If you're not interested, I understand."

"That's not it," he said.

"You mean you must ask permission from the bishop?"

He shook his head with a devilish grin.

"Then you must seek the Earl of Larkton's permission?"

A deep rumble started in his chest. At first she thought it a growl, then she realized it for what it was. He was laughing. Goose bumps broke out across her arms. Whether it was from the cold or the sudden onset of disquiet, she couldn't tell. She hadn't said a single word that could be construed as funny.

Finally, he wiped his hands down his face. His fingers were uncommonly long, and his hands were huge. He leveled the most mesmerizing gaze her way.

"No. My brother always looks out for my best interests as family should." His voice was so low, it practically sounded like he was humming in a deep baritone. "I refuse because it was you, *Lady Warlock*, who asked."

She tightened her stomach at the hateful name. "I know all about you, your hunt for an heiress, and your tomcat ways." She threw the proverbial gauntlet down and waited for him to accept the challenge. She would not, in no uncertain terms, allow him to stay.

"My reputation precedes me, I see."

"One well deserved, I have no doubt." She straightened in her seat. It was time to strike the fatal blow. "Surely, you've seen the articles in *The Midnight Cryer*."

He nodded with a sly grin that reminded her of a mouser out for a midnight stroll, one on the hunt for perverse pleasure.

She'd not let him succeed.

"I'm particularly fond of the description 'a debauched lecher who has mastered carousing.' But between you and me"—he bent forward as if divulging a secret—"it may be gauche, but I've kept all the ones that featured me. I do enjoy reading about my escapades."

"Like the time you were caught swimming in Lord Peters's fountain with Lady Peters and Mrs. Hemsley completely naked?"

"Someone had to save them from drowning. As I recall, I was still wearing clothes," he said. "I can't vouch for the ladies' attire."

"Oh really?" She stared in disbelief. "What about you stealing a kiss from the Duchess of Southart in front of her duke?"

"There was mistletoe. Come now, my lady, you wouldn't deny a man a simple holiday merriment?"

His expression reminded her of a guilty child feigning innocence.

"The article that said I was 'sniffing' after the Countess of Eanruig's hand is incorrect." He leaned back in his chair and grinned as if pleased with himself. "She was sniffing after me."

Unbelievably, she found herself leaning forward to hear his words, hungry for his gossip. She exhaled silently. Best to get ahold of herself before she lost her nerve and her advantage.

"Sir, we don't need your stench of scandal in Thistledown. You're a wild rake."

"As in untamed?" He arched one brow.

"Uncouth," she proclaimed.

The most devilish half grin graced his lips.

"And wicked," she huffed while looking down her nose, but really it was more looking up as he was so tall.

"Birds of a feather . . ." he murmured.

"Careful, Vicar. You're showing how provincial you really are."

"I consider it 'pastoral.'" His deep voice softened as if charming the devil's minions.

"You and your reputation are not welcome in our community." There. She'd said it. The words to drive him away. She didn't want to insult him, but sometimes it was best to go for the jugular, as they say. He didn't need to know that she was the only one in Thistledown who subscribed to *The Midnight Cryer*. Nor did he need to know that she watched for articles about him as fervently as he did.

"How ironic? You do realize that you're welcoming me by gracing me with your presence. Speaking of reputations, what does that say about you?" He tapped the indentation in the middle of his perfect chin with one long, masculine finger. "I think it suggests you're interested in me." He had the audacity to laugh.

"I'm interested in getting you to leave." The clipped words echoed around the room.

"You haven't lost any of your rudimentary charm, Lady Warlock. You'll just have to try harder." He narrowed his eyes. "I'm staying. Now, when shall I meet the marquess?"

It is war's prize to take all vantage.
                              Henry VI, Part 3

Chapter Three

A wise Oxford don had once given Devan Farris a piece of advice that had stayed with him. *"A true gentleman, no matter his circumstances, must invest his hard-earned coin in one piece of clothing that proclaims his rightful place in the world."*

For Devan that extravagant piece in his wardrobe was a fine black wool morning jacket adorned with silver buttons. It was tailor-made and had cost a pretty penny. He'd saved for two years to purchase such a garment and had taken meticulous care of it. It must have been God's providence that forced Devan to pull the beautiful coat from his wardrobe and wear it today. He only wore it on special occasions, but today had predicted to be a little out of the ordinary.

When it was announced that Avalon Cavensham Pearce, the Murchioness of Warwyk, waited for him in the entry, Devan had said a little prayer, thanking the Almighty for his divine intervention. Devan would need every ounce of wit, charm, and persistence to do battle with the plucky woman.

Though they'd met several times through the years, Lady Warwyk hated him. In turn, he'd called her Lady Warlock as a way of needling her. Though his life was devoted to the church and its teachings, Devan believed that God accepted exceptions to the rules—particularly when it was all for the greater good.

For instance, the greater good required that he tease Lady Warlock relentlessly whenever he found himself in her presence. Though her charity work showed her fine character, the woman took herself much too seriously. Perhaps such a trait resulted from her insufferable marriage to the previous marquess. However, it was entirely possible that she'd relied upon her own company for so long that she'd become completely one-dimensional, much like those paper dolls children played with.

He'd scored a direct hit by calling her Lady Warlock if the tic that played and teased across one corner of her mouth was any indication. It must have been his imagination, but she seemed to shimmer in his presence with outrage. He fancied this version of Lady Warwyk rather than the stiff board that had first entered. When her emotions ran high, she was uncommonly becoming.

With thick brown hair elegantly swept off her neck except for one expertly styled curl that hung loose, she held herself regally, like a queen surveying her kingdom. The stance emphasized her long neck. Her green eyes had brightened to a color similar to an English garden in the spring. Her heart-shaped face and pert nose were delightful, and her pink, plush lips reminded him of pillows.

The functional navy gown seemed to be a shield proclaiming her practicality. It did nothing for her figure. A brilliant bronze or a spring green would better complement her perfect complexion and set off her delicate features, particularly her nose, which she favored tilting in the air as often as she could.

"What are you laughing at, you pious—"

"Tsk, tsk, my lady." He leaned a little closer to inspect the pulse pounding in her neck. "Don't say prig.

You have used 'pious prig' too many times in the past. It's lost the ability to shock or wound, wouldn't you agree? I expected something more original." He picked up the teapot, then lifted his eyebrows as if offering more. When she didn't budge, he replaced the pot. "I think if we're to work together successfully in the parish, we should come to an understanding."

"We will never come to an understanding, Mr. Farris," she huffed, the sound like a whisper of air. "I want you gone."

"My dear lady, as much as I'd like to oblige, I'm afraid that just won't happen." He pursed his lips as if concentrating. "Both the bishop and I are concerned about the added financial strain the parish must bear because of your new residents. It's no secret that Thistledown has turned into a haven for women of a certain . . . occupation who happen to find themselves . . ."

"Without a home?" She arched a single perfect brow. "With child?"

He bit his lip to keep from grinning at her contrary action. She was purposely trying to shock him.

"I fail to see that it's any concern of the church when the community has accepted the responsibility." She leaned closer, her sharp gaze like an ice pick. "Nor is it any of yours."

"That's where you're wrong." He lowered his tone to the one that he always used when counseling parishioners who needed help settling an argument. "The Earl of Larkton specifically asked me to take this assignment, not only for the good of the church, but for the good of the Marquess of Warwyk."

"What does my ten-year-old son have to do with this, Mr. Farris?" She leaned back, distancing herself from him.

He'd obviously touched a nerve. "As the guardian and

conservator of your son's estate, Larkton shoulders the responsibility to protect the marquisate and your son."

She dismissed him with a wave of her hand, clearly trying to take the upper hand once again. "There's no need to worry about that. I have my own money. The marquisate is healthy, and the wealth continues to grow from wise investing." Her smile didn't reach her eyes. "So, there's no need for you to 'supervise.'"

He wanted to get a rise out of her so her beautiful eyes would blaze again, but the slight vulnerability in the wobble of her voice stopped him. It was more than her dislike of him. His mere presence worried her.

"It's no trouble, my lady. Supervision is what I do best." He tilted his head and offered his most charming effervescent smile. "Speaking of which, I understand from Mrs. McVey that the Thistledown Ladies Auxiliary holds weekly meetings."

"It does," she answered warily.

"And Mr. Knightley attended those meetings as part of his responsibilities to the parish?"

"Mr. Knightley was a wonderful vicar and a mentor to me when I was young and the new Marchioness of Warwyk. He helped me create the Thistledown Ladies Auxiliary. I still lead the weekly meetings." She shook her head slightly. "There's no need for you to attend, Vicar."

Now she referred to him as "Vicar" instead of Mr. Farris or even "pious prig." The woman was definitely trying to distance herself from him, and he didn't like it one bit. But they'd soon be working together. Warwyk was a wealthy parish, one renowned throughout the church hierarchy as devoted to helping others. To Devan, it meant he'd see Lady Warwyk regularly.

He'd always found her at social events they attended.

She'd stiffen like a crested porcupine whenever she saw him. He'd tease her, hoping to get a reaction that would break her out of her ice-cold reserve. He hadn't been successful until last spring's wedding breakfast that they'd both attended. It'd been the most entertainment he'd had in months. When it became obvious she'd grown angry, he'd immediately quit pestering her. But there was something about her he'd always found intriguing. Every nuanced expression and complicated layer she possessed made him want to examine each one carefully until he figured out the puzzle that was Avalon Warwyk.

Frankly, he could care less if she wanted Thistledown to become a haven for prostitutes. That was Larkton's concern. It made no difference to Devan. However, as a member of the clergy, he had to protect the church.

"My lady, did you know that in old times, prostitutes would find a parish outside of London and deliver their babies? The parish leaders had been known to place a pregnant woman in a wheelbarrow and roll her and the unborn babe on to the next parish. For whatever parish the baby was born in, then that parish took responsibility for the child."

She blinked in response.

"Once the women were well enough, they'd go back to London, leaving the parish responsible for rearing and caring for the infant until they could be placed either at an orphanage or a foundling home."

"And the point of this history lesson?" she asked curtly.

"If others in similar plight see how generous you are, then they'll flock to Thistledown."

"They're not geese seeking refuge for the winter. I expected more empathy"—she regarded him from head to toe—"from such an exalted member of the clergy."

He could practically see her defensive shield being raised. "Without knowing the extent of the church's coffers at this point, I'm trying to ensure that the church could bear the financial weight of such an endeavor."

"I haven't sought the church's assistance. I'm financially responsible. Thank you for your concern, but it's my business," she countered.

"But it's *my parish*." He lifted an eyebrow in challenge.

She huffed in response.

"You can see why I want to know more. Thistledown welcomes these women unconditionally. I understand you're thinking of building special housing for them, along with an offering to learn a new trade such as sewing garments or learning lace tatting."

"Lace tatting is highly sought after by the dress makers in London and Paris. It's good business," she said.

"You're going to pay for all of that?"

She nodded briskly.

"I see. Then I completely support teaching them a new profession so that they could leave prostitution while raising their own children. It's a noble cause that the church should wholeheartedly embrace. From what I've heard and seen in my brief time here, the parish's efforts are filled with love, compassion, and generosity, all Christian values with moral correctness. I just want to help *you*. Won't you allow that?"

Her jaw clenched in response.

"Lady Warwyk, it would be my absolute honor to attend the Ladies Auxiliary meetings with you. I'm of a mind that it will quickly become the highlight of every week, except of course, my weekly sermon. I can't let you have all the fun," he teased.

Her cheeks heated to a beautiful crimson color reminiscent of ripened apples, his favorite fruit to eat.

"There's no need to interrupt your days for our meetings." Lady Warwyk stood to leave. "You must still be busy meeting all the parish members."

"Of course I can make time in my day for your meetings, my lady." He leaned close, and his nostrils instantly flared at her delicate scent of roses mixed with her essence, the warm fragrant scent of a woman. "Perhaps you would introduce me to the members of my new parish before Sunday's sermon. I'd hoped to invite them personally to church. Remember, I'm still hunting for an heiress. Perhaps you could point out a few?"

"Spare me, Mr. Farris." Though she spoke with a low voice, there was no mistaking the growling in her throat. "There are no heiresses in our parish except my sister. Stay away from her."

"Lady Warlock, I beg to differ. There are at least two." He escorted her to the door. "*You* and your sister. No need to worry about Lady Sophia. I don't rob from the cradle. I want to marry a woman with enough gravitas and experience with the world to make the effort worthwhile."

"What effort?" Lady Warwyk turned elegantly and faced him with a cool detached manner.

"The effort of marriage, my dear lady." He opened the door and swept his arm in front of him, inviting her to precede him, "As a gentleman, I must see the patroness of the parish to the front door. Is that where you left your maid? I assume she kept Mrs. McVey busy while you made your generous offer."

He concluded right then and there that Lady Warlock was a sly one. Which made him all the more eager to find out her business.

"I think I'll look for a bride while I'm here." He couldn't help but grin when her cheeks again resembled fall's first ripe apples. Truly, God was gracious to have put this woman in his path.

"You'd have better luck finding a wife in London. But just so we understand one another, this is my parish. Whatever it takes, I'm prepared to do so you'll leave us alone," she murmured. "We're not done with this conversation, Vicar."

"Lady Warlock." He lowered his voice. "I can't tell you how happy I am to hear that. Such a pity I never recognized it before, but *you* are simply delightful. I'll rectify my lack of observation skills when it comes to you. I'm positive you have much to teach me. I predict sharing time with you will be the highlight of my time in *your* parish."

Without another word, Lady Warwyk swept through the front door with her maid in close pursuit. Devan paused and looked for a carriage. Not a footman or black lacquered coach in sight. The good lady of Warwyk Hall had walked to his humble abode. It didn't escape his notice that today was the chilliest of the month so far.

He'd have offered to drive her and her maid himself, but as he was a vicar, there was no coach. However, he did have his loyal steed, Devil. The black stallion was all Devan needed as his transportation needs were simple. Since it was less than an hour's ride to London, Devil could easily accommodate him when Devan made the monthly trip to see his brother to report on his findings here within Thistledown.

Lord, he was tired of the church's special projects that only he seemed to be "fit" to handle. What that meant was that he was the only clergy who wasn't married and had enough brains to solve whatever problems various parishes had seemed to create amongst their neighbors.

He certainly didn't want to destroy what Avalon had created here. From what he'd seen in the last couple of days, the parish and its residents were healthy, happy, and genuinely caring. A lovely place that Devan could easily see wanting to call home forever.

Lady Warwyk was a conundrum if ever there was one—a beautiful one. It didn't take a genius to figure out that she didn't want him prying into her special projects, specifically the Ladies Auxiliary. Whatever that group did, Avalon was the undisputed leader and didn't want to share those responsibilities with anyone.

Including him.

However, she'd been very close to his predecessor, Mr. Knightley, and had welcomed him with open arms into her group. She didn't distrust all men. Perhaps just him. Devan rubbed his hands together to ward off the cold. He couldn't wait to attend next week's Ladies Auxiliary meeting. Mrs. McVey had already told him when and where it was held.

He'd do whatever he could to help her.

As a wise man once said, "Even the mighty must fall."

"My lady, I think it's gotten colder since we arrived at the vicarage," Henri said as her teeth rattled. She clasped her black wool cloak tightly.

"When we get home, I want you to sit in front of the fire, and I'll send for a nice pot of tea. I don't want you catching cold, Henri. I need you."

Her lady's maid laughed. The chuckles broke the air into puffs of frosty white clouds.

"Don't you worry, my lady. I'm fit as a fiddle." Henri thumped her chest with her gloved hand in a show of strength. "Healthy as a horse."

Avalon stood just shy of five feet and six inches, but she appeared to be a giant beside Henri. Though short in stature, Henri had a personality that more than made up for it. Her brown eyes always twinkled from merriment. She could find joy in the simplest to the most complex of things. But her steadfast loyalty was her greatest strength in Avalon's eyes. Whatever Avalon needed her to do, Henri did without question.

Avalon hadn't noticed the cold as she was still fuming after her conversation with Devan Farris, the most disagreeable man on the face of the earth. She let out a breath and an arrow of white steam shot straight in front of her. His brother, the Earl of Larkton, had to be the second most disagreeable man on earth she'd ever come across.

When it had just been the earl that she'd had to deal with, things had been so much easier. Avalon had handled Thane's guardian and conservator with an aplomb that even the most experienced of diplomats would have envied. The earl wrote regularly, and she'd answered each query or suggestion about the estate management or Thane's upbringing with a rational explanation of why the earl's thoughts weren't sound. But now that Devan Farris had arrived, it made things all that much harder. He'd constantly be watching her.

If the vicar discovered how it came to be that prostitutes settled into Thistledown, then Avalon's morals and her skills as a mother of a fatherless young peer might be cast into doubt. She'd become friends—no, allies—with her husband's mistress over the years. The biggest risk was that if Devan discovered their true respect for one another, it might give the earl additional ammunition to take Thane away and send him to Eton.

Devan Farris, blighter extraordinaire, insisted upon interfering into her affairs where he wasn't wanted.

However, her efforts to forge Thistledown into an ideal community would not be dismantled.

Everything she'd planned for her loved ones and

community hinged on her coming up with a spectacular offer, one that Devan Farris, the heiress-hunting vicar, couldn't refuse.

But something kept gnawing at her.

Devan was the first man she'd actually noticed in years. When was the last time she'd actually looked at a man and admired his form? She couldn't remember. Her heart pounded a little more forcefully in answer. Avalon shook her head slightly.

Her time would be better spent finding another way to purge *her parish* of the new vicar instead of listening to her heart.

Be not overly righteous, and do not make yourself too wise. Why should you destroy yourself?

Ecclesiastes 7:16

Chapter Four

A light dusting of snow had fallen the night before, coating the terrace outside Warwyk Hall's breakfast room. Everything seemed to glitter as the sun threatened to appear and melt the sparkles. It mimicked Avalon's mood completely. For the moment, her happiness had brightened with Thane to her left and Sophia to her right as they shared breakfast. It was a common ritual, one that Avalon looked forward to every morning.

"*Maman*?" Thane's soft question broke her reverie.

Avalon leaned close. "Yes, darling?"

"Mr. Waller's dog whelped four puppies yesterday. He said I could have one if you'd allow it." Thane slowly blinked. "My birthday is next month."

He brushed a long dark curl away from his eyes. His hair had seemed to grow overnight, just like the rest of his body. Thankfully, he took after the Cavensham side of the family with hair as dark as night and deep blue eyes.

"Avalon, I think it a marvelous idea." Sophia turned to Thane. "What would you name it?"

"Simon. Mr. Waller says he'll keep a male for me." Thane's soulful eyes captured her gaze. "Simon's white with liver spots. Mr. Waller says he'll be a fine hunter and water spaniel."

How could she refuse such a request? Thane had no one close in age to play with, and the idea of his own dog meant that he'd learn how to be responsible for someone besides himself.

"Would you care for it? You'd have to feed Simon. You'd have to take him outside. Make certain he'd receive lots of love, attention, and exercise. Even in March, it'll still be cold and rainy." Avalon poured herself another cup of tea. "You'd have to train him. I can't have a dog running amok through the house."

Thane scooted to the edge of his seat. "I promise." He crossed his heart with his right index finger. "You have my word as a"—he stared at the table as if summoning his most persuasive argument—"marquess." He nodded once as if that one word made it an unbreakable contract.

"A very sound argument for your mother's consent, my lord." A deep baritone broke the quiet.

Thane and Sophia whipped their gazes toward the door. Avalon didn't have to look as she would recognize the vicar's voice anywhere.

"Then it looks like Simon will be part of the household," Thane announced. Before Mr. Neville, her butler, could announce the intruder, Avalon's son did the honors. "You must be the new vicar. Are you here for my lesson?"

"Thane," Avalon gently chided. "Allow Mr. Neville to properly announce our visitor." Which was a nice way, if she did say so herself, of introducing the interloper.

"If I may, my lady, Mr. Farris has come calling." The butler beamed at the vicar, much to her dismay.

Thane stood and placed his serviette to the right of his plate. "Please come in, Mr. Farris." His gaze shot to Avalon's for approval.

She nodded in response and smiled at her son. He would soon be accustomed to answering to Warwyk instead of Thane. Some days she wanted to stop all the clocks in the house to see if she could hold on to his childhood a little longer. While he desperately wanted to become a man, she just as greatly wanted to hold him in her arms again.

"Mr. Neville, would you ask the footman to bring another place setting?" Avalon asked politely. "We weren't expecting company, but company has found us." Hopefully, the man understood that she meant *unwanted* company.

His lips tilted in a sly grin. He reminded her of a fox about to pounce on an innocent rabbit. She wouldn't be at all surprised if he licked those perfect lips as if salivating for the kill.

He bowed his head briefly in her direction as if acknowledging her barb, then turned to Mr. Neville. "If it wouldn't be an inconvenience, I'll just take coffee. I've already broken my fast at the vicarage."

"I'll bring it myself, then." Mr. Neville bowed his head, then headed quickly out the door.

Mr. Farris rounded the table to Sophia's side. His dark gaze captured Avalon's and he arched a single eyebrow as if baiting her—daring her not to introduce her sister to him.

Before Avalon could start the introduction, Sophia stood, then dipped a deep curtsey. "We've already met. Mr. Farris, it's so wonderful you've come to visit today."

In answer, he sketched an elegant but subdued bow. "The pleasure is all mine."

Sophia blushed prettily.

The vicar rounded the table, ignoring Avalon, and approached Thane. "You must be Lord Warwyk."

At the sound of the name Warwyk, Thane puffed his chest out a little. "I'm happy to meet you, Mr. Farris. I'm anxious to start my lessons."

Avalon's eyes widened at his statement. Thane hated his lessons, particularly anything having to do with Latin. The man would naturally have to charm her son also. Wasn't anybody besides herself immune to his allure and beguiling manners?

She took a deep and steadying breath. She'd not allow him to rile her today. His business this morning would hopefully be brief so she could proceed with her day as she'd planned. After breakfast, she had wanted to visit Annie and see how she was faring. When Avalon had visited her two days ago, she seemed tired and still in the depths of deep grief.

Mr. Neville arrived personally with a tray bearing a cup, saucer, and coffeepot. He efficiently set a place beside Thane, then bowed to the vicar as if he were the newly arrived sun-king. Which was an appropriate analogy as the sun decided in that moment to appear in its full glory as if it too were mesmerized by the handsome Mr. Farris.

"Thank you, Mr. Neville," the vicar acknowledged. As he sat, the butler poured him a cup of the black brew, then fussed with the offerings of cream and sugar, both of which Mr. Farris politely refused.

After Mr. Neville's performance was finished and he swept from the room, Mr. Farris turned his full attention to Thane. "I'm ready to start our tutorials, my lord. I thought today you could show me your study area and your books. I've brought some of my texts to see if I can supplement what you already have."

Thane's eyes grew wide, and to Avalon's chagrin, he nodded a bit too eagerly. "I'd like that, Mr. Farris."

"Excellent." The vicar smiled in answer.

It wasn't a patronizing smile but one that bespoke enthusiasm for the task set before him. Immediately, Avalon's senses went on alert. Why would a sophisticated man of the world like Mr. Farris be excited with the task of tutoring her son?

Rumors from *The Midnight Cryer* swirled around him like bees pollinating flowers. There was always a hint of the forbidden about him. Murmurings that he loved to lavish attention on women, and in return, gloried in their return affections. She'd even heard that he'd had numerous lovers. But the simple fact that he was a man of the cloth made him deserve their respect— though grudgingly on her part—until he proved otherwise.

Still, she had no doubt that he'd had experience with women. Didn't all men?

Her heart tripped in her chest as if acknowledging all she'd missed in her life. Marriage to a loving husband, intimacy from a simple touch, pleasure from a fond kiss—she silently sighed—a partnership only found from a husband who shared one's goals.

Such musings were a waste of time. She had everything she needed and wanted in her little corner of the world. She didn't need a man, nor did she need a certain vicar to complicate her life any more than he already had.

"Would you like to start now?" Thane pushed away from his chair with such exuberance that it threatened to fall over.

Not taken aback at her son's enthusiasm, Mr. Farris settled the chair on all four feet, then elegantly rose from the table. "Lord Warwyk, please lead the way."

Sophia also rose from the table. "Avalon, if you'll excuse me, also. I have several letters to write. Several of my friends from Lady Diane's Finishing School are making their introduction to society next Season. It will be lovely to see them all again."

Avalon also stood as the others prepared to leave. "Mr. Farris, shall I escort you both to Thane's nursery?"

He turned and regarded her with a lifted brow as if challenging her. "Thank you, but no, my lady. That won't be necessary. We are not going to the nursery. Instead, Lord Warwyk will take me to his schoolroom."

Thane, the Marquess of Warwyk, sheepishly opened his nursery room door on the west wing of the third floor, then entered, keeping his head buried in his chest the entire time. When Devan strolled through the doorway, he immediately saw what would cause the young lord's embarrassment.

The room was exquisitely appointed but decorated more for the tastes of a two-or three-year-old and not a young boy of ten. Rocking horses, building blocks, along with books and a couple of dolls lay neatly arranged as if on a permanent hiatus in a mausoleum. However, someone had touched them in the near past as there was a complete absence of dust on the furnishings.

On the floor, a set of tin infantrymen and their mighty steeds were the only indication of play in the room. Devan ignored the rest of the room and knelt beside the army of soldiers. "This is quite a formation. What is it?"

The boy dropped to his knees beside Devan. "It's the square formations that Wellington used at La Haye Sainte. Napoleon's army kept attacking in waves, and Wellington was forced to retreat when our army ran out of ammunition." He tilted his head and caught Devan's gaze. The seriousness in his expression was rare for a young man his age. "I'm studying it in hopes to discover a way to keep the British from losing so many men."

Devan picked up one of the tin soldiers painted in the British redcoats dress. Carefully, he examined the metal piece. The soldier's expression was one of determination. How many of the loyal British army had worn that same expression while dying on the field? It had been Devan's most ardent wish to join them in the army, but Larkton had refused, saying he couldn't afford to buy Devan a commission along with other excuses.

With care so as not to ruin the formation, he replaced the soldier in the line with the others. "That's amazing, my lord. Not many boys your age would study such strategies. You're quite the tactician."

"Would you call me Thane?" The boy's soft voice didn't hide the yearning.

"Of course." Devan grinned, then stood. "Thane, would you be kind enough to show me the rest of the schoolroom?"

The boy jumped to his feet, and with a wave of his hand, Devan invited the boy to proceed. Quickly, Thane showed Devan his books, papers, chalkboard, and even his previous Latin exercises.

Devan could only come to one conclusion. The boy had never been challenged by his previous tutor. His texts were ideally suited for children far younger than Thane. He needed an entire new library in order to be prepared for the academic rigors of Eton.

They sat at a small table set in front of a warm fire. Devan gave him several simple assignments in conjugating Latin verbs. Only missing a couple, Thane proved to be a willing and serious student.

Devan quizzed him on mathematics and history. Thane answered each question quickly and thoughtfully, once again proving that he had a strong grasp of his subjects. He only needed guidance and instruction from a tutor who would test and challenge his abilities.

After finishing his last assignment, Thane looked at Devan a little sheepishly. "Mr. Farris, I was wondering something."

"What might that be?"

"How long do you think you'll be assigned to the parish?" The boy sniffed, then rubbed his nose across his jacket sleeve.

"As long as the church and the parish see fit. Hopefully, I'll be here until I retire." He reached into his pocket and withdrew a handkerchief. He gave it to the boy, then walked to the far bookcase to study the titles contained within the literature section.

"Are you married?" Thane asked. He studied his paper in a not-so-subtle act of nonchalance.

Devan stopped his study, then turned his attention to Thane. "No. Are you?"

The boy giggled. "Of course not. I'm only ten."

"I suppose you'll need to wait awhile." Devan grinned. "Why do you ask?"

The boy shrugged his shoulders, then started doodling on the paper before him. "I'm just curious. Do you want to marry?"

"I do someday. When the right woman comes along." Immediately, his parents popped into Devan's thoughts. "My mother and father were deeply in love, and their marriage was a true gift to my siblings and me. They taught me so much."

Thane blinked slowly. "Like scripture?"

As one side of his mouth tugged upward, Devan debated whether to proceed or change the subject.

"Please tell me," the young lord said. "There aren't many who share important things with me."

Lord Warwyk had to be lonely. Devan hadn't met any

boys the young lord's age yet. "My parents gave me a wise piece of advice that I've followed. They told me to wait for my heart's true match, and so I am."

How surprising that he was sharing more of himself with a boy whom he'd just met hours ago than he'd ever shared with any of his friends or family. However, he'd not share all of his secrets, particularly the one that would cause his friends to reel in laughter if they ever discovered the truth.

It was something he'd only share with his wife: He was a virgin and would stay that way until he found that one true love, the woman he wanted to share the rest of his life with.

"Maybe that's what my mother wants." Thane looked up from his papers and captured Devan's gaze. "Maybe she's waiting for her one true love also. I don't think she loved my father."

"Why would you say that?" Devan asked softly.

"She never talks about him." The boy blinked slowly. "I always have to ask about him."

Devan's gut tightened. "Does your mother answer your questions?"

Thane straightened in his chair. "Indeed. She tells me that he was a man who protected his loved ones and ensured that our tenants and lands were well cared for. She says that my father loved me."

The fact that the marchioness protected her son's image of his father, a man she despised, surprised him. It had to be an incredible feat not to tell the boy the truth about his father. "Would you like for your mother to marry?"

He nodded briefly, as if answering aloud would be forbidden. "Don't tell my mother because I wouldn't want her to worry. But I'd like to have a father. I'd like to have brothers and even sisters, too."

Devan smiled slightly. "Anything you say to me stays confidential. That's what vicars are known for. We keep secrets." He made a fist and placed it over his heart. "Anything you tell me stays here. I may share with God in my prayers, but it'll go no further."

Thane examined him as if deciding what type of man stood before him. After an intense moment, he must have reached a decision of some sort, then nodded. "Thank you. Though I have Aunt Sophia and *Maman*, sometimes I'm lonely. It'll be nice having you here."

Devan let out the breath he hadn't realized he'd been holding while allowing Thane to study him. He wanted the boy's approval. Thane Warwyk possessed a kind spirit, and he yearned for more. Something deep inside Devan's heart made him want to help the boy attain his happiness.

"Do you have any friends close to Warwyk Hall?" Devan asked.

"Not many." His gaze shifted from his papers to Devan. "There aren't many boys my age around here. Except for the Wessex twins. They're fifteen years old."

"Who are they?"

"They're my friends and the sons of one of my tenant farmers." Thane continued, "They take me fishing when they have a day off from working the fields. Would you like to come with us some time?"

"It'd be my pleasure."

Thane smiled and nodded his approval.

So, Lady Warlock allowed her son to mingle with the estate's tenants. As much as Devan didn't want to, he'd give her a proverbial nod of approval. The young lord's friendship with the Wessex twins will ensure they have a reason to stay at Warwyk Hall and help their families.

Devan drew his eyebrows together. But it was more. The marchioness's support and friendship with the women making a new life in the village was a perfect example for her son and how he should treat those who relied upon him. A perfect example of respect between the classes and how we're all the same in God's eyes.

"Do you have any interest in going to Eton?" Devan asked.

Thane's eyes twinkled with excitement. "Oh yes, Mr. Farris. *Maman* doesn't want me to go. She says she needs me here, but I'd like to meet other fellows my age."

"Excellent, my lord. Then you and I shall start on your lessons immediately so you're ready to attend that noble institution when you and your mother come to an agreement." Devan leaned until he and the marquess were eye level. "But you're going to have to work hard. Are you ready to do that?"

The boy nodded vigorously.

In a couple of days, Devan would meet with the marchioness and discuss his thoughts. Her son should not go to Eton. At least not until Devan had the boy ready to face the mass of privileged and spoiled children who attended the prestigious institution.

Otherwise, the Marquess of Warwyk might be decimated by the bullies who resided in its hallowed halls within a week.

He couldn't wait to see Lady Warlock's flabbergasted expression when he told her his conclusions.

He would tell the Marchioness of Warwyk that, for once, he was in complete agreement with her.

*As you turn the other cheek, just remember that
there's no rest for the truly wicked.*
                    Mr. Devan Farris's theme for the Sunday
                              sermon to his pious flock

Chapter Five

As the last notes of the opening processional hymn
hung in the air, the Thistledown parish members
openly sighed in contentment. It could only be described
as a rich sound, one that should have provided Avalon
peace. Her community was happy with their parish and
their new vicar.

The vicar's clear baritone rang through the sanctuary
in welcome as he extended his arms wide as if enveloping them in his embrace. Devan Farris appeared larger
than life in his black-and-white vestments. The bell-
shaped sleeves of his cassock emphasized his long arms
and hands while the pristine white collar contrasted
nicely with his dark hair.

But it was the breathtaking smile on his face, which
highlighted his perfect white teeth, that had female
sighs and flutters joining in a chorus of undeniable pleasure at the countenance of their new vicar.

It was enough to make Avalon want to tilt her head to
the heavens and ask why.

Why did the pious killjoy have to reside in her community? At any moment, she expected him to call her

out by saying that God wanted to cast Lady Warlock from their midst so they could worship in peace.

Which would be perfectly acceptable to her as she thrummed her fingers atop the hymnal. She'd rather be anywhere else but here this morning. Sophia, Thane, and she had arrived late for the service, and instead of making a spectacle of themselves by parading down the aisle in the middle of the opening processional hymn to reach the pew reserved exclusively for the Warwyk family, they sat in the back of the church.

The view from there was certainly different than from the Warwyk pew, the first pew on the right side of the sanctuary. From where Avalon sat, she could see everyone in attendance. She made a mental note that from now on while Devan Farris resided in town, she'd prefer to sit here during services. It meant she could make a timely exit and leave the church before the irreverent vicar could lead the congregation through the recessional hymn.

However, it would not do to act so contrary because of his presence in her community. She needed to be here in church every Sunday. These people were hers, and she'd not shirk from the responsibility of caring for them.

As Mr. Farris spoke about his good fortune in moving to their parish, something that didn't hold her interest in the least, Avalon's gaze settled over the parishioners. The entire female population sported gaudy new bonnets and sparkling new ribbons in hopes of capturing the vicar's attention. If they'd only asked Avalon, she could have spared them their wasted time, money, and effort. The new vicar was only interested in one type of female, a rare breed, indeed—an heiress.

His effect on the masses explained egalitarianism to those unfamiliar with the term. Ladies, gentleman, girls, and even the babies in attendance drooled—*yes, drooled*—over Devan Farris. A gaping mouth on a lady in her ninth decade makes one either lose one's appetite or want to roar in disapproval.

In fairness to her and the well-being of the parish, Avalon should be the one in the pulpit, proselytizing about the evils of falling under the vicar's influence.

There was no denying he was handsome this morning, and everyone, including his conceited self, was aware of that fact. It was as if all intelligence in the fairer sex decided to fly out the window in his presence, if the fluttering of eyelashes and coy smiles were any indication.

The thrumming of her fingers grew loud enough that several members turned in their seats to see who was disrupting the vicar's speech.

Beside her, Thane's cheeks heated. "*Maman*, they think it's me making that racket." His whisper grew louder. "Will you please stop?"

Without turning her smiling face from the vicar's direction, Sophia discretely placed her hand over Avalon's, which immediately made Avalon cease her thrumming.

She huffed a silent protest. Simply put, while he stood there waxing and waning about "turn the other cheek," he was corrupting every moral female in the congregation with his potent wry smile.

But to keep peace within her family, she clasped her hands together and caught the vicar's knowing gaze. He tilted his head and directed a blazing but wicked smile her way as if saying *aha, you've been caught*. Unable to bear it without protest, Avalon tilted her chin up a notch to show him she'd not turn the other cheek and listen to his sermon. Instead, she directed her attention to the congregation.

Miss Sally Marcy, a middle-aged woman who'd never married because she took care of her hypochondriac mother, had slid one foot out into the aisle, giving Avalon a clear view of her half-boot. The poor woman had a hole the size of an egg on the sole. With Henri's help, a new pair would somehow mysteriously arrive on the woman's front step. Sally would never accept charity, but if an anonymous benefactor helped, she couldn't refuse. Avalon also added Sally and her mother to the list of villagers who received weekly baskets from Warwyk Hall.

Avalon searched the pews in both directions for Annie Dozier. It wouldn't be likely that she'd attend today as she'd been under the weather for the last several weeks, but Avalon had prayed that Annie would surprise them all with her appearance.

Well, it gave Avalon all the more reason to exit the service early, then deliver her weekly basket. Byrnn had been teething and fussy the last time Avalon had stopped by. She was anxious to see how the poor woman had fared over the last couple of days.

A slight giggle drew Avalon's attention. Penelope Rowley sat next to her aunt and uncle, completely fixated on the vicar. The sudden flutter of her lashes either meant she'd managed to attract a dust storm while sitting in their family pew, or she was flirting with the vicar.

Immediately, Avalon's gaze flew to Devan Farris's to see if he was encouraging such a silly reaction, or God help them all, if he was returning the girl's affection.

For heaven's sake, his attention was directed toward Avalon.

She stilled in her seat. From across the sanctuary, his green-eyed gaze pierced hers. Her heart pounded from the embarrassment of being caught allowing her concentration to wander. The truth was, it was his fault. He shouldn't give such boring sermons. She straightened in her seat and stared right back at him. She'd not allow him to upset her. So what if she'd garnered his attention?

It made all the difference in the world. Any weakness she divulged made her vulnerable.

The man had the ability to make her life miserable, but more importantly, he wielded influence over his brother's decision regarding Thane's education. She swallowed the sudden thickness in her throat. How long had it been since she'd felt such unease because of a man?

Particularly one who was so handsome.

It had been ten long, lonely years.

She clenched her gloved hands into tight fists. She would not allow his visage or his perfect body in the prime of life to ruffle her world. Nor would his warm, deep voice affect her.

She glared at him in defiance. The rogue hadn't the common courtesy to call on her to discuss Thane's curriculum or his conclusions about her son's readiness to attend Eton. Though it was a foregone conclusion that he'd recommend whatever his brother thought best for Thane. Blood was always thicker than water.

Finally, the organist pounded out the recessional hymn. Avalon realized she was the only one in the congregation still sitting, as the others were standing and singing their hearts out to God, the church, and undoubtedly to their new vicar.

Horrified that she'd allowed her musings to lead her so astray, she stood quickly. Before she could gather Thane and Sophia to steal away before the vicar led the procession to the vestibule, he passed her pew. He winked at Thane, who grinned in return and gave a small wave. Avalon could hear Sophia's giggle behind her. With a look of pure impishness, he smiled and nodded her way.

The man gave a sound reason to avoid church altogether. She could feel a megrim a week from now coming on. It would be a massive one, she could already tell.

Hopefully, God would empathize when she missed next week's sermon.

Whether the vicar would understand wasn't her concern.

He could go to the devil.

When he reached his position in the vestibule to greet the exiting members of his congregation, Devan took a deep breath and exhaled. The parishioners had enthusiastically received his first sermon. Judging by their reactions, he could have stood at the pulpit for at least another hour and recited the vicarage's recipe books without losing anyone's attention to a catnap.

He frowned slightly. One of his flock hadn't been as enamored with him as he would've liked. The preoccupied marchioness had fidgeted endlessly throughout the entire service. Perhaps she missed sitting in her pew and reigning over his flock as if it were hers.

A smile tugged at his lips. He loved the gall of her. She was not in the least impressed with him and let him know it with her expressions of disdain. However, when she thought he wasn't looking, she couldn't keep from glancing in his direction. Just a discreet smile or an innocent wink caused her to bristle like a hedgehog under attack.

He couldn't wait until she passed by. Inevitably, she'd try to sneak through the side entrance without talking to him, but he had his own plans. He'd try to finagle a dinner invitation from her for this evening. As her son's marquisate sponsored him, it was her responsibility to invite Devan to dinner on the evening of the first Sunday sermon to his new congregation.

As a flurry of parishioners approached, he greeted each one by name. Thankfully, he had a gift for remembering names and faces, and it had come in handy with all of his travels throughout the kingdom. Perhaps sometime in his future he'd settle and not have to rely on such a talent. The idea of becoming part of a community permanently wound itself around his heart like a warm embrace. He could easily see himself as the vicar serving this flock until his dying days. As he grew grayer, so would his benefactress. He had little doubt she'd still be a beauty at the age of seventy.

"Mr. Farris, we're so fortunate that God has graced us with your presence." Miss Sally Marcy shyly smiled.

"I consider myself the fortunate one, Miss Marcy." Devan clasped her chilled hand with his. Immediately his brow furrowed. Did the woman not have a warm enough cloak? "How is your mother? I didn't see her in attendance."

"She thought she was catching the ague but wanted me to ask if you could stop by sometime this week." Miss Marcy grew suddenly serious. "She does love her scripture, Mr. Farris."

"It would be my honor," Devan answered.

The next parishioner to demand his attention was Miss Penelope Rowley. The girl had shamelessly tried to flirt with him throughout the service while her aunt and uncle sat beside her completely oblivious. He exhaled slowly and prepared himself.

"Mr. Farris, your sermon has inspired me to look within myself to see how I might be able to forgive those who trespass against me." She dipped her eyes in a show of modesty, then instantly raised them to his, pursing her lips together as if sending him a kiss.

"How clever to recite the Lord's Prayer in relation to today's sermon." He kept his voice even in hopes there wasn't a hint of sarcasm in his answer.

"I'm honored you think so," she said with feigned modesty. "But you have a way with words that touches me deep inside." She placed her hand over her chest, then patted it as if trying to draw his attention to her bodice.

No doubt she could turn the head of any of the young men in the congregation, but Devan wasn't interested. He glanced to his side where Mr. Edward Grant, a somewhat wealthy young farmer, gazed from afar at the young woman.

"It's through the Lord's work that you found inspiration, Miss Rowley. Not mine." Devan smiled sincerely but couldn't help but notice that the young miss was fair of face and figure. She had to be at least twelve or fourteen years younger than his thirty-one years. Why she would even flirt with him was beyond his comprehension.

"Oh, how insightful, sir." She blinked twice, then three times rapidly.

"Is something in your eye?" he asked. Before she could answer, Devan's attention was directed to Lady Warwyk, who scurried away from him. He quickly nodded to Miss Rowley, then stepped toward Avalon. "My lady, might you have a moment?"

The marchioness stopped midstep, as if a thief stealing away in the night. She straightened her shoulders, then turned slowly toward him. "Of course, Vicar."

Thane and Lady Sophia drew alongside.

Thane nodded in greeting with a wide smile. "Will you come to tea or dinner?"

"Oh, you must, Mr. Farris," Sophia added. "We'd be delighted, wouldn't we, Avalon?"

The marchioness turned the full force of her delightful green-eyed gaze his way. "I apologize, but—"

"Avalon, it's customary that the sponsoring family . . ." Sophia whispered.

"I know," she whispered curtly to her little sister.

"Please, *Maman*," Thane added.

Avalon studied her son, then nodded to Sophia before

she turned his way. "Mr. Farris, would you come to dinner this evening? It'll be an informal affair, I'm afraid. I have several errands to attend to this afternoon."

"How delightful, my lady." He presented his most charming smile, then dipped a slight bow in her direction. "Dinner will be perfect as I've a few visits I must make myself."

"Excellent," Thane announced. "I have several new books that I'd love to show you. They're on military campaigns."

Devan squeezed the boy's shoulder. "I look forward to it, Lord Warwyk. I see you have a great deal to teach me about long-term strategy."

The boy beamed in response.

Thane and Sophia turned to Miss Rowley, who had demanded their attention. It left Devan the perfect opportunity to speak with Avalon privately.

"Wouldn't you say the long game is worth studying, my lady?" Devan turned his attention to Avalon.

"It would depend upon what you were fighting for," she said without blinking.

"Domination. After a long battle, perhaps the spoils of war would be domination of the other side?" Devan said, fully intending that she understand he spoke to her exclusively.

Her eyes widened.

"What do you think is worth fighting for?" he said softly. "Perhaps both sides want the same thing?"

She stared at him, and it was just the two of them as all others seemed to disappear. Her eyes blazed in challenge until her bravado melted before his eyes. For a brief moment, trepidation replaced her earlier temerity. Immediately, he wanted to withdraw the innuendo. For heaven's sake, he'd just taught a sermon on why one should turn the other cheek. Now, he stood before her trying to challenge her—wanting her to know that he found her . . . what?

What did he want her to know? That he found her desirable and interesting?

She'd laugh him out of church and out of Thistledown if he ever said such a thing. He almost thought she truly was a witch. Did she realize the power she held over others? Her wealth was only part of the equation. Her real influence lay in her stalwart demeanor seasoned with kindness for others.

The truth was she could conjure and beguile a banshee from its hiding place.

As a mere man, he had no resistance to her or her power.

Before he could issue an apology, she dismissed him with a tilt of her head. "Economics. This is the answer to your question. Every war boils down to money. Money is power. Men believe it's worth fighting for, Mr. Farris." She leaned a little his way and lowered her voice. "You do realize who holds all the power between us, Vicar?" She didn't wait for an answer. "It's me and my money. Now, shall we say six o'clock, then? We keep country hours at Warwyk Hall."

"Until then, my lady," he answered.

Without another word, she swept through the side entrance as if she were the Queen of Sheba and he were simply one of her lowly subjects. He couldn't help but grin. She was stronger than he gave her credit for. She had a few chinks of vulnerability in her armor, but she was a worthy opponent.

When he arrived at her home later in the day, he'd apologize for his outlandish comments.

Then what fun he and Lady Warlock would have this evening.

He couldn't wait to find out more about her.

The Golden Rule

In everything do to others as you would have them do to you . . .

Matthew 7:12

Chapter Six

A valon brought the horse to a gentle stop with a slight pull of the reins. The small cart creaked as she threw the fur rug aside and jumped to the ground. Henri did the same and soon stood by her side.

"My lady, you had cook load the wagon full this time. Are you expecting a blizzard?" A sly smile tugged at her lady's maid's lips. "Perhaps we should have asked the vicar to join us. With those brawny arms of his, he could unload the wagon in half the time . . . well, speak of the devil." Henri nodded in the direction of the north pasture.

There in all his glory, their vicar strolled across the furrowed field with a basket in his hand. Dressed in a black greatcoat, he appeared larger than life. The shoulder cape rippled from the cutting north wind, but none of it seemed to bother him. He raised a gloved hand in greeting, and a genuine smile graced his lips.

She and Henri raised their hands in return.

Shortly, he stood before them. Only his red cheeks indicated that the mighty wind had any effect on him.

So perfect in color, he appeared as if he were blushing from a kiss inflicted by the brisk wind.

Avalon shook her head, desperate to clear such thoughts. She had to quit reading Lord Byron's romantic works so late at night. It was all bother.

No. Devan Farris was all bother and nonsense.

"Good afternoon, my lady." He bowed slightly, then did the same to Henri.

Henri grew flustered for a moment, then quickly recovered. "Vicar. This makes the second time today we've had the pleasure of your company."

"No, I beg to differ, Miss Calvert. The pleasure is all mine. Plus, I'll even have more pleasure this evening when I come to dinner and see you again."

Her lady's maid blushed like a schoolgirl.

It was a sweet gesture to acknowledge her maid with such a greeting, and for an instant Avalon felt her own cheeks heat at the display. Henri was so dear to her, and the fact that the vicar acknowledged her thusly pleased Avalon immensely.

"Mr. Farris," she answered in greeting. Just then an ear-piercing screech rent the air around them. "That sounded like Byrnn." Without waiting for the vicar or Henri, Avalon rushed to Annie's door, which guarded the outside world from the simple but sturdy cottage.

"Annie!" She banged on the door with her fist all the while praying that all was well inside. The infant's wailing grew louder and more pitiful, as if he was truly in distress. "Annie?" she called again, this time louder.

But then Devan and Henri had joined her. The maid peeked into one of the glass windows that framed the door. It was an extravagance, but Avalon had insisted that each cottage had a way for the inhabitants to look outside, plus it had the advantage of making each cozy cottage appear a little larger from the inside.

"I don't see Annie, but Byrnn is sitting in the middle of the floor." She stole another peek then bit her lip. "He's mighty upset, my lady."

Without a thought, Avalon pushed the latch, but the door didn't give. "It must be locked from the inside."

"Stand aside," Devan's deep baritone announced behind her.

Avalon did as asked, expecting him to ram his shoulder against the door. Instead, he dropped to his knees and pulled from his pocket a pin of some sort. Immediately, he put it in the lock and fiddled with it. In seconds, he swung open the door.

Her eyes widened as she glanced between him and the open door.

A sheepish grin broke across his lips. "I learned this trick at Eton."

Without a word in answer, Avalon swept around him and rushed into the main room. Without hesitating, she scooped the baby boy into her arms. He was wet and his diaper soiled. He shivered in her arms and she cuddled him close. "Sweetheart, what's happened," she cooed.

Dried tears left streak marks on his tender cheeks, and a new tear fell as he let out another cry of distress. She kissed his cheek, then handed him to Henri. "Will you change him? Annie keeps his clothes in the basket by the hearth. See if you can find something for him to eat."

Devan was already at the fireplace building a new fire. "My lady, would you like me to go into the bedroom first?"

They all knew what he was saying. Whoever went into the bedroom first would find Annie. If she'd passed away, then the sight might be something none of them would ever forget for the rest of their lives. Quickly,

Avalon shook her head as she made her way to the bedroom.

When she opened the door, she sucked in a deep breath. Annie lay in the middle of the bed curled into a ball as if in pain. Avalon rushed to her side and sat on the bed.

"Annie," she soothed as she brushed her hand over the woman's wet brow. Immediately, the sweat reappeared as if staking a claim on the woman. The fiery flush colored her cheeks from a fever.

"My lady?" Annie's weak voice gave way to a bone-chilling rattle of a cough. Her teeth started chattering immediately after. "I fear the baby's coming."

By now, Devan had come into the room. Avalon didn't need to see him as she sensed his presence behind her.

"On the oak chest is a clean blanket. Will you fetch it?"

Within seconds, Devan was by her side again and carefully spread the blanket over Annie's curled body.

"It's too early," Annie whispered.

"I know, but help is here now." Avalon grabbed her cold hand and squeezed. "When was the last time you ate?"

"Hmm . . ." Annie turned away from her. "I don't want anything."

Henri came into the room still holding the baby. "My lady? What do you need?"

"Go find the midwife and tell her to hurry. See if you can find a wet nurse." Avalon reached into a concealed pocket on her cloak and brought out a clean handkerchief. She wiped Annie's brow again. Heat radiated from the poor woman's forehead. "Take Devan with you, he can drive the cart."

"No, my lady," Henri said. "I'll put Byrnn in a basket next to me. Mr. Farris should stay here with you."

"I agree," Devan answered behind her and handed her his handkerchief as hers was already sopping wet. "I can help you more here."

Avalon nodded.

"I'll be back as soon as I can." Henri's words floated to nothing along with Byrnn's whimpers as Avalon's maid quickly took her exit. The sound of a door closing soon followed.

"Tell me what to do, Avalon." Devan's deep baritone seemed to surround her.

Her own heart raced as she didn't know what to tell him. She didn't even know what she should do herself. "Pray."

"I'm already doing that," he answered.

Numb, she sat for a moment stroking Annie's forehead with a trembling hand. Her stomach twisted itself into knots. She'd never seen anyone this ill before. "I can't think of what else we should do."

"Avalon, let's change Mrs. Dozier's bedding," he said gently. "Perhaps she'd be more restful in dry clothes. I'm sure that would help."

She nodded once. She stood and pulled Annie closer to her. Devan rummaged through the chest until he found a clean set of linens. Within minutes, they had changed the bedding. Devan left the room, leaving Avalon alone with the ill woman.

Annie's shivers increased until her entire body shook. She clutched her swollen belly as if in pain. As best she could, Avalon tried to hold her in support, but Annie shook her head, spurning any comfort.

Devan returned with a basin of steaming water and several clean clothes. "Here. Why don't you try to bathe her. It might help with the fever."

Unable to speak, Avalon nodded as her throat had closed with fear. The pregnant woman seemed to be lapsing in and out of consciousness.

"Shall I step out of the room, or do you need my help?" He placed his hand on her shoulder, and in response she placed one of her hands over his, drawing strength from his composure.

"Why don't you step outside?" She turned to him.

He watched her with a grim face. "You're doing everything you can for her."

She shook her head as guilt seeped into every crevice of her body. "I should have been here every day. I knew she wasn't well."

"Hush." He lowered his voice. "You're here now."

He squeezed her shoulder once, then left.

Avalon swallowed as a sense of desolation swept over her. She pushed her guilt aside as best she could, then proceeded to clean Annie. Chills racked her prone body, and Avalon completed the task as quickly as possible. She pulled a clean nightgown over her, then brought the covers and the extra blanket over the woman. She unhooked her cloak, still warm from her own body, then draped it over her.

Annie reached one trembling hand out from under the covers and took Avalon's hand. Annie's grip tightened, and Avalon matched it.

"Thank you, my lady," Annie whispered.

"My pleasure." Avalon continued to hold her hand as Annie squeezed even harder before she loosened her grip.

The baby was coming and there wasn't a thing any of them could do to stop it. By her calculations, the baby shouldn't come for a least a month or a month and a half. Avalon bowed her head and prayed while still holding on to Annie's hand. As long as she held the woman's hand, Annie would know that Avalon was there by her side, and she wasn't alone.

Foolishly, she thought that if she continued to hold

the woman's hand, then death couldn't come and steal her away.

"Don't be concerned about Byrnn," Avalon said, trying to keep the worry from her voice. "Henri has him. She's feeding him and making certain he's warm. All you have to think about is you and the baby."

Annie didn't respond, and Avalon squeezed her hand.

Suddenly, a flurry of activity erupted on the other side of the door. In an instant, the door swept open and the local midwife, Mrs. Jennings, came in with Patricia, her oldest daughter.

"Hello, dear Annie," she said with a firm voice. "What's this that you're ill and the baby is coming early?" She sat across from Avalon on the bed. Her hand reached to touch the woman's brow. "She still has a fever."

Avalon nodded. "I bathed her, and that brought it down. She's resting, but I think the baby is coming."

Mrs. Jennings waved her daughter into the room. "Why don't you wait outside with the vicar, Lady Warwyk? My Patricia will help me. We'll see where Annie is in the birthing process."

Avalon stood and bent over Annie. "I'll be right in the next room."

She waited for a response, but when none was forthcoming, she took her leave. After she closed the door behind her, she leaned against it and closed her eyes. From nowhere, tears streamed down her cheeks.

Suddenly, strong arms enveloped her and, unable to resist such comfort, she leaned into the embrace. Devan offered a comfort she sorely needed but doubted she deserved. Without a word passing between them, she stayed enfolded in his arms.

His arms were like steel bands, and all she wanted in that moment was to take the solace and warmth he offered.

"Come and sit by the fire," he coaxed. "We can't have Lady Warlock taking a chill. We all need you too much to allow that."

Her normal umbrage failed to make an appearance at his teasing. She allowed him to lead her to the two chairs set in front of the fire.

"I should have visited her before this." She wiped her tears from her cheeks. "I failed in my duties to her."

The skin creased between his eyes. "Why would you say that? Do you think you could have stopped her fever or kept that baby from coming?"

"No. But I could have prayed for her more. I could have arranged for the midwife to come sooner. Perhaps she wouldn't be in so much distress now." Her tone turned challenging. "At least, Byrnn wouldn't have had to suffer so."

"Perhaps. But why do you think the entire responsibility falls on your shoulders?"

"Because, these are my people." She clasped her hands tightly. It was the only thing she could control at the moment as her heart felt as if it were breaking into pieces. "I'm responsible for their welfare. Every effort they expend upon the Warwyk estate or the commerce they provide benefits *my* community."

"Is it only yours?" His poise never wavered. "Doesn't this village, this parish, belong to all of us?"

She let out a deep breath. "Of course. But you know what I meant. They welcomed me when my very own husband didn't want me. I'd do anything for them." She turned her gaze from her hands to his face. His patient countenance held no judgments, and for a moment, she wanted to rail at him while simultaneously taking every comfort he offered. "Tell me this, Mr. Farris, why does God heap so much suffering on people like Annie Dozier?"

She saw him flinch when she formally addressed him. Their earlier ease in calling each other by their Christian names forgotten or, in her case, ignored. She was incensed at herself and God for Annie's sufferings. Unfortunately, the poor vicar happened to be the one who would bear the brunt of that anger.

He studied her as if he could see every hurt and slight and agony she'd ever borne. In defiance, she stared back, waiting for some trite saying of scripture or prayer to come from him so she could challenge him again. At this moment, she could care less if either Devan Farris or God himself called her a heretic and faithless in spirit.

He leaned forward until there was no more than a foot that separated them. The green of his eyes seemed to smolder, whether in anger or shock made little difference to her.

"People suffer, Lady Warwyk. Why God allows others to bear more than some is a question that I can't answer, and I won't even try."

She blinked slowly, wondering how to reply.

"But I can tell you this. I believe He knows best. None of us can fully understand, but He sees everything and knows infinitely more than we do. My faith derives from that knowledge. When I doubt"—Devan's gaze turned tender—"and we all, including me, doubt at times. We're human. But Paul gave us this thought: 'Only in heaven shall we understand God's will.'"

She released a breath and allowed the comfort of his words to console her.

"Remember, Avalon, even you, the mighty Lady Warwyk, who believes she is responsible for everyone, can't keep watch over all your people at the same time. The universe doesn't work that way."

Before she could respond, the front door opened, and

Henri entered. "Vicar." She nodded, then turned her undivided attention to Avalon. "My lady, I dropped Byrnn off at Mr. and Mrs. Stevens's house. Mrs. Stevens says he can stay with her as long as Annie needs him to."

Mrs. Jennings came into the room, and Avalon and Devan stood.

"My lady, you and the vicar should go home. Patricia and I will take care of Annie now. I believe the babe will come tomorrow. If something changes, I'll send someone to fetch you."

"Would you like me to stay?" Devan offered.

"No, Mr. Farris. We'll see you tomorrow." The midwife smiled at them, then addressed Avalon. "My lady, we'll get her through this."

Avalon nodded. "I'll send a footman to stay with you. He can help with the fire, fetch food, and come get me when you need me."

"That would be much appreciated, my lady," Mrs. Jennings said. "Have him bring more linens, if you don't mind."

"Of course," Avalon answered.

Mrs. Jennings gave her the cloak laid across her arm. "You'll need this, Lady Warwyk."

Devan reached and took the garment from the midwife's outstretched hands. Without a word spoken, he draped it around Avalon's shoulders, then proceeded to don his greatcoat.

Avalon took one last look at the cottage inside and said a silent prayer.

One was for Annie and her unborn child.

The other was a thank-you for delivering a certain vicar into their midst.

The ordinary sense of words should be adhered to unless it results in some absurdity that makes no sense whatsoever.

The personal musings of Mr. Devan Farris

Chapter Seven

❧

As Avalon asked the midwife to inform her immediately of any change in Annie's condition, Henri and Devan unloaded the cart with the food and supplies for Annie's house. Avalon had completely forgotten that she'd packed the cart full for Annie and Byrnn's use.

When the cart was empty, they said their farewells, then all left the cottage together. Henri stood waiting for her mistress to join her on the ride back to Warwyk Hall.

"I'm going to walk back, Henri. I need the exercise," Avalon called out.

Without a word, Henri nodded then hauled herself into the driver's seat. She grasped the reins then turned to Devan. "Vicar, may I offer you a ride to the vicarage?"

"No, thank you. If the marchioness doesn't mind the company, I'll walk with her." He stole a glance in Avalon's direction as if asking permission.

She waved Henri on. "I'll take your company, Mr. Farris."

Her maid smiled as if happy with the arrangement,

then with a click of her tongue engaged the team of horses to set off for home.

The wind whipped Avalon's cloak tightly around her legs, but she barely noticed as she crossed the field toward home. Her thoughts whirled with Annie and what she should do to help the woman and her family. Only when Devan held his arm out, once they reached a stile staircase over the ha-ha, did she give him any notice.

"You must think I'm horrible company," she said as she took his proffered arm and neatly climbed the three steps to the next field.

"Not at all. You have much on your mind." He followed her ascent, and they continued their path to Warwyk Hall. "Once I see you home, I'll take my leave."

"What about dinner?"

A smile tugged his lips. "Well, after today, I'm not certain you'd want any further intrusions on your evening."

"Nonsense. I invited you to dinner." She stopped and turned to face him. The light of the day had faded but it was still bright enough to caress his cheeks. The soft glow only enhanced his attractiveness. She could easily see why women were enamored with him.

She shook her head slightly. It was as if a magical wood nymph had cast some sort of spell, making Avalon soften her regard for him. But why should she be so surprised? He'd been comforting and helpful when she'd needed assistance with Annie. He'd not allowed her to wallow in self-pity when she'd questioned God's plans.

There were still a few hours before dinner. "I know it's early, but Thane will be sorely disappointed if you don't come."

"I never asked him, but does he know how to play chess?" Devan's gaze grew bright.

"I don't believe so, unless one of his governesses or tutors taught him." They proceeded to walk to the house. "Do you play?"

"Every chance I can get." He beamed.

His sudden smile radiated warmth, and she wanted to bask in it. If she wasn't careful, he could easily become a habit she could grow accustomed to.

But that tiny spec of doubt, the one that sought refuge around her heart, awoke. No good would come from trusting this man too much. His brother wanted to send her son away. Only she knew what was in Thane's best interest—not the Earl of Larkton or his brother, Devan Farris. Besides the old vicar, Mr. Knightley, all the other men in her life had disappointed her. It was too early to tell what kind of a man Devan Farris was. He could be just like the rest of them.

"I'd like to teach your son how to play. With his interest in strategy, I think it'll help with his logic skills, which inevitably would help him with his studies." He stopped and surveyed the land in front of him.

She stood beside him. "I guess there's no harm in that. There's really no risk involved. I'm not in favor of Thane learning skills of chance."

He didn't turn from his study of the massive garden and the accompanying maze.

"Capability Brown designed the park for the previous marchioness, my late husband's mother. I've never had cause to admire it before. It truly is a lovely landscape, one that invited people to enjoy the view as they walked the grounds."

"It's a beautiful home Lord Warwyk has inherited," he said amiably. "Your responsibility is immense, as it is you alone who bears the task to teach him how to protect his ancestry." He turned his gaze to hers. "And his fortune, while keeping the estate profitable."

His green eyes seemed to flash as brilliant as any emerald she'd ever seen in her life.

"Shall we?" He extended his gloved hand as if inviting her to continue their walk.

Without answering, she continued their walk at a brisk pace. With his long stride, he easily caught up with her, then adjusted his steps to match hers.

"I don't know how to say this without being plainspoken, so please forgive me."

The hairs on the back of her neck stood at attention, and it wasn't from the cold, as she'd pulled her fur hood to cover her head. "Go on."

"Your son should not go to Eton."

She stopped immediately at the happy news and placed her hand over her heart. "Thank you. I don't know what else to say. I'm simply delighted that you share my opinion about the suitability of Eton. Thane wouldn't be happy there."

He narrowed his eyes and shook his head once. "You misunderstand."

"How so?" she asked warily.

"He shouldn't go to Eton because he's not ready."

"He's not ready?" Avalon drawled as she narrowed her eyes.

Devan nodded briefly. "He'd be eaten alive by the other fellows if they even sniff how much he's been coddled by you. Believe me, they'll ferret it out."

"Coddled," she exclaimed. "He's a sweet, gentle young man—"

"I know he is. That's part of the problem. I was just like him when I attended Eton. On the first day, I was beaten to a bloody pulp. The other boys could sense my weakness. When I came home on break, Gavin taught me how to fight."

"My son will not become a barbarian." She took a

step forward, and Devan stopped her progress by taking her hands in his to garner her full attention. He gazed down upon her, and the glimmer in his eyes reflected true concern.

"I didn't have the blunt necessary to fraternize with the wealthier boys so I learned to compromise. I charmed them with my wit and good nature. Gavin and my other brothers, Niall and Hearne, taught me. I was fortunate to find true friends there. Lifelong friends. It could have turned out so different for me without my brothers."

For a moment, she lost herself in the green depth of his eyes, then forced herself to turn away. She'd not be persuaded to change her opinion on Eton. "Thane is not suited to Eton. I need him here. There's much to learn." She let out a breath. "He'd never fit in."

He gently tightened his grip on her hands. "Those are just excuses. What is the real reason you don't want him to go?"

She bit her lip and slightly shook her head. The real reason was simple. She didn't want Thane to be humiliated when he learned that his father had a bastard he loved more than him. She'd spare him such pain. She didn't want to see Thane become embittered once he went away to school. Nor would she allow Richard and his edict that both sons attend Eton together have any impact on her son. He was hers to love and cherish.

"Thane wants to go to Eton. Doesn't that count for something? He doesn't have the support of older brothers, but I'll help him. Avalon, he needs to learn how to interact with his peers."

"I didn't give you permission to call me by that," she said sternly. It wasn't from outrage, but a defensive position, as no one had ever faulted her as a mother. Now she had a too-handsome vicar who was a self-proclaimed heiress hunter trying to give her lessons on the proper manner of being a mother to her child.

"You didn't, but when I called you by your name at Annie Dozier's home, you didn't object." With care, he squeezed her hands. "I thought you were allowing me such a personal address, as I heard you call me Devan." His gaze searched hers. "I liked hearing my name on your lips. I thought perhaps . . ."

She stared at his gloved hands holding hers. Through two layers of leather, she could feel the heat of him reaching her—filling her with a warmth she desperately needed. She closed her eyes to concentrate on his touch. "I apologize for my outburst," she said. "I'm out of sorts."

"It's perfectly understandable. I apologize for my timing. I shouldn't have brought up Thane and Eton with everything you've gone through today." He squeezed her hands again briefly. "Forgive me?"

Surprised by his unpredictability, Avalon forced her gaze to his. He took her breath with the honest sincerity on his face. This man was dangerous on so many levels. If she possessed any sense, she'd send him on his way, then write the Earl of Larkton and say his brother was too familiar for her tastes and wasn't a good fit for Thistledown.

Instead, for the first time in ages, she felt connected to a person outside of her family and staff. A man, no less. One who had a horrible reputation as a rake and a rogue, not to mention a man who possessed a talent to pick locks that thieves would envy, yet she clung to him like a buoy in a rough sea.

He'd proven his worth to her this afternoon with Annie. He hadn't shied away when she'd needed his help even though it was common knowledge that Annie had a dissolute past. Perhaps he wasn't as sanctimonious as she presumed.

"I forgive you if you do the same for me," she answered.

He smiled, a true smile that seemed to light him from within. It made him breathtakingly handsome, and she inhaled deeply, catching a scent of orange, spice, and the musky scent of a man that combined into a fragrance she didn't think she'd ever tire of. With his hair too long, and his eyes gleaming, she could easily see him sailing a ship as a privateer determined to find his fortune or perhaps that elusive heiress he sought.

For that singular moment, she wanted to be that heiress. She wanted to belong to him, and he to her in return.

My God, what was she saying? Too much fresh air had rattled her senses. This was Devan Farris, the Earl of Larkton's brother, and all six feet plus however many inches of him were the biggest thorn she'd ever had in her side. His duty to his brother required he spy on her. He turned up wherever she was—invited or not. Plus, he called her Lady Warlock.

But most importantly, somehow during this walk on a chilly afternoon with a gray sky over their heads, the new Thistledown vicar had made her believe for the first time in a long time, she might have someone who was on her side.

Which made him not just a thorn, but a very dangerous one at that.

"Come, let's continue before you catch a chill." Devan took Avalon's arm and walked toward the manor.

She nodded briefly, not really paying attention as it seemed her thoughts had traveled elsewhere.

He dipped his head to garner her focus. "Forget what I said about your son."

"No, I want to hear your thoughts." She exhaled a deep breath and a rush of white vapor plumes escaped. "It's getting colder." She tilted her gaze to his. "Do you think Annie and Mrs. Jennings are warm enough?"

"I would wager on it. By now, your Henrietta has probably sent over two footmen to keep watch over the house." He patted her hand that rested lightly on his arm. "I wouldn't be at all surprised if during dinner we hear that she's delivered a healthy baby girl."

"How would you know about such things?" she challenged.

"I'm a vicar. We know everything. Including all the gossip. The odds are two to one at the village pub that Mrs. Dozier will have a girl this time." He offered this last tidbit as a way to summon a smile from her.

And was rewarded for his effort.

"I suppose you've had your fair share of births and deaths in your line of work," she acknowledged.

"Some of the happiest and saddest times of my life." He dropped her hand and held up a low-hung branch of an oak tree that blocked their path. "But the truth is I wouldn't trade it for anything. Do you know why?"

She shook her head and preceded him on the path. He carefully dropped the branch so it wouldn't hit either of them in the backside, then quickly caught up with her, securing her hand around his arm once again. "It reaffirms life and all its glories."

"I can understand that thought." When she tilted her head to his, her hood fell back, revealing those luxurious brown curls.

It took every piece of willpower he had not to stop and feel the texture of her hair. The locks glowed like dark brown satin, and his fingers itched to play with them. Suddenly, an urge, a want, slammed into him, something that could only be called desire surged through him, heating his blood, making him want to kiss her right then and there in the cold air.

After all those years of learning how to subdue his desires, his willpower had seemed to have gone on a holiday over the last week. He swallowed and studied the landscape. He forced himself to ignore her rose scent. More importantly, he convinced himself to ignore the softness of her hand that was barely concealed by her leather gloves. The simple touch of her hand resting on his arm burned through the wool of his greatcoat and his black morning coat. It singed the linen of his shirt until his skin felt on fire.

In an act of self-preservation, he took his other hand and placed it over hers, the one resting on his arm. Though the truth was that deep down inside, he had to touch her. For this afternoon, a truce had been called between them. How long it lasted was something he didn't want to hazard a guess at.

"What would you know about gossip?" she asked.

"Hmm?" he responded, completely distracted by her.

"You said that you knew all the gossip." She bent closer and lowered her voice. "How would you, a new-comer to our town, know any gossip?"

"Never doubt my powers, my lady."

She stopped and studied him with a seriousness that made him smile.

"What?" he asked.

"I believe you."

"Meaning?" he asked.

"You do have special powers." Her gaze drifted from the top of his head to his well-worn boots. "The only question I have is whether it's a power from heaven or from the devil."

He couldn't help himself. He leaned back and laughed at the sky overhead. Though it was almost dark, the sky had turned into a marble of grays, white, and a tinge of red from the setting sun that broke through the clouds and demanded attention.

"Perhaps a bit of both," he said through his laughter.

"I knew it all along," she said, joining in with his amusement. "After all, I am the resident witch."

"And a lovely one at that," he murmured with a grin.

An eye for an eye and a tooth for a tooth.

Exodus 21:24

Chapter Eight

Dinner turned out to be a delightful, intimate affair that Devan enjoyed sharing with Avalon and her family. Thane had been enthralled with every word he said, and the same could be said about Lady Sophia.

However, Avalon reigned over the head of the table like a queen, one who sat consumed with dark thoughts. Devan could practically see the gloomy gray clouds of worry appearing over her head. She ate practically nothing, added little to the conversation, and when the meal was at an end, she'd escorted them to a private salon adjacent to the small dining room.

Thane eagerly found a chess set, one that had to be worth a small fortune. Every piece had a burnished gold-leaf bottom that captured the glow of the fire, making the pieces almost appear as if alive when they moved across the board.

Sophia sat comfortably next to Thane and read a novel while Devan started teaching the young marquess how to play the game. Devan's seat on the navy brocade sofa was strategically located so he could gaze at Avalon while still conversing with Thane and Sophia.

Avalon sat in profile on a small velvet chaise longue before the fire. Occasionally, Thane would ask his mother a question. She'd answer, but only after dragging herself from thoughts that seemed to hold her captive. Eventually, Sophia announced she would retire, leaving Devan with Thane and a very-distant Avalon.

"Mr. Farris, come to dinner tomorrow?" Thane's eyes blazed in the reflection of the warm fire as he replaced the pieces in their wooden box. "We could continue our game."

"Perhaps," he answered noncommittally. He'd like nothing more than to attend the family again, but Avalon might not like the familiarity of his presence on a regular basis at her dining table. "Do you ride?"

Thane dipped his head in a feigned sudden interest in the white knight. "I love to ride, but *Maman* only allows it when she's at the stables with me. She's so busy that I don't get to ride as much as I'd like."

Devan studied the boy. "Do you have your own horse?"

"I have a pony named Aster. I'm anxious for a horse"—he let out a soulful sigh—"but everything in time. *Maman* just gave permission for a puppy. Perhaps I should have asked for a horse."

Devan leaned close. "Sometime this week, I'll stop by and you could show me your stables. Perhaps we could find a suitable mount for you there."

Thane's eyes grew wide. "Would you? There's a beautiful gray mare by the name of Storm who's gentle and sweet. I feed her treats every day. Perhaps with your help, I could convince my mother to let me ride her."

It was the first time that Devan could recall the boy referring to his mother as such. Though the French endearment of *maman* had nothing wrong with it, a boy Thane's age and position in society had to be careful of referring to his mother as such. The boys at Eton would tease him endlessly if they heard such a term used by a marquess.

Devan's attentions returned to Avalon, and the need to draw her out of her melancholy grew acute. Avalon had shifted positions. She leaned into the corner of the chaise longue and her head rested on the back. "Lady Warwyk?"

She didn't move an inch at Devan's gentle inquiry.

"She's asleep." Thane stole a glance at his mother. "She falls asleep down here all the time. Sometimes if I wake up in the middle of the night, I find her there, curled up. I keep a coverlet hidden under her chair in case she's cold."

Devan nodded. "That's what the man of the house should do. Take care of his family."

Thane sat a little straighter at Devan's praise.

"Do you ever wake her up so she can go to bed?"

Thane shook his head. "I have in the past. She just smiles and says, 'Thank you, but I'd rather stay here.' I don't think she likes her bedroom." Without another word, he stood and walked to his mother. He leaned over and pulled a velvet throw from under the chaise longue. Carefully, so as to not wake her, he spread it over her sleeping form, then kissed the top of her forehead.

He returned to Devan's side and smiled sheepishly. "I don't want her to catch a chill."

Before Devan could respond, Mr. Neville entered the sitting room. "Vicar," he said quietly.

Devan stood, and along with Thane, they walked to Mr. Neville.

"One of the footmen has returned from Mrs. Dozier's home. The midwife has asked for your attendance. Mrs. Dozier delivered the babe, but Mrs. Jennings fears the babe needs you."

That could only mean one thing. The midwife didn't believe the child would make it through the night. "Any word on how Mrs. Dozier is doing?"

Mr. Neville shook his head. "The footman is waiting in the hallway to escort you. Mrs. Jennings asked if the marchioness could come."

Devan glanced at Avalon. She hadn't moved an inch from her position, still asleep. "I think it best if we allow Lady Warwyk rest. It's been an eventful and upsetting day. I'd hate to cause her any further distress by asking her to come with me this evening. I can stop by in the morning with news."

Mr. Neville nodded.

Thane sidled close to Devan's side. "May I go with you?"

Devan squeezed his shoulder. "I think it would be best, my lord, if you kept watch over your mother."

Thane reluctantly nodded. "I'll be waiting for you in the morning." He turned his full gaze to Devan. "I'm so glad you're ours. I know my mother is too."

Such simple words, but the power of the boy's statement filled an emptiness in Devan that had been his companion for years. "There's no place else I'd rather be, my lord."

And he meant it. A certain perplexing marchioness had somehow woven her way into his life.

If he wasn't careful, she'd use her witchery and steal her way into his heart.

The continuous bonging of the longcase clock woke Avalon. She tried to count how many chimes, but she had to have missed some. She swung her legs over the chaise longue, then stood. The velvet coverlet Thane hid for her fell into a plush heap on the floor. She made quick work of folding it, then put it back in its hiding place, all the while smiling at her son's thoughtfulness.

When had Devan left and what did he think of her,

his hostess who fell asleep after inviting him into her home for dinner?

Really, did she care?

The truth was she did. Not only did she want his good opinion for herself so her work could continue in Thistledown, but she wanted him to agree with her about Thane's future education. She stretched her hands over her head in an attempt to get the crick out of her neck, then glanced at the clock that had made the infernal racket that woke her up.

Just past midnight, the night was still young and the fire robust in her sitting room. One of the footmen must have built the fire up to keep her in comfort. She felt a warm glow flow through her. Naturally, it was from the fire but also gratitude that her staff cared enough about Sophia, Thane, and herself to see to their comfort always.

Avalon went in search of Mr. Neville. He always stayed up as long as she was downstairs. She'd tried to break him of the habit years ago, but he refused. He'd always reminded her that while he was butler at Warwyk Hall, he'd be the last to go to bed.

She found the stalwart butler with a footman. "Mr. Neville, when did the vicar leave?"

"My lady," he acknowledged with a slight bow. "Mr. Farris left a little after nine o'clock. Mrs. Jennings called for him and you. Mrs. Dozier delivered the baby." He bowed solemnly. "The midwife wasn't certain the baby would last through the night."

Her heart fell to the bottom of her chest. Annie couldn't bear much more grief in her life. "Why didn't you wake me?"

"Mr. Farris instructed that you sleep," Mr. Neville answered sheepishly.

"Since when does he employ you?" Immediately, she wanted to withdraw the words. "We'll discuss this when I return." She turned her attention to the footman who stood next to the butler.

The young man's gaze fell to the floor.

"Will you fetch my cloak and gloves?"

"My lady, if I may be so bold?" Mr. Neville clasped his hands in front of him. "I didn't mean to overstep my authority, but you were so exhausted."

"It's fine." She let out a tremulous sigh. The only thing she wanted to address at the moment was the walk to Annie's cottage.

When the footman, Jasper, returned with her things and a lantern, she asked for his company on the walk. They didn't speak along the way as Avalon repeated a prayer over and over asking for mercy for the Dozier family. Within a quarter hour, they stood outside Annie's home. She knocked, then let herself inside.

Jasper stood on the doorstep waiting for his instruction. "My lady, shall I stay?"

She shook her head. "There's no need. I'll stay here until daybreak."

He nodded, then turned for home. Inside the main sitting area, the midwife's daughter sat at the kitchen table with her head resting on her folded arms. Fearing the worst, Avalon rushed into Annie's room.

Mrs. Jennings was the first to notice her and waved in welcome. "Come in, my lady," she said in a whisper.

Avalon's gaze darted to Annie. The woman sat in her bed with a tiny bundle close to her chest. "Come, my lady, and meet my daughter. I've named her Nessa after my James's mother." The joy on her face melted any remaining tinges of illness.

Avalon sat on the bed next to Annie, and the new mother tilted the bundle in her direction. A tiny red-faced baby appeared. Avalon stroked the newborn's soft cheek with the back of her finger. "She's beautiful, Annie."

Annie nodded in response, then tears welled in her eyes. "We were worried about her earlier as her breathing was shallow. But once the vicar arrived and said a prayer for Nessa and me, she started getting stronger. I don't know how to thank you. If you hadn't shown up when you did, I don't know what would have happened to us."

"Don't thank me." Avalon felt the guilt start to raise its ugly head. "I should have been here sooner." She placed her hand on Annie's arm and squeezed gently. "I promise I'll stop by more frequently."

She caught Devan staring at her from across the room. Instinctively, she returned the stare before she recovered her manners and turned to the midwife. "What can I do to help, Mrs. Jennings?"

"My lady, we're fine here. Patricia is sleeping in the front room, and I'm going to make a cot beside Annie and Nessa. We all need a good night's sleep to set everyone back to rights." She turned to the vicar. "I believe Mr. Farris was just about to leave also."

"Indeed." Devan pushed away from the wall. "If your footman or lady's maid is not in attendance, Lady Warwyk, then allow me to escort you home."

Ignoring him, she said goodbye to Annie and Mrs. Jennings. Without waiting for Devan, she walked out the front door, then proceeded in the direction of Warwyk Hall.

"Lady Warwyk," he called out behind her.

In response, she walked faster away from him. Thankfully, the wind had died down so she wasn't fighting against it, too.

"Avalon," he said directly behind her. "Wait."

Suddenly, she stopped and turned around, almost bumping into him. The force of her movement caused her cloak to whip around her legs in an angry movement. "Don't you dare *ever* try to circumvent my actions again, *Vicar*."

The befuddlement on his face would have been amusing if she wasn't so livid. Not since Richard had sent her to Warwyk Hall after they were married while he frolicked in London had she ever been this angry.

"And pray tell, what has brought out this mood, Lady Warlock?" Though it was night, the moon was bright enough that she could see his face where one arrogant but perfect eyebrow arched. "I thought we were long since past this." He tilted his head and stared into the sky. "But that explains it. It's a full moon tonight."

"You sanctimonious, pompous arse," she seethed. "How dare you try to undermine my authority and my right to do as I please."

He rubbed a gloved hand down his face. She could hear the leather scraping the evening bristle that had grown since yesterday morning when he'd probably last bathed and shaved. "Help me, Avalon. What have I done?"

She leaned a little closer, and he matched her movement. His eyes twinkled in the moonlight, and she puffed a stream of white steam in exasperation.

"Mrs. Jennings asked me to come to Annie's the same as you. You unilaterally made the decision that I was to stay home."

"You were asleep," he offered.

"*It wasn't your decision.*" She kept her voice low, but it trembled in outrage. "I make my own decisions, and no man will ever take that right away from me ever again. Do you understand? *Never again.*" She pointed her forefinger toward the middle of her chest. "I can see into the hearts of others, and I know you were trying to usurp my authority. I will not stand for any of your manipulations, sir." Her eyes skated from the top of his head to his boots. A moue of displeasure curled her lips.

Silence descended between them as the last of her clipped words disappeared like a puff of smoke into the night. He stood close enough that she could feel his warmth. Only inches separated them, but at the moment the chasm between them had to be wider than a mile.

He studied her with a seriousness that made her want to run and hide in fear he'd discover everything about her—all the hurts and fears she'd suffered in the past along with all her hopes for the future.

Immediately, she covered her mouth with her hand. She'd allowed her innermost thoughts to slip free.

"Something tells me we're talking about more than my decision to let you sleep after you came home exhausted from Mrs. Dozier's last night." The softness in his voice made her even more wary.

She stood frozen.

"Tell me," he coaxed.

The smoothness in his voice, like a perfect panel of silk, floated over her, encouraging her to confide in him. It begged the question whether all clergymen possessed such dangerous talent or was it just him, a silver-tongued devil who could lure all the snakes out of Egypt.

She willed herself to fight against such magic and against him. To say anything to Devan Farris about her experiences with Richard or the Earl of Larkton, or even how her own father had circumvented the happiness of his own daughter by betrothing her to Warwyk for purely mercenary reasons could impact Thane's future. Larkton could call her unfit to make any decisions for Thane since she despised men in authority. Because she wouldn't bend to a man's erroneous belief that he had

an inherent right to make decisions for her. She'd fight
to her last breath before she'd allow any man to take
control of her son.

How could she have lowered her guard around Devan
Farris earlier? It was as if she wanted him to charm her.
For heaven's sake, she'd practically begged him to come
to dinner with the excuse that Thane would be disappointed. The truth was she didn't want him to go for her
own selfish reasons. She'd found strength in his presence at Annie's.

She'd found comfort in his arms. She'd allowed herself to think of him as a friend and perhaps something
more.

For God's sake, what was happening to her? Every
piece of common sense she possessed flew down the
road in chase after Mr. Devan Farris like autumn leaves
caught in a gust.

"Avalon, tell me." He took one of her hands in his and
intertwined their fingers together.

Such a simple action possessed so many different meanings. Lovers held hands like that when they
couldn't keep away from one another. Sweethearts who
were just discovering the depth of their feelings might
twist their fingers together as if testing how the description of beloveds fit them. Of course, friends held hands
in a show of tenderness, understanding, or simply true
concern.

None of those terms described her and Devan, so she
snatched her hand from his. Such a show of affection
was probably an everyday occurrence to him as a flirt.
But that didn't diminish the loss of his touch. Her throat
tightened and her eyes stung. Suddenly, everything
turned blurry.

Were those tears?

She quickly wiped her eyes against the cloak covering one arm. She was turning into a simpering fool, and it was all Devan Farris's fault.

"What have I done?" He held his arms out away from his body. "What do you want?"

"I want you to leave me alone."

"Well, that's not going to happen," he answered.

"How much money is it going to take for you to leave me alone?" she hissed.

"How much do you have?" He lifted both brows, waiting for her answer. "Larkton wants me to become a rector. You need to make it worth my while for me to say yes."

"More than enough, you despicable lout," she said, keeping her gaze glued to his. "Rector," she scoffed. "More like rectum."

"I didn't *wreck them*." He lifted an arrogant brow, but his lips twitched in mirth. "For your information, I killed them." Then as if he couldn't help himself, Devan laughed aloud as if enjoying her name-calling. "What a charming sense of humor you possess for a warlock. If I didn't know you better, I'd think you're growing sweet on me."

"You're delusional," she retorted.

"Someone needs to expand their vocabulary out of the *d*'s. Tomorrow, I can tutor you." That aggravating lopsided grin appeared. "I wager we can finish the *e*'s if *you* work hard."

"You're diabolical," she murmured.

"I heard that," he quipped. "But no need to show your prowess on the *d*'s. Remember I've heard you call me the devil before."

She pursed her lips into a thin line. The man drove her crazy. "I now understand your role in our community."

"Oh?" He tilted his head and smiled. The grin emphasized his full lower lip.

For an outrageous moment, she wanted to bite it. "Indeed. Mr. Greatwell's livestock won't be needed for next year's nativity scene. You can easily stand in for his prized ass."

Instead of her words angering him, his smile grew even bigger. "Wonderful. It means you still want me here. I'll be in your delightful and witty company for another year."

"You are a dreadful menace. You endanger anyone's sanity if they spend any time at all conversing with you."

"An *e* word." He winked at her. "Bully for you. You'll be a star pupil in no time." He held out his arm for her to take so they could continue on their way.

She slowly examined his arm, then turned up her nose.

It was all she could offer to end their ridiculous conversation. Without a look back, she made a half turn and continued on her way toward Warwyk Hall.

"Avalon, wait. I'll see you home."

"There's no need, nor do I want you to, Vicar." She pulled the neck of her cloak a little tighter.

"There's every need." The silkiness of his voice seemed to surround her. "What if you fall?"

"Suit yourself." Avalon turned abruptly and locked her gaze with his. "But if you fall, you're on your own."

Completely perplexed, Devan had no choice but to follow Avalon to Warwyk Hall. He purposely stayed a good ten or twenty yards behind her. After she'd left him, clearly upset, he couldn't as a gentleman allow her to make her way in the dark. Not that there was anything that could hurt her, but if she fell and sprained her ankle, he wanted to be there for her. She'd known he was there. Several times she'd turned around to see where he was. She never said a word. Afterward, she'd faced forward and continued on her way.

When they reached the massive courtyard that surrounded the Palladian manor house, he'd hung back until she mounted the steps and was safely inside.

Moments later, a footman ran toward him. "Vicar?" The man held out a lantern. "Lady Warwyk asked that I give you this. She said she didn't want you to worry about falling."

The words punched him in the gut, and he grinned. The way back to the vicarage led through a small forest that would be pitch-black even with a full moon. "Tell Lady Warwyk I appreciate the gesture."

Devan turned and took the path toward home, slowly shaking his head. Though she was clearly angry, she'd not see him hurt either. His chest tightened. He'd seen her cross with him through the years, but never once had he seen tears of frustration and anger mar her face. The sight had practically brought him to his knees. She was such a strong woman and for her to be that upset, he'd hit a wound that had never healed.

In fact, he'd sliced it right open.

He'd hope by teasing her that she'd forget whatever had upset her. He'd seen enough in his years as a man of the church to know that her sorrow came from a place deep inside, and he doubted she'd ever shared any of it with anyone she was close to. Her sister and son didn't seem to be affected by such trouble, but her son was sensitive enough to know that something bothered his mother. It was apparent to the young lord that whatever haunted his mother kept her from attaining any type of happiness for herself—including marriage.

Indeed, why would a beautiful young woman like her still be unmarried? Many a woman who'd lost their husbands had played the merry widow, but not Avalon. If anything, with her purported outlandish spending habits, she played the merry widow before her husband had died.

When Devan had seen her last spring at Lady Prydwell's soiree, she'd seemed cool and calm. They'd even talked briefly. Though he called her Lady Warlock to her face, her anger hadn't made an appearance as it had tonight.

She hid her fragility well, but she'd exposed herself tonight. He'd have to be more careful with her as he discovered her secrets. The first meeting of the Ladies Auxiliary since he'd arrived into town was scheduled for Wednesday afternoon.

For some reason, he thought they might be able to help other. She'd help him find a place within her community, and he'd help her battle the loneliness that seemed to be her ever-present companion.

He'd just have to tame his wild urges to kiss her until he cracked that protective veneer she surrounded herself with.

Unfortunately, his urges were growing stronger.

Or maybe it was fortune smiling down on him.

Heaven did move in mysterious ways.

She is clothed with strength and dignity; she can laugh at the days to come.

Proverbs 31:25

Chapter Nine

S ophia, why don't you and Penelope arrange a sitting area so Jasmine and Flora have someplace where they can drape the dresses?" Avalon asked as she straightened the table in the main salon.

Sophia and Penelope immediately started to arrange several brocade chairs in a semicircle. Avalon nodded her approval, then directed the assisting footmen to move a table and chairs to the opposite side of the room.

Jasmine Sinclair and Flora Leona would arrive with the dresses they'd designed and created for the winter party fundraiser. They were the newest members of their small village. Due to their fathers' early deaths and no other family to take them in, they found themselves in London seeking work. As with many a country miss who hoped to find gainful employment in the city, their opportunities were few. Within a short period of time both women found themselves as prostitutes for a very nefarious bawdy house.

Avalon made her way to a small drum table where she kept the journal that contained all the notes from the previous Ladies Auxiliary meetings, when she heard Penelope's whisper loud and clear.

"Though I'm not planning on staying in London for

the Season, I do want to see the dresses on display."
Penelope patted her hair in a hanging mirror while Sophia
moved another chair. Penelope bit her lower lip, then
pursed her lips together as if preparing for a kiss. Next,
she pinched both cheeks in an effort to bring a blush to
the surface.

"Why don't you want to experience the Season?"
Sophia's bafflement was clear in her voice. "Don't you
want to meet the most eligible men of the *ton* and pick
one out for a husband?"

"There's only one eligible man for me," Penelope
purred. "I found him right here in Thistledown."

"Are you referring to Edward Grant?" Sophia asked.
"I always thought you carried a *tendré* for him."

Penelope shook her head. "No. I have no need for a
boy. I want a man."

"Who is it?" Sophia asked.

By now, their conversation had grown even more
discreet, but Avalon could still hear every word.

"The vicar. I expect him to propose any day," Penelope boasted.

"Mr. Farris has shown interest?"

Avalon found herself stock-still as she waited for
Penelope to answer.

"Of course. Every time we meet, he makes an effort
to talk to me." Penelope laughed in a manner that reminded Avalon of all the young women she'd met during her first Season who were confident in their beauty
and allure. They were the ones who could charm a man
into pledging his troth with little effort. These women
possessed a power, almost a sorcery, to make men fall
for them.

Something Avalon had never experienced in her life.
What that magic must feel like—the ability to have a
man see only you in a crowd of hundreds. She let out

a breath. Such an idea was a wasted effort. She had too much to do with the remaining days before the Thistledown annual charity soiree. It would be held at Warwyk Hall, and all the proceeds would go toward building a home for women who wanted to escape London and find another way of life. She'd even planned to build an attached nursery of sorts so that their children could be close while the women worked on their lace and dressmaking endeavors. Avalon had already picked out several loving matrons in the village to act as nursemaids during the days. It would be a place that would represent shelter, love, and new beginnings for these women.

While Avalon had never known hunger or cold, she'd experienced the same type of displacement these women had felt. Whatever she could do to ease these women's burdens, she'd gladly expend time and money for their benefit. Her annual charity soiree was an event that she looked forward to all year. She'd not allow Penelope Rowley to put a damper on her spirits.

Thankfully, the two guests of honor arrived with their beautiful dresses and all the fine accompaniments. As the footmen brought in the trunks of clothes, Jasmine and Flora came to her side.

"Good morning, my lady." Flora dipped an elegant curtsey. Blond, petite with big blue eyes, Flora was the epitome of an English beauty. Her quiet ways might fool some, but underneath she was a shrewd businesswoman who was comfortable negotiating with the posh retailers of trim as well as the secondhand clothing stalls that lined the London streets during market days.

"Lady Warwyk, we can't begin to tell you how excited we are. To think that our dresses and hats will be part of your benefit is a dream come true." Jasmine's red cheeks glowed with enthusiasm. A beauty with flawless skin, black hair, and startling brown eyes, she'd been a favorite amongst the men. But when one of the girls had died of the pox, Jasmine had begged Flora to escape with her, and they'd gone to Mary.

Mary had contacted Avalon via a letter brought by one of her bodyguards. She'd requested help in getting the women out of London for good. As the Covent Garden Rose, Mary Bolen was one of the undisputed leaders of the demimonde. She was renowned for her negotiating skills. Particularly when paramours were through with a mistress or a long-lasting relationship with a favorite prostitute. Though they didn't work for Mary directly, Flora and Jasmine had come to her asking for help in leaving such a life behind.

Without hesitation, Avalon had agreed to help as she had done in the past.

The reasons were simple. Compassion for the women, but also as a tribute to Mary.

At the most desperate time of Avalon's life, Mary had been the only one who'd ever defended and protected her.

Providing a haven had given Avalon a sense of purpose, a calling almost, to help the women. Though their circumstances weren't the same, Avalon identified with them at some level. Each of them had been forced to sell themselves.

She for a title, but Annie, Flora, and Jasmine had to sell their bodies for money, food, and shelter while subjecting themselves to the risk of disease, illness, and, just as terrifying, abuse.

"My lady, come see what we brought." Flora took Avalon's hand and led her to the trunks of dresses. She pulled out a midnight-blue gown that had a black lace netting covering the silk. Throughout the lace, jet-black jewels were sewn. Intermingled with the black jewels, tiny seed pearls were attached like hidden stars in a night sky. The entire ensemble twinkled like the heavens above on a snowy night. The gown was breathtaking.

Jasmine pulled out a gown the color of spring's first pink peony. The rich satin shimmered like a river kissed by the midday sun. White ermine framed the portrait collar, and the sleeves tapered to the wrist. Any woman who wore this gown would feel like a queen while looking like one.

"These are magnificent. Your skills and creativity make these works of art." Avalon reverently touched the satin. "How can I ever thank you? These will fetch a high price I'm certain."

"My lady," Flora said. "It's us who should thank you. This is a dream come true. If you hadn't taken us in . . ." She took Avalon's hand in hers and squeezed.

"You'll have more business than you'll know what to do with." Avalon squeezed her hand in turn.

"Then we'll just bring more girls up to Thistledown, won't we, my lady?" Jasmine winked.

"Yes, we will," Avalon answered.

Sophia and Penelope oohed and aahed over a bronze gown with a brocade bodice of green and dark orange design. Matching bronze lace lined the circular-shaped neckline. In the center of the bodice, an antique topaz stomacher brooch lay nestled so that it dangled between the lady's bosoms. It was decadent, simple, and seductive at the same time.

As Avalon glanced at the treasures the women brought, it looked like she'd stepped into a mantua-maker's shop on Bond Street. Everywhere she looked, gorgeous gowns, matching satin shoes, and reticules lay draped over the chairs.

"Good afternoon, Miss Sinclair and Miss Leona."

At the sound, Avalon looked up to see Devan saunter into the room as if he owned it.

He greeted Sophia and Penelope, then finally turned to her. "Good afternoon, Lady War*wyk*."

The slight deepening of his voice on the last syllable made her stand a little taller. For a moment, Avalon thought he'd call her Warlock.

Before she could respond, he continued, "I do hope I'm not late. I think you might have forgotten to mention the time that the auxiliary was to meet. Thankfully, my housekeeper reminded me that it's every Wednesday at two o'clock."

The smile on his face could only be described as wicked. "Where is everyone else?"

"They're not coming today," Jasmine answered. "Mrs. Marcy isn't feeling well, and Miss Marcy is attending her."

"My aunt had to go to London today so she sent me in her place," Penelope added.

"Shall we sit down?" Avalon waved Jasmine and Flora over to the table where a tea service waited for them.

When Penelope sat, she pulled her chair to the side, practically pushing Sophia away from the table. "Mr. Farris, why don't you pull up a chair and sit beside me."

Shocked at the forwardness of the woman's behavior, Flora whipped her gaze to Jasmine as her eyes grew wide.

Devan lifted a hand to stay all their efforts on his behalf. "There's plenty of room next to Lady Warwyk. Please don't trouble yourself."

He turned that wicked smile to Avalon, and held her gaze a little too long. That man was positively ruthless. In response, she arched one brow as if daring him to come sit by her.

His smile turned brighter, and she knew then that

he'd accepted her challenge. With a sigh, she picked up another cup for him as he came to sit by her. She poured the hot tea, then handed it to him.

He accepted it and nodded in thanks. He leaned close and whispered, "You remembered how I prefer it, hot and strong, just like you."

Her breath caught at the words, and her gaze shot to his. One of his irritating half grins tugged on one side of his mouth, emphasizing the dimple in his cheek. Without a word, she turned her attention to the ladies. Penelope simply stared at her, the look so sharp that for a moment, Avalon felt the prickles of a hundred needles. The young woman's eyes narrowed, then she turned to Sophia and whispered something. Avalon's sister nodded without any real interest, then continued her conversation with Jasmine.

Avalon dismissed her unease and sat her cup and saucer on the table in front of her. The ladies immediately quieted.

Avalon smiled. "This year's event promises to raise more money than we have in the last five years combined."

Before she could say another word, Penelope piped up. "Vicar, thank you, also for attending. Will you become a regular member?"

"Yes. I plan to follow the practice of my predecessor, Mr. Knightley. He didn't miss a single meeting."

Avalon thrummed her fingers on the tabletop as he kept talking. Even in her own home, the man commandeered her authority. Over her dead body would he replace Mr. Knightley, the kindest man she'd ever met.

Devan leaned so close that she could smell his fresh scent, orange and spice probably attributed to his soap. An image of him running that soap over his naked body came to mind—which meant him bathing. How could he fit his long muscular body into a regular slipper tub? He'd stand and reach for linen toweling while the water slowly sluiced from his body, not wanting to let go. His chest would glisten. . . .

"What's your opinion, my lady?" His deep baritone surrounded her.

A flash of heat ignited through her body and crept up her neck to her cheeks. She had no idea what he was asking, so she took a sip of tea before looking at him. The smile on his face hinted he knew what she'd been thinking.

"That's fine." Immediately, she returned her attention to an apple tart next to her cup.

"What's fine?" Laughter rumbled in his chest, but he kept it contained. "We were debating what colors to decorate the ballroom. Miss Sinclair likes gold and silver while Miss Rowley thought crimson and plum perfect. I wanted to know your opinion."

She forced her gaze to his. Ready to offer a stinging rebuke at his teasing, she halted before she uttered one perfectly sharp word. His eyes sparkled, and there was undeniable warmth there. For that scant moment in time, she saw him as someone who could bring laughter and heat into her lonely and cold life. His smile reached deep inside of her. For the first time she could ever remember, she felt like a desirable woman. This was a direct contrast to her usual detachment from all except her family and a few in the community she considered friends.

In answer, she returned his smile. "It's my opinion"—she waved a hand toward all the beautiful gowns that decorated the sitting room—"that we decide on something that will enhance the beauty of each and every single one of these masterpieces. I vote for the silver and gold decorations."

"Excellent." He turned in profile. "Miss Rowley, what if we have hothouse roses and dried lavender set strategically around the room?"

Everything proceeded in an organized manner after that. The guest lists were reviewed, along with the food and drink that Avalon would provide. A trio of musicians from London had been engaged for the soiree. The entire list of auction items was catalogued. Eventually, with her mind on the benefit, Avalon managed to wrestle control over her pounding heart and traitorous emotions.

Soon, the entire group rose to better inspect the dresses.

Penelope studied the rose satin with obvious envy.

"Avalon," Sophia said in wonder. "If I had my choice in gowns, I'd pick the green velvet with the black satin ribbon trim. Which one would you choose?"

Avalon decided then and there that she'd bid on the dress for her darling sister. It would be a perfect gown for the next holiday season.

"They're all so beautiful, I have a hard time choosing."

Sophia nodded before asking Flora a question on where they managed to find such excellent trim for the dresses. As the two started a discussion on seed pearls, Avalon's attention strayed to the bronze gown that had first caught her attention.

She ran her fingers across the silky texture while she admired the shimmering metallic material and gold thread. The antique brooch caught the light and the facets of the stones twinkled. Calling it beautiful didn't do the garment justice. It should be housed in the Tower of London with all the royal jewels. Only such finery would complement the masterpiece.

"I wish I had that heiress in my life now. I'm thinking a wealthy aunt would be quite useful." Devan's whisky-dark voice caressed her like a lover.

She vowed then and there to fight such thoughts. When she turned around, he stood close beside her as if he were an intimate.

"And why is that?" She took a precautionary step away.

"Because I'd buy that dress for you. I'd like to see you dressed in such finery. You'd be stunning."

"That would be highly inappropriate," she answered curtly.

"Inappropriate for whom?" His eyes had a devilish twinkle. "Wouldn't you like to see men fall to their knees and pledge allegiance to you?"

"Of course. But the question that begs an answer is whether you would?" The words escaped before she could rethink what she was saying.

"I'd be the first, then go to the back of the line to be the very last. Afterward, I'd ask for the honor of a dance and fight off any rivals."

"Why would you do that?" she asked.

"I thought you'd know, Lady Warlock," he softly chided. "Didn't you tell me you could see into the hearts of others?"

When Penelope demanded his attention, he clasped his hands behind his back and strolled away. He turned slightly and winked at her.

The odious man had turned Avalon's words against her. Why did she lower her guard around him? He was the only man who affected her so. Without hesitating, she decided she'd bid on that dress also. She'd invite him to dinner, so she'd have an excuse to wear it. She'd like to see him in awe of her.

Perhaps then she'd have the upper hand for once in their sparring.

Within the half hour, Devan took his leave to meet

Thane at the stables as promised. Sophia escorted Penelope to her room, leaving Flora and Jasmine, who stood beside Avalon.

Flora and Jasmine sighed in displeasure.

"Thank goodness, she's gone," Jasmine murmured under her breath.

"Who?" Avalon asked.

"Penelope," Flora said. "She wants us to make more dresses for her. Though her money is helping us repay you for all the fabric and trim you purchased for us, she's a nuisance."

Jasmine nodded. "If I hear how much the vicar loves her and wants to marry her one more time, I think I'll scream."

"She said that?" Avalon's stomach twisted in knots and she smothered a moan.

"Oh, yes. Apparently, he visits the house quite often," Flora said.

Then, it was true. Devan was interested in Penelope, proving once again that he was nothing more than a big flirt. Before she could ask more, Flora efficiently swept across the room to the bronze gown.

Jasmine waved for Avalon to come with her.

Flora held the gown in two hands and peered over one shoulder of the garment. "My lady, this is for you."

"What?" Avalon asked incredulously. "You shouldn't do that. Sell it at the auction."

"Nonsense." Jasmine took the gown and held it up to Avalon's body. "We made it for you, my lady. You've given us a new life. At least allow us to give you a gown to celebrate such an occasion."

"That's what friends do for one another," Flora said, then hesitated. "If it's satisfactory that we consider you our friend?"

"Of course." Tears welled in Avalon's eyes. "I'd like nothing better." A grin tugged at her lips. "However, I'll not take advantage of friends. I'm paying for the gown."

The two women beamed in approval.

"All right, then." Jasmine took Avalon's hand in hers.

Flora scooted closer and a knowing smile graced her lips. "I know men, my lady. That's one benefit from working in London. With that knowledge, I think it's safe to say that a certain vicar might appreciate you wearing such a frock the night of the auction."

"He's not interested in me." She shook her head in denial at such a ridiculous thought. "It's Penelope."

"He didn't take his eyes off you the entire time he was here." Flora smiled knowingly. "We both saw how he leaned close and whispered in your ear. He didn't do any of that with her."

"Well, if he's not interested in you, won't there be other men at the soiree?" Jasmine asked, then laughed. "Perhaps a mysterious man who'll sweep you off your feet. Let's have you try on that dress and see if it needs any alterations."

Avalon nodded as a fiery heat filled her checks. "I do like mysteries," she murmured as she tried to put Devan out of her thoughts.

When life throws you a surprise, settle in, grab a bottle of wine, and enjoy.

Devan Farris

Chapter Ten

After the tumultuous afternoon at Avalon's home, tonight's dinner had been a subdued affair. Thane had invited Devan to join them. He'd gone to the vicarage to answer a few letters from his brothers, then returned to Warwyk Hall. After dinner, he and Thane had retired to the sitting room for another chess lesson. Sophia sat nearby and sketched dresses after finding inspiration in the creations she'd seen in the afternoon.

Devan found himself becoming more comfortable in Warwyk Hall. Thane had a gift for bringing smiles to his mother's and aunt's faces. Plus, the boy had a mind that reminded Devan of a sponge. He soaked and retained everything taught to him. Within a year, the young marquess would be an excellent chess player, one who could become a master if he continued the study of the game. His interest in battles and strategy served his understanding of logic well.

Much to Devan's dismay, Avalon had excused herself to prepare for her guests' arrival in three days. The entire Cavensham clan would descend upon Warwyk Hall and attend the charity auction.

When the longcase clock had struck the hour of nine,

he'd taken his leave and gathered his greatcoat and hat, but an urge to see his benefactress, his Warlock, stole into his thoughts. After he'd flirted with her this afternoon, she'd become flustered and a beautiful flush had colored her cheeks.

He'd never thought her a woman who would charm him, but her strength and allure wove a magic like an enchantment around him. Though what to do about it confounded him. She hated him, or at least, didn't trust him. Could he even pursue whatever this was between them? Was it an infatuation, a tenderness, or something deeper with a promise of a lifetime devotion?

Would she even see him worthy of her affections?

A footman escorted him down to the wine cellar. Holding court, Avalon stood with Mr. Neville and the myriad of wine bottles that were carefully stored in wooden cases and racks that lined the walls of the room.

"Lady Warwyk?" Devan stepped into the cellar room. "I thought to take my leave this evening."

She turned her attention from Mr. Neville. "Mr. Farris, what time is it?"

At the sound of her honeyed voice, his entire body seemed to vibrate like a church bell.

"A little past nine," he rasped. Such a reaction to Avalon was becoming a regular occurrence. He cleared his throat, hoping to stave off any indication that she affected him in such a manner. But it was becoming harder and harder to deny the attraction he felt for her.

Mr. Neville nodded in greeting, then turned to Avalon. "My lady, if you'll excuse me for a moment? I promised Cook I'd attend her. She had several questions about the preparations for the soiree."

"Of course," she said. "I can finish this by myself."

Mr. Neville bowed slightly before he took his leave.

Now that they were alone in the cellar, Avalon's attention focused on him, and in turn his attention focused on her face. The light from the candelabra sitting on a small table next to her flickered across her cheeks as if kissing her. In that moment, he wanted to replace the light with his lips.

He cleared his throat again. "I wanted to thank you for the dinner and hospitality." He took a step near to take her hand. It provided a rare occasion where they could touch without the interference of gloves.

When he extended his hand to her, she hesitated for a moment. "You may not want to take my hand."

"Why is that?" He grinned slightly. She was quite fetching when she was a little unsure of herself.

"My hands are cold," she said with an answering smile and a slight shrug. "Mr. Neville and I were deciding which wine to serve for the soiree."

Without a second thought, he took her outstretched hand with his and gently rubbed. Not only to warm her skin, but for his benefit too—he could indulge in caressing her soft skin. He examined her hand slowly as he lifted it higher. He frowned slightly in feigned concentration. "I'm shocked."

"I warned you," she said.

"It's not what I expected. I thought all war—"

"*Do not say it*," she bit out with a laugh.

"What? Warlock?" he answered innocently. "Of course, I wouldn't say that. I was going to say that I thought all warmth was absent from down here, but you are the exception. I can see the glow on your cheeks. That must come from a warm heart."

"You, Vicar, are a dangerous man."

He placed a hand over the middle of his chest. "Madam, you know how to wound me."

She shook her head in silent laughter, then slowly

grew serious. "Devan . . ." She studied him as if debating something. Finally, whatever silent war she waged within herself, she'd made a decision.

He bent closer and lowered his voice, delighted she called him by his first name. "Whatever you want to say, please speak freely."

She nodded once. "I overheard Penelope say she expected a marriage proposal from you any day." She studied their still-clasped hands.

Instead of pulling away, she stepped a little closer, and he wanted to rejoice that she felt comfortable enough with him to confide in him.

"Perhaps you shouldn't spend so much time here if you're pursuing her. I could tell she didn't like the way we chatted with one another this afternoon."

He shook his head. "She's misunderstood my attentions. This has happened a few times before in my other parishes." His eyes captured hers. "I didn't encourage their affections or Penelope's. I know I have a reputation with the ladies, but I'd never compromise a woman, especially someone as young as Penelope."

Avalon's lips curved upward. "I'm not shocked that you would have admirers amongst the young women in your parishes. You're an attractive . . ."

Her words trailed to nothing as if she was afraid she'd revealed too much.

"An attractive what? Reprobate? Rake? Soon to be rakish rector?"

The words caused her to laugh, and he knew in that moment that he'd never tire of the sound.

"An attractive man, you vain peacock," she retorted softly, but her blush returned in full bloom on her cheeks.

He chuckled. "That wasn't so difficult, now was it?"

"Quit teasing, Devan, and listen," she scolded. "Penelope is here because her aunt and uncle have offered to sponsor her in a Season while her parents live abroad in Italy. She's rather impressionable."

"Thank you for the advice. I don't want to cause any trouble within your—" Before he could finish the thought, the cellar door slammed shut behind them.

"What on earth?" she cried as she rushed to the door and pushed against it. When it didn't budge, she pounded against the thick oak paneling twice. "Hello?" she called out. "You've locked us in."

A haunting silence descended, with only the hiss of a candlewick decrying their circumstances.

Avalon turned around and rested against the door with her hands behind her. The position had the unintended effect of accentuating her breasts where a hint of cleavage peeked from her square neckline. The purple satin of her dress glistened in the candlelight like a starry night, and the woven wrap around her arms draped in a manner that had the unintended effect of seducing him.

Good lord, he was mad if a simple garment could entice him with such sensual thoughts.

"We're locked in." Her voice didn't waver in alarm, but there was a hint of astonishment in her tone.

"Locked in," he repeated. How fitting as his emotions were currently locked in a battle. His mind warned not to think about asking to kiss her. But his heart disagreed and encouraged him to cross the room and take her in his arms then kiss her repeatedly until they both agreed that there was an undeniable attraction between them that had to be addressed.

This was desire with a strength to burn him alive, and he wanted to go up in flames—as long as it was with Avalon, the one woman in his life who with just a look or a simple word could ignite an irrefutable passion within him.

That was the problem with Avalon. Her presence caused his self-control to fly out the window like a prisoner escaping the Fleet Street Prison. One glimpse of her hair, a mellifluously spoken word, or even the perfect arch of a single eyebrow in his direction made every one of his senses come to attention.

"Shall I see if I can pick the lock?" As soon as he said it, he wanted to withdraw the offer. He'd much rather stay in here with her alone.

She shook her head, then pushed away from the door. "There's a sliding bolt on the outside of the door. Your skills as a locksmith won't help us here. Hopefully, Mr. Neville will discover us. He never retires until he knows everyone is abed. Perhaps if we bang on the door, he'll hear us."

Devan crossed the room to stand by Avalon, then they pounded the door with their fists. No one rushed to their aid. He turned to her, and she blinked slowly as if trying to understand what had happened.

"I wonder who would have locked us in?" She banged the door once for good measure. "If it is open, then everyone knows someone is in here."

"They'll find us."

"If worse comes to worst, Mr. Neville will open the door sometime tomorrow morning. He'll have the footmen bring the bottles to the small ballroom." Lines of worry radiated around her eyes. "We'll have to make do until then."

He waved his hand in a half circle. "At least we won't go thirsty with all this wine around."

Avalon grinned reluctantly. "I suppose not. Do you want a glass of something? The only glasses we keep down here are small for tasting." She knotted her wrap around her shoulders.

"I'm fine for right now. Are you cold?"

"A little."

Devan reached her side, then draped his greatcoat over her body. Unable to resist, he adjusted the coat, allowing his hands to slide gently across her shoulders. With her hair up in an elegant chignon, she looked like a small soldier wearing a hand-me-down extra-large army coat. "Better?"

She nodded, then swept her gaze around the room. "There's no place really to sit."

"Let's see what I can do." Devan strolled in search of something on which they could rest. Quickly, he arranged eight wooden crates into a formation that resembled a chaise longue, then laid a rug across the top. "It's nothing fancy."

"I think it's brilliant." The smile on her face was simply lovely.

"Madame, for you." He swept a hand toward the makeshift sitting area. "Would you care to sit?"

In two short steps, Avalon was by his side. Carefully, she scooted across the rug. She whipped off his greatcoat, then patted the crate beside her for him to join her. Without further encouragement, Devan slid upon the makeshift longue. Hip to hip and leg to leg, they sat beside each other. The heat of her body warming his. She neatly folded his coat and handed it back to him.

"Don't you want it?"

"I thought perhaps you might be cold." She pulled her shawl a little tighter to her body.

"Let's share." He whipped the coat out, and soon they were nestled underneath it together.

She turned her gaze to his. The endearing expression on her face was surprisingly sweet, if unsure of what was happening between them.

"I promise I'll be on my best behavior." He waggled his eyebrows and managed to receive one of her delightful laughs in payment.

"That's not what I'm worried about," she warned. "You could have your pick of any woman you wanted. I would not be the right choice."

He adjusted his hip so he faced her profile. "Why would you say something like that?"

She let out a tremulous sigh. "I know how you and others see me. Nothing more than a money-sucker, a woman thirsty for material wealth."

"Avalon—"

She lifted one hand and laid it on top of his coat, thrumming her fingers softly. "It's the truth. But I didn't keep Warwyk's money or gifts for myself. Everything I bought with his money, I sold after he died. I used it for Warwyk and Thistledown. It was my insurance if I didn't receive my dower. I wasn't certain he'd uphold the marriage settlements. He hated me so much, I wouldn't have been surprised if he didn't provide for me after his death."

He leaned closer. "Your marriage was an unhappy one."

"Unhappy makes it sound like a walk in the park. It was hell for both of us."

She shrugged in a defensive action that tore him up inside, the pain evident on her face. He'd never seen her so open and honest before. Certainly, never like this with him.

"I owe you an explanation for the other night when I was so angry with you."

"When you told me to never circumvent your decisions again?" He didn't hide the sincerity in his voice. The growing intimacy between them made him drunk with emotion. He wasn't happy she had been miserable, but he relished the fact that she thought enough of him to confide in him. After all these years, he was coming to know the real Avalon Warwyk.

"After I left Richard"—she trained her emerald-green eyes on him, and for a moment, it reminded him of his mother's descriptions of her home in Ireland—"it's no excuse, but I promised myself I'd never be vulnerable again to anyone's manipulations or allow anyone else to make decisions for me about my own welfare."

He didn't respond for fear it would break this moment between them.

"I know you've disliked me for years because of what I did to William. But I had no choice." She straightened slightly and the movement caused his greatcoat to slip down her shoulders into her lap. "My father and my own mother told me that my duty to the family required that I make the best match possible, and *that* was to marry Richard. They told me if I didn't, then I'd never be able to see Sophia again, nor would I ever be welcomed into their home." She studied her hands as she twisted her fingers together. "They coerced Richard into marrying me, and he hated me for it." She clasped her hands tightly, then turned her gaze to his.

Pain radiated from their green depths.

"Go on," he encouraged, keeping his voice low.

"My father had won a property from Richard in a card game at a fall hunting party earlier that year. The only way they'd allow him to buy it back was by marrying me." Her mouth tilted in a grim smile. "The people that should have protected me used me like a piece of chalk in a billiards game. I was only useful if I helped them play. Would you like to know how it came to be that I helped Annie and the others?"

He nodded.

"It was Mary Bolen."

"But how is that you and Mary . . ." His words trailed to nothing.

"I'd met her right before her son was born. I didn't know who she was, but I immediately liked her and thought we might be friends." She waved a hand in the air as if it didn't matter, but the pain in her eyes betrayed the truth. With an elegant ease, she let it fall to her lap. "Remember that day you and Larkton found the three of us in the sitting room? Several of Mary's girls were there also. Richard wanted to move Mary into our London home and told me to return to Warwyk Hall. I purposely made him angry."

He nodded. "I don't know what happened."

"Richard raised his fist to hit me, but Mary stood in front of me, thwarting him." Her eyes darted to her hands. "It was the first time anyone had come to my defense." She forced herself to hold his gaze. "That's when you and Larkton walked in. For all my days, I'll never forget the utter shock and resulting fear. That's why I won't let any man have any say over me."

Devan squeezed her hand with his. "I'm sorry if I caused you additional pain that day."

She nodded as if forgiving him. "Years ago, Mary contacted me. That's why I started my charity. In one of her letters she asked if I could take Annie, as the man who got her with child was threatening her. Mary said I was the only one she could turn to for help. Since my parents sold me to Richard, in some sordid way, I knew what Annie felt. Several months ago, Mary sent Jasmine and Flora my way. I'll always help those women because they're my friends. I'll never refuse Mary anything because when no one was there to help me, Mary was."

"My God, I had no idea," he whispered.

"Please, don't share this with your brother."

"Never," he answered. Before he could say another word, she turned and stared at the light from the candelabra that danced around the drafts in the cellar.

"I'm feeling sorry for myself." She turned her attention back to him, and that mask she wore that protected herself from outsiders had returned. "Many women have the type of marriage I was subjected to. Though it was horrible, he never struck me."

The silence stretched between them.

Devan stayed absolutely still, afraid any movement on his part would break this fragile bond between them.

After a moment, she continued, "I walked into his home after the wedding ceremony and realized that I had nowhere to escape. Do you have any idea what it feels like to be hated for who you are? To be hated by your spouse? Perhaps I should have tried harder to win his affections." She forced her gaze to his, and the shimmer in her eyes betrayed her anguish. "Instead, I made certain he knew I despised him in return. That's the type of person I am." She dipped her head and studied her clasped hands. "It's humiliating to discuss."

"I'm a vicar. I hear people's darkest secrets and deepest regrets all the time." He bent closer, and her sweet fragrance rose to meet him. "I'd like to know what happened." The dead bastard had hurt her, and though he couldn't do anything on earth, a well-placed prayer asking for vengeance wouldn't be out of line in his opinion.

She swallowed, and that tiny movement almost undid him.

"It's a miracle that Thane was even born." She lowered her voice and still refused to look at Devan. "Finally, after two weeks of marriage, Richard came to my room, the only time he ever did. He was so disgusted that he had to get foxed to come to my bed. I was a nervous wreck waiting, wondering if he'd ever consummate the marriage. He didn't even talk to me. He made me feel like I was nothing more than an animal. At the end, he said one word."

"What was that?" Devan took her hand in his.

She blinked slowly and sniffed gently to keep her tears from appearing. "He cried out 'Mary,'" she whispered. She took a deep breath, then slowly released it.

Avalon was a proud woman, and the effort to confess the shame she had taken upon herself laid it bare for him. She squeezed his hand as if collecting strength.

The fact she shared such a memory with him left him in awe of her. "Warwyk didn't deserve you," Devan said. "I'm glad you're free of him. One thing I've discovered in life is that sometimes people only see in others what they fear is within themselves. He was ashamed of his own weakness so he blamed you."

She didn't move but stared at his hand in hers.

"Your parents didn't deserve you either. They should have protected you from such a life."

She slowly lifted her gaze to meet his. "My mother told me it was my duty, and that a 'bargain had been struck.'"

"Some things like a daughter's safety and happiness are far more valuable than a king's fortune." Slowly, he brought her hand to his lips, then whispered against it. "May I share a secret with you? It's something I've never told anyone."

"Of course. I'll keep it in confidence, like I'll hope you do with mine."

Devan nodded, then furrowed his brow as he wondered how to begin and how much to tell. There was a part buried deep within that whispered encouragement to open all his secrets and share that part of himself he'd never done with another. With a deep breath, he smothered the urge. Only his wife would be privy to his choice to save himself for their wedding night. Though the urge to share with Avalon was becoming harder and harder to resist.

"I always wanted a military career, and Larkton refused to buy me a commission. He always said my position as the fourth and youngest son of our family meant I should have a career in the church."

"That's why you stay upstairs for hours with Thane analyzing various battles. I wondered why you were so bloodthirsty."

He waggled his eyebrows. "Now you know the true me. I'm a *vicious* vicar."

The silken lashes of her eyes flew up in surprise and laughter.

"Allow me to tell you the sad tale. After arguing with my brother and not making any headway, I walked out of his study that day and never returned until he summoned me. He apologized for his decisions, then proceeded to tell me that he'd secured an appointment at Oxford seminary for me. I railed at him for his highhanded manner and asked him who had appointed him God. I told him I'd just enlist like any man could."

"I imagine his eyebrow lifted over that remark," Avalon said.

Devan smiled and tangled their fingers together. The warmth of her fingers against his was a comfort he could easily grow accustomed to. "He became agitated and started pacing the room all the while screaming at me."

Avalon's hand flew to her chest. "That must have been deeply concerning."

"More like alarming. I'd never seen him that angry before. Though we fight like dogs over the choicest bone, it's half in jest." He smiled slightly. "You might find it unbelievable, but I love my brother. That day when I really looked at him, sweat covered his brow, and his hands were shaking." His gaze darted to hers. "He was frightened."

"About you leaving?" she asked.

"Yes. I asked him what was wrong." Devan looked to the far corner of the room as the image of Gavin crumbling before him crept into his thoughts. "He collapsed into a chair and held his head in his hands. His shoulders shook, and I thought he was laughing."

Avalon's eyes widened. "He was crying, wasn't he?"

He squeezed her hand in acknowledgement. "I went to sit beside him and put my hand over his shoulder. He told me that he just couldn't bear to go through what he had with my older brothers, Niall and Hearne, once more. He couldn't sit idle and watch another brother leave—the worry, the waiting, and not knowing if I was safe or dead on a battlefield somewhere. So, he refused to buy me a commission. He said he'd never wish that anguish on anyone again." He smiled. "Because I'm the youngest and the other two came home safe, he believed I would have been killed if I fought. He said fate would come to collect its due if he allowed me to become an officer."

"He was trying to protect you," she soothed.

"We never spoke of our previous confrontation again," Devan answered. "But I understood his decision. More importantly, I could see the toll it had on his life. He's never married. He only worries for the family and estate. In that order, I might add." He rubbed his thumb over the softness of hers, drawing comfort. "Our father had ensured that money had been set aside for each of his younger sons to buy a commission. My older brothers, Hearne and Niall, had served in the navy, and both were rewarded for their bravery in battle. I wanted that." He exhaled slowly. "But I accepted my position in the church and celebrated my ordination like any young man ready to spend his life doing God's work. It wasn't a hardship, but it wasn't what I wanted. Yet, I couldn't make Gavin suffer anymore."

"Don't you like being a vicar?" she asked.

"I like to help people, and I think I'm somewhat successful. Though I seem like a soft and capricious fellow—"

"Don't say that," she whispered. "What you did for Annie"—she turned toward him—"and me that night took a true talent. You sense what people are feeling and instinctively help them feel better. If you hadn't gone into the church, have you ever thought about the lives that would have been changed for the worse because you weren't there to help them?"

The look in her eyes made him feel ten feet tall. "You exaggerate, madam."

"Look at Thane. He's come alive under your tutelage. I'm amazed at his progress and eagerness to learn. He's matured in just the few sessions you've taught him."

"Be careful, Lady Warlock," he murmured. "You'll make me full of myself."

Instead of stiffening when he called her that, Avalon relaxed slightly. "I wouldn't say such things if they weren't true." She lowered her voice. "Believe it or not, I like it when you call me Lady Warlock. You make me think I do have some type of special powers." She studied their entwined hands for a moment. "I didn't know anything about the true you," she said softly. "But I'm starting to learn."

He kept himself still as she examined him. For some inane reason he almost wanted her to see everything about him. More importantly, he wanted her approval.

Her eyes flared in the candlelight. "May I ask you a question?"

He nodded.

"Why did you tell me you wanted to marry an heiress? If your brother has found one for you, why do you dismiss them out of hand? Seems to me, you'd find one who would be a good match."

"Because not just any heiress will do."

Devan leaned back, and Avalon wanted to protest the distance between them. The magic he created just by talking and sharing his life with her could weave into an enchantment she wasn't sure she could fight.

Nor was she certain she wanted to.

He stared at the ceiling for a moment, then trained that deep gaze on her. "I want to share another story with you. One you might find offensive."

"I doubt that. I've shared all my horrid, well, most of my horrid secrets with you," she said. Now he had her curiosity piqued. What could the vicar have done in his life to warrant such trepidation?

"That's reassuring." He smiled slightly, the humor giving his voice a lovely lilt. "I was known for my locksmithing skills while at Eton and Oxford. I decided to act as judge and jury for my peers"—he turned toward her and rested his shoulder against the crate— "particularly the ones who couldn't manage the rigors of the academic curriculum. But those were young men who loved the church and would serve God every moment of their lives. I had no doubt."

"Go on," she said softly.

He took a deep breath and continued, "One early morning"—he tilted his head and stared into space— "the head don of the seminary school walked into his office and found me. I'd broken in and was caught redhanded changing the grades in his record book."

"What?" she asked incredulously. "Wasn't that grounds for expulsion?"

"Indeed. When Mr. Wilkens asked what I was doing, I did the only thing that came to mind. I told him the truth."

"What happened?"

"The don was a kind man. When I explained my reasons, he listened intently, then gave me a blistering lecture. Afterward, he told me that he'd not tell my brother, nor would he expel me. He'd give me a second chance because my heart was in the right place, even though I was a misguided youth full of himself to make such decisions." He chuckled, then a fetching smile tugged at his lips, making him even more handsome than he had a right to be.

"From that day forward, I promised myself and God that I would always give people second chances. I learned that I didn't possess the knowledge or the infinite wisdom to make such decisions. Only God does."

"I can understand such reasoning, but that doesn't answer my question about your desire to marry an heiress."

"Clever lass," he teased. "I thought maybe you'd forget that part."

He winked at her, and everything within her softened. He was a dangerous but charming man on so many levels.

"I also promised myself that day that I'd find a way to help those fellows like me, third or fourth sons of gentlemen who wanted a military career but couldn't afford to buy a commission. I want to start a scholarship. Those young men could valiantly serve their country without the worry of whether they can afford to be there or not. An heiress would allow me to do that. But I want to fall in love with her and she with me. Just like my parents."

"That's a lovely thought. I hope you find her."

He nodded. "Do you want to hear another secret of mine?"

"Yes." She leaned closer, waiting for him to divulge another piece of himself he kept hidden.

"Larkton sent me to spy on you. See how you spent money on your charity and where it came from."

"I expected as much," she answered.

"I let him know that I'd come here, but I'd not hide the reasons from you. He'll hear nothing you shared with me tonight."

"Thank you." Avalon bit her lower lip, then smoothed the tender skin with her tongue.

His eyes blazed in response. In that instant, everything between them changed. She waited, tensing her body as if preparing to hear a pistol shot. She knew what was coming but had no idea when it would happen. The stillness between them seemed to keep them suspended as if each waited for the other to make the first move.

He stared at her mouth, then his gaze slowly rose to hers. The heat in his eyes, one that suggested he saw her as a woman he wanted, wove a fervent thread between them. It reminded Avalon of a spider's web, thin, silken, yet possessing an unbelievable strength.

The fullness of his lips called to her and, without hesitation, she leaned toward him. He matched her movement.

A slight moan escaped.

She had no idea whether it was from Devan or her, and she didn't care.

There was only one thing she desired in that moment.

More than anything else, Avalon wanted Devan's arms around her as she kissed him until the sun came up the next morning.

You have witchcraft in your lips.

Henry V
Act 5 Scene 2

Chapter Eleven

❦

Avalon's breath hitched as Devan moved closer. Her entire body felt as if a burst of electricity had arched between them, setting her alive. For the first time in ages, she wanted a man to hold her. She wanted a man to kiss her. She wanted to lose herself in Devan's arms and never be found.

Inch by inch, he moved nearer. In response, she did the same with her heart pounding in approval. With his breath fanning her lips, she forced her gaze to his. "Devan, I want . . ."

The words came from a place inside so deep, so forlorn, that she hardly recognized herself.

Without answering the undeniable plea in her voice, he closed the distance between them. Like a touch of a feather, he brushed his lips against hers. Before she could grow accustomed to the indescribable heat of his mouth against hers, he drew away and looked at her as if memorizing every feature of her face.

This time she did moan in protest. After so many years to be denied the feel of lips against hers was a sin against humanity. She leaned forward shamelessly to capture his mouth against hers again. Awkwardly, her nose bumped against his chin. "I'm sorry."

"Don't be. I want to kiss you as much as you want to kiss me." He moved closer, and his mouth descended to claim hers deliberately and with tender care.

This time his lips pressed against hers, and she could do nothing except push her body close to his as if seeking him—ready to claim him. He tasted of brandy and mint, and she wanted to drown in it. Instinctively, her arms curled around his neck, holding tightly while she pressed her chest against his. Immediately, her breasts grew heavy, aching for him as her nipples tightened into painful points as if pouting for him to give them attention.

When his arms encircled her waist, she sighed against his mouth and he pulled her tighter against him. The buttons of his waistcoat were a delicious torment, and she wiggled against them, seeking relief.

He nipped her lower lip playfully, and she tried to return the gesture. When she opened her mouth, he slanted his mouth over hers and his tongue slipped inside. It was heaven. For the life of her she couldn't remember ever sharing anything so personal and intimate with another person. His tongue slowly danced with hers and she groaned in appreciation as hers matched each intricate movement.

He drew back slightly, and she could tell by his rapid breath that he was as affected as she was. "Avalon," he whispered.

The sound of her name made everything inside her soften to molten heat. With infinite care, she kissed him again. At first, she teased him by sweeping her lips across his. When he made to deepen the kiss, she pulled away. He allowed her to play before capturing her lips with his. The caress turned sweet and tender, then, like a wildfire, it became a force to be reckoned with.

Eventually, he was the first to pull away, and she protested with a whimper. His breathing had grown ragged, and he rested his brow against hers.

"We must stop." He pressed his lips against her forehead.

Her own breath raced as if trying to keep up with her frantic heartbeat. "Why? Am I doing it wrong?" Even to her own ears, she sounded like a petulant child having a treat taken away. "You could teach me. With your experience, it shouldn't take long."

He pulled away from her.

She'd been denied such pleasure all her life. For once in her life, he made her feel and believe she deserved it. She'd never coveted a physical closeness with another like she had with him tonight.

"It's not a matter of experience, Avalon. These aren't ordinary kisses, are they?" He waited for her to answer.

Instead she pressed her face against his neck cloth and inhaled deeply. The smell of starch and orange bergamot along with the stiffness of his cravat combined into a maelstrom of sensual excess. She wanted to bury herself in it.

"Are you afraid to do more because I'm your benefactress? Please don't be." God, she wanted more kisses and more of him. It was paradise in his arms, and his kisses tasted of ambrosia straight from the gods. But a startling truth grabbed ahold and woke her from the sensual dream they'd created. If he told his brother Larkton what she'd said or done, Thane would be ripped from her and Warwyk within a week. After one last deep inhale, she forced herself to back away from him.

The sharpness of his gaze told her he missed nothing when he studied a person. He was much too intelligent not to know how much she wanted him.

"I got carried away," Avalon offered. She pressed a hand against her pounding heart with the unintended effect of her arm pressing against her hardened nipples. How would she survive the cold of the night and the deluge of new sensations that were her new companions?

"We both did," he answered. The tenderness in his voice immediately made her wary.

One kiss from Devan Farris, and she'd turned into a lovesick fool. No wonder he was so popular with ladies. She straightened her shoulders as she struggled with how to address what would happen next.

"This whole night should stay a secret. If word got out, I'm concerned . . . your brother would take Thane." Memories of Richard's threats that he'd take her son resurfaced. The fears and horrors of his rants grew. She gulped a breath of air, desperate to flush away the haunting reminder.

He silenced her with a finger against her lips. It only took one look at the affection shining from his eyes, and she felt as if she were falling endlessly headfirst down the tallest cliff at Dover.

"Avalon, what happened between us is no one's business but ours. Larkton will never hear of it from me. If you choose to tell him, that's your prerogative."

She swallowed the fear that had lodged in her throat. "I'd hoped we could keep this private."

"Of course." He dipped his head until his gaze met hers. "But this does change things between us."

"How so? Aren't I just another in the long line of women . . ." She let the words trail to nothing as she immediately regretted their tartness. "That was unbecoming of me."

He trailed a finger down her cheek as he slowly took in every one of her features. "What am I going to do with you?" The affection in his voice was mesmerizing. "I know you well enough to recognize the defensiveness in your tone. You don't have to shield yourself from me as there's nothing to fear. I won't hurt you." He traced her lips with his forefinger, the touch incredibly erotic. "Do you want another secret of mine?"

She nodded as if mesmerized by him.

Which she was—completely and irrefutably entranced by him tonight.

"Do you know why I call you Lady Warlock?"

Without her gaze leaving his, she shook her head slowly.

"Because like a witch, you've completely enchanted me."

She blinked slowly. Was he just saying it out of kindness or did she dare hope there was a kernel of truth in his words? Her heart thudded so loudly against her chest Devan had to hear it.

He took his greatcoat and spread it around them. "Now, I think we'd best figure out a way to stay warm."

Unable to hold his breath any longer, Devan slowly exhaled. By now, Avalon's breathing had taken on a regular pattern. She was sound asleep.

Somehow or other, the Marchioness of Warwyk lay between his arms with her body encased between his legs. Her delicious backside was nestled up against his groin. If this was heaven's idea that he needed to glimpse the amount of temptation Christ had to resist from the Devil, there was no need.

The wooden cases he rested against dug into his backside, and frankly, he could have cared less. All he could think about was Avalon's soft body lying against his. Her sweet scent warmed by their combined body heat filled the air and made his nostrils flare. His arms tightened an infinitesimal amount, as if already claiming her as his while his body had magically matched her rhythmic breathing.

Of the smattering of kisses he'd experienced in his life, nothing matched the touch of her lips against his. She was sweeter than the finest wine he'd ever tasted. He could have easily spent their entire night together learning what she liked.

But as sure as the sun would rise in the morning, a hundred kisses would never be enough to learn all the secrets of Avalon.

But not everything was heaven.

Devan's own body betrayed him with a raging erection that had kept him awake all night.

Every move or sigh on Avalon's part caused the damn thing to swell as if trying to reach her. He'd tried to move once or twice with the end result of Avalon moaning slightly against him as his cock dug into her perfect backside.

Once he'd made the foolish mistake of leaning until he could bury his face into the soft skin of her neck. He wanted to trace the slope of her neck with his nose until he reached her ear, where he'd tell her all the things he'd imagined he could do with her.

Only, in his imagination, they were married. He let out his own sigh, and in response Avalon burrowed deeper against him.

Which caused his cock to twitch like a racehorse ready to break free from its stall.

This was pure and simple torment, but it was incredibly sweet and sincere. If someone had told him a week ago that he would have kissed Avalon then slept with her all night, he'd have called them a fool. But tonight, just that very thing had happened. What made it all that more astounding was that she'd wanted more of him—more kisses, more of him, everything.

He did too. But as the vicar of the community and as

a person who believed that marriage came first, he had to stop before he betrayed his values.

Avalon twisted again and moaned. She rested her head against his chest, and her midsection rested against his groin now. Of course, his cock was currently throwing a temper tantrum as heaven waited so near to his pant falls, yet so far. Gently, and with as much ease as he possessed, Devan turned her slightly away.

Once she was settled again, Devan allowed himself to stroke her hair. She'd taken it down, or more aptly, it had fallen down on its own. Unable to resist the rich, luxurious chestnut locks, Devan allowed his fingers to glide through the silken softness of her curls.

Her chignon had been pinned so tightly, it was a miracle she could turn her head and didn't suffer from a headache. But Devan had watched as her hair fell out of its rigorous confines. As if sprung free from jail, the soft curls seemed to bounce with glee down her back.

Funny, but his Warlock's hair style suited her perfectly. It was tight and controlled on the outside, but on the inside that's where all the softness resided. Just like her.

After tonight, so many things made sense. Avalon had attacked him the night that Annie Dozier had her baby because she'd thought he'd been making a unilateral decision without consulting her—without considering her wants and needs.

Devan *had* made the decision singlehandedly, but only because he'd been concerned for her welfare. No wonder she'd lashed out at him in anger. When she'd confessed what she'd suffered in life with her parents and Warwyk, Devan had been filled with fury. After hearing the story, all he'd wanted to do was get out of the cellar where he'd have been free to dig up the Marquess of Warwyk out of the ground, then damn him to hell.

Which was probably a wasted effort since that's where the former marquess surely resided. All the people she'd had in her early life, the ones who should have protected Avalon, probably gave more consideration to their hunting dogs than to her.

Without giving it a second thought, Devan pressed his lips against the crown of her head. He breathed his fill of her sweetness, then held it as long as he could before releasing it. For all of his days, he'd remember this night when perfection resided in his arms. He pulled her a little tighter against him, and she mildly protested with a moan.

He lightened his grip and she snuggled closer.

"Devan," she whispered, turning until they lay chest to chest.

In response, he rubbed his lips across her head again.

"Have you heard anything?" she murmured.

"No. I've been listening." The heat of her breath against his linen shirt felt as if she'd just kissed him.

She pushed against his chest, creating distance. Every instinct told him to pull her tight, but he let her go.

"I can't get comfortable," she grumbled in a sleepy voice. "There's something prodding me." She wrestled with his coat and sat up slightly. She reached between them, and before he could stop her, she pushed against his swollen member.

He grunted in response, then grabbed her hand before it became any more unbearable while his cock struggled against the falls of his breeches. It took every ounce of self-control not to pull her hand to him.

"Oh heavens," she whispered. "Did I . . . Are you in pain?"

"Ignore it," he drawled slightly. "It's always seeking attention."

"What if I can't ignore it?" She dipped her head and looked intently at his breeches.

"Don't stare. That'll only make it worse," he sighed. "It thrives on being the center of attention."

"You talk as if"—she waved her hand toward his groin—"it has a mind of its own."

"It does," he answered, then blinked in earnest.

One lone candle hissed as if entertained by their conversation.

She shook her head, then raked her fingers through her hair, trying to tame the wild curls. The sight was another lesson in erotic torture.

"Did I cause that?" she asked without looking at him.

He'd be lucky if he survived the night.

"The simple answer is yes. All night, it's been having its very own soiree." Desperate to touch her, he reached up and pushed several renegade curls behind her ear. "It can only be described as a rout." Could their conversation about his member become anymore ridiculous?

Her attention was devoted to the lone candle that remained lit. Though there was little light, he could plainly see the flush that kissed her cheeks.

She tilted her head and examined him. A hint of a smile tugged at her lips, making her even more attractive than he'd ever seen her before. With her tousled hair and the beautiful blush on her cheeks, she looked like a woman who'd been loved thoroughly and completely.

Not that he would know what such a woman would look like, but he did have an imagination. And in his dreams, his lover looked like her—right now in this very moment before him. The urge to take her in his arms grew, but he fisted his hands.

"Devan." The sultry, sweet sound of his name on her lips must have been what those sailors from long ago had heard when the sirens' song called for them to leap to their doom. He'd willingly go overboard if he could hear his name on her lips again in that same intimate and seductive manner.

He ran a hand over his face. For heaven's sake, he needed to get control of his body and the situation. He should be tired after no sleep. He was a vicar and not a schoolboy with his first crush. He should act accordingly.

"I want to thank you." The sound of her whispered words pierced his chest and hit the bullseye on his heart.

"Why?" he managed to croak out.

She dipped her head shyly. "You're the first man who has ever had . . . that type of affliction because of me."

He groaned. Forty days with the devil breathing down his neck would be child's play compared to eight hours with Avalon.

Sometimes a rescue is nothing more than an entrapment.

Lady Warlock

Chapter Twelve

❧

The door bolt slid, then the hinges squeaked in protest.

Avalon shot up off Devan's chest at the noise. Though he grunted at her abrupt departure, he slowly rose in tandem with her. She rubbed her cheek where lines of sleep from lying against his chest marred her face. Though she looked a bit disheveled, as anyone would from spending the night in a wine cellar, he thought her radiant. Immediately, he wanted to kiss her again.

A lone candle lit the doorway and a small black head of hair peaked around the door.

"*Maman*? Are you in here?"

"Thane," Avalon cried as she rushed forward. "Thank goodness." She dropped to her knees against the cold floor and hugged her son. "You found us."

The worry on the boy's face made Devan's chest tighten. "Who's us?"

"Mr. Farris and I."

"Did you spend the night in here?"

"I did." Avalon kissed his cheek. "But I'm right as rain, my love."

Then the lad focused on Devan, his eyes round as saucers. "Are you going to marry her?"

Avalon stood and shook her head in denial. "Darling, I'm not ruined."

Thane blinked twice in confusion. "Did you spend the night alone with him?"

"Well . . . yes." Avalon's gaze darted to his. Soundlessly, she mouthed, "*Say something.*"

Devan closed the distance between Avalon and Thane, praying he'd find the correct words to calm the boy. His chest tightened. This was a situation he had no experience with.

"Thane, it's perfectly understandable that you're a little bewildered." Devan knelt beside the young boy and placed an arm on his shoulder. "It's admirable how worried you are for your mother's reputation. If it was my mother, I'd feel the same way. Shows you're taking the responsibilities of the marquisate to heart."

Immediately, the boy stood taller.

"Allow your mother and me to have a conversation." He cleared his throat. "When two people think about marrying, there are numerous things to consider. She and I would need time to make certain we were compatible. We'd want to ensure that we could build a good life for you."

"And each other." Thane smiled brightly. "Of that I have no doubt. We'd make an excellent family. When you discuss the wedding, I should like to attend. I'll make certain you have all the information necessary to make the decision."

"Thane, there's no need." A flush swept across Avalon's cheeks, and the crispness in her voice signaled her prickliness had returned after its hiatus from last night. "The vicar and I are two adults who don't need chaperones. We'd have to . . . No harm was done." She blinked slowly, then straightened to her full height under her son's unrelenting gaze.

"Mother, your dress is skewed and gaping in the bodice." The boy's voice had a sudden deepness that sent chills running down Devan's back. "Your hair is down. Don't worry. The vicar will do what's necessary."

Avalon's brow pinched into neat lines.

"Don't you want to marry him, Mother?" Thane asked earnestly.

"Thane," Devan said with as much kindness as he could muster under the circumstances.

"He's a good man," Thane urged. "You'll be happy."

Avalon's cheeks turned a deep pink.

"Don't embarrass your mother." This time there was a little more emphasis in his words.

The young lord turned his razor gaze to Devan. "I'm making an observation, that's all."

"My lady," Henri exclaimed as she rushed into the room. "We were so worried when we couldn't find you. When I came into your chambers this morning and discovered you hadn't slept in your bed, I immediately summoned Mr. Neville."

The butler followed right behind her. "I'd thought Mr. Farris had left and you'd gone to bed." The poor butler wrung his hands. "The young master was the one who suggested we search down here. I should have never left your side."

"There's no need to worry, Mr. Neville." She smiled with an ease that gave assurance that all was in order. "Both Mr. Farris and I are so happy you have found us."

But after last night, Devan knew she was like a capsizing ship desperately trying not to go under. Her son meant the world to her. If Avalon thought that last night would give Thane a false expectation they'd marry or confuse the boy about the truth of their friendship, she'd put distance between them. His stomach roiled at such a thought even if it was understandable.

"The vicar and I would like to freshen up," Avalon said in her most efficient voice. She turned to Devan. "Afterward, will you join me for breakfast, Mr. Farris?"

Now they were back to addressing each other as Mr. Farris and Lady Warwyk. He wiped one hand down his face, hoping to erase his fatigue. The bristles on his face reminded him he had a fright. He needed a shave and bath immediately, but unfortunately under the circumstances, he needed to speak with Avalon in private before Thane's concerns were addressed. He nodded, and instantly, Avalon swept from the room with her entire entourage, including him, falling in step behind her.

Within the half hour, Devan found himself seated in the Warwyk Hall small breakfast room after seeing to his immediate needs. The intimate dining area, the one reserved for family, featured peach silk wallcoverings and lent the room a soft touch, one that reminded him of Avalon.

She took a sip of tea, then folded her hands. "I must apologize for Thane's behavior. He's trying to protect me the best way he knows how." The tightness around her mouth gave away her discomfort at having to discuss last night. "My staff is loyal and won't say a word about our spending the night together."

"If you're worried about my housekeeper, Mrs. McVey, don't be." He leaned his elbows on the arms of the chair and leaned back against the blue velvet upholstery. "It was her customary night off."

The chair's softness was a perfect antidote to the wooden cases he'd slept against last night. But nothing could replace the feel of the vital, warm woman across the table who he'd held in his arms. He shook his head to clear such thoughts. He had more important things to discuss.

Avalon carefully laid her serviette next to her untouched plate, then regarded him. "Sophia won't say a word. I'll stress how important it is not to share this with others. As a sister, her loyalty is unquestionable."

He nodded. "I have little doubt of that. Her affection for you is great."

"I'm more like her mother than our own was." Avalon leaned toward him. "There's nothing to worry about. I promise."

The air that separated them still possessed that crackle of awareness that arced between them. Every part of him seemed primed to act. It would take little on his part to cross the distance and kiss her again. He'd never felt as alive as he had last night when he'd made love to her mouth with his.

There was no other way to describe their kiss. For a thousand times last night and today, he thought of making love to her. Images of her supple body beneath his while he lost himself in her embrace conjured all sorts of pleasurable torture. But last night could not be repeated, so the quicker he accepted that fact, the quicker he could set aside such thoughts.

Who was he fooling? There was something unique about Avalon, and he was determined to find out more about her. But he'd not force her into anything she didn't want. She possessed a painful past with memories that wouldn't be erased with one night together.

"Avalon." He cleared his throat, then slowly took her hand in his. Smooth, soft, but with a hidden strength. He tightened his fingers around hers. "What do you want to do? Should we consider marriage?"

"There's no need," she said lightly as if he'd made a comment about the weather. Her perfect mouth curved into a smile. "I do hope we can remain friends. I have so few in my life."

"I will always be your . . . friend." He bit his lip to keep from saying any more. The sting of disappointment dug into every inch of him. For that singular moment in time, he wanted her to say yes. He wanted her for his wife. It was a strange feeling considering they'd been at odds for so long. But somehow, they created something very special between them because of last night, a bond he'd cherish forever.

Before Avalon could respond, the door opened.

As if the Almighty found hilarity at his expense, his two best friends, Paul Barstowe, the Duke of Southart, and William, Lord Cavensham, who'd recently been named a baron, sauntered into the breakfast room with the cheekiest grins plastered on their faces. Reluctantly, Devan let go of Avalon's hand.

The two men immediately sobered when they saw his face.

"Who died?" Lord Cavensham asked.

"By the looks of it, I'd wager it was his dog, but he doesn't have one," Southart drawled.

Avalon almost felt normal after taking a hot bath and changing into a fresh gown. Her muscles still protested the damp cold of the wine cellar if the stiffness in her lower back was any indication. "When did the Duke of Southart and Lord Cavensham arrive?" She eased into the slipper chair that sat directly in front of her dressing table.

Her lady's maid pulled Avalon's hairpins from her pocket and laid them on the table. She picked up her brush and started to work on untangling the knots that currently resided in Avalon's hair. "His Grace made mention that they'd gone to the vicarage first, and when no one was around, Lord Cavensham thought it wise to come see you about the charity event."

"Well, I'm glad they were here, when Dev—the vicar took his leave. The poor man looked like he couldn't walk to the end of the drive let alone the mile back to his home."

"What exactly happened down in the cellar?" Henri pretended to be interested in arranging Avalon's hair, but she knew that innocent but niggling hint of curiosity in Henri's voice.

"Nothing." Avalon closed her eyes and took a deep breath. She could still smell Devan's musky essence. She released it on a sigh. "We fell asleep next to one another under his greatcoat."

Without any noticeable response, Henri continued to fuss with Avalon's hair. She took an unruly curl between her fingers, then pinned it in place with a jeweled hairclip. Though it looked expensive, both of them knew it was a piece of paste jewelry. Avalon had sold the real jeweled hairpins a year after Richard had died. They were the last pieces of jewelry to be sold. She'd hated to part with them, as they were her favorites, but the money went to a good cause. It helped establish Annie in her lace business.

"My lady, may I make a suggestion?"

Avalon caught Henri's gaze in the mirror. "Of course."

"Have you thought about taking a lover? You're so young to give up finding happiness for yourself."

"I'm a mother raising her son to take over this vast and beautiful estate. I don't have time for a lover. Besides if Larkton found out, he might take Thane from me." She shook her head, vehemently dislodging the same unruly curl that Henri had fixed before. "It's out of the question."

"Nothing is ever out of the question, my lady." Her maid's eyes darted to the curl and with an efficiency gained through the years, she pinned it back in place with two pins, thus ensuring it wouldn't fall again. "You should allow yourself a little joy in your life." Henri stopped fussing with Avalon's hair and propped a hand on her hip. "By my way of thinking, the Lord knows you work hard enough. Perhaps He sent you the vicar as a little reward on this heavenly earth. Have you ever thought of that?" Henri raised her eyebrows, challenging Avalon to refute her logic.

"He's a vicar. Mr. Farris isn't that type of a man, Henri." Avalon blew out a breath. "I'm not even certain he likes me. He calls me Lady Warlock."

For the first time that morning, Henri laughed. "My mother always said that you tease the ones you love."

"He doesn't love me." Perhaps there was a glimmer of truth in Henri's words. Last night his tender attentions let her believe he truly cared for her.

"Don't be so certain." Henri raised a single eyebrow in challenge. "Something happened in that cellar last night. You're different this morning."

"Of course I am." Avalon turned in her chair and faced Henri. "I barely managed to get an hour's worth of sleep last night. The soiree is only two days away, and guests will soon arrive. I'm a little unsettled, and I'm sure it's showing on my face."

"That's not it." Henri studied her face. "Your eyes are brighter, and cheeks are rosier. You look happy."

"Of course I'm happy." Avalon waved a hand in dismissal. "I'm happy to be out of the wine cellar."

"You're not telling me something. Did he kiss you? Or did something more than kissing happen down there?"

Henri kept on staring at her, and Avalon refused to look away.

After critically evaluating Avalon, Henri broke the

silence between them. "You are a good woman who deserves to have a man care for you. You need someone who will teach you what I and the rest of your family already know." Henri reached forward and affectionately tapped Avalon in the chest. "You are a worthy person who deserves love. You don't have to tell me what happened. I shouldn't have pried, but I want you happy."

"Thank you, Henri." Tears welled in Avalon's eyes. Without meaning to, Henri tore away the carefully constructed barriers around Avalon's heart with her loving words and revealed Avalon's real weakness.

How many people in her life thought she was a worthwhile person? The answer was simple. Henri, her son and sister, the women she'd helped, and perhaps a few of the villagers thought of her that way. She'd created her own haven here in Thistledown, and she was proud of it.

It was enough. It had to be. She couldn't afford anything else, not until Thane was old enough to manage things on his own. Then perhaps she'd think about moving back to London. Hopefully, Sophia would marry and live in the city. Avalon would find ways to fill her days. It was a waste of time to wish for more.

Yet, she yearned for someone of her own to share all the moments of her life with. Someone like Devan.

Henri closed the distance between them and hugged her.

Avalon hadn't even realized it, but tears streamed down her face. That her future promised nothing more than a bleak and lonely existence was a bitter truth she had to accept. She sobbed aloud, then brought a hand to cover her mouth. She would have given every last penny she possessed to have a man see the real her. A man who could see all her faults and still love her.

Last night she'd pretended Devan was that man and it'd been heaven.

How was she ever going to look at him again without wanting him in her life?

Devan rubbed a hand across his cleanly shaven chin, then leaned back in his chair. Across his desk sat Paul Barstowe, the Duke of Southart, and William, Lord Cavensham. Both men stared at him as if he'd suddenly sprouted horns atop his head. "Larkton practically begged me to come here. He wants me to spy on her."

"Are you?" Paul took a sip of his coffee.

"Yes and no. I told Larkton I wouldn't do it without telling her, and I told her what Larkton wanted to know. It's safer to tell the truth, I think."

"Are you still calling her Lady Warlock?" Will asked.

Paul shook his head in dismay, then raised an eyebrow in Devan's direction. "I thought you used your talents as a clergyman to help and comfort people, not insult them. What happened to you and your supposed talent with the ladies? Bad form to insult Lady Warwyk with name-calling."

"'Warlock' is a term of affection," Devan protested.

William looked around the well-appointed room. "She's paying for all of this, isn't she?"

Devan shook his head in annoyance. "Will you both stop?" He poured another cup of black coffee, then held up the pot in offering to the other two.

William waved a hand for another cup, and Paul declined.

"Devan, after what you've said about the young lordship wanting you to marry his mother, how are you going to keep tutoring him without it being awkward?" Paul leaned back in his chair. With his elegant clothing, light hair, and blue eyes, he looked like an archangel that had stopped by for a visit.

Devan rested his elbows on the desk, then studied his steaming cup and hoped the vapors might reveal some piece of wisdom. "I don't know. I'll disappoint him if I'm not a more permanent part of his life." He looked up at his two friends. "She loves her son. He's her whole world. She doesn't want to marry me."

"The soiree is in two days. My entire family is coming up here for the event. Since I married Thea, she's made certain that Avalon, Sophia, and Thane are treated like a part of the Cavensham clan." William took a sip of coffee. "I'm acquainted with the young marquess. He's a good fellow. I don't think he'll hold a grudge against you."

Devan tried to damp his unease, but it was like a burr. No matter how he tried to shake it off, it stuck to him. Perhaps if he discussed what happened with his friends, they could make sense of it.

He'd wanted Avalon to say yes to marriage. As he'd waited for her answer at the table, a million images flashed through his eyes as he envisioned a life with Avalon and Thane. But he was a vicar and she was a marchioness. She'd never have accepted, even if she had feelings for him. Besides, she was scared of marrying again.

"After last night, I want to marry her."

"Really?" William's voice deepened. "So, the wild vicar is ready to be tamed."

"Appearances aren't everything." He'd kept his secret from his friends—whether it was pride or something else made little difference. A part of him only wanted to share such a truth with his wife. But his friends wouldn't judge him for allowing the rumors of his experiences with women to manifest in a persona that he willingly hid behind to keep Larkton from hounding him to marry. "I'm not that experienced with women."

"We assumed as much." Paul closed the distance between them and stood before Devan, halting his pacing.

"How?" Devan asked, clearly shocked.

"For someone who has always talked of marrying an heiress, you are awfully picky." Paul's mouth tilted in a half smile. "Too picky, in my opinion. Which leads me to believe you were perhaps uncomfortable. Maybe shy?"

"Shy?" Devan took a small step back. "No, it's nothing like that. As I became an adult, I appreciated the marriage my parents had. I wanted the same."

"You should be picky," William offered in support. "My parents taught me and my siblings the same thing. The right woman can turn a life into an amazing, beautiful adventure."

The duke then grabbed him by the shoulder. "You can convince Avalon you're the right man. Use that silver tongue of yours and bring her around."

Devan exhaled, then turned his attention to the fire. "No. I'm far beneath her station."

"Nonsense," William said as he joined them, then knelt to attend the dying embers. His gaze shot upward to Devan. "But I will say this, she's one of a kind."

"Did you know that her parents forced her to marry Warwyk?" Devan asked.

William shook his head. "No, but I'd heard rumors to that effect." He stood and brushed his hands together. "I'm a perfect example of a man who married above his station. I married a countess before I was made a baron."

"He's right. You shouldn't be concerned about marrying above your station. Besides, you're an earl's son." Paul nodded in agreement, before one eyebrow arched perfectly. "You always did want to marry an heiress. For some odd reason, I think you and Lady Warwyk would be perfect for each other."

"It would require a miracle for that to happen," he murmured.

Paul's eyebrow shot up. "Isn't that your specific calling, Vicar?"

"I'm not certain God involves himself in matters of the heart," Devan answered.

"Don't be a fool," William gingerly chided. "We all need a little help at times. Particularly in matters of love."

"I'm not in love with her." The objection left a metallic taste in his mouth.

"Still honest as the day is long, aren't you, *Vicar*?" the duke asked as he deliberately tapped one finger against his chin. "Brings to mind the old saying, 'Be careful or all your chickens will come home to roost.'"

Indeed.

Every thought, action, or innuendo that supported the lie that he was a man of the world with the ladies would soon make a fool out of him.

"Perhaps a ride would clear some of the cobwebs that seem to be cluttering your thoughts." William wrapped an arm around Devan's shoulders.

"Excellent idea," Paul answered.

Within minutes, they were astride their horses and strolling through the village. Devan veered his black stallion over to an empty field where Avalon stood with a gentleman who clutched several drawings in his hands. He pointed to a location across the way, then back to the drawing.

Immediately, Paul and William followed Devan toward Avalon.

"Look there, Vicar," Paul murmured. "Divine intervention at work. Here is your chance to do a little wooing."

Without answering, Devan approached Avalon and the gentleman. Just seeing her again caused his heart to gallop in his chest. All signs of fatigue disappeared like the faint wisp of a cloud in a summer sky. When he dismounted, he quickly tied Devil to a branch. As soon as Avalon saw him, she smiled and waved.

"Good afternoon, Lady Warwyk," Paul called out as he and William both dismounted from their horses.

"Your Grace," she answered. With an elegant ease, she turned to Lord Cavensham. "Good afternoon, William." Finally, she turned to him. "Hello, Vicar."

It might have been his imagination, but Devan could have sworn her smile became a little brighter when she greeted him.

"Avalon, it's delightful to see you again," William answered. He came forward and executed a bow.

"Gentlemen, may I introduce Mr. Christopher Strong. He's helping me with the plans for the new workroom and nursery I'm building." She turned to the architect. "Mr. Strong, this is His Grace, the Duke of Southart, Lord Cavensham, and Mr. Farris, our local vicar."

A distinguished-looking man in his late forties nodded and sketched an abbreviated bow to the men. "The pleasure is mine."

Soon they were all discussing her plans for building a two-story building. The workroom would be on the main floor with the nursery above. As Mr. Strong was showing Paul and William the modern plumbing planned for the building, Devan leaned closer to Avalon. "Hello, Vicar? Are we back to formal terms?" He spoke in a low tone, ensuring they wouldn't be overheard.

"Would you prefer something else, then?" she teased.

"I'd prefer to hear my name on your lips," he answered.

"Mr. Farris, then," she quipped with a grin. "Come, I want to show you something." Without waiting for him, she briskly walked to a part of the field that had been marked with painted sticks. As soon as he drew to her side, she continued, "This will be the view from the playroom I've had Mr. Strong design for the children and their nurse-maids. While their mothers are working below, the children will have an excellent view of the river from the second floor." She pointed across the field. The glow of excitement in her eyes was breathtaking. "They can see the valley from this direction."

Devan gazed in the direction she pointed. Indeed, the bucolic beauty of the Warwyk lands couldn't be hidden even in the dead of winter. "It's beautiful, Avalon. They'll be enchanted. I'd wager their mothers will have a hard time getting them to leave at the end of the day."

She bit her lip in an adorable way as she considered his words. "I hope they're all happy here."

"I have little doubt," he said.

She nodded slightly. "The rest of the floor will be split into small apartments for women who are newly arrived and need housing."

Suddenly, a gust of wind blew his hair into his eyes. Before he could brush it back, she did the honor for him. The touch, intimate as a kiss, stole his breath. He caught her hand before she lowered it and brought it to his lips. "Avalon, what you're doing here is remarkable."

Her gaze locked with his, and her lips parted slightly. She released a deep breath, not breaking eye contact. "Thank you. I wish I could do more."

"How so?" He studied her face once again. The determination and pure joy that shone from her eyes made him want to sweep her into his arms and kiss her again just like last night.

"I'd like to help the girls who have nowhere to go before they find themselves on the London streets," she said wistfully.

"Perhaps you could start an apprenticeship for young girls. I could ask the parishes around here if any girls are alone or appear vulnerable. We could offer employment before they travel to London. From what I've seen of Miss Sinclair's and Miss Flora's talent, they'll soon be inundated with dress orders. They could use several assistants, I wager, and perhaps even more." Determined to help, he continued, "Mrs. Dozier could teach some of them how to make lace. Perhaps some of the girls would help the matrons with the care of the children."

"Devan, that's brilliant," Avalon said softly. "I love the idea."

"I love hearing my name on your lips." He stepped closer, and she answered in kind. He could hear Paul call his name, but Devan didn't dare break this moment between them.

A half grin tugged at her lips. "You mean 'Mr. Farris'?"

"Come, Lady Warlock, enough of your witchery." He held out his arm for her to take. "Let me escort you back to Mr. Strong."

She slipped her arm through his. Touching her was the antidote to his fatigue.

But he wanted more.

He wanted another night in the wine cellar with Avalon.

Out of the mouths of babes comes wisdom with a
healthy jolt of stupefying clarity.

Devan Farris

Chapter Thirteen

❧

Last evening, the Duke of Southart and Lord Cavensham had dined with Devan at home before returning to London. This morning, after Devan had visited Annie Dozier and her family, he walked the familiar road to the vicarage. Only a few whistles of wind through the bare branches accompanied him as he strolled through the country lane. He had little interest in the weather as all of his thoughts were consumed by a certain woman with chocolate-brown hair, mesmerizing green eyes, and a complicated disposition to match.

Tomorrow night at Avalon's benefit soiree, he'd be in company with her again. He planned to dance with her as many times as she'd allow. As a widow, she could do whatever she wanted, but she always kept herself a tad aloof from the others. But he hoped for her first and last dance. His plan would require that he arrive early and talk to the small orchestra Avalon had hired for the event. A carefully spoken request would ensure that those dances would be waltzes.

Never one to worry about his upcoming sermons, Devan had plenty of time to prepare for the upcoming Sunday's church service. He'd chosen to discuss tolerance and affection. There was a wealth of material for divine inspiration in the community, including the perfect accord he and Avalon had reached. It'd be lovely to discuss how animosity could grow into tolerance and eventually—he hoped—deep affection.

How could one woman consume his thoughts so completely? He shook his head gently as he tugged his gloves a little tighter. Such was the power of Avalon.

"Mr. Farris?" a female voice called from behind.

He slowed his gait to a stop and turned around. The voice belonged to Lady Sophia Cavensham. Miss Penelope Rowley had her arm linked with Sophia's as they approached.

"May we walk with you?" Penelope asked.

Sophia's interest was consumed by the large elm tree to the right of them. However, Penelope looked at him boldly, as if daring him to deny them.

"Of course." Devan bowed slightly. "I'd enjoy the company. Are you going into the village for a little shopping or are you visiting a friend?"

Sophia's interests shifted to her feet. The young woman still had refused to look him in the eye. It was unusual behavior for Avalon's sister. Normally, she wasn't bashful around anyone, particularly him.

Devan studied her a little while longer, then turned to Penelope, who, with a practiced smile, devoted all of her attention to him.

"Lady Sophia and I were just returning from visiting Miss Sinclair and Miss Leona." Penelope lifted an empty basket in her free hand. "My aunt and I baked bread and included fresh butter and a jar of jam." She released her hold of Sophia and came to stand nearer. "They've been so busy with tomorrow's soiree, we thought they might need some help." She batted her eyelashes. "I'd like to bake some for you."

Avalon's words to take care around this young woman rushed into his thoughts. "A lovely offer, Miss Rowley, but I would hate to offend Mrs. McVey. My housekeeper loves to dote upon me." He chuckled. "Perhaps you could bake some for Mrs. Dozier. Mrs. Jennings and Miss Jennings are still staying at her house. I'm sure they would appreciate the kind gesture, and they need it more than I do."

"Would that please you?" Penelope asked.

The dulcet but sickening tone sent chills racing down his back. Without any hesitation, he took a step back from Penelope. "I'm of no concern, but I'm certain the Almighty would look favorably upon such a kind act. Perhaps, Lady Sophia could—"

"Oh goodness. I forgot my reticule at Miss Sinclair's and Miss Leona's home." Sophia turned around, then ran as if her house were in flames.

Without a glance back at her friend, Penelope came to his side. "Would you see me home?"

"Perhaps we should wait for Lady Sophia?" Devan said.

Penelope shook her head. "She told me earlier that she wanted to look at Miss Sinclair's and Miss Leona's gowns again."

Devan released a silent sigh. He was no actor, but he'd seen enough drama in his life to know that he was about to see quite a performance from Miss Rowley. He nodded once, then clasped his hands behind his back, refusing to offer his arm. "Shall we?"

She nodded and fell into step beside him.

"Are your aunt and uncle home?" he asked.

"Yes, they are. Why? Do you wish to see them?" The hopefulness in her voice was unmistakable.

"I thought perhaps to ask them to help sponsor the church altar centerpieces for the upcoming month."

"*Ooaf.*" She grabbed his arm in an apparent attempt to keep from falling.

As a gentleman, he had no recourse but to help her stay upright.

With little warning, she leaned heavily into him, causing them both to be caught off balance. Suddenly, the world tilted, and they both fell to the hard ground. Devan twisted to take the brunt of the fall.

Penelope landed directly on top of him. With their legs tangled in a seemingly hopeless knot, she pressed her chest firmly against his. "I think I twisted my ankle on a rock."

Her gaze captured his and the intensity in her eyes sent warning bells clanging. Without preamble, Penelope pressed her lips against his. "Oh, Devan," she murmured.

Immediately, he took her arms and carefully pushed her away. He sprang upright like a jack released from its box. "Let me help you up."

What else could he say? *Unhand me, you wench.* Perhaps a better retort was called for. *Have you lost your bloody mind?* Surely heaven would excuse the use of profanity in this instance.

When he held out his hand, she placed hers in his and squeezed.

Ignoring the gesture, he hauled her to her feet perhaps a little abruptly as she stumbled forward again. He sidestepped her to keep from having her fall into kissing him again. "Can you walk?"

Her eyes narrowed for an instant, then a cool smile graced her face. "Devan, I've known for quite awhile that you wanted to kiss me. Just like I wanted to kiss you."

"I didn't give you permission to address me so intimately." The words sounded guttural to his own ears, and he didn't hide the curtness in his tone. Her face fell in response, betraying her hurt and emphasizing her youth.

He wiped a hand down his face. He'd had women throw themselves at him in the past but not literally. There was only one solution to nip this disaster in the bud. He had to address what she'd done. "Miss Rowley, you've misconstrued any attention I've given you in the past."

Any embarrassment she possessed disappeared like a ship sailing into the fog when her lips thinned in anger. "Every time we're together, I catch you glancing my way."

"You're mistaken," he said. Warily, he regarded her. "I have no romantic feelings for you. Nor shall I ever have such feelings, I'm afraid."

She stared at him defiantly, then quickly schooled her features. "You're just embarrassed. Don't be." Her tone turned gentle. "You share the same regard for me as I have for you."

He shook his head. "I'm afraid not." She took a step closer, and in tandem, he took a step backward, keeping distance between them. "You should turn your attentions to someone who would welcome them. Perhaps Mr. Grant."

"He's a boy. I want a man. I want you."

Devan stared at her for a moment. Immediately, the image of the female snake-haired monster Medusa came to mind. Her young age didn't hide the covetous gleam in her eyes. Never before had such foreboding pummeled him with a need to take care around a woman.

"Miss Rowley, I have no doubt you have much to offer another." Her cheeks warmed at his praise. "However, don't waste them on me. I don't share your affection. Besides, I'm much too old for you."

"I like older men," she said.

"And I like older women," he countered. "You're too young for me."

"What does age have to do with attraction? If two people find an undeniable attraction"—she tilted her head and examined him much like a succulent pastry—"I'd say an undeniable bond is a better description. How can we resist?"

"Miss Rowley, please." His patience had worn thin. "Whatever you think it is you feel for me, it's misguided. I can only offer friendship. You're going to have to accept that fact." He bent and retrieved his beaver top hat. Unfortunately, it had been a casualty of his fall. The brim had a nasty bend on one side. Without his usual fanfare, he placed it on his head with a firm tug.

Her eyes widened, and her mouth gaped like a fish out of water desperate for air. She stuck her nose in the air, then with a huff for good measure, she turned and strutted in the opposite direction. No doubt she had a rendezvous with Lady Sophia to discuss the failure of her conquest.

Amazingly, her gait was smooth without a hint of a limp as she sauntered away.

Without a look back, Devan proceeded to the vicarage, where a warm brandy would be a welcome balm for this troublesome interlude with the young woman.

Penelope Rowley threatened his peace of mind, and he didn't want any interference from her and her wild imagination as he concentrated on his friendship with Avalon.

Friendship was such an innocuous word when it came to describe his feelings with a certain marchioness. While Avalon may think they were friends, it didn't define his feelings.

Ever since they'd spent the night with one another, he couldn't get her out of his thoughts.

Amazingly, three weeks ago she'd circled around him like a gladiator preparing for an epic battle against a lion until one of them fell in defeat. How things had changed.

Perhaps the best course for both of them would be to listen to the organs in the middle of their chests. It could teach warriors a thing or two—specifically, how to be valiant when the call to arms turns into an engagement of the heart.

"Mother, I don't want to do this." Thane's gaze slid away from Avalon to his boots.

They'd been standing outside the vicarage door for the last five minutes as her son had grappled with finding the courage to knock.

"Confessing our wrongs makes us stronger," she said. She bent slightly so she could gaze directly into her son's eyes. The way Thane was growing, it wouldn't be too much longer before he'd be the one who would have to bend to look her in the eyes. "It's best to get it over with and try to put it behind us. I meant . . . best to put it behind you."

In bed, she'd twisted and turned all last night as she weighed what was the appropriate action to take with Thane. After wrestling with it, she'd finally decided this morning that they'd both go together to see Devan.

"He'll think I'm weak."

"No, he won't. He'll think you're a young man who accepts responsibility for his actions."

Thane slightly shook his head in disbelief.

"Mr. Farris will appreciate it, and he'll respect you more." She spoke the truth. After spending the night with Devan and telling him all her secrets and Devan sharing his secrets with her, she knew more about the man and his integrity.

They'd also come to accept a truce between them. The bond that they'd shared that night had been something tangible, and she didn't want Devan to worry that he'd done something to alienate her son.

Thane took a deep breath as he raised his hand to the door and knocked twice. He returned his gaze to hers, and Avalon nodded in approval. "You'll survive this, I promise."

"I hope so," he muttered to himself.

Instead of Mrs. McVey answering their knock, it was Devan, who, with one hand, was buttoning his waistcoat.

"Come in, please." He stood aside and quickly motioned for them to enter. With his height, the entry of the vicarage seemed to shrink. He quickly put on his morning coat, and the garment seemed to melt onto his body—much as she had that night two days ago. "Pardon my appearance. I was writing to my brothers." Immediately, he frowned slightly. "Is anything amiss? Mrs. Dozier?"

Avalon shook her head. "We've just come from there. Annie is fine, the baby is growing by leaps and bounds, and Byrnn is back to his old jolly self." She turned to Thane, who looked everywhere and anywhere except at Devan.

"Thane," she coaxed, keeping her voice low.

He nodded once, then forced his gaze to the vicar. "Mr. Farris, I was wondering if I might have a moment of your time."

"Of course. Let's adjourn to my study." He held out a hand for them to precede him.

Just then, Mrs. McVey entered the vestibule. Drying her hands with a linen toweling, she appeared to have come from the kitchen. "Pardon me, Vicar. I didn't hear the door. I just baked some fresh tarts. Let me prepare the tea service."

"Thank you, Mrs. McVey." His mouth curved upward. "Your extraordinary tarts would be perfect."

At his words and kind smile, the housekeeper flushed liked a young girl who'd just received a compliment from the handsomest boy in the village.

Remarkable that he had that effect on everyone. Such a revelation caused Avalon's heart to kick into a jig. He had a God-given talent to make any person—man or woman—feel as if they were special. He showed such kindness to everyone. It would be wise on her part to remember such wisdom and not let their frivolous flirtation and previous intimacy make her feel singled out for special attention.

Avalon touched Thane's shoulder as a sign for the boy to proceed to the study as Devan talked to Mrs. McVey. The boy visibly swallowed but led the way. Avalon's heart tugged at such a gesture. He was scared, but there was nothing she could say or do to stop what had to happen. It was the only way he would learn his lesson.

As soon as they had settled into the two chairs that faced Devan's desk, he entered the room and sat down. The fire crackled in greeting as if glad to see him—just as she was.

"Mr. Farris, my mother and I are here today . . ." Thane looked to her, and she nodded in encouragement. "I owe you an apology."

Devan leaned back in his chair. It was the one that the previous vicar, Mr. Knightley, had used. With the old vicar, the worn leather chair had seemed too large for his frail body, but with Devan, the exact opposite was true. Devan appeared too large for it. The breadth of his upper body completely hid the back and the arms.

"How so?" Devan asked while keeping his gaze firmly locked on Thane.

"Well, you see, Mr. Farris . . ." Thane pulled his neck cloth away from his neck as if the offending piece of linen was choking him. "Mr. Farris," he repeated.

Devan leaned forward and rested his elbows on the desk. "Just say it, my lord. I find that getting it out is relief in and of itself."

The boy's eyes widened, then he nodded. "Well, you see . . ." He studied the floor for a moment, before turning his attention back to Devan. "It was me who locked you in the cellar with my mother the other night."

"You?" Devan asked quietly. "I don't understand."

Thane's cheeks heated in embarrassment, and so did Avalon's in empathy. "Thane and I had a conversation last night, and we wanted to come visit this morning." She dipped her head toward her son. "Go ahead," she encouraged.

He nodded, then exhaled loudly. "I wanted you to marry my mother so you'd come live with us. You spend time with me, and frankly, I look forward to it every time you visit. I wanted more so I locked you in together overnight so you were both ruined, and you'd have to marry."

Devan didn't say anything, but the kindness on his face never wavered.

"I could hardly sleep as I waited for morning to come. I was the first one up in the household, and I woke Henri asking where Mother was. When she became worried, I went to Mr. Neville as I knew he'd calm Henri down." Thane's voice grew quiet. "I led them down into the cellar to witness that you both were together. I'm sorry for trying to orchestrate such a situation and making assumptions about what would make you both happy."

Devan rose, then stood beside Thane. He knelt on his haunches and rested his hand on the arm of Thane's chair. "I accept your apology, Lord Warwyk. But as long as I am the vicar in Thistledown, you never have to worry. I'll always be your friend, and I promise to visit Warwyk Hall as long as I'm welcome."

Thane sniffed back a tear and wouldn't look at either of them.

"I appreciate your honesty." Devan lowered his voice. "But there's no harm done."

Finally, Thane turned slowly to face Devan. "I don't want you to be my friend."

"Thane," Avalon admonished. "That's cruel."

Her son shook his head. "I don't want him as a friend. I want him as my father."

As her son's words hung in the air, she saw the incredulous look on Devan's face and heat blazed across her cheeks. Her back instantly became ramrod straight. It was the only way she could prepare herself for the discussion that would follow.

A puff of wind would have knocked Devan over after young Lord Warwyk had proclaimed that he planned the entire night in the wine cellar so Devan would marry Avalon. The longcase clock in the room ticked like a hammer on a stubborn nail ad nauseam as he'd tried to think of an appropriate response.

Avalon's cheeks flushed scarlet and her eyes widened at her son's declaration.

Devan bit the inside of his cheek when the boy's shoulders and head dropped at the confession. "Thane," he soothed. "Your mother and I . . ."

Both Thane and Avalon turned their gaze to him. It could have been his imagination, but each had a hopeful glint in their eyes. He had little doubt that Avalon wanted him to disavow the boy's wishes. But for the life of him, he couldn't form the words.

"Thane," Avalon murmured. "Just because you wish it doesn't mean we'll marry."

"I know." The young lord sniffed. "But you've been happy since the vicar moved to town, and the same for me. I thought we could always be that way if you married him. He's the only man who truly takes any interest in us. I'm surrounded by women. It's nice to have someone to ride with and learn things from besides you, Mother." He bowed his head. "I love you, but I want Mr. Farris, too. Is that so wrong? Do I have to apologize for that also?"

"Here we are." Mrs. McVey entered the room with the tea tray, then carefully set it down. "Oh, dear. I forgot the tarts."

Disbelief had robbed Devan of speech. Thankfully, Avalon answered for him. "How wonderful. Thane, will you follow Mrs. McVey and bring back the tarts?"

The boy nodded, then stood and followed the housekeeper out of the room. When the sound of their footsteps quieted into nothing, Avalon collapsed against the back of her chair.

"I'm mortified at his confession. He told me he thought I should marry so I'd have someone." Her eyes glistened with emotion. "I apologize, too. I had no idea that he wanted a father." Her gaze darted to her tightly clasped hands. "Nor did I think he'd ever do such a thing. You must think I'm a horrible mother." She shook her head slightly. "If it's any consolation, based upon what Thane shared, I believe I'm a horrible mother, too."

"Avalon." He deepened his voice, wanting to comfort her. "What Thane did has no bearing on who you are or what type of a mother you are. He shared with me one day that you say kind words about his father. I know how difficult that must have been for you."

"He'll find out soon enough about his father from

others," she murmured. "He doesn't need to hear it from me."

"That's a lovely gift you've given him, and it says volumes that you had him come to me today to apologize. It shows that you're teaching him what's morally right."

"He wants a father." The shock was visible on her face. "It's just incredible." She stood slowly. "Perhaps I shouldn't have harbored the women I brought up from London. Maybe my charity work is taking too much time when I should have devoted more to my son. Mayhap I should consider giving your brother more authority over Thane's upbringing. I'm floundering here and didn't even know it."

Never had he seen her so defeated. His Warlock had always had steel in her backbone, but her son had just brought her to her knees.

In two strides, he reached her side and took her hands in his. "You are a wonderful mother." He squeezed her hands in reassurance. "You've provided Thane with a loving home and family who cares deeply for him and his upbringing. You've performed the roles of mother and father with aplomb and gravitas. Never question your ability to raise that boy," he added softly.

She lifted her head and searched his gaze as if wanting to believe it, but something held her back. "How could I have presumed that I knew how to raise and protect him when I had such poor examples for parents?" A renegade tear dropped with the speed of a shooting star in a night sky. She turned her head and wrenched her hands from his to wipe the offending wetness off her cheek. "I must go."

"Don't, please. I'd like your company." The vicarage possessed an undeniable energy in it when she graced its doorway.

Good Lord, he'd always had a fondness for her, but

now the only thing he knew was that he wanted more. She was like a life-affirming miracle water, and he wanted to swim in it—with her beside him.

For a moment, she seemed to consider staying longer, then shook her head. "I have to prepare for the soiree, and Sophia and I have calls to make this afternoon. I'll collect Thane. We won't interrupt your day any more than we already have."

She turned to leave, and he stopped her with a single word. "Avalon."

With her head down, it became apparent that she'd lost her fighting spirit.

"You may run from me, but you can't hide." His voice deepened in a husky whisper. "I see the real you, and I won't let you forget who you are either. I bid you adieu, my Lady Warlock."

His farewell had the intended effect. That one affectionate word, and a smile tugged at her lips.

She was back.

His Lady Warlock.

Many a wise woman would forgo their queendom for a dress.

source unknown

Chapter Fourteen

∽ ♦ ∽

A valon smoothed a hand down the front of her beautiful bronze gown, allowing her fingers to skate over the antique jeweled stomacher brooch. Never before had she felt like a princess at a ball, but wearing this dress tonight made her feel regal, as if she were the queen of everything in her domain. More than a hundred had accepted her invitation to the soiree, and her small ballroom was filled to capacity. The undeniable success of the evening was helped immensely by the Cavenshams.

Her third cousins, the entire Cavensham clan, had come *en masse* to her charity event and were the first to arrive. Hugs and smiles had been freely given, and for the first time all day, Avalon allowed herself to relax. Everything about this evening would be perfect.

At least, she'd prayed it would be. No doubt it would all depend upon how Devan treated her after she'd scurried out of the vicarage with Thane beside her.

That was entirely the wrong attitude to take this evening. She was the Marchioness of Warwyk, and it was her responsibility to make all her guests feel welcome, even if one was a vicar who made her feel slightly off-kilter.

Sophia came to her side and kissed her on the cheek.

"I'm so proud of you. It's simply astounding how you've helped these women transform their lives. You're amazing."

"Nonsense," Avalon answered.

"I beg to differ, Lady *Warrrwyk*."

Devan's silken voice wrapped itself around her from behind.

Sophia dipped a quick curtsey. "Mr. Farris, it's so lovely that you're here."

He took Sophia's hand and delivered a perfect courtly bow. "Good evening, Lady Sophia," he said.

"If you'll excuse me? I see Flora and want to chat before the auction starts." Without waiting for an answer, Sophia turned and walked in the direction where the gowns were displayed.

Not to appear too eager at Devan's arrival, Avalon forced her gaze to the golden and silver silks decorating the windows. The yards and yards of material glittered as if vying for his attention. The red roses from the Warwyk Hall hothouse were breathtakingly lovely and filled the entire room in a delicate floral scent.

But Devan stood close enough that a hint of his familiar cologne along with a clean pure scent of male wafted her way as he waved a hand around the room. As if delighted he'd finally arrived, her pulse pounded in welcome. She leaned slightly backward, and his hand rested on the small of her back—as if claiming her as his. With only Devan and her with their backs to the ballroom doors, no one could see such an intimate caress. The rest of her guests were milling around the dresses and other items for auction in the center of the room.

She closed her eyes and inhaled deeply. Though it was scandalous, she'd fantasized about Devan nightly, her thoughts wild and salacious as she imagined all the things they could do to pleasure each other in bed.

Her traitorous body melted at his slight touch, and all she wanted in that moment was to lean against him and luxuriate in his warmth while his arms surrounded her. Immediately, she stepped away to increase the distance between them. Ready for the evening, she was happy and slightly nervous for the event to start. With him so close, everything seemed to be amplified.

"Avalon, are you wary of me?" Devan's soft words floated around them.

She didn't answer. Somewhere in this ballroom, she'd lost her mind as the memories of the wine cellar flooded her with heat. That had to be the answer for her lack of poise this evening. However, she'd put all that bother aside. This was a special night, and she'd do what she pleased.

"Welcome, Mr. Farris," she purred. She pivoted to face him, and as a result, the sweep of her bronze silk skirt kissed his legs with a *swish*. "Why would I be wary of a man such as yourself? A man whose sole purpose in life is to guide others to the pearly gates that promise joyous rapture to all." She tapped her chin twice and regarded him. "Makes me wonder who guides you? Perhaps it's best to ask who you would *desire* to guide you?"

His eyes widened at the innuendo in her voice. "Guide me in what?"

"Oh, come now, sir. I think you know the answer," she teased. She lightly caressed the jeweled brooch to keep from betraying the shaking of her hands. She'd never in her life flirted so shamelessly with a man before.

His gaze darted to the exposed skin of her décolletage and his nostrils flared. That one movement on his part told her that her flirting was having its intended effect, and she'd never felt so alive.

"My, my." His green eyes twinkled. "Lady Warlock is in rare form this evening."

"Indeed," she answered and flipped open the matching jeweled fan Jasmine had given her to accompany the dress. "It's such a relief," she sighed dramatically.

"Pray tell, what do you find a relief?" he asked with an unmistakable hint of laughter in his voice.

"You didn't call me 'my Lady Warlock.' Finally, you understand I'm not yours." She leaned toward him slightly as if sharing a secret. "But perhaps I'll accept the title of Lady Warlock. It's so much easier to be bad when everyone expects it of you."

His gentle laugh reminded her of a caress, one she felt all the way to her bare skin.

"You spoke of 'pearly gates' earlier." His gaze swept slowly over her gown. You look like heaven."

Caught off guard by the vibrancy in his voice, she stared when his eyes smoldered with the promise of forbidden pleasure in their depths. This man wasn't a simple country vicar, but someone who had the power to turn her world upside down.

Avalon wanted that promise this evening. She'd allow herself to experience all the simple pleasures she'd missed in her life like harmlessly flirting with an attractive man, and how perfect it would be if Devan would fulfill such wishes. Such power promised to be a heady aphrodisiac, and she wanted it—tonight—with him.

"Do you want to experience heaven, Devan?"

His lips tugged upward, revealing two deep dimples she immediately wanted to explore with her lips. "Are you offering paradise?"

"I can act as gatekeeper." Without taking her gaze from his, she closed her fan. Without looking, she flicked her wrist and opened it panel by panel. "Open my gates, and you'll find bliss."

He exhaled slowly as he tightened his own hands into fists as if trying to maintain control. "Lady Warlock," he murmured. "You're playing with fire."

"You can put it out," she countered.

"You'd best be careful, or I'll do just that." He stepped a little closer, and his heat enveloped her like a lover's embrace.

"I'm certain we'd both enjoy it." She took a deep breath, the movement emphasizing the bared skin of her chest. "But be forewarned. I'll start another blaze between us."

"And I'll put it out again and again. All night with relentless pleasure . . . for both of us."

His word conjured all sorts of salacious and redolent images. She could imagine his hands skating slowly down her skin, learning all her body's secrets as she learned his

The small orchestra started to play a waltz.

"Avalon." Her name on his lips was a plea for what they both knew couldn't happen but seemed inevitable as the seconds ticked by. "Dance with me."

Before she could answer, Sophia sidled up to them and Avalon took a small step back. Devan blinked as if he himself were coming out of a trance.

Without any awareness of what she'd interrupted, Sophia turned to Avalon. "Jasmine and Flora need your help. After this dance finishes, Mrs. Rowley wants to make an announcement about the auction."

Sophia nodded again to Devan, then headed toward the dais set up for tonight's event.

Avalon nodded also, but with more reserve than Sophia had exhibited. It was time to return to the real world. "Vicar."

"Don't you dare put distance between us." Devan stepped closer. "Please don't," he whispered. "You've shown me your true self, and I'm enchanted. I'll be waiting until you return to my side."

"What if I never do?"

"I think you will." He took her hand in his and brought it to his lips. The warmth from his hand burned through the satin of her gloves. "But I have no objection to taking the lead on this delightful path you've introduced us to."

"I've always enjoyed exploring new paths." Without waiting for his answer, Avalon returned to her guests. All the while, his intense gaze burned a hole straight through her heart.

She now understood the power contained in Cupid's quiver.

Devan watched Avalon cross the room. With a gentle sway of her hips, the magnificent gown she wore shimmered in the candlelight. His body burned deep inside with each subtle movement she made. He'd known desire for a woman, yet always he'd been careful and able to keep it under lock and key.

But not this magical night. His Warlock called to him like no other had ever done before. The charming interlude they'd created deserved to be nurtured.

He smiled as she elegantly and efficiently managed the ladies of her committee while they twittered about the mounds of dresses up for auction. Though Avalon had other women as part of her committee, everyone knew that it was Avalon and her plans that had created this marvelous evening to benefit her charity, and specifically Annie Dozier, Jasmine Sinclair, and Flora Leona.

Every now and then, she'd glance his way and catch him staring. Unwilling to break the magic they'd shared, he'd smile. Each time, a beautiful blush colored her cheeks, and in response his heart would beat harder as if demanding to break out of his chest and fly straight to her. If she were his, then after tonight when all the guests had gone home, they'd fall into bed together where they'd discover all the wonders of sharing each other without any barriers between them. Skin to skin, mouth to mouth, they'd finally join their bodies together in a dance older than civilization.

He'd make her hunger for no one but him. Just like he hungered for her.

Restless, Devan released a sigh, one born of patience. He and Avalon were so similar, and frankly, he was surprised that he hadn't seen it before now. It had nothing to do with their good works for others, but more about the growing desire for one another. They both wanted to be careful in seeking a partner. He had little doubt that once she gave her heart it'd be forever—just like him. But unlike her, Devan had never been hurt. She carried scars that he'd give anything to soothe. Whatever she needed, he'd gladly give her, and they'd both be the richer.

"Vicar?" A woman's voice broke his reverie.

He looked down to discover Penelope Rowley before him. "Good evening, Miss Rowley." He clasped the hand she'd lifted and offered an abbreviated but expected customary bow. At once, he took a slight step backward.

Her brows grew together at his coolness, but she offered a small smile. "I'd wondered if you'd like to sit with my aunt and uncle and me. The auction will soon start, and my aunt has promised to bid on the pink satin for me. She says it's perfect for me as it will enhance my complexion. I'm afraid I may become overcome with all the excitement. Your presence would help calm me, I'm certain."

Before he could politely decline, his friend Paul, the Duke of Southart, drew to his side. "I'm afraid, Miss Rowley, that my duchess and I have already coerced Mr. Farris to sit by us."

A scowl twisted her face as her brows knitted together. She dipped a small curtsey. "Your Grace." Without taking her leave of Devan, she scurried back to the auction proceedings.

Paul watched her retreating form. "Devan, I've had my share of experience with women, both good and bad, before I fell in love with Daphne. But I remember enough to know when I see trouble brewing. You'd best be careful with that one."

"She's just a young girl." Devan's gaze immediately drifted to Avalon, who stood center in the front of the room as the auction began.

"She's been lurking, waiting for you and Avalon to finish your discussion before she approached you. As soon as the marchioness left your side, Miss Rowley rushed to join you," Paul said. "But enough of that." His gaze followed Devan's to the front of the room. Immediately, one of his lopsided smiles appeared. "Avalon is looking lovely this evening, isn't she?"

"Your Grace, you may have a difference of opinion, but she's the most beautiful woman here."

"I feel the same way about my duchess." Paul looked to his wife, Daphne, and immediately his eyes glowed with tender affection. "A piece of advice. Opportunity waits for no one. Bold moves require bold actions."

Devan laughed in spite of himself. "When have you ever seen me bashful?"

Paul regarded him, then held out his hand for Devan to accompany him to their seats. "I'll answer your question with one of my own. Why are you hiding in the back of the room with a look that you obviously want her?"

"That noticeable, is it?" Devan answered distractedly.

"I know you better than anyone else, and I've never seen you this way. I believe you're smitten. Perhaps you're finally in love with a woman."

"A spectacular one at that," Devan murmured.

"You prove my point," the duke said in return. "I should know. I found one of my own."

As the duke settled in next to his duchess, he turned to her and a charming smile adorned his face. The duke's face had softened with a look of desire that couldn't be mistaken for anything else.

Devan shook his head slightly. There was a huge difference between the two of them. Paul was deeply in love with his wife.

His heart tightened. He couldn't be falling in love with Avalon this quickly. Could he?

*Nothing is more perfect on this Earth than to hold
a Warlock in your arms and dance. It gives a whole
new meaning to "make a joyful noise."*
                    Mr. Devan Farris's personal notes of Lady
                                        Warwyk's benefit soiree

Chapter Fifteen

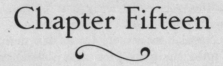

"Sold! The pink satin with ermine trim to the Duke of
Langham for one hundred and twenty-five pounds!"
Mrs. Marcy hit the gavel on a block of wood to amplify
the sound. Simultaneous cries of laughter and sighs of
disappointment filled the room. "That concludes the auction." The brilliant smile lit her face as a round of ap-
plause filled the room and slowly died. "On behalf of
the Ladies Auxiliary, we thank each and every one of
you for your bids. Now, let's continue the dancing as the
orchestra is about to start their next set."

The Duchess of Langham's face glowed as she turned
to her husband. "Thank you, Sebastian. I dearly wanted
it, but I didn't want to bid against the others."

"I had a hunch you liked it, Ginny." The duke took
his duchess's hand and raised it to his lips. "It's for a
worthy cause. Besides, I have a selfish reason for win-
ning it. I want to see you wear it. You'll make the beautiful dress stunning."

Avalon stood near enough to hear the exchange and
bit her lip to hide her smile. That's what a loving marriage should be. The love and care the duke and duchess

shared for each other was apparent to all who attended tonight. Avalon's heart skipped a beat at the lovely gesture that showed everyone that the Duchess of Langham was and would always be the most important person in the duke's world.

To have someone who cherished you in that way would make your life a success whether you were rich or poor. She glanced at the other Cavensham family members in attendance, then stood still. For heaven's sake, she'd never really considered it, but all of the Cavenshams' marriages were so blessed. Each and every one of them had married their heart's true love and had the same type of marriage as the duke and duchess.

Why couldn't she have had the same type of luck in love? She quickly dismissed the envious thought. She had more than enough blessings in her life—her son, her sister, her community, and her charitable work. That was enough, and she should be thankful for all of it.

Her heart stuttered in protest, but she ignored it.

The reason the Cavenshams had been so successful in love is that they had a beautiful example in the Duke and Duchess of Langham. When she eventually had the conversation with Sophia about what to expect in marriage, she would use the duke and duchess as the perfect ideal. She'd also do the same with Thane when the time came. It would be her greatest achievement if she could ensure both her sister and her son had the gift of a loving spouse.

But at the moment, her greatest challenge required she collect the bid sheet that recorded the monies earned this evening, then give it to Miss Marcy to record in the Ladies Auxiliary's bookkeeping journal.

"Avalon," Sophia whispered in her ear. "Thank you for purchasing the green gown for me."

She turned and found her lovely sister stroking the

silk of the gown Avalon had managed to win. The bidding had been fierce for the beautiful garment, but Avalon had budgeted carefully this month. She wanted Sophia to have it. "You're so welcome. I can't wait to see you in it. I imagine you wearing it with a husband adoring you during your first Christmas together."

Sophia's gaze widened. "Whoever he is, I'll make certain that he knows that I have the most wonderful sister in the world." She turned suddenly serious as her fingers danced across the soft velvet bodice. "I don't tell you this enough, but I love you. It had to be difficult taking me in as a child while you were raising Thane after losing Richard. You're the best sister anyone could ever have."

Avalon dipped her head until their eyes met. "Enough of such talk. I'd not have had it any other way."

Sophia's eyes grew misty.

The sight caused the same with Avalon. "Besides," she said, sniffing quietly, "I beg to differ. You're the best sister anyone could have. Who else would have helped me with Thane when he was a baby?"

Sophia's natural buoyancy returned. "Remember when he wanted me to write him a personal bedtime story every day? I think that was the hardest but most rewarding thing I've ever done."

"You're a dear to have done it for him," Avalon said.

"He's relentless when he wants something," Sophia said. "He reminds me of you."

"Me?" Avalon asked.

Sophia nodded and pointed to her new gown. "When you wanted to win this gown, you got it. When you believed that there should be a charity for women who'd fallen on hard times, you created it. There's not a thing you can't do when you put your mind to it." She directed her attention behind Avalon. "I should speak with Penelope. She's upset that the Duke of Langham bought the pink gown for his duchess."

"Will you take this sheet to Miss Marcy for me, dearest, on your way to see her?"

Sophia took the sheet, then left with her beautiful velvet gown draped over one arm. Once again Avalon stood by herself. The solitude didn't bother her. She listened to the orchestra warm up for the next set and let her gaze sweep across the room. Of course, she wasn't looking for a certain naughty vicar.

But she hated to call herself a liar.

"Looking for me?" Devan murmured behind her.

She turned slowly and there he stood in all his glory before her. His hair was a tad long for conventional wisdom, and black evening attire was a little too somber, but with that smile he graciously bestowed her way, he was the most handsome man she'd ever seen. His every move and nuanced word sent a thrill running through her that settled into a molten heat that centered low in her belly. All she wanted for the evening to be perfect was to once again be in his arms.

"Why, Mr. Farris, I wondered where you'd run off to. Didn't you mention something about a dance?" She tilted her head and delivered her best smile.

"You and I think alike." He extended his hand. "Allow me to escort you to the dance floor."

She placed her gloved hand in his and allowed him to lead her away. Her small hand fit nicely in his. The music started for the next dance, a lively reel.

Devan slowed their pace and leaned in close. "That's inconvenient. I wanted a waltz."

She didn't hide the disappointment in her voice. "I did, too. But I could request one after this."

"I have a better idea. Isn't the music room close by?"

She nodded. "Two doors down."

"Come with me. If I'm not mistaken, there's a waltz about to start there."

"What are you about, Devan?"

"Do you trust me?" he asked. His green eyes flashed in mirth.

Right then and there she linked her arm with his.

"I'm not certain." When he looked down at her, she winked at him. "But since you're my vicar, I believe you're trustworthy . . . at least for the next five minutes."

He tucked her arm closer to his as they left the ballroom. The lively reel filled the hallway with sound. When they reached the music room, Avalon opened the door, and Devan followed her in. Without a word, he pushed the door shut, locking out the boisterous music and the outside world. Along with a few candles, a cozy fire cast the room in a soft, warm light.

Avalon propped her hands on her hips and regarded Devan. "There's no orchestra or even a pianist to accompany us. We can't waltz without music unless you want me to play for you while you twirl around the room with a pretend partner."

"I don't want a pretend partner when I have a lovely, vibrant woman before me who wants to waltz. I'll provide the music."

"How?" she asked.

"When did you become so impatient? You're like a child on Christmas morning," he playfully teased. Devan placed one arm around her waist and she answered in kind by placing her hand on his shoulder. Her fingers itched to squeeze his solid muscular form, and slowly, she allowed herself the luxury. His shoulder tensed at her inquisitive touch, and Devan smiled down at her. Together, they clasped their other hands together. Her chest met his when he pulled her close, and her pulse quickened at such an intimate touch, one that many married couples shared in their everyday lives together. How much she'd missed by not having someone to share such ordinary things with.

Softly he hummed a little ditty as he gracefully twirled her around the music room, the movement slow and sensual as their bodies touched each other's—leg to leg, hip to hip, and chest to chest.

She'd never been seduced, but this had to be what it felt like. She could only describe it as heaven on earth, and she never wanted him to stop moving or humming to her. Eventually, the perfect dance drew to a close when Devan slowed his steps and brought them to a complete stop.

"I should never doubt you when you say you'll do something. I loved your music, and you, sir, have been blessed with a beautiful voice," she whispered. Though they were the only two in the room, a whisper seemed more private and deserving of the moment between them.

He leaned close and brushed his lips over her earlobe. "Thank you. I've been singing since I was a little boy." He released a soft sigh, and his warm breath on her neck caressed her. "It helps with your parish members, particularly the choir, if you can carry a tune." He dipped his head lower, then placed his lips on the pulse of her neck. "Does it help me with you?"

She shivered, then moaned slightly. Heat exploded in her center then settled between her legs. Instinctively, she pushed her body against his.

Devan brought his hand to the small of her back to anchor her close. With a slight lean away, he examined her, taking his time to memorize each freckle sprinkled across her face. In time, his gaze eventually settled on hers. Only inches separated them.

She dared to take her eyes off his to study his rich, full lips. "Your mouth is perfect and deserves to be bitten."

A deep rumble started in his chest, and his eyes flashed. "Do you want to bite me? Is that what you're asking?"

"Perhaps." She shook her head slightly while locking her gaze to his. "But I want to kiss you more."

Those perfect lips tugged upward, but he didn't move or say a word.

With each rhythmic breath, her chest brushed against his. All she wanted in this moment was to lose herself in his kiss and feel every inch of his body covering hers.

"What are you waiting for?" he finally asked.

"A sign, a hint, or something . . . that you're receptive to my forwardness."

"Lady Warlock, you'll always have my blessing to kiss me senseless," he said.

She answered him by tilting her head to his and wrapping her arms around his neck. Slowly, she pulled him to her. When her lips met his, her heart fluttered in approval of her bold actions. She deepened the kiss, and Devan groaned his approval. He opened his lips to her, and her tongue met his. She learned everything she could about his likes while finding pleasure for herself. Taking control of their kiss was such a heady experience, one she would never forget.

He pulled her tighter against him. With only evening clothes between them, it was easy to feel his arousal pushing against her midsection as if trying to reach her.

The man she held in her arms wanted her.

For her dancing, for her kisses, for simply being herself.

Did he have any idea that she'd give him everything?

The moonlight fell across his face as if worshipping him, and Avalon wanted to explore and touch every part of his face and body. From the hunger in his eyes, he wanted to do the same.

She kissed him again and moaned into his mouth, the small sound either a demand or a plea for mercy.

Either way, he took control of the kiss as if starving for her.

Somehow, they'd moved from the center of the room to one of the walls. His arms encircled her as his lips found hers again. Their kiss grew in intensity and she pushed against him, seeking relief from the delightful torment they'd created. Devan settled in between her widened legs.

"Closer," she demanded softly as she pulled his hard body tightly against hers.

"Whatever, my—"

"Do not say 'warlock.'" Her breathless sigh escaped.

He chuckled against her lips as she tilted her hips to meet his. The need to feel him next to her became unbearable. She adjusted her position until his erection pressed against her cleft.

"Avalon." He whispered her name like the holiest of devotionals.

"Please," she answered, not caring that she begged him for relief.

Their mouths met, and their tongues tangled as their movements became more frenzied. He pushed her against the wall, and she pressed harder against him—grinding and rubbing until she found a cadence that made the promise she'd soon soar. To where, she had no idea. But women found pleasure in lovemaking, and Avalon was determined to join their ranks.

She concentrated on every touch, every push, and

every sensation they created together as it washed over her. Every part of her body circled higher and higher as if in an eddy that drew her closer to completion.

He possessed her in a kiss like a man starving for nourishment, then cupped her breast through her gown. He brushed his thumb over her nipple, and sensation flashed like a star bursting overhead, stealing her breath and all sanity.

She cried out his name.

Drunk with all the swirling sensations, she leaned her head against the wall and allowed her body to float back to earth. Devan cupped her cheek and rested his forehead against hers while the evidence of his desire pulsed against her stomach.

"Devan?"

He hummed in answer, then leaned slightly, keeping his body pressed against hers. His eyes devoured hers as he cupped her cheeks. "Did you?"

She couldn't keep the ridiculous smile off her face and nodded. "I've never . . ."

He smiled with an arrogant lift of his lips. "Look at me."

She tilted her gaze to his.

"Always remember that tonight there was no one else here except you and me. This was as unique for me as it was for you."

She nodded her acceptance. "Is there anything I can do for you?" She swept her hand down alongside their legs. "Like you did for me?"

"Just let me hold you for a moment or two." He brushed one of her loose curls behind her ear, then gathered her in his arms again. "I should be the one to thank you," he said.

"For what?" Her voice had acquired a faraway dreamy quality she was unfamiliar with.

"For proving that you really are a warlock, a powerful one at that." He rubbed the back of his finger in a leisurely manner against her cheek, threatening to whip her body into another frenzy at his tender touch. "I'm completely under your spell."

She swallowed the words that threatened to escape. It was safer this way. He didn't need to know that she felt the same way about him. His reputation led her to believe that one day he'd turn his attentions to another. When it happened, she didn't want to be pitied as she picked up the pieces of her broken heart.

Fools rush in where angels fear to tread.
      Alexander Pope in *An Essay on Criticism*

Yet, overthinking a situation is highly overestimated. It takes away all the fun.
      the personal observations of Devan Farris

Chapter Sixteen

❦

It hardly mattered that yesterday's church service was a blur. With his boots propped on his desk, and his hands behind his head, Devan smiled like a fool while staring at nothing. Which wasn't surprising as he'd suffered from the affliction for the past two days since he'd returned home from Avalon's soiree. When she'd come in his arms, it was momentous for several reasons. She'd never experienced such pleasure, which meant she'd never really explored desire on her own. He'd never brought a woman to orgasm before. Together they could change the earth's orbit.

Well, perhaps they couldn't do that, but they could stay in bed and try.

He released a contented sigh. Not only was she passionate, beautiful, and, simply put, amazing, but Avalon was mesmerizing. He could talk and listen to her for days on end. He tilted his head to the ceiling and said a silent prayer thanking the good Lord above for Gavin, the biggest millstone around Devan's neck. For without his brother, who sent him here, Devan feared that he and Avalon would still be snapping at one another from afar.

All of his earlier misconceptions that she was self-centered had flown out the window as soon as he realized how committed she was to her family and community. She was a woman who loved deeply and without reservation.

He'd decided last night as he lay in bed that he'd not be intimidated by the chasm that existed between their social statuses. While she was a marchioness by marriage and an earl's daughter, she treated him as an equal. After the soiree, he knew that his path was to pursue whatever this was between them.

And he would relish the chance to win her affections.

Suddenly, the door to Devan's study flew open as if an explosion had rocked his home. Immediately, he was on his feet.

In the doorway stood Gavin, with his black hair standing on end and his cravat tilted like a windmill as if he'd rushed to dress. With a feral look in his eyes, Devan's brother simply stared.

"What's happened?" Devan rounded the desk. "Is it Hearne or Niall?" When Gavin didn't answer, Devan's skin crawled. "Elizabeth?"

"Nothing about the family. Do you have anything to drink?" Gavin choked the words out.

Without answering, Devan moved to the sideboard and uncorked the brandy bottle. He poured a glass.

"You better pour two. You're going to need one also." Gavin rubbed a hand down his face.

Without disagreeing but having no intention of touching liquor this early in the morning, Devan did as asked. Whatever had unnerved his brother had to be monumental. Otherwise, he'd have never graced Devan's threshold so early in the morning.

Gavin lowered his body into the chair, then rested his elbows on his knees and hung his head as if defeated.

Immediately, Devan sensed something dire had happened to his brother. "Whatever troubles you, I'll help."

Gavin picked up his glass then drained it. Finally, he turned his gaze to Devan. "That's not it. It's your troubles, and how I'll fix it."

"Meaning?" Devan settled behind his desk and leaned back in his chair. "If this is another lecture, spare both of us."

"This is trouble." Gavin shook his head. "Do you know a Miss Penelope Rowley?"

Devan's body tightened as if preparing for a punch. "She's a member of the parish."

Gavin trained his hawklike gaze on Devan. "Her uncle demanded to see me at the ungodly hour of six this morning. I was still abed."

"It's unfortunate that your sleep was interrupted. We both know you need your beauty sleep—"

"*Goddamn me, Devan*. Will you cease the jabs and listen?" The panic in Gavin's voice echoed around the room.

Devan blinked slowly but didn't respond to his brother's outburst.

"Miss Rowley claims that you seduced her the night that your housekeeper had off. Her uncle is furious. He threatened to call on the bishop, then tell *The Midnight Cryer* what you'd done. I spent an hour calming his ire, but he threatened to destroy you if I don't step in and make the situation right. He says his niece's reputation is ruined."

Devan stood and began to pace in front of the fireplace. The flames jumped and the fire crackled, mimicking his unease. Five days ago, he'd spent the night with a woman, but it wasn't Penelope.

That was the night he'd spent in the wine cellar holding Avalon in his arms.

"Well?" Gavin queried.

"Well what?" Devan snapped in answer.

"We both know it's not true. You're a good man, but I need to hear it from your lips."

"The girl is lying through her teeth," Devan said.

Gavin exhaled. "How are we going to prove it?"

To protect Avalon, he'd not disclose the truth. He'd never allow her morals to be questioned by Gavin, which would occur if he revealed where he was that evening.

"I don't know if I can. Everyone in the entire village knows that Mrs. McVey takes that night off every week. She visits her daughter's family." Devan threw another log onto the fire. The burning logs hissed at the newcomer's interruption.

"Tell me what you did that evening."

Devan shrugged his shoulders. "That evening I attended a dinner at Lady Warwyk's home. I spent the day tutoring Lord Warwyk." He'd stick as close to the truth as he could since Mrs. McVey had known his schedule for the day and anyone could easily verify it through any of the staff at Warwyk Hall.

"What time did you return home?" Gavin volleyed.

"I don't remember."

"Did you see anyone else?" His brother lowered his voice. "Were you with anyone else that evening?"

Devan closed his eyes as the room became unbearably hot. He was standing too close to the fire. Both literally and figuratively. He nodded his head.

"Who was it?"

"Why does it make any difference?" Devan asked snappishly. "It's my business."

"It's Penelope Rowley's word against yours," Gavin argued. "If you think it makes a difference who is telling the truth, then you're more naïve than I give you credit for."

"Meaning?"

"If you don't have a corroborating witness, then you have no choice. And neither do I. You're going to have to marry her. Otherwise, your career is over."

"I'll do no such thing," Devan answered in his most curt voice.

"You will if I hold a gun to your head. Because otherwise, little brother, that's exactly what Mr. Rowley wants to do to you. He's livid and demands satisfaction."

"Dear God in heaven," Devan muttered.

"Exactly," Gavin agreed. "Say every available prayer you have." His brother rose and joined him by the fire. With his arms clasped behind his back, the Earl of Larkton was a physically imposing man, with a large personality to match. But today, with worry etched across his face, he appeared defeated. "Devan, look at the benefits. You'll get the heiress you always wanted. Rowley told me his niece is worth over ten thousand pounds. That's a nice fortune that will keep you comfortable for the rest of your life."

"Are you out of your mind?" Devan answered. "I'll not marry her. She tried to compromise me two days after she claims I seduced her."

"How does a woman compromise a man?" his brother asked with a hint of skepticism.

"You're an idiot if I have to explain it to you." Devan rolled his eyes. "She conveniently found me walking alone, then forced herself on me and tried to kiss me. I told her then that I had no interest in her." Devan started to pace again. "She's retaliating for my refusal. I wouldn't marry her if she was the last woman on this green earth. Tell her uncle to go to hell."

"Tell me who you were with." Gavin nudged him again. "I need to know."

Devan's hands knotted into fists. What he wouldn't give to punch a hole in the wall for all the trouble that Penelope Rowley had stirred this morning. Perhaps then, he could maintain some control over his anger. He wasn't upset for himself but for Avalon. He wouldn't drag her into this. "I already told you. Stay out of my affairs." He stared Gavin straight in the eye, not hiding the menace in his voice.

"Those rumors of your prowess and charming ways with women have conveniently played right into Miss Rowley's hands."

"It's no one's business but my own," Devan declared, not bothering to dispute his brother's assessment.

Gavin shook his head, then forcefully grabbed his greatcoat and hat. "Have it your way."

"What does that mean?" Devan challenged.

Gavin turned back to him as he put on his coat. He tugged his beaver hat snuggly on his head. "If you think I'm going to let my little brother's career and reputation be destroyed because you have a lover you refuse to name, think again."

"Stay out of it," Devan growled.

Without a look back, Gavin exited the room in the same ominous way he'd entered. Only this time, he slammed the door shut.

Which was perfect in Devan's opinion. His brother could go to the devil.

He picked up the brandy, then drained the glass. He put it on the side table beside him. "Damn me," he uttered to the empty room.

How in the hell had Penelope Rowley even come up with such a preposterous idea? Then he remembered how she'd stared at him when he and Avalon had spent time together in the back of the room. Her gaze had bored straight through them as if she were throwing a thousand daggers with her eyes. The truth slammed into him with such force that he took a step backward. The pure hatred on her face wasn't directed at him, but at Avalon.

He'd best go directly to the Rowleys' home and discuss what had occurred. If he asked how the girl could sneak out at night and meet him, it might jar some sense into her aunt and uncle. There was no way that any self-respecting young woman who wanted to be introduced into London society the next Season would ever risk her reputation with a vicar, even if he was the brother of the Earl of Larkton.

Devan chuckled to himself. Perhaps that's where Gavin had headed. He could easily see his brother sacrificing himself by asking for Penelope's hand in marriage to save his youngest brother's reputation.

Suddenly, his chest felt as if it were in a vise. What if his brother wasn't visiting the Rowleys' home? What if, instead, he'd gone to discuss the matter directly with Avalon? As his benefactress, she had a right to know what was occurring within her parish.

Without waiting another second, Devan grabbed the handle of the study door and wrenched it open.

At that moment, poor Mrs. McVey had the misfortune of walking past carrying a stack of clean linens in her arms. His housekeeper windmilled her arms, then she pressed her back against the wall to get out of his way.

"Mr. Farris, you scared me." She placed her hand over her heart as the clean linens scattered to the floor like a fresh snow.

"I'm sorry, Mrs. McVey. Something urgent has come up and I need to go to Warwyk Hall."

She nodded her acceptance of his apology. "It's certainly a popular place. That's exactly where the earl said he was headed."

Devan grabbed his coat and hat, then ran out the door. If his brother said one word about him that would turn Avalon's regard for him into disgust, it would give Devan the excuse he needed for fratricide.

"My lady, the Earl of Larkton is downstairs and says he needs to speak with you immediately." Henri twisted her fingers into knots as she always did when worried. "I think he's come to discuss 'you know what.'"

Avalon patted her hair as she glanced at the mirror, not really concerned with how she looked. It was a nervous tic to keep her own hands busy. Mr. Neville had come to her immediately upon her wakening to share the news about Penelope Rowley's accusations. As Avalon's butler was close friends with the Rowleys' steward, the story had come to Warwyk Hall first thing this morning, and Mr. Neville had reported it to her directly.

Penelope was trying to force Devan into marrying her. Avalon didn't know the specifics of the girl's accusations, but whatever she'd said, it had sent waves through the Rowleys' house that expanded into her own home. Avalon took a breath in an attempt to calm the racing of her pulse.

"Show him into my study. Will you make certain that Thane and Sophia are busy? I really don't want to be interrupted this morning."

Henri nodded, then left.

Avalon stood and smoothed her dress. Her glance

skated down the brilliant blue wool skirts of her gown. Yesterday, Jasmine and Flora had come to alter it along with several of her older gowns, ones that Avalon never thought would see the light of day again. She'd bought them when she was married to Richard and had never bothered to wear them. However, the women had magic in their fingers. Within the space of an hour, they'd re-created the dress with a basket of trimmings that would make the queen envious.

It was another masterpiece, in Avalon's opinion, and perfect for meeting the earl this morning. Though she'd wanted to save wearing it for when she knew Devan would be here, she'd decided the best course was to don it today. Whatever the purpose of the earl's visit, she wanted to look her best. Not to impress him, but it would make her feel better, giving her standing as an equal if she had to negotiate anything with him.

She made her way down the stairs to the first floor. At the bottom of the stairs, Mr. Neville waited to escort her to the room.

"Could you decipher his mood?" she asked quietly.

"He's clearly upset, my lady," Mr. Neville answered. "He's been pacing the room like a caged animal since he arrived."

She nodded. They drew to a halt in the hallway outside the study. With the door open, Avalon could see Devan's brother clearly. Indeed, he was worried if the lines marring his brow were any indication. There was a definite resemblance between the two brothers. No one could deny that Larkton was handsome with his dark brooding looks, but he couldn't hold a candle to Devan.

Avalon nodded, and Mr. Neville stepped out of the way so she could enter.

"Larkton, good morning," she called out. "For what do I owe the pleasure of your company?"

He stopped his pacing immediately, and in several long strides reached her side. With a deferential bow, he took her hand. "Lady Warwyk, thank you for seeing me. How are you and your family?"

"Fine," she answered. "But that's not why you're here. You normally send correspondence if you want to vex me."

With a charming lopsided grin that reminded her of Devan, he dipped his head in acknowledgment. "My brother Devan warned me about you."

"Excellent. He calls me 'Lady Warlock' for a specific reason. Let's make ourselves comfortable." She preceded him to the two matching teal sofas that flanked the robust fire. "Would you care for refreshments?"

"No, thank you." He waited until she was seated first, then took the sofa opposite hers.

She nodded once to Mr. Neville, who bowed slightly as he took his leave, closing the door behind him.

Though he wasn't as tall or as fit as Devan, his body seemed to consume the piece of furniture as he rested against the sofa. "There's some trouble in the parish and the village that you should be made aware of."

"Go on," she coaxed.

"A young woman by the name of Miss Penelope Rowley has claimed that the vicar has compromised her." He rested his head in the palm of his hand, "This is somewhat painful."

She drew her lips into a thin line. "When did this allegedly happen?"

"Five days ago. She said that he sent her a note to meet him at the vicarage at ten o'clock that night."

Avalon stilled at the timing of when Devan supposedly compromised Penelope. That was the night he spent in the cellar with her. There was no way he could have met the girl then. "Are you certain about the date?"

"Yes, I am. Her uncle came to see me in London this morning. Apparently, the girl confessed all, their first secret meeting along with all the other sordid affairs that she claims happened."

She could tell by the tilt of his head that Devan's brother cared deeply for him. It was the first redeeming quality Avalon had seen in the lout since she'd met him.

"Devan mentioned that he'd tutored Lord Warwyk that day and stayed for dinner with you and your family."

Avalon straightened her back while wondering what else Devan shared with his brother. "Yes, he did."

"Were there any others who attended? Mayhap they left the same time my brother did?" He sat on the edge of the sofa, anxious for her answer.

"He was the only guest who came to dinner that evening." Then, he'd spent the night with her locked up with bottles of wine for company until Thane had come to let them out. If that story leaked, Larkton could use it to his advantage against her.

"I see." With frustration clearly marking his face, the earl raked his hands through his black hair.

She should tell Larkton what had happened. However, to give Devan's brother any ammunition to use against her went against her nature. Perhaps it would be best to go on the offensive. "Lord Larkton, I do not and never will approve of your actions of installing your brother into our happy and secure village for the purpose of spying on me."

As she delivered the stinging rebuke of the earl's behavior, he had the decency to flush in embarrassment.

The sight emboldened her to speak out on Devan's behalf. "However, your brother has become a part of our community, a very vital part if I do say so myself. He visits the sick and spends time with the elderly. He always has a smile on his face for everyone. Perhaps

Miss Rowley misunderstood his kind manner and tender heart."

Larkton shook his head. "It makes little difference at this point. She's claimed he's ruined her, and her uncle is pressuring me to convince my brother to marry her. I just came from the vicarage, where I spoke to my brother."

At his words, a swarm of butterflies took flight in her stomach. She swallowed in an effort to ground them. "What did Mr. Farris say?"

She didn't believe that Devan would share that they'd spent the night together. But she had no idea if he'd agree to a marriage to Penelope Rowley. One thing Avalon had learned in her time with Devan is that he was a man of honor. He'd do the right thing, namely, marry Penelope, if the situation required it. Such a thought made her heart stumble in her chest. She bit her lip as she waited for the earl's answer.

The earl fisted his hands. "He denied every allegation and refused to marry her."

Avalon quietly let out the breath she hadn't realized she'd been holding. "I see."

Larkton stood and started to pace again. "I don't think you do. The truth is that if he doesn't marry her, then his career is ruined. I'm afraid that Miss Rowley's uncle left my house threatening to go to the bishop with the news. He assured me that the bishop wouldn't stand for a man like Devan ruining a young innocent girl, and I'm afraid he's right. Devan faces dismissal from the church."

Larkton's pacing had increased in speed. The sight of the grown man practically racing up and down her study made Avalon squirm in her seat. The only right thing to do was to tell him that Devan spent the night with her. She couldn't let Penelope ruin Devan.

"But I thought the bishop was his mentor, his friend."

"The bishop is, but neither he nor the church can suffer a scandal. The only way out of this is to prove where he was that night. Devan is adamant that he can't and *won't* prove where he was." Larkton turned his gaze to hers.

She couldn't help noticing that the earl's eyes were a blue color similar to a summer sky while Devan's eyes were saturated in deep green, the color of emeralds, her favorite jewels.

"I believe he was with someone."

"Who?" The word sounded like a squeak when she said it.

Perhaps Cain had the right of it when he said he wasn't his brother Abel's keeper. Such a shame that my own doesn't abide by those rules.

From the personal notes of Mr. Devan Farris

Chapter Seventeen

L arkton, *enough*." Devan strode into Avalon's sitting room.

Leave it to his brother to make a bigger mess of the situation. Under no circumstances would Devan abide Gavin making Avalon a part of the farce he currently found himself embroiled in with Penelope Rowley. Without waiting for either Avalon or Gavin to invite him in, Devan sat next to Avalon. Her sweet scent rose to greet him, and he inhaled deeply. Since he'd left her Saturday night, her fragrance had left an indelible mark on him. Everything within him came to attention when he was by her side.

"What are you doing here?" Devan didn't hide his displeasure. "I told you all I wanted you to know about the situation. I've decided to handle it directly."

"And get your head shot off in the process, I'll wager," Larkton said. "If you're too pig-headed to see—"

"What I see is an earl who acts more like an old hen." Devan's retort ricocheted through the room. "Go manipulate someone else's life. Perhaps while you're scratching around the proverbial barnyard, you'll find someone else to control."

"Devan," Avalon soothed. "He's just trying to help."

Gavin's eyebrows shot skyward. "You two are on intimate terms?"

"Is that so surprising?" Devan taunted. "Hard to believe that I could actually form a friendship with a woman?"

Avalon turned to Gavin and tilted her head. "What can I do to help?"

"Tell me your personal knowledge of what happened that evening."

"Do not get her involved." Devan made a move to stand.

Avalon's attention stayed riveted on Gavin as her hand shot out and grabbed Devan's arm. "This is my business, too."

Her touch calmed the beastly urge inside him to pummel his oldest brother to pieces. "Avalon, do not become involved just for my sake."

"He was with me," she said, her voice clear and resolute. "We were locked in the wine cellar that night."

"Don't say another word." Devan stiffened beside her.

Gavin's eyes widened. "Can you prove it?"

"Yes," she said.

Neither Gavin nor Avalon acknowledged his warnings. It was enough to make Devan growl. "Do not—"

Just then the door opened, and Mr. Neville entered with His Lordship, Bishop Marlowe. Devan felt his anger sail right out the window at the bishop's entrance. By summoning His Lordship to Warwyk Hall, Gavin had blocked Devan's growing self-righteous indignation at the earl's interference. Any chance Devan had to handle the situation by himself had been stolen like a clipper ship blocking another's access to the wind.

In essence, Devan's position of strength was dead in the water.

The bishop controlled his career and standing within the clergy.

His Lordship approached and they all stood. Avalon extended her hand in welcome, and the bishop gave the perfunctory bow, then greeted both Gavin and Devan. He settled next to Gavin when they all took their seats.

In his mid-thirties, Bishop Marlowe was a handsome man, though the trials and tribulations of his position were readily apparent by the premature graying of his temples. By special assignment, he was responsible for parishes throughout the church that seemed to be floundering. That's how Devan received his appointments. But a sense of calm always seemed to surround the bishop, and just by his presence, this incident would be resolved one way or another.

Unfortunately, his mere appearance in Thistledown this morning meant that the situation was dire for Devan.

Gavin spoke first. "Thank you for coming."

Bishop Marlowe waved a hand in the air. "It was the right thing to summon me." He turned his attention to Devan. "What's this I hear that you've managed to attract a little trouble?"

"It's nothing you need concern yourself with, Your Lordship." Devan sat on the edge of his seat while he addressed the bishop. "My brother reacted too quickly in calling you here. I'm about to go to the young woman's house and settle the situation myself."

The bishop regarded Gavin, then turned to Devan. "Whenever there's an allegation of compromising a young woman, it's never too soon to react. I know the answer, but protocol requires I ask anyway. Is it true?"

"No, sir," Devan answered.

Avalon straightened in her seat. "He was with me all night." At the bishop's quick intake of air, she held out her hand in an appeal to be allowed to continue. "I was explaining to Lord Larkton that Mr. Farris and I were locked in my wine cellar the night that Miss Rowley claims to be compromised. There's no way he could have been with her. We have corroborating witnesses in my staff. My son was the one who found us the next morning."

"Thank God," Gavin sighed.

The bishop shook his head. "It's not all good news, Larkton. While he didn't compromise the girl, clearly, there is still the allegation. There's only one solution by my way of thinking." His gaze bounced from Devan's to Avalon's direction. "He marries the young woman."

"What?" Devan shot off the sofa. "You can't force my hand."

The bishop narrowed his gaze on Devan. "Otherwise, you can't continue in your duties to the church. You've already managed to attract enough scandal swirling around you to blow asunder the good work that this parish has accomplished in the past several years." He leaned back against the sofa. "From the simple fact that Lady Warwyk has chosen to help ladies of questionable reputations make a new life for themselves here, your unfortunate circumstance will forever tarnish her good deeds."

Avalon released a sigh, then stood. She crossed the room to her desk, then opened a drawer and brought out a journal of some type. His gut tightened with the elegance of her movement. Whatever he had to do, he'd protect her even if it meant giving up the only career he had. Immediately, an image of him working the fields as one of her tenants intruded. By God, he'd do manual labor for the rest of his life if it meant he could still be near her while protecting her reputation.

To hell with his own.

The cruel reality was he faced real ruin. There was no one who would welcome them into their society if they thought him a lecher who would ruin a young woman then refuse to marry her. Penelope Rowley had executed a perfect plan when she came up with the ridiculous tale. She would force his hand into marrying her or he would be without a livelihood.

By then, Avalon had returned to her seat. Her soft gaze fell on his, and the warmth of her smile made him believe that whatever decision had to be made, they'd do it together. He let out a tense breath.

"You don't have to do this," he murmured for her ears only.

She nodded slightly. "Devan, if you'd be so kind as to allow me to converse with Lord Larkton and His Lordship privately, I'd be in your debt."

"What are you about, my lady?"

"I'm trying to save your career." She lifted one eyebrow as her spine straightened in defiance. "Now, will you leave on your own or shall I have two footmen escort you out?"

Avalon watched silently as Devan left her study. She set her accounting journal on her lap.

"Your Lordship," she addressed the bishop. "Unfortunately for me, Lord Larkton is the male guardian of my son and the conservator of the estate. He orchestrated Mr. Farris's move to my village for the sole purpose that Mr. Farris discover where I receive the funds to do the work around the parish. He believes that I may be using the marquisate's funds for my own."

Not refuting her statement, Larkton had the decency to look ashamed.

Coyly, the bishop smiled. "Larkton and I became friends as boys. I'm very familiar with how he operates. Mr. Farris's appointment had to be approved by the church."

"And you were the one to approve it on recommendation from the earl?"

The bishop nodded.

A movement caught her attention. With his head bowed, Devan cut across the drive, heading back to the vicarage. She'd hated to send him away, but he would have protested every word or thought she'd present to undo the damage that Penelope had inflicted on all of them today. There really was only one way out of the situation, but before she'd agree to anything, she would negotiate on Devan's behalf. Though the two men before her thought they could force Devan to do their bidding, they couldn't force her to do anything.

But she'd do the honorable thing and protect Devan's reputation. Though his every action had been designed with her in mind, Devan was mistaken when he thought he had to protect her. The truth was she had to protect him.

"We recently had our annual benefit auction, and I'm proud to say it was a monumental success."

She handed the journal to the bishop. His Lordship pulled a pair of glasses from his waistcoat, then proceeded to look at the page that she had opened the book to.

After a few minutes, he looked up and shook his head once in disbelief. "This is a staggering amount of money." He passed the book to Larkton.

The earl looked up and gave the journal back to Avalon. "Fine. You've proven you know how to run a successful charity."

"I've never taken a shilling from the marquisate other than what was needed for the upkeep of the property and the welfare of the people who live here."

"And the point of this?" Larkton asked warily.

"Before we proceed any further in our discussion over your brother, I want to make something perfectly clear. I resent the fact that you thought I'd take those funds for my own use. From my own son, no less."

"My lady," he said smoothly. "I know your reputation."

She nodded her head vehemently. "Indeed, you do, sir. Because you helped create it when you were best friends with Lord Warwyk. You allowed him to say whatever he wanted about me without trying to discover the truth. You two were thick as thieves then."

"What do you mean?" Larkton asked.

"Richard provided the town house and the jewels to me so I'd keep quiet about his mistress. He moved her into our home, into my bedroom, and forced me elsewhere. Not to mention, to keep quiet about his abysmal treatment of me."

The bishop's eyes widened in shock. "My lady, these are matters best left for another time."

"I respectfully don't agree, Your Lordship." Avalon would not back away from confronting Larkton. "Everything we discuss, every bargain presented will not have my agreement unless we all understand each other."

"I promised Warwyk before Thane was born that I'd look after his son if the need ever arose. I thought you preferred to live here." The look of utter shock on Larkton's face took her aback.

"You truly didn't know, did you?" For the first time, she saw the man before her not as an irritation but as someone who was trying to do what was right for Thane and his legacy.

He shook his head. "Richard was always one to exaggerate, but he showed me the bills and said you'd left him. He told me that he begged you to come back to London, and you refused."

"Hardly. You were there the day he threw me out of London and away from my sister. I was sent here to Warwyk Hall to have Thane with specific instructions not to leave. I had no support, company, or even a single confidant. I found no succor in my situation. That's why I've worked so hard on this community. The people on the estate and in the village welcomed me with open arms. They were my salvation." She forced herself to take a deep breath. "I want you to know all this because we can't find a solution to Devan's problem without you knowing the truth about me. You'll never trust me otherwise."

Larkton rested his elbows on his knees and buried his head in the palms of his hands. "I had no idea he'd done that to you."

"I was seventeen years old, Larkton. What experience would I have had in terms of spending money? My father and mother kept me under lock and key." She snapped her journal closed. "However, it's water under the bridge."

The bishop, who had kept quiet during this time, cleared his throat. "My lady, from what you've shared today on how you benefitted from Thistledown, it's easy to see that its people benefitted greatly from *you* and your endeavors."

"Thank you," she answered. "But the parish has blossomed under Mr. Farris's guidance, also. He brings a vigor and energy sorely needed by the town's residents. He's a good man who deserves to continue in his chosen career. I say this not only as a concerned member of the parish, but also as a person who knows what it feels like to have someone else ruin their standing and reputation within society. My deceased husband was a perfect example. I won't let such a thing happen to Mr. Farris. He doesn't deserve it, nor does he deserve to be pushed into a marriage that's doomed to failure from the start."

"My lady, that's all well and good, but he's a member of the clergy. He's held to a higher standard," the bishop argued.

"As he should be," Avalon agreed. "However, he should be allowed to make the decision. He's the son and brother of an earl. If Miss Rowley has her dates wrong and what she says is true, he's aware of what's expected of him." She let that last little bit hang in the air. "But at the very least, let him defend himself."

When Larkton wiped his hand down his face, she knew she'd hit the mark. "Perhaps there's another way to save Devan's reputation without him having to marry the Rowley woman," Larkton said cautiously.

"Penelope is young." Avalon sat on the edge of her seat. "Let me speak with her and try to discover why she's said those things. I can try to persuade her to withdraw her allegations."

"I'm afraid that won't work." Devan's brother shook his head. "The damage has been done. Even if you refute Miss Rowley's claim, you put yourself in jeopardy."

"But her uncle's anger would be diffused," Avalon argued. "Besides, it's the truth I was with him."

"My lady, you could marry him and explain that you were locked together in the cellar the night she claims she was ruined." Larkton turned to the bishop. "What do you think, Marlowe? It'd save his career. If the Rowley woman doesn't make any further accusations, then everyone would win in this situation."

The bishop's eyes flashed, and a smile graced his face. "That's brilliant, Larkton."

They both turned to her with such eagerness on their faces, it reminded Avalon of dogs begging.

"And why, pray tell, why would I want to marry Mr. Devan Farris?" She was quite pleased with the calmness of her voice.

Larkton leaned back against the sofa with a new ease. "You have to marry him or both of your reputations will suffer. People will talk."

"I'm a widow in control of my own fortune." She clasped her hands a little tighter. "I have a young son to raise."

"A young son who happens to be my ward," Larkton responded. "I could whisk him off to London at any time."

"Are you threatening me?" She stared at the earl, then raised an eyebrow.

"Of course not, my lady," the bishop said smoothly. "Larkton is many things, but devious, I think not." The bishop clasped his hands together and a peaceful expression colored his visage. "Lady Warwyk, the church has invested a great deal in Mr. Farris's career, not to mention we have high hopes for his advancement. Whenever there's a special project that is a delicate matter to handle, we assign Mr. Farris. I know he seeks to have a more permanent position within the church. If he was married to you, Mr. Farris's career would be saved, and he could assist me in London since he'd be living so close. Your interests and charities could continue as they are, and everyone could go back to normal."

"But I'd have a husband, one who would control me and my fortune just from the fact that we were married." She straightened in her seat. "Why would I do that, gentlemen? If either of you were in my position, you'd have walked out the door by now."

The bishop slowly swung his gaze to Larkton. "What

would you offer to help the marchioness make the right decision?"

Larkton nodded curtly, then turned to Avalon. "I'll offer not to send the boy to Eton for another year." He leaned back against the sofa, but the tension in his shoulders was readily apparent.

"That's not enough," she shot back in answer. "Your brother would be my husband and have constant contact with Thane," she argued. "You'd still have control."

Larkton shook his head. "Come now, my lady. I have control now and always will until the lad reaches his majority. Marriage to Devan wouldn't change that. Besides, you've personally seen how Devan and I relate to one another. He doesn't do anything I ask. You'd still be raising the young marquess the same way you are now. Marrying Devan will at least give you more time with your son before he goes to school."

"Only a couple of months," she said.

"My brother is quite fond of the boy," argued Larkton. "He'd not contradict the boy's interests. You know that about him. If he says Warwyk isn't ready, I'll listen to him."

Indeed, Devan had not only tried to charm her, but he'd completely captivated her son. Thane would be delighted if they'd married. But what about her? She couldn't deny how lonely she'd been over the years. It'd be wonderful to share her interests and life with someone, particularly Devan. With a single word, he could tease her into laughter. But he could also be a good listener when she was troubled.

But a husband?

"Think of my brother as an ally you'd have an opportunity to woo. I have every faith you'll be able to do the impossible."

She couldn't bear to have another marriage like she

had with Richard. She'd not do it. She'd not give up her freedom just for another man. She'd have to find another way to wrench Thane's guardianship from Larkton.

But the truth wouldn't be denied. She'd yearned for someone to hold her close on cold winter nights and hold hands with her on long summer walks. When Devan glanced her way and smiled, he made her feel as if she were the only person in the world.

Which was probably what he did with all the women who caught his eye. What if he found someone else?

He called her "Warlock," for heaven's sake and thought her prickly. At first, his teasing was unmerciful, then it became playful and affectionate. Devan cared for her—of that she had no doubt. But she couldn't risk another marriage where love hadn't been openly declared.

Yet, Devan had also held her and felt anger for what she'd gone through with Richard. It would be wonderful to have a willing partner to experience life with plus share the physical intimacy of marriage while never having to fear she was always second best. Yet, how could she secure such a promise from someone like Devan?

He was a pure rake, albeit a religious one. He loved women and thrived on flirting and made no secret about it.

She released a sigh.

Larkton cleared his throat and looked down at his hands. "What's it going to take, Avalon?"

"Twenty thousand pounds," she announced without hesitation. Let them think the worst of her. "I want twenty thousand pounds to marry him."

Larkton choked on her words. "Why am I not surprised you asked for that?" He stood with such a force that she felt a gentle wind blow across her face. "I don't have that type of money. It's a fortune."

She'd clearly upset him, as he started to pace in between the two sofas.

"I know. Your brother wanted to marry an heiress. Since my fortune is tied up in investments that pay for my charities, I don't have anything to give your brother." She stood and returned her journal to her desk, then returned to her seat. "Surely you understand my reasoning."

"I do," Larkton admitted. "That amount would bankrupt my estate." He stopped pacing and stared at the floor. After a long moment, he returned his attention to her. "I could take out a mortgage," he said reluctantly.

"Don't worry yourself over bankrupting the earldom. I have some discretionary funds available plus money of my own. I don't want to lose a man like Devan." The bishop's focus settled on Avalon. "I'll make certain you receive it, Lady Warwyk, but on one condition. You must marry by special license by tomorrow evening. I don't want any more of a scandal to erupt in that gossip rag, *The Midnight Cryer*. It wouldn't do any of us any good if we let this situation fester, particularly the church."

"I'll have my solicitor draw up the marriage agreement," Larkton said with a tone that indicated that the matter was settled.

"Though you didn't ask for my answer, I'll marry him." She didn't care that her tone sounded curt. "But I'll have my solicitor draw up the documents." Then she smiled sweetly, hoping to disarm them from becoming suspicious. "We don't want any loose ends, do we, gentlemen? If you'll excuse me, I've business to attend to."

Namely, asking Devan to marry her. Without another word, she gracefully walked out of the room, leaving the earl and the bishop with their mouths open.

As soon as she was out of the bishop's and Larkton's

sight, she found herself walking briskly all the while hoping she was doing the right thing. She hadn't had feelings for Richard and he'd dismantled her into pieces with his loathing. She blew out a breath. Devan was a different man, a better man, and she cared for him. But still, there were no guarantees for a happy life. With her affections already engaged, wasn't she risking her happiness, her future if things turned ugly?

She was risking everything. Avalon donned her cloak and gloves, then continued walking to the vicarage because she wanted him.

The unbelievable circumstances that she would be married tomorrow to a devilish, dashing vicar consumed her thoughts.

Of course, that was only if he'd have her.

She didn't care if she did have a tendency to use an excessive number of words that began with *d*.

Moreover, Avalon wouldn't *delude* herself.

Devan Farris was a *delicious devil,* and she'd have him in her bed tomorrow.

Another bargain was struck.
Only this time, it was on my terms.

Avalon Warwyk

Chapter Eighteen

❧

As soon as Devan arrived home, he'd sent Mrs. McVey on a shopping errand to collect a few things the house needed. She didn't need to know he'd made up the task in order to have privacy, thus ensuring he could rail to the heavens without interruption. It was simply beyond the pale that the bishop and his brother thought they could manipulate his life without any regard for what he wanted.

Well, damn them to hades because he'd not be forced into anything, particularly marriage to Penelope Rowley because of her lies. Nor would he allow Avalon's reputation to be tarnished because of Thane's poor misguided plan to have them marry.

He lowered himself to his chair and rested his head in his hands as he considered his options. His career in the church was finished, which left him without a way to make a living. Besides begging Avalon to allow him to stay on at Warwyk Hall in some type of menial capacity, he could consider settling in Ireland where he still had family from his mother's side. However, who would welcome a defrocked vicar?

No one.

Unable to contain his restless energy, Devan abruptly stood to retrieve his greatcoat and walk. Where, he had no idea, but the thought of being cooped up in the house alone no longer held any appeal. As he made his way to the entry, a soft knock sounded on the front door. Whoever the interloper was, he fully intended to send them on their way. If it was Gavin, he'd slam the door in his face.

As a second knock sounded, this one a little more insistent, his ire settled somewhat. He'd not turn away a parishioner in desperate need of his help. When he swung open the door, Avalon stood with her head bowed. She raised her gaze and smiled slightly. Instantly, his heart galloped in his chest at the welcome sight.

"What are you doing here?" He looked past her to see if anyone, particularly his brother, had accompanied her.

"I'd hoped you would spare me a few minutes." She glanced behind her. "I'm by myself."

"Mrs. McVey isn't here." The petulance in his voice was unmistakable.

"Good." The humor in her voice was a direct contradiction to his peevishness. "That's fortunate for me as I want to discuss something with you that requires complete privacy."

He stood aside and waved her in. Without a glance his way, she swept past him and walked to his study. He followed.

Devan closed the door behind them in case Mrs. McVey returned early and interrupted them. However, he relished the alone time with his Warlock. She'd always had an ability to cut to the chase of matters. Perhaps with her guidance, they could find a way out of this mess.

Instead of sitting behind his desk, Avalon chose the

small sofa that framed the fireplace where a freshly made fire blanketed the room in a toasty warmth. The flames crackled, sending sparks in the air like fireworks—a spectacular greeting of welcome just for her. He seconded such a salute. For the first time all morning, he felt his mouth tug upward. Only she could make the dreary day brighter.

He sat next to her and rested his arm on the back of the sofa.

A needed distraction, it amused him that the distance between his outstretched fingers and the soft tendrils of hair that had escaped her elegant chignon was mere inches. With a slight stretch, he could grasp one wayward curl and tease it between his fingers.

"Well, what did the 'powers that be' decide for my future?" He lowered his voice. "I'll not marry Miss Rowley. It would be akin to admitting that I was guilty of such an abominable crime."

"You accuse me of using an excessive amount of *d* words while you seem to be stuck on *a. Akin, admitting, abominable*." Her eyebrows lifted, revealing the enchanting green of her eyes.

He couldn't help but laugh. Whenever he saw her, he found a brilliance surrounding them that was mesmerizing. Never had he needed such loveliness more in his life than this morning after his whole world had exploded into bits. "I'm so happy you're here. You make me smile."

"I feel the same." She shyly tucked her head as if collecting her thoughts in a neat, orderly pile.

"Tell me what my esteemed brother and His Lordship have decided." He'd best find out what had happened, though he knew it would ruin this perfect moment.

"They believe you should marry tomorrow." Finally, she lifted her face, and the sight stole his breath.

The humor and radiance in her eyes held him entranced. For a moment, he concentrated on her and nothing else. Eventually, her statement cracked the contentment that surrounded him. "Mark my words, I'll not marry her, Avalon."

"I understand." She tangled her fingers together. "But that's not whom they want you to marry."

"Who then?" He sat up straight and leaned toward her. She had his full attention now. "Who in God's name would they pick besides Penelope Rowley?"

"Me."

"You?" The incredulity in his voice fractured the ease between them.

In answer, she leaned back as if slapped. "I didn't know it would be so repugnant."

He knew her well enough to recognize the hurt in her voice. He wanted to kick himself. After all she'd confessed in the wine cellar to him about the marquess's horrid treatment and disdain of her, he shouldn't be surprised at her response to his outburst. "Avalon, I didn't mean it that way. I apologize. It's no excuse, but you took me by surprise."

She clasped her hands so tightly that he could see the white of her knuckles.

He placed his hand over her clasped ones.

Slowly, she raised her wary gaze to his.

"After our kisses in the wine cellar and music room, look deep inside me. Use your talent to look inside my heart."

"Now you're mocking me." She tilted her head to the ceiling. "I thought we'd be able to discuss this like adults."

"I'm serious. If I recall correctly, I asked you to marry me once," he said. "But truthfully, why would you want to marry me?"

"Larkton told me that he'd take Thane," she said softly.

He released a sigh. "Leave it to my brother to force everyone to bend to his will. Let me talk to him again. You can't marry me. I'm a low clergyman destined for near poverty."

She shook her head vehemently. "Stop that. You're a wonderful man with a bright future. You have a God-given talent to help people." She turned her gaze back to his. "You've helped the people of this village, and me. You're the son of an earl, and I'm a daughter of an earl. Doesn't that put us on equal footing?" Avalon waited a moment before she continued, "I think you should listen to what I have to say."

"Go on." He scooted closer and clasped his other hand over hers. He adored it when she took charge like this. It amazed him that she thought them equals though the differences in their respective societal positions were wider than the Thames.

"I told both your brother and the bishop that I didn't think it was right for Penelope to win. I couldn't live with myself if I didn't tell the truth of what had happened that night. Your brother asked if I'd consider marrying you, and I said yes, for the right price."

Devan couldn't help but laugh. The thought that Gavin would pay for him to marry Avalon was comical, to say the least. "If my brother wouldn't buy a commission for me, I can't wait to hear what he said in response to paying you to marry me." Her gaze shot to his. "Why would he pay if Miss Rowley would do it for free?"

She leaned closer and he wanted to take her in his arms and hold her until this nightmare was over for both of them.

"He was considering mortgaging the earldom for you," she said softly. "He doesn't want you to be ruined.

But he won't have to bear the brunt of the finances as the bishop said that he personally, along with the church, would pay for your marriage settlement. He doesn't want to see your future ruined, and I don't either."

The affection in her voice was unmistakable. He felt like a peacock whose display of tail feathers had won the prize peahen. "Go on. I'm intrigued."

"I'm having my solicitor draw up the papers. They want us to marry by special license by tomorrow. The bishop believes this will help keep the rumors silent."

"What are the terms?" he asked nonchalantly, though he prepared himself as if ready to receive a punch. "What did they have to offer to convince you?"

"Devan, don't belittle yourself. I'm not. I asked for twenty thousand pounds, and they agreed."

"I didn't realize I was such a catch," he murmured.

"You're worth more. And you should know that Larkton said he'd listen to you if I can convince you that Thane should stay with me instead of Eton," she added with a smile.

"That will be an easy task on your part." Almost hesitant to ask for fear of her answer, he kept still and continued, "What are you going to do with the twenty thousand pounds?"

This time she leaned closer to him. "Devan?" His name on her lips sounded like a prayer.

He couldn't help but close his eyes, wanting her to say she'd marry him without any thought of money or other benefit. But he was living in a fantasy world to hope for such a declaration from her. He'd taunted her through the years with that ridiculous nickname of Warlock, and it was only natural she'd be leery of him. She had to protect herself, particularly since she'd been hurt by a husband before.

"It's none of my business," he said finally. "Forget I asked."

"Now I'm asking that you look at me," she said.

Slowly, he turned to her and waited for the answer. Whatever she said, he promised himself he wouldn't react.

"I'm giving the money to you."

His lungs burned with the breath that he hadn't realized he'd been holding. With an exhale, he relaxed. "Why? You could use it for your charity."

Her cheeks heated to a beautiful pink, and the sight made him want to lean over and take her in a scorching kiss that would make both of them burn.

"The charity is doing fine, and I'll have more than enough to help more women and their children." Suddenly, she clenched her jaw as if girding all her hard-fought resolve. "I have one condition regarding the fortune." The slightest hint of a tremble colored her voice.

He narrowed his eyes and stared at her, desperate to understand why she felt the need to protect herself. "What is it?"

"If you ever seek the company of another woman, you forfeit all the money to me." She didn't flinch as she said the words. In warning that this was a tenuous moment for her, a sudden breeze howled as it traveled down the fireplace, and the flames diminished as if escaping the wind's wrath. In its wake, a coolness descended through the room.

He nodded ever so slightly, then leaned toward her. "May I hold you?"

Her shoulders relaxed ever so slightly, the first indication that she would let her guard down. She nodded tentatively, then scooted closer to him.

Carefully, he wrapped his arms around her waist and brought her close. She nestled her head under his chin. He pressed his lips against the top of her head where her soft hair tickled and teased his face.

"My wife will never have to worry about that." He kissed the top of her head again, then pulled away so he could gaze into her eyes. The hint of vulnerability reflected there tore him into pieces. "I'd never hurt you, and I'd never share myself with anyone but my wife." He'd take a bullet before he'd ever cause this woman such pain.

A breathless sigh escaped her, and her eyes grew misty. "You have no idea how difficult that was for me to say. I know it sounds ridiculous."

He traced the outline of her mouth with his thumb. The softness called to him to take her in a kiss, and he would kiss her with such tender regard that she'd have no doubt of his sincerity.

But not yet.

Not until she understood completely. "It'd be an honor to share a bed with you, Avalon. But the greatest honor would be to share my life with you."

She leaned into his touch, and a slight smile replaced her earlier sadness.

"There's my girl, my Lady Warlock."

Her soft laugh turned his insides out. He had little doubt that she'd always have the power to turn his world upside down, a true facet of her powers.

"Then there's only one thing left," she said.

"Tell me," he coaxed as his lips brushed hers.

"Will you marry me tomorrow?"

"I thought you'd never ask," he whispered against her lips.

She moaned slightly, then nipped his lower lip. She pulled him closer and the heat of her body enveloped him like warm sunshine breaking through the clouds. He inhaled her as if consuming her. Every breath of Avalon's scent intoxicated him, drawing him deeper into her spell. He deepened the kiss and she opened to him. Their tongues tangled and mated in a magic that neither could resist, nor did he want to. He cupped her head between his hands and angled his own to kiss her harder, longer, until he marked her as his.

Avalon broke away and stared into his eyes. Her befuddlement over their kiss pleased him. Gingerly, she touched her fingers to her lips, as if not believing that they'd just shared a kiss that could melt an iceberg in a snowstorm. She appeared cool on the outside but her eyes blazed with the passion they'd ignited on the inside.

From now on, he'd ensure that she knew every day that he burned for her with the same need and fire. He took her again in a kiss designed to leave them both senseless.

The entry door opened, and Mrs. McVey called out in greeting.

Reluctantly, Devan broke away, but not before stealing another of Avalon's delightful kisses.

She blinked slowly. "What just happened?"

He laughed while nuzzling her neck. "I think we decided to marry."

"So, is that a yes?" she whispered.

"If my answer wasn't clear earlier, pardon me." He studied her red, swollen lips and decided then and there that tomorrow wouldn't come soon enough. "Let me say it again."

"You wicked man, stop. Your housekeeper is here." She straightened her gown, which had become twisted, then patted her hair into place. "How do I look?" she whispered.

"Like you're ready to be devoured," he answered.

She laughed. "You're incorrigible."

"Thank you. I think that's the nicest compliment you've ever given me."

She playfully swatted his chest. "I'll send you the settlement agreement first thing tomorrow."

"I want to add a term."

Avalon tilted her head. "Of course. What would you like to have in the document?"

Devan exhaled dramatically, then took her hands in his as he stared into her eyes. "I want it added that tomorrow we both dress with the other person in mind."

"Meaning?" She arched one perfect eyebrow.

"For our mutual sakes, we should wear clothing that will be easy to disrobe." He tried his damnedest to appear earnest and forthright.

"You're simply devious." She laughed. "I adore it." She stood and shook her head. "I'll see you tomorrow. I need to tell Thane."

"Shall I accompany you and help explain it to him? I don't want to leave you with such a responsibility alone."

"That's very kind, but if you don't mind, I'd like the evening with him." Avalon swept her cloak around her. "It'll be our last night as two. Tomorrow, we'll be three," she said with a grin.

"That's a beautiful sentiment, Avalon."

Her eyes brightened. "Even warlocks like a bit of sentimentality every now and then." She opened the door and greeted Mrs. McVey.

As he watched his bride leave, Devan felt a euphoria, one that he'd never experienced before. He had no doubt that he'd made the right decision to save himself for marriage. Life with his Warlock would never be dull.

A half lie is nothing more than a half truth. Just like a half empty glass is really half full.
The philosophical musings of Rev. Devan Farris

Chapter Nineteen

ᕗ

Devan paced in the entry of his family home, now Gavin's domain. Avalon should have arrived more than an hour ago. After meeting at her solicitor's office and signing the marital settlement documents, they'd parted. She'd had an errand, and Devan had needed to secure the special license. Bishop Marlowe had met Devan at Doctors' Commons and had been instrumental in securing the license. He would be the one to perform the wedding service.

When Devan heard the carriage rumbling up the drive, he stole a peek through a window. Without hesitation, he opened the door and bounded down the steps where Avalon and Henri stood outside the carriage.

"Finally, I found my bride. I thought you might have gotten lost," he said taking Avalon's hand.

She shook her head slightly. Something was terribly wrong as her face had paled since the last time he'd seen her, and her eyes had grown wide, as if she'd seen a horrible specter. "We must talk."

Henri nodded in his direction. "Are Lady Sophia and Lord Warwyk inside?"

"In the study with my brother and the Lord Bishop," he answered, never taking his gaze from Avalon.

Henri proceeded as he drew Avalon close and helped her up the steps. Through her thick winter cloak, Devan could feel the trembling in her limbs.

"Everyone is waiting in the study," he said. "Do you need to freshen up?" Before he took another step, Avalon halted.

"Where can we talk?" Her voice wobbled in panic.

Devan led her to an anteroom off the study. Without saying a word, he closed the door.

She'd taken off her cloak and was dressed in a beautiful ivory gown trimmed in pink silken roses and matching ribbon.

For a moment, he couldn't speak. "Avalon." His voice cracked as it deepened. "I've always thought you beautiful, but today you're breathtaking. I'm the luckiest man in the world."

"You're not lucky." She blinked as if seeing him for the first time since she arrived. "I can't do this. I can't marry you." The frantic words tumbled from her lips. "I don't know what I'm doing. I'll make a terrible wife."

"I beg to differ. You'll make a wonderful wife." He tried to pull her close, but she pulled away.

"No. You don't understand. My parents . . . they had a horrible marriage. My father had mistresses, and my mother had lovers. I don't know what a good marriage looks like. I couldn't bear it if our marriage failed like my first one."

"Your marriage wasn't your fault." He held her hands and studied her face. A little color had returned, but that wild, forlorn look in her eyes was still there. "Do you trust me?"

She nodded hesitantly.

"What if I told you I've seen this type of anxiety before with other couples right before the service?"

He rubbed his thumb across the soft skin of her hand, soothing her. "It's perfectly natural—"

"No, it's not," she protested as her gaze searched his. "I've done this before. Remember? I'm incapable . . ."

"Darling, I know you're scared, but will you do something for me?" He raised his hand and cupped her cheek.

Hesitantly, she nodded. She was so frightened that all he wanted to do was hold her in his arms. Instead, he lightly pressed his lips to hers, then drew away.

He looked deep into her eyes. She squeezed his hand as if desperate for strength.

"Listen to what I have to say. If afterwards, you don't want to marry, then we won't."

She barely nodded but her eyes never left his.

"I was fortunate to have a wonderful example of marriage in my parents. They loved each other deeply and were fully committed to one another throughout their lifetime together. They taught me what a good marriage is and how it's done." He smiled gently. "Our marriage will be different from your first one. We're a different couple. We care for each other. Rely on me to get you through this. Rely on me whenever you need me. Whether it's today, tomorrow, next month, or the next decade, whenever it's too much, let me take the lead. Will you do that?"

A brief smile graced her lips. "I'll try."

He couldn't help but grin in return. "I've waited my whole life for you. I promise, starting right this minute and all the others that follow, I'll do everything in my power to protect you and make you happy."

He pulled her into his embrace and this time she wrapped her arms around him as if she'd never let go. Her familiar scent rose to greet him, and he knew with her in his arms he was home. Never had anything felt so right before. God save him if she didn't want to marry him.

"You don't know what you're getting into." She stood close and whispered in his ear. "But will you marry me?"

"A thousand times yes." He pressed his lips against her cheek.

Slowly, she pulled away. The earnest look on her face took his breath away. "Thank you for having patience with me."

Devan took Avalon's chin and lifted her gaze to his. "Thank you for making me the happiest man in the entire kingdom." He lowered his lips to hers again. The touch was sweet and filled with promise. Unable to resist, he deepened the kiss. She responded with a slight moan, inviting him in. Devan pulled her closer, never wanting to let her go. His hands slowly traced a path down her back.

A knock on the door sounded. "Mother? Are you in there?"

Avalon rested her forehead against Devan's chest. "Thane."

He kissed the top of her head. "Are you ready?"

She pulled away and nodded, never once breaking her gaze from his.

Today, he would be trothing his life to her, and she in return to him. For all his days and nights, he'd never forget this blessing.

He took her hand in his, then they both went to meet Thane. Grinning from ear to ear, the young lord stood outside in his formal suit. Without hesitating, Avalon walked by Devan's side as they entered the study.

Acting as witnesses, Gavin and Henri stood beside Bishop Marlowe, who held his Book of Common Prayer open. Thane stood beside Devan, and Sophia stood beside Avalon.

The bishop's deep voice echoed through the room. Since Devan knew the words by heart, he concentrated on his lovely bride. As His Lordship performed the ceremony, Devan embraced the awe and thankfulness that swelled in his chest. Indeed, he was the luckiest man alive.

He would not fail her.

Devan stole a quick glance around the room. Thane's excitement made the smile on his face glow. Henri and Sophia wiped their eyes as tears of joy escaped. Even his brother Gavin seemed overcome with emotion as he cleared his throat. A heartfelt smile creased his lips as his gaze met Devan's.

His own heart beat strong for the love that surrounded Avalon and him. It boded well for their new life together as a couple.

"I now pronounce you man and wife," the Lord Bishop declared with a smile on his face.

Without missing a beat, Devan took Avalon in his arms and kissed her.

For in his arms he held his life, his happiness, and his future.

He held his wife.

Sitting on the velvet bench next to her, Devan leaned close with his arm around her waist and waved with his other hand at Gavin and the bishop. Sophia and Henri had taken the other carriage with Thane, who had chattered like a magpie after the ceremony.

As soon as they were out of sight, Avalon sighed.

Her lips still burned from the incendiary kiss Devan had given her at the end of the ceremony before they'd signed the marriage register. Now, with evening closing in, they were on their way to the vicarage, where they'd spend the night and consummate their vows. Not that Richard had ever visited her at Warwyk Hall, but under no circumstances did she want any remembrance of him on her wedding night with Devan.

Henri and Sophia would mind Thane this evening, and Henri had thoughtfully brought a few items of clothing and toiletries for the night to the vicarage.

Still, the stark reality of what she'd done today settled around her like a midnight London fog. She had married Devan Farris, a man who just a month ago she'd have called her biggest menace.

"It was a lovely ceremony." She turned to Devan and sniffed back her tears, but she didn't hide her smile. She wouldn't describe her mood as euphoric, but she was happy and had high hopes for their future, particularly after he'd said such sweet things to her to calm her fears. "We're married. Do you believe it?"

"No." He brought her gloved hands to his lips. "I finally have a wife."

"And I have a husband." Reverence leaked from her voice. "Our lives will never be the same."

With his clear, bright eyes, he studied her. "Are you having second thoughts about your decision?"

She shook her head. "It's just . . . everything has changed in just a short amount of time."

The gentle rocking of the carriage did little to lull her anxiety. Nor did the intensity of her husband's stare. An unsettling notion nipped around the edges of her thoughts. She'd had complete freedom for the last nine years, and now she'd have to consider Devan's wishes whenever she made a decision. Whether something as inconsequential as what to serve for dinner or something incredibly important as to how she'd raise Thane or what her plans were for the parish's charities, any and all of it, she would need to seek his opinion. That's what a good wife would do.

She tamped down the unease. Her new husband was correct. The fault of her first marriage didn't lie with her, but with Richard and her parents. They made decisions that deeply impacted her life and future. But Devan treated her as an equal partner. He was a man who'd never given her cause to doubt his true motives and desires. She vowed then and there, she'd do everything in her power to make their marriage a success.

"Let me ask you in turn, are you having second thoughts?" Though it was silly to be on pins and needles as Avalon waited for his answer, she felt herself on edge and quickly filled the silence between them. "You didn't have much choice in the matter."

In no hurry, he tugged his gloves free. With an ease that suggested they'd been together for years instead of hours, he cupped her cheek, the caress a command for her to look at him. Ironically, the warmth in his fingers sent a chill through her.

"Avalon, never." The softly spoken words were clear and vibrant through the creaking of the carriage as it picked up speed now that they were through London and racing to the vicarage. "For all my days, rest assured that every day I'm on this earth, I'll make certain I show you what you mean to me." He dipped his head until their gazes met. "Starting tonight."

He pressed his lips against hers. The touch as light as a butterfly's wings against one's finger. She sighed faintly against his mouth as the kiss ended. Devan Farris had just proven that her conception of marriage was completely wrong. For the first time in her life, she had hope for happiness in her future because she'd married a very naughty, irreverent, but tender vicar, a man who promised he'd devote his life to making their marriage succeed.

She and Devan had decided they would live permanently at Warwyk Hall instead of the vicarage or the dower house on the estate. She'd instructed the staff to open the state bedroom on the family floor. It could be a new home for both of them. Living at Warwyk Hall, she could continue her work, and Devan could still meet with parishioners either at the vicarage or at the Hall.

They rode the rest of the way in a peaceable silence while holding hands. One thing she'd noticed about Devan, he liked to touch her. After so many years of being alone, she relished the close contact with another human being. For heaven's sake, she sounded like a woman who'd let her heart out of its cage and the thing was running wild circles around her. She grinned to herself.

The carriage pulled up to the vicarage, and Devan didn't wait for the Warwyk footman to open the door. He jumped down and held out his hand to hers. With a deep breath and a smile, she placed her hand in his and stepped out of the carriage.

This was the start of the rest of her life.

Devan had seen to her every convenience when they'd arrived. He'd prepared a bath for her while he prepared a small meal for them to enjoy since Mrs. McVey wasn't there. Overjoyed at the news of their marriage, the housekeeper had offered to stay with her daughter and family this evening, leaving Avalon and Devan alone.

As she soaked in the tub in his bedroom, her hands trailed over her body, lingering over her breasts and nipples until they puckered into hard peaks. Her body tingled with the realization that soon she'd make love with Devan. Heat pooled into a delicious liquid warmth that settled low in her body. She closed her eyes and surrendered to the delicious and wicked thoughts of his body touching hers, covering hers.

Soon, the water grew cooler, and she reluctantly stood and dried herself with linen toweling. The cloth wasn't as fine as the ones she was used to at Warwyk Hall, but they were Devan's. He used the same ones to dry his own body. She released a gentle sigh as she brushed the toweling over her tender nipples, imagining his hands replacing the cloth.

She slipped on a ruby-red satin dressing gown trimmed in black ribbon. Henri had said she looked striking in it, and she wanted to look her best for Devan tonight. How long would she have to wait before he came to her? Her pulse quickened, and her knees weakened. What if she was the type of wife who didn't enjoy lovemaking?

A firm knock sounded against the door.

She hesitated for a second. "Come in."

Devan entered, and his gaze locked with hers. The soft glow of candlelight in the room seemed to kiss his cheek. He wore the black silk banyan she'd purchased for him in London today as a wedding gift. The shop had delivered the lovely garment this afternoon.

She swallowed as his compelling green eyes locked her in place. Magnificent was too tame a word to describe him.

He went back into the hallway and returned with a tray. "There's wine, cheese, bread, and a beautiful fruit cake Mrs. McVey baked in celebration of our wedding." He closed the door with his elbow, then entered the room and set the tray on a table.

Any and all words lodged in her throat.

His riveted gaze returned to her face, then slowly traveled the length of her body. "You're beautiful, Avalon."

"So are you." He looked like a warrior coming to conquer everything in his path. Her throat tightened at the thought.

He glanced at the banyan he wore. "Thank you for this. Was this the errand you had to finish?"

"In the marriage contract, you asked that we wear clothes easy to shed." She grinned.

"My wife is brilliant." The joyful sound of his laughter filled the room.

She nodded once in thanks. "Anything you need, I hope you ask."

"I need you."

Her heart tripped in her chest at the deep rumble of his voice. When his gazed locked with hers, she stilled.

With a wicked smile, Devan poured a glass of wine and offered it to her. When her fingers touched his, electricity shot through every inch of her and she felt rooted in place. Never before had she ever been so aware of another.

"To us. May we have a long and happy life together." His sinfully dark voice resonated through the room with a self-assuredness that made her envious. Why couldn't she be as confident as he? Hurriedly, she took a sip. If she didn't get her unruly emotions under some type of control, they'd never be able to consummate their marriage.

"Are you nervous?" He took a sip of his own wine.

She nodded slightly. "There's no earthly reason for it, but . . ." She let the words trail to nothing.

"What is it?" A deep crease between his eyes marred his beautiful face.

She cleared her throat in hopes that the flutter of butterflies in her stomach would settle for the night. "I'm uncertain if I'm any good at this." She waved her hand between the two of them. "What we're going to do."

He put his wine down, then stepped to her. His large hands rested on her shoulders, commanding her to look at him. She'd never regarded herself as a coward and wouldn't start now.

She lifted her face to his, then took a deep breath. "I've only done this once, and it was a disaster," she admitted.

"I highly doubt that, darling." The endearment on his lips caused the sweetest sensation to rush through her veins, rekindling the fire she'd started in her bath. "For all the years I've known you, I've admired your passion, temerity, and strength. I find it all so desirable." His lips touched the side of her cheek. "I find you so desirable."

She closed her eyes at his touch, then forced her gaze to his. Never before had she bared her weaknesses to another. "I want us to make love, but I'm afraid I'll disgust you like I did Richard—"

He placed his forefinger against her lips. "He was a fool not to see the treasure that you are. There is not a single part of you that would disgust me." He pulled her close. "This is the first time for both of us." His hand slowly trailed up and down each vertebra of her back. Eventually, his hand cupped the back of her neck, and his mouth met hers.

It was unlike any kiss they'd shared before. The sweet touch of his lips promised that whatever happened tonight, there would be no judgments. No rejections. Just a celebration of the two of them. "I'd like that," she whispered against his lips.

"It will be for me."

She stared at him, and he didn't look away.

"It's true." He lowered his voice and bit his lip. "I've never in my entire life lain with anyone."

"What?" she asked incredulously. Her mind reeled

with such a shocking revelation. "You're known as a consummate ladies' man."

He slowly shook his head. "My parents . . ." He tilted his head to the dark ceiling and stared at nothing as if hoping to gather more courage to proceed with his tale. "They told me never to waste the opportunity to share such a glorious gift as love by squandering it on someone who didn't mean anything to me. I've taken their advice."

She shifted closer and only inches separated them. "How can that be? You're known throughout society for being a . . ."

"Ladies' man? A naughty vicar? London's most lustful clergyman?" He laughed. "It's quite freeing to discuss. You, who have a reputation as an avaricious ice queen, and I, who have a reputation as a 'Jack among the maids,' prove that the gossip rags, in particular *The Midnight Cryer*, don't have the faintest clue who we are as real people." He turned his stalwart gaze to hers. "I think such a union between a man and woman should be honored and cherished. I'll not waste such a precious gift on anyone other than my wife."

"That's a lovely sentiment," she said quietly.

The hesitant smile on his face showed a rare vulnerability that she'd never seen before. The fact that he shared it gave her hope for the success of their marriage.

"This moment makes me thankful that I didn't waste it. I want you, my lovely wife, to be my first." His gaze penetrated hers.

Though he was the one without any experience, she felt like an untried virgin herself. Suddenly unsure what to say, she simply nodded.

"Avalon." He pressed his lips against hers again, then deepened their kiss, igniting a need within her to explore and feel every inch of him. His touch threatened to spin all her senses out of control, and she didn't care. Never before had she felt this way. He made her feel desirable. After all these years, she felt like a frozen maiden breaking out of the snow and into the fire.

With tender care, he broke away, and then, as if he couldn't help himself, he took her mouth again in a scorching kiss. Before she could demand more, he took her hand in his and led her to his bed. While his eyes undressed her, his hand reached and unknotted the tie at her waist. She sucked in a breath as the cool air hit her skin. Instantly, he embraced her and his arms surrounded her. His dressing gown had draped open and his hot skin met hers.

With a tremulous breath, she reached to undo the knot of her hair, but he took her hand in his.

"Let me," he said.

"Are we really going to do this?" she whispered in wonderment.

He slowly pulled the pins that anchored her curls, releasing her hair. His hand combed through her locks. "Unless you don't want to." Before she said a word, he continued, "I don't mind waiting. I've waited all my life for this night. Another day, week, or month makes little difference. Whatever you want."

"I feel as if I've waited all my life, too. I want tonight." She pressed her chest against his. "I want you."

His slow, seductive smile made her stomach turn flips. "Then let's not tarry, wife."

He swept her in his arms and laid her on the bed as if she were the most fragile piece of china in the kingdom. She allowed her gaze to sweep down his body. His chest was bare underneath his banyan, and the breadth of it caused her breath to hitch. He was beautiful in so many ways. Not only was he handsome, but his body was a work of art. A smattering of hair down the center of his chest called to her, and she reached toward him. Her fingers instinctively combed through the coarse hair before her hand pressed against the center of his chest where his heartbeat pounded strong and true.

He smiled, then placed his hand over hers. "I like you to touch me, but I warn you in advance to be careful." The deep thrum of his voice lulled her into exploring him more.

"Why?"

"I don't want the night to be over before it begins. I want to make love to you all night."

"Oh." What else was there to say? Her husband thought her desirable and wanted to be with her. If he'd showered her with endless jewels and strings of pearls, they couldn't compare with the sweet tender gift he'd just given her.

"Now, let me see you." With a whisper of a touch, he pushed away the gaping dressing gown. She forced herself to watch as his eyes meandered over her body. He traced a line down the center of her chest until he reached her breasts. Without looking, she knew her nipples had puckered, begging for his touch. With the gentlest of touches, he skimmed her nipples with the backs of his fingers. They grew even heavier at his ministrations. She sucked in a ragged breath.

His eyes widened at her response. "Am I doing it wrong?"

"I like it. I don't think anything you do tonight will be wrong."

His lopsided grin tugged at the corners of his mouth, and she felt herself falling into an abyss she wasn't certain she ever wanted to climb out of. Never before had a man looked at her the way Devan was this evening. It made her drunk with a feminine power that she'd never experienced before.

With infinite care, he covered her body. Instantly, she became aware of his smell. He must have shaved and bathed in another room as his cheeks were smooth. The subtle scents of lemongrass soap and the musk of his skin combined into an alchemy that filled her with a needy ache for him inside her. His massive thighs framed hers while his arms enfolded her in his embrace. As he took possession of her mouth, his hardness pressed against her stomach.

Like a starved man, he moved his mouth down her neck, licking, biting, and sucking. Such exquisite torture. Begging for more, she moaned as her hands traced the curves and contours of his shoulders.

He wove his way down to her breasts. The swirl of his tongue around her nipple made her see stars. Seeking purchase, she combed her fingers through his hair, the dark, damp strands as familiar as her own.

They both groaned as he turned his attention to her other breast. The cool air did nothing to tamp down the fire that was roaring through her veins. Devan pushed his shaft against her leg in an act that mimicked lovemaking. He was hungry for her, and there was no denying she wanted him.

He trailed his mouth lower and kissed her stomach before going lower. His lips traced one hip bone. His eyes locked with hers as he inhaled deeply. "I can smell your arousal."

She stopped touching him and simply stared. "What do you mean? How do you know?"

Never taking his eyes from hers, he traced a small delicate pattern through her curls, his fingers slipping closer and closer to her sex. "That night at the soiree when we were in the music room, and you found your pleasure, I smelled you then. I'll never forget it. It was like the sweet fragrance of honey, and I wanted to taste it. I wanted to taste you."

Her heart pounded against her ribs, trying to reach him. She should be shocked at his words, but they excited her more. His legs straddled hers, and he leaned forward until his head was close to her sex.

Through the candlelight, she could see his erection pulsing with need—with desire for her. A drop glistened at the tip, and after what he'd just said, she wanted to return the favor.

Before she could say a word, he rose to his knees and kissed her *there*. His eyes never left hers as he ran his fingers down the cleft of her sex. Heat and want flooded her body.

"Show me where to touch you." If possible, his voice had deepened from desire.

"Well, I'm . . . not certain." Her cheeks heated, and her voice hitched in answer.

He rested his hands beside her head and bent down for a quick kiss. She could taste herself on his lips.

"You've touched yourself before?" he asked.

She nodded ever so slightly. "But I never allowed myself . . ."

"Show me," he demanded softly. "I want to learn what you like. How to please you. Then, together, I want to help you find it like we did the other night."

She searched his eyes, waiting for his laughter but there was none—only sincerity, which wiped away all remnants of her embarrassment. She moved her finger between them, and he lowered himself to her sex once more to watch. Without hesitation, she showed him the sensitive nub that had brought her so much pleasure when they'd been in the music room together.

"Let me try."

One stroke of his finger, and she wanted more. One leg fell open in invitation.

He brought his fingers to his mouth and sucked. Fire seemed to alight from his eyes, and he groaned in pleasure. "Good?"

"Very," she answered.

"I'll let you in on a secret. I was right. You *are* sweet, and I've waited so long to satisfy my hunger." He dipped his head and soon his tongue darted out and circled the pulsing center—possessing it while possessing her.

"Devan," she whispered. Whether it was a prayer that he never stop, or an ode to his lovemaking, she didn't care. Raw need for him to continue his relentless pleasuring pounded through her, building, then cresting, and eventually rising again. As he continued the tender ministrations of his tongue, he groaned. The vibration of the sound against her tender sex amplified her pleasure into a fiery hunger that demanded to be satisfied. She tilted her hips and Devan responded to her demand by sucking harder. He eased two fingers into her sex, and she closed her eyes at the exquisite torture.

"Don't stop," she whispered. Her body reached for something, building, pushing, demanding satisfaction. Suddenly, it was like a starless night had exploded into daylight as pleasure took possession of every inch of her body. When she finally found her breath and her sanity, she looked to Devan, her lover. The amazement on his face made her hungry again for him.

"How does a virgin know how to do that?"

He fit his body perfectly against hers as he took possession of her lips again. He tasted of her and the forbidden, and she wanted more.

He leaned over her and chased several damp curls from her cheek. "I learned it from scripture. Did I ever tell you what an excellent student I was in seminary school?"

"Scripture?" she murmured as if lost in the aftereffects of the pleasure Devan had given her.

"Indeed," he murmured. Unable to resist, he swirled his tongue around one pert nipple, then did the same to the other as he fisted his hand over his member. The urge to pleasure himself was near nigh impossible to resist, but he couldn't help being transfixed by the flush of her face.

Sensual gratification made her face glow. He'd always thought her beautiful, but seeing her thus, she mesmerized him. Though his cock throbbed, demanding attention, Devan wouldn't rush this night. Avalon's half-lidded eyes made him want to pound his chest that he'd given her an orgasm that they'd both remember.

"I've never read anything about pleasuring a woman that way in the Bible," she playfully challenged as she wrapped her legs around his waist and pulled him down into the cradle of her hips.

"Song of Solomon." Somehow, he managed to rasp aloud the words as her hand clasped around his shaft. When her thumb circled the crown of his member, spreading his leaking seed, he groaned. Paradise had to be highly overrated when compared to being in bed with Avalon.

"I thought that was a love poem." She gently sucked her thumb and moaned. His bollocks tightened, warning that he was in real danger of not surviving the night. An image of her with her mouth on him, bringing him to completion, roared into his thoughts.

"It is a love poem, but it also instructs how a married couple should pleasure"—he groaned louder as she squeezed a little harder—"and honor each other."

She didn't answer as she guided him to her sex. He balanced on his elbows as he stared into her face. He'd remember this moment for the rest of his life. His body, hot and sweaty, covered hers, and she didn't seem to mind. She moved her hips as if she wanted him closer. His blood seemed on fire as it raced through his veins, encouraging him to take what he wanted. What he needed.

Her.

He needed to possess every inch of her.

He pushed, barely entering her. He stopped and studied their joined bodies. "Look at us," he said in awe.

She tore her gaze from his and glanced where their bodies joined. "More," she whispered.

Never before had he felt such wonder and hunger for another. He thanked God it was Avalon because, truthfully, he never could imagine himself with anyone except her.

With infinite tenderness, he gripped her hips, then pushed into her. Her muscles tightened as if denying him entrance. Avalon tilted her hips, making it easier. He was in another inch. His blood pounded and sweat covered his brow. Nothing in his life had ever felt as right as this moment.

Like a beast finally released from its cage, he wanted to pound into her. Take her, seize her, and mark her as his.

His wife.

Needing to lose himself within her, Devan took her mouth in a scorching kiss as he thrust until he was completely seated within her heat. Her moan caused him to come out of his frenzy. He'd never forgive himself if he hurt her. He searched her face, and her eyes blazed with a need that matched his.

"Don't stop," she pleaded.

He withdrew, leaving only the tip of his cock in. "Say my name," he growled, proving he was an animal.

At least in her arms.

"Devan," she commanded as she thrust her hips, showing him how much she wanted him.

Unable to restrain the desire that burned like fire through every inch of his body, Devan grabbed her hips with his hands as if never letting go, then thrust again. Her eyes widened as her body clamped down on his cock, milking it in an attempt to control it.

He was close to coming and stared into her eyes. She nodded slightly, instinctively knowing what he wanted. Without relenting, he withdrew then drove into her again and again. Each time she rose to meet him. A charring heat started in the base of his spine and spread like molten lava across his skin until his bollocks felt like they were going to explode.

"Devan," she begged in the sweetest voice, like a siren calling him home. He grimaced, then closed his eyes as the searing heat of his seed spilled within her like an endless flooding river. This was one of the most intense orgasms he'd ever experienced as he pumped more and more until he filled her with a part of himself that was only hers . . . forever.

He inhaled deeply, struggling for breath as he opened his eyes. As they calmed the tempest they'd created, their hands stroked and petted one another. Her breathing matched his as she held his gaze.

"So, what do you think of making love?" he asked, hoping he hadn't disappointed her.

"Are you looking for a compliment?" She lifted an eyebrow in a playful challenge. Without waiting for his reply, she continued, "I'd say an amazing effort for a first time."

When a delightful smile graced her face, he laughed

out loud. "Well, I'm always ready for more instruction. Let's do it again."

"You are such a rake, one with very refined tastes that are hard to satisfy. Lucky for you, I'm up for the challenge." Avalon pulled him down for a kiss.

Before their lips met, he pulled back and rested his weight on his elbows. "I never imagined it would be this wonderful. But seriously, did I hurt you? I'll never forgive myself if I left bruises on your hips."

She rose slightly, then rubbed her nose against his cheek. She worried his ear lobe with her teeth, driving him mad. "I won't break. You were marvelous. In a way, this was my first time, too." Her eyes searched his, pressing him to believe her. "With my husband who . . ."

"With your husband who wants you desperately." He couldn't resist this woman, his Warlock. He took her in a kiss designed to show her all the passion he felt for her. Eventually it turned tender as if they were having a conversation with one another. The feel of her lips against his nurtured a part of him that perhaps had always hungered for her.

For in these sweet, spectacular moments, he found himself fulfilled for the first time in his life.

He finally felt like he belonged somewhere.

He was home in his wife's arms.

Perils of the past have a way of designing the future.

Lady Warlock

Chapter Twenty

A dull gray morning greeted Avalon, but she smiled in return. With a full body stretch, she slightly grimaced as muscles she hadn't even known existed protested. Her husband, Mr. Devan Farris, had made love to her, Lady Avalon Farris. For once in her life, she felt desired and more.

She felt satisfied.

She looked around the room, hoping he was still there, but as soon as she awoke she felt an emptiness in the room, as if some vibrant star were missing from the night sky.

He'd taken her twice more last night and afterward, each time, he'd washed, then fed her or brought her something to drink. He'd taken care of her like she was a precious gift. While he'd bathed her, he'd kissed her knees, her hips, her hands, anywhere and everywhere. Frankly, she thought herself a princess in a fairy tale. For someone who never believed she'd find a husband who would treat her with respect and admiration, she had been proven wrong by fate.

"Good morning, my lady," Henri called out as she knocked on the door. "Mrs. McVey is cooking you breakfast, and I'm here to help you dress."

"Come in," Avalon called out. "Where's Mr. Farris?"

"He had to make a call to the Satterlys' home." Henri shook her head and clucked in worry. "The elderly Mr. Satterly had a troubled night. His son asked for the vicar to see his father this morning. It seems Mr. Satterly wants Mr. Farris to read some scripture to him this morning in case he didn't make it through the night." Henri clucked her disbelief. "The devil himself will have to come from hell to retrieve that old goat. He'll outlive us all. Just you wait and see."

"Henri," Avalon scolded.

"The truth will set you free, my lady." Henri bustled in with the efficiency of a general preparing the troops for battle. Avalon smiled at her loyal maid's demeanor. Without any question, Henri was dying to know what had happened last night, but Avalon refused to start the conversation.

Her maid prepared a bath in the small slipper tub. While Avalon soaked in the hot water, Henri laid out her clothes. Avalon dried herself, then Henri held up a chemise for her mistress to pull over her head. When she handed the garment to Avalon, Henri's eyes grew huge, and she bit her lip in mirth.

"What?" she asked.

Henri pointed to her shoulder, then held up a hand mirror for Avalon's inspection. Several small red marks appeared in the reflection where Devan had nipped her in the throes of passion. "Does Mr. Farris have the same, my lady?"

"Wouldn't you like to know," she playfully retorted.

Henri shook her head and smiled. "Someone is full of vinegar and spice this morning. All I suggested was that you take him for your lover, but you ended up marrying him." She helped slip the chemise over Avalon's head. "You look different. Blissful. Do you feel happy?"

"It's the first time I've ever felt . . . contented. Fulfilled."

Henri laughed as she picked up Avalon's stays from the bed. "A well-loved woman is a beautiful sight, my lady. You are ravishing this morning."

Avalon's cheeks heated at Henri's observation, and she didn't want to gush about the happenings in their marital bed, but she was happy. She did feel pretty. For the first time in years, she felt a lightheartedness from within and couldn't wait to see her husband again.

Henri wasted no time tying the stays, then helping Avalon with her morning gown. Her matching pelisse lay draped over Devan's bed.

It was their bed. They were married now, and that's what couples did. They comforted and cared for one another. She let out a contented sigh. Who knew marriage could be so rewarding?

At least the bed-sport.

But that wasn't all. It was the way Devan's eyes smoldered as he possessed her. It was as if he could see the loneliness inside and joined his body with hers to fill her emptiness so she'd never suffer such solitude again.

"What are you going to call yourself now that you're married? Mrs. Farris or Lady Avalon Farris?"

"We haven't discussed it." She stopped as soon as she realized what she'd said.

We.

It was a new word in her vocabulary, one she hoped to use every day.

Henri straightened the bed. "The state bedroom is ready for you and your husband. The young master is beside himself waiting for you to return. I don't think I've seen Lord Warwyk this excited since you told him he could have a puppy."

"And Sophia?" she asked.

A crease appeared between Henri's eyes. "She's pleased but worried. She said she had misgivings how Penelope Rowley would take the news." Her lady's maid leaned closer. "That Rowley girl had set her sights on the vicar, and now she's destroyed her good name by trying to ruin him."

"She's young and her actions are unfortunate for all. Especially her," Avalon answered. "After breakfast, let's make a call to the Rowley home and allow Penelope the chance to make things right before the entire village is forced to choose sides."

"Pfft." Henri didn't bother to hide her disdain. "What was she thinking?"

"I don't believe she was." Avalon smiled slightly, not looking forward to the discussion. "That's the problem."

Mrs. McVey was kind enough to have eggs, bacon, and kippers, along with toast and jam prepared for her. After last night, Avalon found herself famished and ate a full breakfast. She finished her cup of tea, then collected Henri for the walk to the Rowley manor house.

Soon they both stood in the entry. It was an elegant home surrounded by granite columns that reminded Avalon of the Parthenon.

"Welcome, my lady," Mrs. Rowley exclaimed as she made her way carefully down the steps to greet Avalon.

Penelope followed a safe distance behind, glowering.

"Good morning, Mrs. Rowley." Avalon kept her gaze devoted to Penelope.

"Come, let's take tea in the conservatory this morning." Mrs. Rowley dipped a small curtsy. "It's the warmest room in the house this time of day." She leaned close to Avalon. "You heard about our poor Penelope, I presume?" Without waiting for a reply, she continued, "We're keeping it quiet so the vicar can make amends. We don't want Penelope embarrassed any more than she already is over Mr. Farris's actions. She's absolutely ruined. We must discuss what we're going to do with the new vicar. I always thought there was something wrong with him."

Avalon's back bristled at the words against her husband, but she bit her tongue. No good would come from speaking too soon that she'd married Devan.

"I won't stay long. But may I have a word with Penelope alone?"

Penelope stuck her chin in the air as if superior to Avalon, then turned on her heel to walk to the conservatory.

Henri raised an eyebrow as she watched the young miss flounce down the hall while her aunt twittered behind her.

"Wonder where she received her deportment lessons? The barnyard?" Henri said under her breath.

Avalon chuckled, but didn't answer as she followed the two women.

Mrs. Rowley waited outside the room for Avalon and stopped her with a touch of her hand on Avalon's forearm. "Begging your pardon, my lady. But my husband and I have tried to get Penelope to talk about what happened. It's just too horrible for her to discuss. She's been distraught since the night of your soiree when she told us."

It wasn't surprising that Penelope wouldn't discuss it, because it never happened.

Mrs. Rowley looked at Penelope, who sat with her back facing them in a small settee. "I hate that she won't confide in me. If you find out anything will you share it with me?"

The worried look on Penelope's aunt's face told Avalon that the woman truly cared for her niece and suffered because of Penelope's lies. "Of course, Mrs. Rowley."

The woman nodded once, then took her leave. Henri sat at the back of the room, more as a witness than a lady's maid who was attending her employer on a social call.

"Good morning, Penelope," Avalon said. "May I sit?"

"Of course, Lady Warwyk," she answered sweetly, but the daggers in her eyes betrayed her true regard.

Avalon settled in a chair next to the settee, then looked out the windows at the gray and dreary courtyard that had captured Penelope's attention. She turned her attention back to the young girl. "Since it's only the two of us, I wonder if you'd like to share what happened between you and Mr. Farris?"

"Why are you interested?" Penelope hissed.

"Because I'd hate to see anyone's reputation ruined," she offered, keeping her voice low. She leaned a little closer. "Do you want to tell me . . . the truth?"

"I know you want him," she snapped, then brushed her hands down the front of her dress as if trying to calm her ire. "Lady Warwyk, what's done is done. Mr. Farris has made it known that he loves me. When he seduced me, he forced my hand."

"Indeed, it would be horrible to be compromised against your will." Avalon studied the courtyard for a second before turning her attention back to Penelope. "Did you tell anyone else?"

"No. It's too intimate to share." Pleased with herself, Penelope grinned slightly. "If you only knew how persuasive he is when he kisses you. Two days after he compromised me, he was so overcome with passion that he knocked me to the ground when we were walking home from the village for a kiss. The man is completely smitten."

Everything within Avalon stilled. "He kissed you?"

"Goodness, yes." Penelope didn't flinch at the question.

Though a sweet smile graced her lips, Penelope's eyes sharpened in their assessment of Avalon.

By now, Henri had silently moved to where she stood behind Penelope without the girl becoming aware.

Avalon needed her to admit it again, so Henri could witness the lie. "Three days before the soiree he seduced you? You're certain?"

"Of course I'm certain. A woman doesn't forget when her virtue has been stolen from her. If you don't believe me, ask Sophia," Penelope challenged.

"You just told me that you didn't share this with anyone. Now you're saying Sophia knew about it."

"You're just trying to trap me. But you'll not succeed." Penelope lowered her tone. "You've wanted Devan as soon as I said I would have him for my husband. But it's too late. He flirts with me every time he sees me, even during church service. He's made it perfectly clear that I'm the one he wants, not you." Her eyes traveled up and down Avalon's body, judging her. "Sophia told me all about your marriage to the marquess. Much like a piece of fossilized wood, you're practically petrified with your airs and all the years you've lived alone. You'd be a cold fish in bed, I'm sure."

"That's enough," Avalon warned as she tightened her stomach. The girl's biting words had their intended effect—they'd weakened Avalon's newfound confidence. But as she'd always done when insulted and made to feel worthless, she lifted her chin an inch and straightened her back. "Tell me the truth about the night you said Mr. Farris compromised you."

"Or what?" Penelope dared to lean forward. "How could you possibly know anything? You weren't there."

"No, I wasn't there with you, but I know the truth about that night and so do you," Avalon said. She drew a deep breath, hoping for patience. Her calm demeanor was ready to snap in two. "I'm confused why you're saying these things. This isn't like you. Do you want me to tell your aunt and uncle?"

Penelope gasped, the slight sound abruptly caught in her throat. "My uncle went to see the bishop and the Earl of Larkton. I expect Devan to propose to me any day now."

"I think it's best if I speak with your aunt and uncle. They're worried about you." Avalon stood, and the swoosh of her satin gown snapped, breaking the eerie silence between them.

The girl's eyes widened as she stared at her. Then her lips trembled as her haughty demeanor slowly melted. "Lady Warwyk." Penelope lowered her voice so only she and Avalon could hear. "Please, do not be cross with me."

Penelope's tormented face reminded Avalon how young she was.

"You've always shown me kindness. Please accept my apology for my behavior." Penelope visibly swallowed. "I don't want to lose your friendship."

"Of course, we'll still be friends, but you must see how this is hurting Mr. Farris," Avalon answered and slowly sat back down.

"My lady . . ." A single tear fell down the girl's pale cheek. "I must marry him."

"Penelope, Mr. Farris and I married yesterday." Avalon waited for the girl's disdain to return.

"What?" She brought her hand to her mouth. "Oh God, all is lost." A tear streamed down each cheek, and she clasped her hands around her waist and rocked back and forth. "All is lost," she repeated.

"Sweetheart, what is it?" Avalon scooted closer. She'd never seen such utter despair in Penelope.

"You don't understand," she cried.

"What don't I understand? Tell me." Avalon glanced in Henri's direction. The maid had walked to the girl's side.

"Miss Penelope, you can share with Lady Farris. She and I will help you," Henri offered.

"It's too late." Penelope choked back a sob. "You see I'm betrothed to a vile creature of a man. It's been arranged since I was a little girl. He grew up next to me in London."

"Who is it?" Avalon's voice turned softer.

"Harrison, Lord Renford. He made a fortune in trade." By then, Henri had given Penelope a handkerchief, and she dried her eyes. "He's a monster." Penelope squeezed the piece of linen tightly in her fist. "As a child he was cruel to his pets and dismissive of the servants. When I was thirteen I looked out my bedroom window . . ."

"Go on," Avalon urged.

Penelope exhaled, the painful sound poignant. "My window overlooked his courtyard. One day, he was beating a maid with the whip he used for his horses. I could hear the leather singing through the air before each strike." She shivered in her seat. "He beat her so badly that blood soaked the back of her uniform. She . . . fell into a heap. He spit on her, then walked away."

"That's horrible." Avalon's stomach churned at Penelope's words. "Did you tell your mother?"

The young girl nodded. "She said it didn't matter. He wouldn't treat me that way." She caught Avalon's gaze. "I couldn't get it out of my thoughts so I had my maid ask one of the servants next door what had occurred to cause such wrath." Penelope's hands were clasped so tight her knuckles were white.

"What happened?" Henri asked.

Penelope shook her head. "No one knows. There

were rumors he beat her so hard she died, then had her body carried out in a cart that night. But I don't know."

"Did you ever find out why he was so furious?" Henri murmured.

The girl's gaze darted to hers. "He discovered she was carrying and unmarried. He called her a heathen whore."

"Oh God." Avalon released the breath she'd been holding. She closed her eyes and pinched the bridge of her nose. "Of course, no one could concern themselves with a maid who disappeared."

"After my parents and I moved abroad, they allowed me to come back to England. I thought I could find someone else to marry." Penelope slowly bowed her head. "I moved here and made friends. Then Mr. Farris arrived, and he was so nice to me."

"Are your aunt and uncle aware of your fears?" Avalon asked.

"They're trying to help me, my lady. That's why my uncle was vehement about forcing Mr. Farris into marriage. My uncle was relieved that I wouldn't have to marry Lord Renford." The girl shook her head. "Renford wants to call the banns, and my parents are adamant that I marry before spring."

Avalon's heart constricted at Penelope's last words. It was exactly what had happened with her and Richard. Her parents' wishes had to be obeyed. Penelope faced the same trap Avalon had been caught in.

"I'm sorry, my lady." The girl bit her lip and forced her gaze to Avalon. "I tried to get Mr. Farris to notice me. He's kind and good. I thought he'd seek my hand, and my aunt and uncle would have allowed us to marry. But I couldn't hold his attention." The girl tried to smile but failed miserably. "He preferred you."

"I'll not let this happen. You won't have to marry Renford." Avalon placed her hand over Penelope's. "I promise."

"No one can help me." Penelope's voice was barely above a whisper. "You see . . ." The girl turned away and stared out the window. "I'm carrying."

A haunting silence echoed around the room.

"Penelope?" Avalon's voice cracked as she wrestled with the news. "Who's the father?"

"I cannot say," Penelope finally answered.

Desperate to find a way to help her, Avalon studied the girl. She seemed lost within her thoughts. "We should go to your aunt and uncle and discuss this."

Penelope's eyes widened. "No. Please, I beg of you. Don't say a word. They'll be so disappointed in me."

Avalon let out a sigh. "I promise. But whoever the father is he has a right to know." She slowly stood and hugged the girl. "Don't you think he'd marry you?"

"It's too late," Penelope murmured.

"Why?" Henri asked.

The girl remained silent.

"You can't keep this a secret. Everyone will suspect that the baby's father is Mr. Farris." Holding her hands in Penelope's, Avalon took a step back and stared into her eyes. "Rumors will soon swirl at the accusations you've made against my husband. I can't let that happen . . . to either of you. Your reputations will be ruined."

Penelope's hand flew to her mouth in fear.

"I'm going to speak with your aunt and uncle and tell them you weren't with my husband that night, but I won't say a word about anything else. But think about what I said. We can find a solution, I promise." Avalon turned to Henri. "Will you see Penelope to her room?"

"Of course, my lady. As soon as I get Miss Rowley

settled, I'll find you." Henri took the girl's hand and led her from the conservatory.

Penelope Rowley would be destroyed if she had to marry Lord Renford, and Devan would be destroyed if they didn't find out who was the father of Penelope's baby. The young woman's words echoed in the recesses of Avalon's heart and mind. After the girl had revealed her secrets, all the old hurt and devastation reared its ugly head. Really, what protection did any married woman have when wed to a fiend?

Plus, the revelation that Devan kissed the girl left a bitter taste in Avalon's mouth. Why wouldn't he have told her?

Just like Richard had married her for Bumble Green, perhaps Devan had married her for money. Though it was the church's money and not hers, she became an easy vehicle to attain his newfound fortune, which was twice the amount of Penelope's dowry. Larkton needed funds. Devan and the earl could have thought the whole scheme up the morning before Larkton came to Warwyk Hall. Both she and the bishop wanted to save Devan. With his brother threatening to take Thane, Avalon would have done anything to keep him. Yet she'd wanted Devan, and everyone knew it.

As her doubts twisted around her heart, she willed herself to think logically. Devan cared for her. He was her husband and a part of Thistledown—her community and her responsibility. Surely, he would explain what had happened if Avalon asked. But right now, she had to think of Penelope.

Whatever Avalon had to do to protect the young woman and what remained of her innocence, she vowed to keep Penelope safe just like Mary Bolen had done for Avalon all those years ago. A footman escorted her to the sitting room on the family floor of the manor where Mr. and Mrs. Rowley waited.

"Did you find out anything?" Mrs. Rowley asked before allowing Mr. Rowley to greet Avalon.

"I did." She turned to Mr. Rowley and nodded gracefully. "Mr. Rowley, thank you for joining us."

He bowed slightly, then waited for Avalon to take her seat before he settled next to his wife. "So, don't keep Mrs. Rowley in suspense. It's all she can think and talk about," he said with an exasperated sigh. "Frankly, I'd hoped that you were the vicar calling. He should be here to ask for her hand. That's the only way to handle the disgraceful way he's treated our niece. I for one will be glad to have the matter over with."

"Herbert," Mrs. Rowley scolded. "Lady Warwyk is aware of what's happened." She turned in Avalon's direction. "What did she tell you?"

Henri entered and sat discreetly in a chair by the door. By her posture, Avalon was certain her maid was poised to hear every word. She wouldn't miss this for anything in the world. That was one of her most endearing traits. She was completely loyal to Avalon and, in return, Avalon was completely loyal to her. However, this was Avalon's battle. Yet, it was comforting to know that Henri stood by her side no matter what.

"I have something to tell you that will no doubt be upsetting, but you must know the truth. I'm afraid that Penelope is telling a falsehood when she says that Mr. Farris seduced her."

"Are you calling our niece a liar?" Mr. Rowley's face turned the color of a ripe beet as he practically roared the question.

"Herbert, please," Mrs. Rowley begged as she twisted her handkerchief repeatedly. "Go on, my lady. I'd like to hear what you have to say. She's said little to us, but she always says the same thing. He seduced her at the vicarage, which I can't fathom how that could have happened. One of the servants would have seen her leave the house."

"The girl could have always left a door or a window open and gone to him," Mr. Rowley added with a nod of his head.

At her husband's remark, Mrs. Rowley lifted an eyebrow. Clearly, Penelope's aunt had reservations about her niece's story while Mr. Rowley wanted to defend her. Well, there was nothing else to do but tell the truth.

"Penelope told me that the seduction happened three days before my soiree."

Mr. Rowley nodded in agreement.

"There's no way that your niece could have been compromised by our vicar," Avalon said while keeping her gaze on Mr. Rowley. "You see, he was with me. We were locked in my wine cellar together all night. My staff and my son found us the next morning."

"She might have her nights confused about when it happened, but our Penelope said he seduced her." He crossed his arms across his barrel chest. "I believe her."

"Mr. Rowley, she told me twice it was three nights before the soiree. The night Mrs. McVey always has off. I asked Penelope if she was certain. My lady's maid was there too and heard her say yes."

Mr. Rowley's gaze shot to Henri, who nodded once in agreement.

"I asked her to come and tell you the truth, but she refused. She's beside herself with fright." Though Avalon didn't know everything about Penelope's story, one fact was certain. Penelope was not compromised the night she claimed. "She doesn't want to marry Lord Renford. I'm afraid she made up the story of being with our vicar to escape the marriage."

Silenced reigned in the room for a moment as the Rowleys' shock had frozen both of them in place.

Finally, Mrs. Rowley bowed her head.

"*Bloody* hell," Mr. Rowley muttered while dragging his hand down his face.

"We owe him an apology." The agony on Mrs. Rowley's face aged her by twenty years. "We owe the earl and Bishop Marlowe an apology too."

"I think everyone would appreciate that." Avalon nodded.

"I'll have a carriage readied so I can make the trip to London this afternoon. No use postponing it." Mr. Rowley's lips drew into a thin line indicating he was clearly confounded with the news. "First, I'll visit the vicar. If he'd still marry the girl, I'd make it worth his while."

Mrs. Rowley's hopeful gaze flew to his.

"I'm afraid that won't happen," Avalon said. Before she could tell them the reason why, a deep baritone she was intimately familiar with came from behind her.

"Because I married Lady Avalon Cavensham Warwyk yesterday," Devan announced.

She inhaled at his words laced with defiance and something she'd never seen or heard from him before.

Fury.

The Devil has an innate talent for interrupting the truth with details.

Devan Farris's collection of bon mots and witticisms

Chapter Twenty-one

Devan had arrived in time to hear his wife cleaning up the mess that Penelope Rowley had made for all of them. He shifted his attention to her as blood raced through his veins. The fact that Avalon had to concern herself with any of it made him see red.

Then her gaze flew to his, and that flash of intelligence, bravery, and empathy that made Avalon so unique combined into a heady mix that stole his breath. It also had the additional benefit of deflating his anger like a popped balloon, and he released his fisted hands as he relaxed his shoulders.

Dear God in heaven, she was a sorceress capable of turning him into a fool who would do her bidding just for a glance his way. She stood and smiled as if he were the only man in the world, and his heart pounded against his ribs trying to reach her.

His Warlock had come to defend him, and he wasn't surprised in the least. The only thing that amazed him was that she'd arrived so quickly. After their bout of lovemaking last night, she should still be asleep.

He'd have to try harder tonight. Just the thought made him grin slightly. There was no denying, he could watch her for days and never tire of her.

"Come in, Vicar," Mr. Rowley called as he stood in greeting. His wife followed suit.

Devan claimed the seat next to Avalon. He moved close enough that they were hip to hip. In response, she stirred in her seat as if uncomfortable.

Perhaps she was overcome just as he was.

He'd never seen her this way, and it enchanted him that his touch could have such an effect on her. There was no denying they were attracted to one another, but to see her react the same way as he did when she touched him made Devan want to crow like the only rooster in the hen yard.

But then she did the unthinkable. She moved slightly away from him, creating distance. Though the breech was a mere inch, it felt like a mile. Propriety's sake demanded it, and he forced himself to relax. "Mr. Rowley, I heard enough of what my *wife* said to deduce that you understand what happened?"

The man nodded once. "Both Mrs. Rowley and I owe you an apology. I went off like a half-cocked pistol." He took a deep breath and exhaled. "Since we weren't blessed with children, our experience is somewhat lacking with how to deal with little Penelope."

Devan lifted one brow in challenge. "Little Penelope" was a misnomer if he'd ever heard one. But the couple before him were clearly distressed over their own actions along with their niece's. It was best to try to put the matter behind all of them.

Devan slowly reached for Avalon's hand. Whether it was all proper, he didn't care. He needed to touch her and hoped she'd grant him this one boon.

"Respectfully, Mr. and Mrs. Rowley, your niece isn't little anymore and her actions over the last several days have caused a lot of heartache for many people I deeply care about," Avalon answered as she squeezed his hand.

Mrs. Rowley sniffed, then wiped her nose. "Mr. Farris, can you find it in your heart to forgive her?"

He stole a glance at Avalon, who nodded discreetly.

"Of course, understanding and forgiveness are requisites for my profession." Devan turned to Avalon. "I think it perhaps for the best if we start for home."

"In a moment." She turned to the Rowleys. "Penelope is desperate not to marry Lord Renford. She's frightened. Based upon what I heard, I'm terrified of him myself, and I've never met the man. We should find someone for her to marry and quickly."

"Pardon me?" Devan stilled in his seat. He'd heard all the sordid and vile rumors that were glued to Harrison Renford. The man was pure evil.

"She made up the story that you . . . compromised her to avoid marrying Lord Renford." Avalon lowered her voice. "She's been betrothed to him since she was a little girl."

Devan turned to the Rowleys. "Can't you write a letter to the man and break the engagement? No one of good breeding will have a thing to do with him."

"I wish we could." Mr. Rowley sighed. "But Renford has given a lot of money to Penelope's parents. He's been fixated on my niece since she was ten."

Mrs. Rowley sobbed, the soulful sound heart-wrenching.

Avalon jerked her hand to her stomach. The sight angered Devan even further. He'd not see her even more distraught at such news.

"Mr. Farris, perhaps you and I could speak about this later?" Mr. Rowley asked as he comforted Mrs. Rowley. The poor woman buried her head against her husband's chest, desperate for comfort.

"Of course. Please send word when you'd like to meet." Devan helped Avalon to stand with him, and the Rowleys joined them.

"Vicar?" The softly spoken word didn't hide the hesitancy in the older woman's teary voice.

He turned his full attention to her while pasting on his usual tranquil smile that a vicar had to carry in his arsenal to comfort his flock. "How can I offer assistance, Mrs. Rowley?"

"Would you consider counseling Penelope?" she asked.

Avalon stiffened beside him. Though no one saw a thing, he felt her withdraw, and that invisible shield she'd don when she felt threatened appeared out of nowhere. Her face froze like a portrait in a stuffy hall at Larkton's house.

"No, Mrs. Rowley. I don't think that would be wise," he answered, hoping not to distress her any further.

"Of course, we understand," Mr. Rowley said.

"However, I can see if a curate or another vicar close by would speak with her."

"Oh Vicar, that would be so kind of you." Mrs. Rowley's soulful brown eyes betrayed her anguish. "We want to help her and do right by her. We're her last chance."

"Meaning?" Devan asked.

"Penelope didn't do well in Italy. We offered to sponsor her for a Season, and her parents accepted. But now, Lord Renford is pressing that they marry before . . ." Mrs. Rowley's voice caught.

"Spring." Mr. Rowley finished her sentence, then put his arm around his wife in a show of affection. "My wife, Louisa, is beside herself."

"I'm sorry if I caused you any additional distress," Avalon said with as much tact as possible. "I thought you needed to know the truth. However, we must find a solution before her reputation is ruined beyond repair. I promised Penelope."

"Of course," Mr. Rowley said solemnly. "I best go see the earl and the bishop before it gets too late. Maybe they'll have some suggestions how to handle this scandal."

"We'll be on our way, then. Anything I can do to lend assistance, please ask." Devan held out his arm, and at first, Avalon hesitated before she wrapped hers around his. Henri followed them to the entry, where Devan helped Avalon don her cloak before he put on his greatcoat.

The contact embodied the myriad of enjoyments about married life—helping his wife with such simple things. It would always give him a chance to touch her.

As she buttoned her cloak, he placed his hands on her shoulders then leaned close to her ear. "What would my wife like to do?" he murmured. "Take the carriage or walk?"

"Walk and work off some of this restlessness."

"Your wish is my command." He brushed his lips against the tender lobe of her ear. "I may have an idea or two of how we could tame our urges."

"Hush," she whispered. "I didn't say urges."

"But I did." The words evoked the response he was looking for.

She whipped her head around and narrowed her eyes. "Behave."

"I never learned how," he answered.

Without another word, she turned to Henri. "Would you mind taking the carriage back to Warwyk Hall? Mr. Farris and I have decided to walk."

Henri nodded.

Soon they were walking back to the Warwyk estate. Without saying a word, Devan took Avalon's hand in his and entwined their fingers together. Though there were two layers of leather that separated their skin, he could feel the warmth of her hands in his. "What made you decide to come to the Rowley home today?"

She slowed her gait.

When her gaze caught his, he inhaled deeply at the brilliance in her green eyes. She was riled. There was no other way to describe her.

"This morning I was abed while you went to see Mr. Satterly. After our wedding night, without a whimper or complaint, you went to see about a parishioner who was obviously troubled. You were giving and kind."

Something happened to her at the Rowley house that bothered her. He could tell by the set of her mouth.

"You couldn't defend yourself while at the Satterlys'. I didn't want Penelope to spread rumors, and I didn't want this situation to fester and end up dividing the community." She stopped and tilted her head up to him. "I saw Penelope first to give her the chance to tell the truth. The girl stayed steadfast with her story until I told her that I would speak with her aunt and uncle. Then she confessed all."

"That was a very kind thing to do for her, Avalon."

"She's facing the same type of marriage I had. Perhaps worse." Her gaze locked with his. "I can't let that happen to her."

"Avalon," he coaxed. "You're not responsible for her lies or her marriage."

"Yes, I am." She took a deep breath, then turned her attention to a barren field with deep frozen ruts plowed from the last harvest. For a while she studied it almost as if lost in thought.

Gradually, she pivoted and faced him. A small but sad smile tugged at her lips and the overwhelming desire to kiss the forlornness away and make her laugh rooted deep in his belly.

Avalon held her hand as if offering him the field. "Some people may see a harvested field where its bounty has been picked, then left to wither and wane in the cold. Others might see a field gathering strength, so it can blossom into a fertile land again. It'll offer huge rewards with spectacular yields for those who tenderly care for it."

"What do you see?"

"I'm not certain," she said.

"Meaning?" He took a step nearer. The distance between them was too great for his tastes.

"It represents a marriage in many ways, but I'm not certain which way," she said matter-of-factly.

"You think ours is an empty barren field?"

"Honestly, I don't know," she answered.

He slowly took her arms and brought her close. "I see everything in that field. I see our future. I see happiness and babies."

"You mean our own children?" she asked. Her voice had dropped an octave, and everything within him vibrated at the resonance of her alto tone.

"Hmm, yes." Desire had darkened his own voice. "We'll have dark-haired girls with green eyes like their mother. We'll have boys who look like you, too. I see marriages in our future for Sophia and Thane. I see grandchildren."

Another small smile graced her lips.

"There will be some heartache as we all must face life's trials and tribulations that are designed to test our mettle, but they'll make us stronger. And I'll be right beside you as we plow that field and create our life together. I see holidays and birthdays and celebrations. I see you and me with gray hair. I see us as always together. Forever."

"That's beautiful," she whispered.

"Like you." Unable to keep from touching Avalon, he brushed his lips across the top of her forehead. I'll do whatever is necessary to make you happy." His mouth found hers. He kissed her once, then looked deep into her green eyes that reminded him of spring fields. She reminded him of all the possibilities for a blessed and full life ahead of them.

He took her in another kiss, one filled with all the passion and desire and respect that he had for her. It came from someplace deep inside, and he was determined that she felt it as much as he did.

With wide eyes, she broke the kiss. Her chest heaved as she tried to catch her breath.

"I feel the same breathlessness as you, Avalon. That's what you do to me. I want to kiss again. I want to make love to you right now. Right here. But you decide when and where. Whatever you want."

She turned and looked at the field with longing. Slowly, she turned back to him. "Right now, I want to ask you a question."

He nodded once.

"I want you to tell me the truth."

"Of course, I will always tell you the truth."

"I hope so." She took a deep breath as if gathering courage, and her eyes suddenly lost their brilliant fire. "Did you and Penelope Rowley kiss?"

Everything came to a sudden halt. The wind died. The lingering fallen leaves stopped rustling. Even his heart seemed to stop, suspended in his chest. Everything waited for him to respond to his wife's question. Even Avalon stood frozen, waiting for his answer.

Without taking his eyes off her, Devan swallowed. Though he had little experience with women, he knew his wife. Whatever Penelope had said to Avalon filled

her with sadness and uncertainty and preyed upon her
great fear that he, her husband, would betray her with
another woman.

"I won't lie to you." Though her face remained frozen, the slight slump of her shoulders revealed that
thread that they'd woven together last night had been
pulled taut. His next words would hurt her more, but he
had no choice but to answer truthfully. "Penelope found
me walking to the vicarage. She orchestrated a stumble
knocking us both to the ground. That's when she did it.
Yes, she kissed me, but I've only ever lain with you."

The wind gusted as if stirred to anger, yet Avalon remained still. Only the blinking of her eyes registered
that she'd heard him.

"Was this before or after our night in the cellar?"
The calmness in her voice warned of a grave danger that
would beset both of them if he didn't handle this carefully.

Of all the times in his life when he wished he had
more experience with women, it was now.

But then, wasn't that the cause of his problem? He
had allowed everyone to assume that he was a favorite
of the ladies and the beneficiary of all their affections
when it was so far from the truth.

"After," he said.

"I see." She narrowed her eyes and her brow crinkled into neat rows like the furrowed field before them.
"Why didn't you tell me?"

"I didn't see that it mattered," he answered. Unable to
determine her mood, Devan held out his arm in hopes
that she'd touch him, reassure him that she understood
what had happened.

She stood still, ignoring his arm. "Did you ever meet
Penelope before you moved to Thistledown?"

"No. Why do you ask?"

"Just curious." She ducked her head and studied the ground as she started down the path, leaving Devan behind to ponder his next words.

"Avalon." He increased his pace until he was beside her. Carefully, he tugged her to a stop. "You can't possibly think that I wanted to kiss her."

"I don't know what to think." She shook her head as if awakening from a dream.

"But you saw my anger when I discovered what she'd done."

"I did," she agreed. "Both of us were pushed into this marriage. I wonder if either of us understood the ramifications."

The lack of emotion in her voice made his blood turn to ice. "What are you saying?"

She started to walk again, and he followed.

"Maybe if we'd let your anger cool and I had taken time to think of your brother's ultimatum, we would have made a different choice. Perhaps you'd have married Penelope."

"This conversation is bordering on the ludicrous. I wanted to marry you." He blew out his breath hoping it would tamp down the anger that had ignited like a wildfire. "What did Penelope Rowley say to you?"

"She made some observations about me, that's all." She huffed a breath, and a steady stream of silver mist rent the air. "Nothing I hadn't heard before," she murmured as she hunkered down in her cloak.

A three-story stone building known as the Warwyk Hunters Lodge lay several hundred feet to the left of the path. By God, he'd find out right now what had her unnerved. At the Rowleys' she'd seemed fine, even happy to see him. "Come. Let's finish this conversation in the lodge. It'll still be chilly, but at least we'll be out of the wind."

This time when he held out his hand, she reluctantly took it. Immediately he wrapped his other hand over hers, hoping that small touch would help soothe whatever had worried her.

Without another word shared, they crossed the distance, and Devan opened the door. Avalon opened a door off the entry. Inside the massive sitting room, a fireplace the length of the entire north wall took center stage. What Devan wouldn't give to have a roaring fire lit at this moment to chase Avalon's chill away. She dropped his arm and crossed the distance to the fireplace. She knelt, then picked up a log to arrange a fire.

"I'll make the fire," he said as he knelt beside her. That's when he saw a lone tear skating down her cheek.

She turned from him, then stood.

"Avalon?" He stood behind her. When she didn't acknowledge him, he gently placed his hand on her shoulder and squeezed.

She slowly turned, but kept her head bent.

"Sweetheart? What's happened?"

At the sound of the endearment, she sobbed. He pulled her to him and she burrowed into his chest as if seeking sanctuary. He held her in his arms and rocked her, offering comfort. After several minutes, she turned to him. Her tears were gone, but the misery in her eyes had increased tenfold.

He went to caress her cheeks with his thumb, then cursed under his breath. He still had his gloves on. With haste and little grace, he ripped the offending pieces of leather from his hands. He had no idea where they landed, and he didn't care. The only thing that concerned him in this moment was his wife. He cupped her cheeks in his hands.

"Tell me what has upset you."

"Perhaps we should speak of it later," she murmured.

"I disagree. I've never seen you this upset before. Now I didn't hide from you when you asked me a direct question. Do the same for me."

"Penelope Rowley called me a piece of petrified wood. She said I'd be cold and offer little comfort in your bed." She feigned a chuckle, then held his gaze.

"Listen to me, sweetheart. After last night, you proved that theory false. I was certainly burning for you. How I wanted you."

Avalon didn't react.

"She's nothing more than a foolish girl."

"I was once a foolish girl, and my first husband said I was a piece of ice in bed," she whispered.

"He was a fool." Devan pulled her close.

"When Penelope described her betrothed as a horrid man who beats, humiliates, and perhaps even murders women, it brought forth all those memories of my parents forcing me." She pulled away an inch to look at his face. *"They forced me to marry a man who didn't want me.* He never did. It made me wonder if I'd forced you . . . why did you marry me?"

He held her face in his hands. The uncertainty in her voice tore a piece of his heart away. Unable to resist, he took her in a plundering kiss designed to show her that she was wild, passionate, and there was no one else in the world he wanted to be with except her.

When she moaned low against his lips, he pressed deeper, harder, and longer. With his hands on her darling derrière, he pulled her closer. His erection pulsed with each hectic heartbeat as he continued to worship her mouth. She nestled closer.

He whispered her name as he moved her cloak to reach her warm body. "Every inch of me burns for you. Only you. From the night in the wine cellar, you have been a part of me. When I see you, I see me. You, darling wife, are entwined in every part of me." He brought her hand to his chest, where his heart pounded for her. "Do you feel that?"

She nodded.

"Every beat is yours."

Her eyes filled with tears and an enchanting grin tugged at her lips.

"Show me then." She brought his hand to her leg and together they pushed her gown and petticoats to her waist.

The world seemed to wobble when her hand touched him to unbutton his falls. He almost came on the spot. This would not be a gentle or long coupling. Theirs would be a joining that would burn them together. He hissed when she released his cock into the cold air. With a jerking, frantic grasp, she brought his erection to her entrance.

With both hands, he lifted her in the air.

She hugged both legs around his hips. "Do it."

He turned slightly, then took a step so her back rested against the wall, then entered her.

"Move, please." Whether it was a command or a plea, he couldn't tell.

She didn't have to say it again. He groaned in pleasure as he withdrew, then thrust inside her again. She tightened around his cock. It was the most exquisite torture, and he wanted more—needed more—needed her. He growled her name as he withdrew, then entered her again. Holding her against the wall, he protected her head with his hand cupped around her hair.

"Touch yourself," he murmured. "I won't last long."

She took his mouth with hers. He felt her hand move where their bodies were joined. The rhythmic movement of her fingers teased him. He imagined her doing that very same thing in their bed as he watched. God, the things this woman could do to him. She made him lose all control.

With a deep breath, he forced himself to wait until she was ready for more. He kissed the exposed skin of her neck, then nipped it. Her breath rushed past him, accelerating. This was the way she'd been last night— wild, demanding, and ready to explode from the fire of their joining.

Stroke for stroke, she matched his movements, tightening her sex around his member as she buried her face in his neck.

Like a beast taking his mate, Devan pounded her flesh until his seed flooded her, marking her as his.

They held each other until his heartbeat slowed, and her breathing calmed. When his cock slipped out of her body, she untangled her legs and stood.

He kept her in his embrace and kissed her again. From his coat pocket, he retrieved his well-worn but clean handkerchief. He dropped to his knees in front of her and lifted his head to gaze into her eyes. Their coupling had brought a beautiful blush to her cheeks, and her eyes sparkled.

With infinite care, he cleaned her, then kissed both thighs in a show of affection, regard, and deep fidelity. After he lowered her skirts and carefully straightened them, he returned his gaze to her. "You are a passionate, giving woman. Don't ever doubt my words. I'm honored to call you my wife."

She didn't answer.

"Do you believe me?"

Instead, with a shaky hand she reached toward him and tangled her fingers in his hair. With the gentlest of touches, she combed his straight locks.

Neither of them moved. Though his legs felt as though they'd frozen to the floor, he'd not move while she kept stroking—touching him. The tenderness in her regard made him want to pledge his undying devotion for all his days to her. Simply put, she undid him into a thousand pieces he'd never known existed, and each one was hers.

They stayed in their respective positions until she shivered slightly.

"Let's go home," he whispered as he stood. He tangled their fingers together and led her from the lodge.

They walked back to Warwyk Hall, not breaking contact. The skies above them grew ominous, portending storms, but to the west, the sun refused to give up its glory.

Avalon kept her silence, but every now and then she would glance his way and smile slightly. His heart tripped in his chest at such a glorious sight.

Containing deer meat, the delicacy is called umble pie. If there's a bit of crow in it, it becomes humble pie.

source unknown

Chapter Twenty-two

While Devan had excused himself to meet a church member at the vicarage, Avalon had sought refuge to pace in her old bedroom. She'd always hated the marchioness suites. With its beautiful ivory walls and exquisite floral embroidery, the room had always reminded her that she'd been an imposter as Richard's wife. For the full two years that they were married, he'd never returned to Warwyk Hall while she was here. He'd always preferred London, where his true "wife" lived.

That was what he'd called Mary Bolen. Indeed, Avalon did feel like a fraud once she found out the truth of her husband's affections for Mary. What would Richard have thought if he'd known that she and Mary had become allies after his death? Probably shock and an overwhelming urge to keep Avalon and her taint as far away as possible from the family he loved.

Though she didn't love Richard, knowing this had turned Avalon's heart to ice. A well-constructed barrier that she'd designed to keep such heartache from breeching her ever again. At least she'd thought it well-constructed until the vicar had entered her life like a hurricane tearing down every obstacle in its path.

Avalon stopped her pacing as her attention drew to

the ornate and ostentatious bed. She'd never lain with a man there. Not with Richard.

Not with Devan either.

When she thought of him, a heat rushed through her. When he'd joined his body with hers, for the first time in her entire life, she felt whole. The emptiness in her life cast aside.

Devan was a man she'd never tire of.

He called her a warlock, but the truth was he'd woven a spell around her that tied her into knots. She now knew how it felt to climb a perilous mountain where one false step could lead to utter destruction. She'd been through heartache before and had promised herself she'd not fall again.

If she took a wrong step with Devan, she wondered if she could survive the ultimate fall, because there was one big difference between her two husbands.

She wasn't just falling in love with Devan. She loved him.

Her traitorous heart had slipped through all the protective barriers she'd created and given itself freely to him.

Later that night at dinner, Avalon stayed unusually reserved. It was apparent to all that she was lost in her thoughts. Devan didn't ask, but he kept a watchful eye. Even his own musings had turned dark. He had the irrational fear he'd turn around and she'd disappear like a puff of smoke.

It was only natural that he be worried about her, but Avalon was by far the strongest woman he'd ever met in his life. She possessed an innate sense of right and wrong and followed her heart. No challenge was too big for her. One just had to look at what she'd accomplished with her charities to see her inner strength. The fact that she was raising her son and sister at the same time was simply awe-inspiring. If there was ever a woman who was a flawless blend of strength and radiance, it was his wife.

Or at least, that was his opinion. He chuckled slightly to himself. No doubt, his friends would argue that their wives were perfect.

But Devan had the vantage. He'd married a witch, a very powerful one.

After dinner, he bathed in front of the fire in the exquisite formal bedroom Avalon and he would share from now on. It was right down the hall from her old bedroom. Suddenly, the bedroom door opened, and she stood before him in her dressing gown.

A smile broke across his face. Slow and measured so he'd not spill water from the slipper tub, he stood. Water sluiced in tiny rivulets down his torso. He reached for the linen toweling and began to dry himself. Not surprising, his member thickened at the sight of her. "Are you ready for bed?"

She stared at his body, then slowly raised her gaze to his. "No."

Though he'd never been one to believe in premonitions, something stirred in his wife's eyes. A decision or an ultimatum. Perhaps he was overthinking why she was there. A little humor might lighten the mood, so he waved a hand down his body. "You have my undivided attention."

She didn't spare a glance at his hand. Instead, she visibly swallowed, betraying her unease, which could have been cut with a knife. "I know you deny you were rushed into marriage, but the truth is you were." Her chest rose and fell in agitation. "And so was I. I've not been able to think of anything else since you told me you kissed Penelope."

"She kissed me," he argued.

"Yes, you told me that." She fiddled with the tie of her dressing gown while her gaze latched to his. "I find that I'm in an awkward position and have been unable to reconcile my thoughts. You see, I'm the type of person who needs the truth, and if that makes me unsophisticated and naïve, so be it."

"I'd never think that. If anyone, that describes me."

"Stop, I beg of you." It became apparent to both of them that she was hellishly bent on finishing her thoughts.

He finished drying, then drew on the banyan, not bothering to button it. In five strides he crossed the great room to stand beside her.

She held up her hand as if commanding him to halt. "You said you wouldn't lie to me, but I've discovered something since you've moved to Thistledown. You've omitted the truth when it's convenient for you." There was little emotion in her soft voice.

"Meaning?"

The heavy sound of her sigh landed on his shoulders. Immediately, his hope to make love to his wife tonight sank.

"I don't . . . know if you're sincere or not. Everyone believes you to be a man of great experience with life and women, but you tell me differently when you're about to bed me."

"You doubt that I was a virgin?" He didn't hide the incredulity in his voice. He was skating on thin ice and could hear it cracking beneath him.

"How do I know?" The hesitation in her voice was undeniable. "I can't. You did things to me that I've never had experience with before. A virgin wouldn't know those things, would he?"

"I made up all those tales of rakish conquests to fit in

with my friends. I was an outsider trying to find a place in the world." He ran his fingers through his hair, praying he was saying the right things to relieve her worry. "It kept Gavin from escorting me to any more brothels. You can appreciate that, can't you?"

"Indeed, I can. Being an outsider describes my life in so many ways." She sighed silently. "Did you tell anyone else your secret?"

"Not until recently. I spoke of it with Will and Paul after our night in the cellar," he answered.

She narrowed her eyes. "Why didn't you tell me?"

"I didn't have time." He exhaled his frustration. Whether it was for her questions or his bumbling reluctance, he couldn't guess. "I was going to tell you when you first asked me to marry you. Then Mrs. McVey came in and you were hurrying away."

"Come now. You couldn't walk me out of the vicarage and tell me?" The hint of challenge in her voice was unmistakable.

"It's not something that I wanted to tell you out in the open when anyone could have walked by and interrupted us." He shook his head, desperate to come up with a way to make her believe him.

"Penelope told me that she didn't share with anyone that you had ruined her until later." Her stare pierced him in two. "But you and I know that was a lie."

"*Avalon.* Don't compare me to her." His sharp voice revealed his frustration.

The proverbial ice cracked open and he felt the cold water slowly seep into his veins. What had he done? All his maneuverings to appease his brother and fit in with his friends as a man of experience while keeping himself chaste were a fool's errand. A deep sense of foreboding joined the cold in his veins. He should have told Avalon immediately before they married. She had a right to know everything. Particularly after she'd shared her experience with her first husband, Devan should have been astute enough to see that she needed to know more about him. For God's sake, as a vicar, it was expected he'd not hide behind a false rumor. Desperate for warmth, he walked to the lit fire and closed his eyes.

"I told you where I learned how to do those things. I'll not deny that I listened when others talked about their experience with women. I wanted to come to my wife pure and ready to give her, meaning *you*, pleasure. Are you going to condemn me for that?" He forced himself to calm down.

"Again, how would I know?" A hint of vulnerability shaded the determination in her voice.

His heart lurched in response. Never did he mean to cause her doubt.

She took a step closer. "I didn't have much choice or time to think through all of this. Neither did you. Your brother threatened me with taking Thane away if I didn't agree to marry you."

"Sit with me." The plea in his voice was unmistakable as he pointed to a miniature settee next to the slipper tub. He'd beg on his hands and knees if it would convince her to come nearer. "It's difficult to discuss such matters with you so far away." He lowered himself to the bench, then patted the seat next to him.

Avalon didn't sit next to him as he'd asked. Like an animal who'd been beaten and was now shy, she came closer, but kept five feet separating them. It was as if she was frightened he might bite.

God, what had he done?

For the first time in his life, he had a caring, beautiful woman, *his wife*, to share his life with, and she didn't trust him.

"I'd always thought I'd have the opportunity to tell

my wife about my virginity before the ceremony. But everything happened so quickly. I'm sorry." He stood and closed the distance between them. When she didn't retreat, he wanted to rejoice aloud. "You can't actually believe that I have feelings for Penelope Rowley, do you?"

"Truthfully, I don't think so."

"Avalon," he murmured. "It was my foolish pride to hide my inexperience and pretend I was someone I'm not. After today and last night, how could you think otherwise?"

She held up her hand to silence him. "Someone once told me that pride was a dangerous trait."

Her gaze felt like a hot razer cutting through him. He'd said those words to her.

"Devan?" She wrapped her arms around her waist as if protecting herself.

"What is it, sweetheart?" he murmured.

She visibly swallowed, then exhaled as if debating what to say. "Penelope is carrying a child."

"Dear God." He ran his fingers through his wet hair. Suddenly, Avalon's hesitation made sense. "You don't think I'm the father, do you?"

She didn't move an inch but continued to stare at him.

"Avalon, talk to me," he begged. The silence between them thickened. Even the fire seemed to lose some of its fierceness.

Finally, after a moment, she broke the silence. "No. I'm trying to make sense of it all. I have to help her. She wouldn't survive such a marriage to that monster." Her eyes widened in fear. "She's part of my . . . I meant to say our community."

"There's only one solution I see," Devan calmly said. "We should leave Penelope's problems to the Rowleys. I'll meet with Mr. Rowley as promised."

"Devan." Her voice cracked in disbelief. "You're the village vicar, and I'm their patroness. I want to help her. She's a family friend and a member of *our* community."

"I'll not see her hurt you or cause a divide between us," he argued. It was bad enough that he had to witness her late husband haunting her, but Devan vowed to protect her from future pain.

She tilted her chin upward. "I remember your first sermon. Wasn't it turn the other cheek?"

"Yes," he said slowly. "But if you remember, dear wife, I also said that one had to make wise choices when you venture into the valley of evil." He lifted one brow. "Did you miss that part?"

"No. I heard it. But it's the 'valley of death,'" she corrected. "You'll fear no evil."

"Exactly. I will fear no evil," he countered. "But I also know when to stay away."

She bit her lip as if debating her next words. When she glanced his way, she'd grown pale. "Did you marry me just for the money?"

"How could you ask that?" he asked incredulously. "Do you not understand what I feel to be married to you?"

"I'm sorry." She clenched one hand in a fist, and the other she held close to her heart as if protecting it. "I have no experience with any of this except for Richard's and my parents' machinations."

"What secrets they kept from you were hurtful, not to mention despicable. But they're not me." He lowered his voice. "Come. You can't tell how much I wanted you last night and today?" Everything he believed he had with Avalon slipped away like sand through his fingers. "I'll want more tomorrow."

They stood facing each other—chest to chest and eye to eye—neither moving. The eerie quiet between them suddenly broke when the logs collapsed in the fireplace. Sparks lit the room in a subtle glow before dying. He prayed it wasn't a harbinger of what would come of their marriage.

He took her hand and brought it to his lips, where he pressed a kiss. Her warmth and scent wove around him like tentacles securing him to her. The simple truth? He never wanted to escape. In her arms, he'd found everything he'd ever wanted.

A wife, a family, a place to belong.

"Do you believe me when I say you're amazing and passionate, and that I'm a lucky man?" He pressed his lips against her forehead, then rested their entwined hands against the middle of his chest. "Do you have an answer for me, Lady Warlock?"

"I'm trying to believe," she whispered. The words floated straight to his heart.

"I'll just have to work harder to convince you." With an audible sigh, he pulled her closer, if that was possible. "Come to bed and let me show you."

The moment she pulled away, his heart tripped in his chest. He adored her softness, her thorns, her doubts, and her convictions. He loved her devotion to family and community.

He loved *her*.

"Sweetheart, I could no more betray you than I could betray myself or God."

With that sterling truth, an unbearable aching took hold. Though he loved her, she didn't believe him true. Indeed, tomorrow, he'd work twice as hard to convince her she ruled his world.

His wife didn't need any witchcraft to accomplish such a fact. All she had to do was be herself.

"I'm sorry if I've impugned your honor. I don't mean to." She crossed the room, then reached for the handle of the door. "But I find great comfort from this one truth. My failings, these wounds I carry don't hurt you. Only me."

"That's where you're wrong. Everything that hurts you, hurts me too. You're my wife, the greatest gift I've ever received."

If there was one thing he desired in his shallow life, he wished he'd have told her that she made him want to be a better person. By allowing misconceptions and telling tales of his supposed debauched life, he'd hurt her and his chances to make her see how much he valued her. He vowed then and there that all of his days would be devoted to showing her how wonderful and unique she was.

"If you desire to help Penelope, then I'll be by your side. Anything that concerns you, concerns me. That's the way I'll always feel." He swallowed the lump in his throat. "I apologize with my entire being if I've caused you pain or doubt."

She nodded once, then slipped out the door.

He closed his eyes and whispered a short prayer for help.

If he lost her, then he'd lose everything of value.

For without her, he had no heart.

I am an enthusiast in my notions of fidelity and fondness.
Alexander Hamilton in a letter to John Laurens
describing the attributes of a perfect wife.

No doubt, Mr. Hamilton was referring to his favorite lapdog.
Lady Warwyk

Chapter Twenty-three

For hours, she'd stared into the salon's fire after tucking Thane's throw around her. The solitude had allowed all those tumultuous thoughts to consume her. Every time she'd thought of Devan, an undeniable truth refused to leave her alone. Devan was so much more than she could imagine. She'd shared her innermost feelings with him, and he'd not condemned her or belittled her. If she'd done the same with Richard, he'd have laughed in her face. Perhaps he would have done it as a defensive gesture, but he would have mocked her until she grew silent or most likely, left the room.

Yet Devan had listened and asked questions until he understood everything she had expressed. Though he hurt the same as she did from their conversation, the strength of his words and wishes for them to build a happy life together flooded her with warmth. Finally, she allowed herself to fall asleep.

Much later, Avalon woke to a fire still blazing in the hearth. She'd come to a decision. It was time to let go of the past and embrace her future with her husband. She would do everything in her power to give him the life he wanted with her. Because she wanted that and so much more with him.

She stretched her hands over her head, then swung her feet to the ground, stubbing her toes against a mound of bricks. The bricks turned out to be her husband, who slept beside her on the floor.

"Devan?" Nothing but a mumble greeted her. "What are you doing down there? How can you sleep on the floor?"

With a groan, he opened his eyes and stared at her. With a grimace, he propped himself up on his elbows. His skin glowed from the light of the fire, which outlined the slight stubble of his evening beard. When he smiled, the dimples that kissed his cheeks appeared. Immediately, her breath caught. His green eyes seemed to shimmer with mirth. In answer, her heart thudded in her chest at the sight. It had to be her imagination, but the man grew more handsome every day.

"I wouldn't call it sleep. I'd say the floor and I made our acquaintance. I'd get settled, then it would squeak. Then, I'd grumble, and it would squeak again." He shrugged his shoulders, then leaned closer, propping one arm on a bent knee. "It was quite a lively conversation. I'm surprised I didn't wake you up."

She couldn't help but laugh at his charming tale. "Why would you sleep there?"

Devan leaned closer as he took her hand and lifted it to his mouth. "Because wherever my wife sleeps, that's where I sleep."

His eyes never left hers as he pressed his lips against her skin. Her breath caught. For in that moment, she realized she'd married the man of her dreams. Though they'd argued, he didn't want to be away from her. "I feel the same way. Thank you for staying with me."

"You're welcome." He released her hand. "But might

I make a suggestion? Can we finish the night in our bed?"

"That's the least I could do to show my appreciation of your gallantry." She grinned.

He stood slowly, then entwined their fingers together. Without hesitating, Avalon led him up the stairs to the state bedroom and entered. Whatever happened in the room would define her and Devan's marriage for the rest of her days.

"In for a penny, in for a pound," she whispered under her breath.

"If I may have a say, then let's go for the pound," he answered. He kicked the door closed as he pulled her into his arms for a kiss.

Though his words teased, the kiss was gentle and considerate. Before things progressed further, she pulled away and fiddled with the lapel of his banyan. "Tonight, I made some decisions. My marriage to Richard was my parents' choice, but my marriage to you is mine. I'm going to do everything in my power to build a happy life and marriage for us."

He dipped his head so their gazes met. "Good. You deserve all the happiness life can bring you."

"I do. And so does my husband." Avalon smiled. "I want to learn to trust," she said softly.

"That's an excellent start." He took her hand to keep her from playing with the buttons of his coat, then held it to the middle of his chest. His eyes searched hers. "When you look at me, I want you to know that I only see you. I love you," he murmured.

Blood rushed through her, causing a faint lighted-headedness much like riding a horse over an unfamiliar jump. All her life, she'd wanted to hear those words. She took a deep breath, hoping to hold on to this moment forever.

Devan's gaze never faltered as he brushed her hair from her eyes. "I love you," he repeated as if reassuring her.

Their bodies nestled against one another in a perfect fit. Like a starving person, she needed Devan. He was as vital to her well-being as air and water. For the first time in her life she felt tied to a man. She belonged to him, and he belonged to her. After so many lonely years, she'd not waste another night. "I love you," she answered. "Let's go to bed."

Hours later, chest to chest, her heart pounded against his as if sharing all her secrets. This time, their lovemaking was as sweet and unhurried as a wandering bee discovering the new spring blossoms. The way they'd pleasured one another reminded her of something precious and sacred that only they could share together.

He swept a disobedient curl from her forehead, then pressed his lips in that same spot. "That curl reminds me of you. Willful. Rebellious. Defiant."

"Be careful," she whispered against his shoulder, then pressed her lips to his. "Such sweet nothings will go to my head." She snuggled closer in his arms, then pressed a kiss in the middle of his chest where his heart resided. She traced a line down the middle of his torso, concentrating on the way his muscles contracted at her touch.

"Who do you think Thane favors?" He swept that belligerent curl behind her ear again, then cupped her cheek.

She turned her attention from his chest to him. "Why do you ask?"

"I think Thane looks like a Cavensham." He bent his arm, resting on his elbow, then propped his head on his hand. "We probably need to think about how to tell Thane he has a brother."

The words trailed to silence when she placed her fingers against his lip. "Please, let's not talk about that."

Devan's knowing gaze studied her for a moment. "Are you going to tell him how Annie, Jasmine, Flora, and the others that came before them came to live here? How Mary Bolen had no one to turn to except you when they needed help, and that you didn't hesitate?"

"He knows. Don't make me out to be a patron saint." Avalon stiffened slightly in his arms. "Taking them in was as much a benefit for me as it was for them. It gave me purpose."

"How so?" he whispered as he trailed the back of his finger down her cheek.

"They had to sell their bodies, and my parents sold me." She broke away from his embrace and settled on her back. Staring at nothing, she continued, "Of course, they faced unspeakable horrors that I could never imagine. Outside of disease, injury, did you know the establishment that Flora and Jasmine worked at was the cruelest to the women? The owner sold their virginity. They offered those women drugged out of their minds, like prized heifers at auction," Avalon said softly. "I wanted to help them have a different life."

Devan clasped her hand. "The Duke of Langham has been trying to close such entertainment down for years without any luck. There are members of the House of Lords who like to imbibe in such sickening entertainment. With any luck, the duke will succeed soon and shut those establishments down. Thane will one day be in the House of Lords. Once he's ready to learn the truth, he could be another voice against such violence."

"Thane is not ready to hear of such horrors now, but you're right, I suppose." She shrugged a shoulder. "Any way I can help women escape such pain, including

Penelope, then it would mean that I had worth to someone."

She could feel Devan's warm gaze studying her. After a moment, he leaned and brushed his lips against hers. "You've always been important to me. But now, I realize how blessed I am with riches beyond comprehension."

It was her turn to study him. She lay on her side and tucked a hand in between her head and her pillow.

"Never doubt your greatness, Avalon Farris." He scooted close until they could stare into each other's eyes. "Your generosity and ability to love are endless. I'm thankful every single day that God put me in your path."

"Perhaps you should thank Penelope Rowley," she whispered. "She's the one that caused all this. Without her, I wouldn't be wedded to a man whose patience and virtue are tremendously impressive. I'm thankful you said yes to marrying me."

"My darling wife, I've said it before and I'll say it again. You've bewitched me completely." He tugged her close. "Let's save our discussion of Penelope until the morning. I've a meeting at the vicarage after Thane's lessons. Afterward, will you meet me for tea?"

Her sleepy reply was a yes. She yawned against his chest, his warm skin and strong arms reminding her that she was in the most perfect place on this earth—heaven.

The next morning, Avalon sat in the small breakfast room and lingered over a cup of tea while waiting for Devan to arrive.

"I'm going to the stables." Thane crunched a bit of bacon. "Sadie had a new litter yesterday."

"Sadie?" Devan entered the room.

Immediately, Avalon's stomach fell like a flight of swallows swooping.

"The barn cat," Thane said while nodding at Devan.

He took a sip of milk. "She won't allow anyone near her kittens except me."

By then, Devan had come to stand by her side. "Good morning, wife. I hope you slept well," he whispered. He kissed her cheek, then placed his hand over her thrumming fingers. She hadn't even noticed that the nervous habit was making a racket. He gracefully sat next to her.

Thane cleared his throat. "Now that you're both here, there is something I'd like to discuss."

"What's that?" Avalon smiled.

Thane looked to Devan, then back to Avalon. "I'd like to go to Eton."

Avalon set her teacup on its saucer, a feat of monumental control when all she wanted to do was throw it across the room.

Before she could answer, her son continued, "Mother, with you marrying, you won't be lonely when I leave." As if the matter were settled, he turned to Devan. "I think I'll be ready academically. My lessons are progressing nicely."

"You are making progress," Devan said cautiously. "But this is a big decision you and your mother should make."

"Thane," Avalon said. "About Eton."

"All I'm asking is if you'll consider it," Thane said without a hint of irritation.

His cool demeanor reminded her that he was growing up more quickly than she realized. "That is fair enough. I shall give it some thought."

"My lord, why don't you go to the schoolroom," Devan said. "I'll be up shortly for our lesson. I have to drop off a basket at Mrs. Dozier's home. We could do it together and ride over there."

"It would be my pleasure." Without any grumbling, Thane rose, then politely bowed to Avalon.

After her son took his leave, Avalon nodded discreetly to the attending footman. Immediately, he left the room.

"My goodness, he's becoming more self-assured every day. Did you have any idea he was going to suggest this?"

Devan shook his head. "We haven't discussed it since the first day I met him. You both should think on it. I know it troubles you, but it's important to him."

"It is." Avalon sighed, then placed the serviette beside her plate. "But right now, I'd hoped we could discuss Penelope's situation."

Devan smiled, then took a sip of coffee. "I've been thinking about what we might do for her."

"I have some ideas too, but you go first." Avalon took a bite of toast.

"What if Larkton invites her to stay in London? He wouldn't let a mouse inside without an invitation. My sister Elizabeth would keep her company."

"That's too dangerous for Elizabeth and Penelope. What if the servants talk about her pregnancy?" Without a sound, she drummed her fingers again on the table. "Your sister's reputation could suffer."

"Good point," Devan agreed. "But I don't think Elizabeth would care a whit. She's strong-willed about how society treats women and babies born out of wedlock."

Avalon nodded. It didn't surprise her in the least that Devan's little sister would be so gracious in her thoughts and deeds. "Elizabeth must take after you."

"Thank God for that." Devan ate a piece of bacon. "My brothers have the manners of a bull in a dining room, but they have good intentions."

She laughed. His love for his family was endearing. "I was thinking about renting a cottage in Cornwall and sending Penelope there with Mrs. Marcy and Miss Marcy. The temperate climate might help Mrs. Marcy."

"But what if Renford finds her? Those women will need protection. Perhaps Niall or Hearne could accompany them." His brow crinkled into neat lines as he contemplated their options. "I wish Penelope would name the father. Mr. Rowley and I could have a conversation with him. If he's unmarried, then we could encourage him to marry her."

"I wish she would share who it is also. Perhaps I should have another conversation with her." Avalon rubbed the small handle of her teacup as if it were a talisman and she was hoping for inspiration. "I'd thought about asking Mary Bolen if I could send her there. Her establishment is a regular fortress. I'm not certain her aunt and uncle would approve though."

"What about Will and Thea's residence in Northumberland?" He leaned forward and rested his elbows on the table. "Renford would never think to consider looking up there. Will and Thea would never let anything happen to Penelope. Their staff is small and settled in the area."

Avalon beamed. "That's brilliant. Do you think they'd do it for Penelope?"

"I know they would if we asked," Devan answered. "Before you join me for tea this afternoon, I'll write to them."

"Let's have a groomsman deliver it and wait for their reply. The quicker we get her away the better." For the first time this morning, Avalon felt herself relax.

"I was thinking the same." Devan stood, then rested one hand on the table as he kissed Avalon's cheek. "I'll take my leave."

After he left, Avalon stood to start her day. She had a multitude of tasks to finish before the afternoon, including the estate bookkeeping she'd send to Larkton. Only then would she visit Flora and Jasmine. She wanted to show them the plans the architect had drafted for their workroom.

By early afternoon, she'd finished the bookkeeping, then set out to the village. Soon, she rounded the corner where the Thistledown church stood before her. Its tall steeple and rugged masonry reminded her of Devan. He'd quickly become the cornerstone of the community and her own life.

Unbelievable that only a week ago, they'd never even considered a life together.

"My lady," a familiar voice called out.

When Avalon pivoted, she found Mrs. Rowley practically running up the path to meet her. "I don't mean to interrupt you, but I was wondering if you'd seen Penelope?"

"Pardon?" she asked and waited for the poor woman to catch her breath.

"Penelope," she answered. Her cheeks flushed a brilliant red from the cold and the exertion of her walk. "Her yellow curricle is gone from the stables. I thought perhaps she and Lady Sophia might be together."

"I don't believe so. Sophia planned to stay home today. I left word with my butler to see if she'd join me at Flora and Jasmine's home later."

"If you see my niece, will you tell her I'm looking for her?" She darted her worried gaze up and down the street. "Lord Renford informed us that he's arriving tomorrow. We received word last night. I want to prepare her for his stay. He wants the vicar to call the first week of banns this Sunday. Mr. Rowley headed to London at first light to talk to Lord Renford about ending the engagement. I'm not certain it'll work, but it's the least we can do."

Avalon took Mrs. Rowley's hand in hers. "We don't have much time. After I finish my visit, I'll find Sophia and ask if she's seen her."

"Thank you, my lady." Without a goodbye, Mrs. Rowley started toward the small pub at the end of the street.

Without wasting another minute, Avalon turned toward Flora and Jasmine's house. After a knock, Flora stood at the door with a beautiful smile welcoming her. "Welcome, my lady."

"Good afternoon." Avalon lifted the roll of plans. "I brought the architect's drawings for us to review."

Soon, she was inside the comfy warm home. With little fanfare, she placed the plans on the table.

Jasmine rubbed her hands together. "I can't wait to see what the rooms look like."

Flora carefully unrolled the packet, then spread the bundle across their table. "Look at the windows." She pointed to the south part of the workshop, where there were chairs arranged in a cozy sitting area along a bank of windows.

"It'll be perfect light for sewing and minimize the strain to the eyes," Jasmine offered. She pointed to a row of built-in cabinets. "Those look big enough to hold the bolts of fabric."

As the two women reviewed the drawings and chatted, Avalon strolled to the window. Outside, there was no sign of her sister. "I hope you don't mind, but I asked Sophia to meet me here."

Flora waved her hand in the air. "We actually thought you were her at the door. She came by this morning and forgot her embroidery basket."

Avalon whipped her gaze to the women. "Sophia was already here?"

"Yes," Flora answered.

"Was Penelope with her? Mrs. Rowley is looking for her. I told her I'd ask Sophia if she's seen her."

Jasmine looked up from the drawing she was carefully studying, then frowned. "We haven't seen Penelope. But we had the strangest conversation with Lady Sophia earlier today."

"What kind of a conversation?"

"She wanted to know about our previous work," Flora said as she poured herself a cup of tea. "Ma'am, would you like a cup?"

Avalon shook her head.

"Specifically, where she could find Mary Bolen's bawdy house in London," Jasmine said.

Flora nodded. "She asked if we felt safe at Miss Bolen's White Dove."

Avalon widened her eyes. "You didn't work there. Why would she want to know that information?"

Jasmine shrugged her shoulders. "We stayed there until you brought us to Thistledown."

Avalon stood, slowly thinking. How odd for Sophia to be asking such questions. They'd discussed Mary Bolen several times, but Sophia had never asked about Mary's business. "Let me leave the plans with you."

"We'll bring them back tomorrow," Flora said.

"Enjoy your tea with that handsome husband of yours," Jasmine called out.

Avalon stopped suddenly. "I didn't mention anything about tea with the vicar."

Flora chuckled. "Lady Sophia told us that you were having tea at the vicarage this afternoon."

The only way Sophia could have known she was having tea with Devan this afternoon was if she'd been outside the breakfast room this morning listening to their conversation about Penelope. After hearing about her earlier conversation with Flora and Jasmine and the fact that Penelope was missing, the only conclusion was that Sophia planned to take Penelope to Mary Bolen's White Dove in London.

With a brief farewell, Avalon left the ladies. She had to talk with Devan. She glanced at the darkened skies where intermittent flashes of lightning streaked across the horizon. However, all she could think about was Sophia.

If only she were a warlock, she could fly to Devan instead of walking briskly, then swoop them both to London immediately.

A good knight knows how to shine his own armor.
Devan Farris

Chapter Twenty-four

When Avalon walked the brick path to the vicarage door, Devan was leaning against the doorjamb waiting for her. Without his morning coat and with the last button of his waistcoat undone, he looked like a man of leisure. However, the disarray of his hair indicated that he'd been running his fingers through his dark locks while working diligently on his weekly sermon.

For someone who let others believe he didn't put any labor into his work, Devan put a tremendous amount of effort into his parish.

"I saw you through the window," he said. His brow creased into thin lines. "I can tell by your expression that something is the matter."

"Sophia's missing. I think she's taken Penelope to Mary Bolen's brothel."

"What's given you that idea?" Devan took her hands in his. Their size and warmth provided comfort, something she sorely needed.

The Warwyk carriage came to a halt in front of them. Devan nodded at the driver, Dalton Sweet, Warwyk's oldest groomsman, who hopped down to help Henri exit the carriage.

"My lady, it looked like a downpour, so Mr. Sweet and I thought we'd come for you." The wind picked up, blowing several strands of her maid's hair loose. Henri smoothed it back into place. "Of course, after you finish your tea with the vicar."

"Have you seen Sophia?" Avalon asked, still holding on to Devan.

"No, my lady. She left early this morning to see Jasmine and Flora. Said she was going to see Miss Penelope afterward."

"Keep the horses warm, won't you, Mr. Sweet?" Devan took Avalon's arm, then assisted her inside. "We won't be but a minute."

"Yes, sir," Dalton replied.

The accompanying groomsman waved his hand in acknowledgment.

Once they were inside, Devan closed the door. "Tell me what's happened."

"Mrs. Rowley said that Renford is coming tomorrow and she can't find Penelope . . ." She squeezed her eyes, stemming the burn of tears that clouded her vision. "I think Sophia heard us discussing Penelope at breakfast. She went to Flora and Jasmine and asked about Mary Bolen's establishment."

Lightning flashed, enveloping the entire room in brilliant light before a crash of thunder rent the air. The carriage horses neighed in sudden fear. Of all the times for it to storm, not now.

Avalon grimaced at the thunder. "Sophia hates storms." She tugged his arm toward the door. "I'm scared. Neither of the girls have been to that part of London before. Let's hurry."

"Sweetheart, we'll find them," Devan answered. "Let me get my coat."

Any other time she'd have basked in the affectionate term, but not now. Not when Sophia and Penelope were likely in danger. Though most in society only saw

London as a fairy-tale place at night with balls, soirees, and musicales to fill their social calendars, Avalon knew better. The dark streets and narrow alleys were a haven for criminals and men who hunted for young women.

Dear God above, let them be safe. Avalon closed her eyes, desperate for the girls to walk through the door.

He led her into his study where papers and half a cup of tea sat waiting for him. He let go of her, and she wanted to cry out at the loss of his touch. He donned his morning jacket, then blew out the candles lighting his desk.

Funny how within a few short days he'd become the person she went to when she was troubled or needed help.

He escorted her to the door, then pulled her close as he whipped his greatcoat over both their heads to keep the stinging rain from assaulting them. Henri waited inside the carriage. Before he could tell the coachman where to drive, Avalon directed him to London.

Devan whipped off his beaver hat, then laid it on the seat beside him. "Perhaps she went to Annie's for a visit. We should make our way there before we set off for London."

"No, I don't think so." Avalon looked at the rain streaming down the carriage windows. The weather was worsening. "She planned to spend the day with Annie tomorrow."

"My lady, let me walk back to Warwyk Hall. I'll search the house, and you and the vicar go on to London." Henri drew her wet cloak tighter. "If she's there, I'll have a groomsman ride to catch you."

"But it's storming," Avalon argued. "I can't allow you to do that."

"Then I'll ask Mrs. Rowley to take me," Henri said.

Avalon hesitated, then nodded.

Henri grabbed Avalon's hands in hers. "Godspeed, my lady." With a nod, she was out the door, running through the driving rain.

Fighting the wind, Devan shut the door, then knocked. The carriage sprang forward.

"Let's go directly to the White Dove," Avalon said. "The girls must be at Mary's bawdy house within the financial district. Mr. Sweet knows where it is."

The air grew dense, like in the moments before a storm unleashed its unyielding power. If she'd said she was carrying a child due to another immaculate conception, she didn't think she could have shocked him more.

"You've been there?" he asked in disbelief.

"Yes." She tilted her chin defiantly. "Will you feel uncomfortable going there?"

"No. I've been there too." His long legs framed hers, and he leaned forward. Though it was almost dark, his gaze pierced hers like a knife. "Larkton went there regularly with Warwyk."

"When I was married to Richard?" She tried to mask any outward sign that she was unsettled by his statement, but a wild twitch below her left eye betrayed her.

Devan placed his hands on either side of her hips, then leaned his weight forward. His face came within inches of hers, close enough that he brushed his nose against hers.

"I'm sorry if I sound abrupt." She didn't pull away at his touch. At this moment, she'd take all the comfort she could get. "Warwyk always brings out the worst in me."

"My brother took me there so 'I could become a man.'"

"How ridiculous," she answered. The warmth in his eyes immediately relaxed her. "Your brother is beyond foolish."

"Your perception matches mine." He chuckled. "Anyway, I sat in the receiving room where all the women appeared. It was like a scene from a comedy. Apparently, my brother told them I was a virgin. Immediately, they all vied for my favors."

"What did you do?"

"I politely told them that they were all lovely, but I wasn't interested as I was saving myself." He bent and shook his head. "All the prostitutes thought it was charming, which increased their interest in me. By the time Larkton was ready to leave, we were all having tea together and chatting away. Mary Bolen sat next to me. When my brother called me a wastrel in front of all those women, I thought they were going to revolt and lead a mob against him. He never took me there or to any other brothel again. But he took me to Warwyk's that day with the same intention. That's when I saw you hurt and upset." He shook his head. "I can't believe I'm telling you this. I've told no one."

She placed her hand on his face. His heat felt like heaven, and the soft hint of his beard soothed her. "I like it that you're sharing it with me."

He turned his head and kissed her palm. "Before the end of the week, you'll know everything about me."

"I know what you're doing. You're trying to keep my mind off the girls." She searched his eyes as her shoulders hunched together in a defensive action.

"Avalon," he murmured. He leaned forward, and in reaction, she leaned forward also. "You don't have to make this trip. I can see Mary Bolen myself."

"No, you misunderstand. You see, Mary Bolen"—she struggled with the right explanation—"came to my home when the solicitor read Richard's will." She looked to the ceiling, unable to look Devan in the eye as she told another sordid tale of her late husband. "In essence, he provided for me as dictated by the marriage settlements, the full dower amount, but nothing more and nothing less. He directed that a special mausoleum be built for him and Mary away from the rest of the family."

She closed her eyes as those memories, every single one of them, came rushing back.

"You don't have to tell any more if it's too painful." He rubbed the back of his fingers against her cheek, his warmth calming her racing heartbeat.

"No. You should know all of it before we arrive in London." She cleared her throat, then studied her hands. "He bequeathed a huge fortune on Mary and her son, Richard Bolen. He even made provisions for him to attend Eton." Her lips tugged into a half smile, though she wanted to crawl into a corner of the carriage and weep. "That's why I don't want Thane to go there. The other boys would be unspeakably cruel when they discover they're half brothers, one a marquess and the other the son of a brothel owner. What if Thane returns a bully like his father? What if Mary's son resents Thane?"

"Avalon," he said, "you can't always protect him. Eventually, they'll meet. Mary's son will become friends with peers who'll come to know Thane when he sits in the House of Lords."

"I know," she said a little defensively. "I couldn't bear it if Richard's son hurt him. Lord knows, Richard was horrible." Her eyes burned with unshed tears. "He never even held Thane the only time he saw him."

"Darling, Thane's brother is Mary's son too. She wouldn't allow him to be cruel. But whatever type of person he is, I won't let you or Thane go through that alone. I promise."

She nodded briefly as she quickly wiped away a tear. "When the solicitor left, Mary was still in the study with me. I was uncomfortable because she was grieving so. Her grief made my own failure as a wife that much more acute. I had to get out of the room. But when I looked at her so forlorn and alone, I went to sit by her. Somehow, I ended up holding her while she shed her tears."

"That must have been difficult." He spoke softly and drew nearer.

"After she finished weeping, she told me if there was anything I ever needed, not to hesitate calling on her." Her gaze locked with his. "This is that time. She'll help us. She has an army of men who protect her and her girls. She'll help us find them."

Another flash of lightning rent the sky, the brightness unexpected. Avalon closed her eyes.

Dear God, thank you for my husband, but if I have any favors left in Your grace, please let us find Sophia and Penelope . . . quickly.

Clean your own house first before you criticize anyone else's domestic skills.

Lady Warlock

Chapter Twenty-five

The horses raced to London, seeming not to mind the inclement weather. Fortunate, as Devan needed them to make haste. He settled against the squab. Though Avalon was worried for good reason, she still maintained her sense of calm.

He tightened his hand into a fist. If that arse of a first husband had just left her alone without being cruel, things would be so much easier for both of them. His heart clenched in his chest as he recalled the look of abject misery in her eyes when she shared what Richard had done to her in the reading of his will. What man in his right mind would inflict that kind of torture on his wife?

He studied the London proper streetlights outside the carriage window. Within minutes they arrived at the White Dove. With little fanfare, Mary Bolen's protectors had personally escorted them into the same sitting room where he'd been all those years ago.

A prim and proper maid dressed in all black entered with a tea tray. Her mode of dress ensured that she faded into the shadows so the women who served Mary's clients could shine like baubles at Christmas.

"When might your mistress arrive?" Devan asked as serenely as possible, though he wanted to search the entire premises then and there without an escort. "We're in somewhat of a hurry."

The maid dipped a curtsy. "I'm not certain, Vicar. But I'll let her know you're here."

Before he could ask more, the door opened. A beautiful woman with blond hair entered, her dress elegant but subdued. By looks alone, she could easily be a member of the *ton* instead of the demimonde.

Without a glance his way, Mary was riveted to Avalon. "My lady, welcome to the White Dove. It's so lovely to see you." She closed the distance between them, then waved a hand for them to sit. "And you also, Mr. Farris," she added almost as an afterthought. "May I offer you some tea?"

"No, Mary," Avalon said quietly as she twisted her gloves in her hand. "We're here on an urgent matter."

"Lady Sophia Cavensham and Miss Penelope Rowley?" She tilted her head, and a kind smile graced her lips. "They're safe and sound. I was about to send a footman to Warwyk Hall with the news they're here."

"Thank God." For the first time since this morning, Avalon seemed to relax. "Are they all right?"

Mary Bolen laughed, and the surprisingly loud sound erupted from such a small but elegant woman. "As I said, safe and sound." Her smile melted into a slight grin. "I'll take you to them. But before I do, how are you, Avalon?" The affection in her voice was unmistakable.

Devan's wife smiled. "I'm well, Mary. And you?"

Mary's eyes twinkled. "I'm excellent. I heard you married again?"

Avalon glanced at Devan with a smile. "Yes. Mr. Farris and I married several days ago."

"Felicitations on the happy news." Mary turned to him. "And no honeymoon with your bride, Vicar," she chided while tilting her head and regarding him as if taking his measure. "Your wife is a woman of the highest caliber and deserves happiness."

"Indeed, Miss Bolen." He took Avalon's hand and raised it to his lips. "I find myself beyond blessed to have married such an exquisite woman."

She nodded her agreement. "I hope you love her."

"I do." Devan's gaze settled on Avalon. "My wife has lived a life where, unfortunately, others have failed to recognize how extraordinary she is. Never fear, Miss Bolen, I see my wife clearly for who she is."

Avalon's eyes widened at his bluntness, but soon, they shimmered in happiness. "And I see my husband the same."

Mary bit her lip and for the first time appeared hesitant. "Lord Warwyk must be growing tall. I've always wondered if he favors my son, Richard."

Avalon's gaze settled on Mary, and she shook her head. "Lord Warwyk looks like a Cavensham."

"If things were different, I'd have you and your husband to a proper tea." Mary waved a hand in front of her. "But none of us can change who we are."

"I beg to differ. We all have that power within us," Devan argued.

"Do you?" Mary asked with a lift of one brow.

Immediately, he thought of how he'd changed over the time he'd been in Thistledown. No longer did he need to hide behind the persona he'd created. He felt grounded and knew he belonged not only to a community but to a person, his wife. There wasn't anything he'd not do for Avalon. "I know so."

"I shall watch you for inspiration, Mr. Farris." The

amusement melted in Mary's eyes, replaced by admiration. "Come and I'll take you to the young ladies."

"One minute before we go," Avalon announced.

One thing Avalon had come to realize in her short time with Devan was that she did trust him. He said he'd help her with Thane, and now was the perfect time to prepare her son for his future.

"Mary, I've changed as well. I've learned how to appreciate how special life truly is." Determined not to allow her resolve to disappear without talking action, she stepped forward and took the woman's hands in her own. "With my husband's sensible guidance, I want to propose that Lord Warwyk meet your Richard. They'll both be at Eton together soon. Now is the time, don't you think?"

Overcome, Mary bit her lip and tears welled in her eyes. She blinked rapidly, then nodded. "My lady, I can't tell you what this means to me. Richard will have no other siblings, and I'm certain he'd cherish meeting his . . . Lord Warwyk."

Avalon's vision blurred with emotion. "Thane will be thrilled to find out he has a brother." She said the words, shedding the burden she'd allowed herself to carry for so many years. "Though Warwyk was forced to marry me, I'm thankful he gave me a son, whom I love dearly. Just as I know you love your son. I'm truly glad that you and Richard found happiness for the short period of time he had on this earth."

Devan stood close, resting his hand on her lower back, supporting her in her decision.

Mary nodded as she wiped away a tear. "Thank you."

Avalon leaned close and pressed a kiss against Mary's cheek. "Thank you for Sophia."

"It's my sincere pleasure to help, Avalon." Mary returned the kiss, then whispered, "With your vicar, I think you've found the same type of happiness I had with Richard."

She paused for a moment and said a silent prayer of thanks. "I'm truly blessed."

Mary nodded, then swept her hand toward the door. "Come. The girls are down the hall."

As Devan and Avalon followed Mary, he squeezed her hand. "You are amazing."

She caught his gaze, then leaned into him. "So are you."

Before she could say more, Mary stopped at the door before opening it. "I'm not the one who found Lady Sophia and Miss Rowley. It was a gentleman by the name of Marcus Leighton."

"I've met him at the Cavenshams before," Avalon answered.

As Mary escorted them down a narrow hallway, she continued, "This is part of my private quarters. No one needs to know our business." She stopped in front of a closed door. "Mr. Leighton brought them here and hasn't left their side for a moment."

Devan's eyebrows shot upward. "Is he one of your regular customers?"

"Vicar!" she scolded.

The train of her dress swooshed against the thick wool carpet beneath her feet as if chastising him, too. Before he could inquire more, Mary waved both of them forward.

"You and I are in the same business, in a manner of speaking. I keep secrets just like you do." She glanced up and winked. "I can't tell you anything about my clientele. However, I can share that he wants to talk to your wife about Lady Sophia." She twisted the ornate gilded doorknob, then stepped back. "If you need anything, please don't hesitate to ask." She turned to leave, then lightly placed her hand on Avalon's arm. "I'm so happy you're here."

"I'll leave you two to finish and see you inside." Devan nodded to Mary, then to Avalon. He entered the room, leaving them alone in the hall.

"Will you write when would be a convenient time to bring Richard to meet Lord Warwyk?" Mary asked, not hiding the hopefulness in her voice.

"I will," Avalon promised. "I can never repay you for your kindness."

"You just did a thousand times over by agreeing to allow my Richard to meet your son." The warmth and sincerity in her voice showed that Mary genuinely cared for her. There was little doubt that their lurid past had tangled into the tightest of knots and would forever keep them bound in some way. "Go see your sister." With those last words, Mary walked down the hall.

A deep sense of relief and rightness buoyed Avalon's spirits. Without a glance back, she entered the room and found Devan next to Sophia in front of the roaring fire that had been built in the formal sitting room. Wrapped in a greatcoat, Sophia had her head bowed. Marcus Leighton stood sentry beside her, murmuring something. There was no mistaking it was Mr. Leighton, a gentleman who made his fortune in imports, as his unique dark blond hair glowed a golden red in the firelight.

A little distance away from the group, Penelope stood with a blanket wrapped around her.

At the sound of the door closing, Leighton positioned himself in front of Sophia as if protecting her, then when he noticed Avalon's presence, he stepped away immediately. Sophia rushed forward. Never taking her eyes from Leighton, Avalon opened her arms and hugged her sister.

Sophia took a step back, then waved a hand down her dress. "Look at me. I'm a drowned rat. When the skies opened in a downpour, we just stood there. If it hadn't been for Mar—Mr. Leighton, we'd probably . . ." Her whole body shivered. "Who knows where we'd be." Sophia walked to her friend. "Pen?"

Penelope sat quietly staring at her hands. With a troubled breath, she exhaled, then forced her gaze to theirs. "I'm not going back."

"You can't stay here. Your aunt is worried. But Avalon and I have some ideas we'd like to discuss with you. We have friends in Northumberland who you could stay with." Devan smiled in reassurance.

"Beggin' your pardon." The maid, who'd entered the room, dipped a curtsy. "If Lady Sophia and Miss Rowley would like to change, Miss Bolen has gowns for them to borrow in the room across the hall."

Sophia took one of Penelope's hands in hers and tugged her to stand. The girl's listless manners matched her pale complexion. She appeared almost lifeless.

"Penelope," Avalon said as she took the girl in a hug. "We'll keep you safe."

"Come, Pen." Sophia put her arm around the girl's waist, offering support. "I don't want you ill."

"I'll have them back as soon as I can, my lady." Immediately, the maid swept Sophia and Penelope from the room.

Devan exhaled a breath as Leighton approached. "Marcus, how can we ever thank you?"

Leighton shook his head. "No thanks needed." His brown-eyed gaze flew to the door where Sophia had just exited, then back to her and Devan.

"Where exactly did you find them?" Avalon asked.

Leighton's expression turned solemn. "They were being circled by two foxed lechers outside another brothel.

They couldn't find Mary's place. If I hadn't arrived when I did, no telling . . ." He pursed his lips. "When I found them, they were soaked to the skin and shaking like leaves. I think Penelope might have been in shock."

"Did Lady Sophia share anything about why they're here?" Devan threw his head in the direction of a side table that held a well-stocked supply of brandy and sherry.

The man nodded and followed Devan. After he poured and handed a brandy to Marcus, he gave one to Avalon.

Leighton took a sip of brandy and closed his eyes as he swallowed. "Sophia said that Penelope needed to stay in London with her." His eyes blazed in anger. "Those men . . ." He let the thought drift to nothing.

Without saying more, he'd described the danger perfectly.

Avalon's hand flew to her chest. "They could have been raped or murdered."

Devan took her hand in reassurance. "But they weren't."

She leaned against him. It was the most natural feeling in the world to have him close.

"The only thing I could think of was to bring them here." Leighton finished his brandy. "I knew they'd be safe."

"Thank God you were there." Devan ran his fingers through the wet locks of his own hair.

Marcus stared straight at Devan. "What were they doing in this part of town?"

"We're not at liberty to say, Mr. Leighton." Avalon smiled in apology. "But my family"—she squeezed Devan's hand in hers—"is forever indebted to you."

Devan blinked slowly at Avalon's words. Indeed, this was his family. Not only because he'd married Avalon but because he genuinely cared for all of them. Sophia was like his sister and Thane was like his son. They were his, and he'd do everything in his power to protect them from harm.

But there was more. In that moment when he thought of Avalon, his heart pounded triple time. She was the light that conquered his lonely darkness. She was everything to him. He loved her laughter, her thoughtfulness, her quirks, but most importantly, he loved her heart and her passion. He loved the way she challenged him in every way possible. Deep within, he acknowledged the truth. This woman owned him thoroughly. Heart and soul.

He'd do anything within his power to be worthy of her.

Leighton stepped forward with his hat in his hands. "My lady, I must be off for an appointment. But I had hoped I might call on you and discuss my intentions toward your sister." For the first time today, he actually wore a smile.

Avalon stared at him, then nodded briefly. "Allow me to discuss the matter with Sophia first."

"Of course." He bowed to Avalon and shook Devan's hand.

After Marcus Leighton departed, Avalon relaxed slightly. "I had no idea he even noticed Sophia before. What do you think of him?"

"I think he's a good man," he answered honestly.

"Then he comes highly recommended," she teased. "But we'll leave it up to Sophia. Let me go see if the girls are ready to leave for Warwyk Hall."

"I have no intention of letting you out of my sight. I'll come with you."

"I'd like that," she answered while squeezing his hand. "It's time to go home."

He stole a quick kiss. "I love it when you talk like that."

One half of me is yours, the other half yours
Mine own, I would say; but if mine, then yours,
And so all yours.

The Merchant of Venice
Act 3 Scene 2

Chapter Twenty-six

After Leighton took his leave, Avalon and Devan went in search of the girls. With her husband behind her, she knocked on the door. When there was no answer, she knocked again, only this time louder. "Do you suppose we have the wrong door?"

Before Devan could respond, the door swung open. Instantly, a pistol was shoved in her face.

"Both of you, over there." An attractive man with light brown hair and shimmering gray eyes that flashed with a wild fury pointed to Sophia and Penelope. They stood in the middle of the room, holding each other.

Panic flared in the pit of Avalon's stomach at the stark terror on their faces. She stood motionless, struggling to make sense of the sight before her. Her heartbeat pounded while the blood in her veins thickened from the cold that seeped into every inch of her.

"What is the meaning—"

Before Avalon could finish, the man aimed the pistol toward the middle of her forehead. "Quiet," he hissed.

Devan darted in front of Avalon, using his body to shield her. "Who are you?"

"I'm Renford, Penelope's bridegroom," he snarled.

"After the maid left us, he found me," Penelope murmured in a small voice.

"As if you could ever hide from me." He waved the pistol in the direction of the young women. "Must I repeat myself? I said *over there*."

Still shielding her body, Devan walked Avalon to her sister's side. He turned to Renford. "How did you get in here?"

"Easy. I paid for a whore, then I walked straight into this room and I found one." Renford glanced sideways at Penelope. "My bride-to-be."

"What do you want?" Avalon tried to swallow the fear that swelled in her throat making it difficult to breathe.

"What's mine." The man narrowed his eyes. "Who are you?"

"Avalon Farris."

"And you?" He pointed the gun at Devan.

"I'm her husband, Devan Farris, the parish vicar of Thistledown."

Avalon locked her knees in place, determined not to show any weakness. She turned to Sophia and Penelope. "Are you hurt?"

Her sister shook her head, but Penelope didn't answer, keeping her gaze fixed on Renford.

"Let the women go." Devan's gaze didn't stray from the madman, but his voice had taken a gentle tone, one designed to comfort someone hurt and wounded. "You don't want to do any harm here."

"Harm?" Renford scoffed. "I'm the one who's been harmed here. I was promised a virtuous bride, but the whore spread her legs and now is carrying a bastard."

Penelope flinched at the hateful words. "How do you know that?"

"Edward Grant waited for me at the gate of your aunt and uncle's house. I didn't even have time to freshen up. He told me all about it. How he loved you, then asked you to jilt me. The fool told me how you came to see him earlier to say goodbye. Lucky for me, he told me you were headed here." Renford waved the gun around the room as his voice grew louder. "You thought to hide in a whore's house?"

Penelope flinched.

He shook his head, waving the gun at her stomach. "A farmer? You gave your virtue to a farmer? Such plebeian tastes," he snarled.

Penelope's hand flew to her mouth. "Did you hurt him?"

With his eyes glowing, he resembled a monster as his hoarse laughter echoed in the room. He slashed his free hand across his neck. "Cut 'em like a pig."

"No," she cried. "Edward's dead?"

"No one takes what's mine." Renford swung his attention to Avalon and Devan. "What am I going to do with you? I was only going to have to get rid of my fiancée's friend. Now, I've two more to dispose of." His upper lip crept up in a sneer. "Penelope, you're not worth the effort, but here I am. Cleaning up your mess."

Avalon took Sophia's hand and squeezed. She tried to make sense of the sight before her. Her heartbeat pounded, sounding the alarm to run, but she stayed still.

Devan held up his hand as if trying to calm the man. "Don't make the situation worse. Let them go, then you and I can discuss this in a civilized manner."

Renford stalked closer to Devan, then aimed the gun directly at him. "I don't consider you and your wife hiding Penelope from me in this brothel anything close to resembling civilized, *Vicar.*" He turned his attention to

Penelope. "How dare you do this to me," he sneered. "I loved you, and in return, you humiliated me."

Her eyes widened in fear. "I'm sorry. Just let them go."

"I'm sorry too." A hint of pure malevolence tinted Renford's voice as he shook his head. "You're such a disappointment."

With Renford focused on Penelope, Devan shot forward. When he went to grasp the gun, the madman backed up quickly. "No, no, no," he chided. "Don't try to be a hero." He pointed the gun at the middle of Devan's chest, then held his coat open. "I have two knives and another pistol ready. "If you even make a move to touch me again, I'll gut your wife like I did Grant."

At the sound of Edward's name, Penelope whimpered.

Within seconds, he cocked the hammer, and Avalon's heart stilled, suspended in her chest. Fear, a kind she'd never experienced before, withered everything within her to ashes. "Dear God in heaven," she whispered.

"You'll meet him soon, I promise." With his eyes glazed with fury, Renford aimed the weapon at the middle of her chest with the powder burning.

Devan pushed Avalon at the same time a deafening shot rent the air. She fell against the wall hard enough that for a moment she saw stars. Another shot rang out, and various yelps and cries erupted around the room. The stench of sulfur and fire smothered the air. Along with the smoke, tears blurred her vision, keeping her from seeing what had happened.

"Devan?" she cried.

A deep groan sounded. Suddenly, Devan pulled her tightly to him. "Are you hurt?" His eyes were frantic as he catalogued her every feature while his hands reverently skated down her body, looking for wounds.

She shook her head, then found the ability to speak. "You?"

He stood slowly and pulled her to her feet. By then, the smoke had lessened. She turned to find Sophia beside her and Penelope enveloped in Edward Grant's arms, who seemed to have come from nowhere. Thankfully, he was still alive.

"Your gown," Sophia murmured, her eyes wide in fright. "Have you been shot?"

Avalon's gaze skated down her skirt. Blood covered her dress, deep red blotches staining the green silk she wore. "Dev—" she whispered as she whirled around.

He leaned against the wall. His heavy breathing reminded Avalon of a chimney bellow. It was much too quick, as if he were nervous. He clenched his arm tightly around his waist. She fell to her knees as he cautiously lowered himself to the ground. Her hands trembled, but she examined him by running her hands carefully over his body just like he had done earlier to her until she found the blood oozing from his side. She hadn't seen the wound immediately as he wore a black satin waistcoat. She pulled one side of her dress up and pressed a handful of her petticoats against his wound. The muslin slowly turned crimson from her husband's blood.

Edward knelt beside Avalon, his cravat bloodstained from his injury. "I'll fetch Miss Bolen."

Devan grimaced and placed one of his bloody hands over hers. The warmth of his fingers helped assure her that he wasn't losing that much blood.

"How badly are you wounded?" She swallowed her fear and focused on his face. His eyes narrowed in pain, but his cheeks were normal in color. Another sign that should have given her reassurance, but didn't.

"He caught my side. I thought the bullet might have

hit you also." He flinched in pain, then smiled slightly. "It just grazed me."

Two footmen burst through the door with Mary and her maid following right behind them.

"Help Mr. Farris to my bedroom," Mary instructed the men, then turned to her maid. "Call the doctor."

"What about the authorities, ma'am?" one of the footmen inquired.

"Let's start with the coroner," Mary said decisively. "He'll bring the magistrate."

Still pressing her garment against Devan's side, Avalon glanced at Penelope and Sophia, who stood huddled together trying to make sense of what had happened. Avalon's breath caught in panic. The danger wasn't over. "Where's Renford?"

Her gaze swept the floor until she found him. With his eyes glazed in death, Harrison Renford lay in a puddle of blood.

"Don't, sweetheart," Devan commanded softly. "Look at me."

She turned to face him as the smell of blood and death surrounded them. "What happened? All I could concentrate on was Renford."

"Edward entered the room and was almost upon Renford when Renford aimed the gun at you. I thought we had a chance to stop him."

"Oh my God," she gasped. "You foolish man." Suddenly, she sobbed at the horror of what she'd almost lost, the love she'd finally found in her life. "You pushed me so he'd shoot you instead of . . . me. I could have lost you."

After the footmen got Devan to his feet, he pulled Avalon to his good side. "No, you couldn't have lost me, especially since I just married you, the woman who possesses my heart. Trust me when I say, I'm not going any-where without you."

Two days later, Avalon and Devan arrived home after the doctor gave his consent that Devan could travel. While Devan had rested at Mary's establishment, he'd found his wife had another hidden talent, nursing. She hadn't left his side the entire time.

Since the journey to Warwyk Hall had tired him, she'd demanded—*yes demanded*—that he immediately retire to their room. Avalon had hovered around him though he'd declared that he could see to his own needs. She'd answered in her commanding way—the one he adored—that he must be progressing very nicely since all he seemed to want to do was protest. Thane had kept him entertained with several games of chess while he was sequestered in bed, but when the day surrendered to night, he'd found he couldn't stay awake.

When the next dawn broke, Devan didn't bother to waste time seeing the sun rise. Not while he held his wife in his arms. He could lay there all morning and just watch her sleep and never be bored. Yet, a rare rising sun called for him to prepare for his day.

He carefully untangled his arms from around Avalon, then pressed a gentle kiss to her temple. For a moment longer, he watched as her deep rhythmic breathing continued. He leaned to open the drawer on his side table. He flinched as the movement pulled the stitches on his side. His wound was healing nicely, but it still gave him fits and starts if he didn't move care-fully. He retrieved the small velvet box that Thane had retrieved from the vicarage yesterday afternoon. The young lord had been instrumental in hiding it from Avalon's watchful gaze. For the fifteenth time since its arrival, Devan opened it to admire the contents, his wedding present to his wife.

Carefully, he put it back in the drawer, then turned to her. Unable to resist, he kissed her lips. "I love you, Avalon." His throat tightened. "With my body, my heart, and my soul. You're a part of me forever."

She moaned in response and threw an arm over her eyes. Quickly, she settled back into a deep sleep.

His chest shook with a silent rumble of laughter. Leave it to Avalon that her hatred of mornings made an appearance when he expressed his love. Tonight, he'd do it properly. He had so much to share with this special woman, and thankfully, he was the lucky recipient of all that made her unique.

Later that afternoon, Avalon had been surprised to discover that Devan had left on his own to visit a parishioner. Mr. Neville had informed her that the vicar's presence at the Garrisons' house had been requested by Mrs. Jennings. Mrs. Garrison, the mother-to-be, didn't need Devan's guidance, but the father-to-be did. According to the note Mrs. Jennings and her daughter, Patricia, sent, Mr. Garrison was becoming somewhat of a problem. Seemed that every five minutes, the poor man would pop his head in the room where his wife would start railing at him to leave her be.

Avalon had half a mind to follow Devan to ensure he wasn't doing too much, but Mr. Neville had shared that her husband would be home shortly as word had spread that the Garrisons' baby had come. Unfortunately, Mr. Garrison had fainted dead away and bumped his head at the news that he had a new son. The midwife now had an extra patient who needed her care.

While Avalon waited for her husband to return, she decided she'd visit her sister's chambers. They hadn't spoken about that night at Mary's yet as all of Avalon's time had been spent tending to Devan.

Sophia sat at the small desk in her sitting room with a journal in front of her. It was a cozy room, and the familiar smell of rose water and clean linen instantly calmed Avalon. Her sister looked her way and smiled grimly. With her wet hair braided in a long queue, Sophia should have resembled a young girl. Instead, she appeared like a woman who'd seen parts of the world that no one should ever have to experience.

Henri directed several maids who were removing the slipper tub from in front of the fire.

"How is she?" Avalon whispered to Henri.

Henri smiled affectionately. "She's stronger than you or I give her credit. She doesn't seem the worse for wear now." A grimace skated across her lady maid's face. "Undoubtedly, she wants to talk to you. I think there's more to the story than what you know." With that, Henri escorted the maids from the room, leaving Avalon alone with Sophia.

"Avalon, come in," Sophia greeted her. "Thane's already been in to see how I was doing." Her voice caught in her throat. "I told him I was feeling a little under the weather."

"Thane's always been observant when it comes to us." Avalon pulled up a side chair and settled in front of the desk. "I hoped we could talk now that it's just you and me."

Sophia nodded as she laid her quill aside. "Of course." She traced a delicate finger around the outer edges of her journal a few times as if collecting her thoughts before leaning across the desk and placing her hand over Avalon's. "You probably want to know why I took Penelope to Mary's place in London." Sophia released a deep breath. "I overheard you and Devan talking in the breakfast room that morning about Penelope's situation." Her sister dipped her head sheepishly. "I'll be the first to admit, I panicked. When Penelope told me Lord Renford planned to visit the Rowleys and have the banns read, I knew I had to get her out of Thistledown."

Avalon scooted closer. "But I don't understand. Why Mary Bolen?"

Sophia shrugged. "I thought hiding her at Mary's would be the perfect solution. Lord Renford would never think to look for her in a bawdy house. You always spoke so highly of Mary, even with your past entanglements." She looked Avalon in the eye. "She was very kind. You'll be pleased that she scolded me once she found out that you didn't know about my plan."

She sat absolutely still, determined not to allow the horrid memories of Devan bleeding in her arms to scald her with fear or anger. Avalon counted the seconds while she commanded her heartbeat to slow its rhythm in time with the ticking ormolu clock that sat on Sophia's desk. She focused on the twin dolphins that supported the face of the clock with their backs, their faces a study of concentration as the creatures carried the weight of the clock as if it were serious business.

Silly animals who had no idea what it meant to carry the weight of the world on your shoulders yet still not able to control anything. She forced her gaze to her sister's face. "Why didn't you tell me your plans? Were you just going to disappear?"

"Once I got Penelope settled, then I planned to come home that evening. But you know the story. When those men accosted us, Marcus helped us."

Avalon closed her eyes, trying to make sense of it all. "I'm so sorry."

"You think this is your fault?" Sophia queried.

"I'm responsible for you," Avalon countered.

"You're not my mother, Avalon," Sophia said softly. "But you are the best sister a woman could have. Please don't try to accept the responsibility for my mistake as your own. Both you and Devan had just married, and I was trying to help a friend out of a frightening situation." She bent her head and shook it slowly, clearly feeling remorse. "I'm sorry. I thought it'd be a short trip, and I'd planned to tell you what I'd done when I returned home. Penelope went to see Edward and told him we were going to Mary's. He told Renford in the heat of the argument. That's how Renford found us." Her voice grew softer. "Avalon?"

"Yes, Sophia," she answered like she'd done a thousand times before when her sister needed solace. She should be scolding her for lying to her, but the truth was Avalon was just happy to have her home safe.

Her sister smiled. "Good hearts and deeds prevailed that day. Mary Bolen protected us and so did Marcus." She fiddled with the edge of her journal again. "But your Devan was a true hero." She looked to the ceiling as her voice wobbled slightly. "I don't know what I would have done if I'd lost you . . ."

The sound tore a rip in Avalon's heart. Tears welled in her eyes. "I was so scared when I saw him bleeding on the floor. I thought I'd lost him."

Sophia rushed to hug her. "I know how much you love him. I'm so thankful you both found each other. I want that."

Avalon clung to her sister. The warmth of Sophia's body anchored her from losing herself in the nightmares that would seize her at moments of her day. "Thank you. You want someone like Devan, darling?"

She lifted her eyes and nodded at Avalon. "Marcus . . . I mean Mr. Leighton . . . he asked if he could call on me. I think he's interested in marriage."

Avalon wiped the tears from her eyes. "Would you like that?"

"Yes." Sophia straightened her shoulders and smiled. "I want to marry him."

"Why?" she asked softly, hoping to convince her sister to take her time. "You won't have a Season. I don't want you to rush into marriage like I did. I want you to experience the world and find love. I want you to find a man who will love and care for you. I want a man who will put you before all others in his life."

"Maybe I found him." Sophia smiled at her impassioned speech.

"No," Avalon said adamantly.

"Avalon, please hear me out."

The resolute tone in her voice made Avalon lean back in her chair. She'd never heard her sister take such a decisive tone with her before.

"I think we'll have a good life together. He's kind and considerate." Her face softened as she spoke of Marcus. "Trust me to make the right decision. I don't want to go through what you did."

"That's exactly what you'll be doing."

"It's my choice," Sophia argued without raising her voice. "You chose to marry Devan." Before Avalon could say another word, Sophia continued, "And I'm glad you did. It's like the leaden cloak of worry and responsibility you've worn for years has finally been untied from around your shoulders. You've shed your loneliness. It's all I've ever wanted for you. I think Marcus can do that for me."

Avalon pinched the bridge of her nose and shook her head. Sophia had matured during her hours in London and had become infinitely wiser. "Devan is a wonderful man and husband. I want you to have the same."

"He's lucky to have you. You're a remarkable woman

who is kind and giving. Look at how you care for others in the village, including Thane and me. You've sacrificed so much for us, and we're better for it. If anyone deserves happiness, it's you. I believe I can have that with Marcus."

Tears ran down Avalon's face and a soft sob escaped. She nodded.

They both stood, and Avalon embraced her. "How's Penelope?"

"She's well and happy. She came to see me today. Edward asked her to marry him again, and this time she accepted."

"Why didn't she say yes the first time?"

Sophia took a step back and regarded Avalon. "Because she thought Renford would kill him if she married him. She thought if she could convince Devan to marry her, he and his brothers could have convinced Renford to leave her alone peacefully." Sophia smiled slightly. "She panicked, and just like me, she didn't think through her actions. But now, she can finally live her life as she pleases. I'm happy for her."

"I'm happy for her too." Avalon kissed her sister's cheek again.

Sophia lifted an eyebrow. "Shouldn't you go find your husband?"

"When did you become so presumptuous?" Avalon asked.

"When I decided that I wanted to be just like my older sister." Sophia guided her to the door. "If you want to sleep at the vicarage, Henri and I can watch Thane."

Avalon whipped her gaze to her sister.

"Precious gifts are to be enjoyed." With that, Sophia returned to her desk.

Chapter Twenty-seven

⁓

Vicars were always in demand.

Avalon took a sip of tea and sighed. Devan still hadn't returned from the Garrison home.

"Why does Devan have to attend the Garrisons? Shouldn't he be in bed by now?" Thane asked as he looked up from the book of chess strategies Devan had given him. The sun was long gone, but the sitting room was cozy from the large fire that blazed in front of them.

"I wish he was home too. But Mr. Garrison needed his grace and support while his wife had the baby. Devan is a loving and giving man who helps others." Avalon set aside her journal and smiled at her good fortune. She had two men in her life that she loved beyond reason.

Truly, she had everything she'd always wanted. She'd made her own family and friends out of the community and the women she welcomed here. Though she hadn't had a worthwhile first marriage, she'd found a true and absolute love with Devan.

"I'm thankful you married him, Mother. He's a good man, and he treats you well. Do you love him?"

"I do, Thane."

"Will you and Devan have children?" Thane's green eyes held hers.

"I hope so," she said. She could imagine Devan holding their child in his arms. "I think he'd make an excellent father."

"I'd like to have a brother and a sister. Then, I don't think you would miss me when I go to Eton." Thane studied the chess set in front of him.

"Trust me, I will miss you always." She scooted across the sofa and put her arm around him. "Would you mind if I give you a hug?"

"Of course. You're my mother."

When she pulled him close, a lightness fell over her, and she laughed. For once in her life, she was thankful she'd married Richard. For without him, she wouldn't have this marvelous son. "Devan and I were talking the other day about your father, and there's something I'd like to share with you."

"Hello," Devan called softly as he leaned against the doorjamb. The look on his face was almost hesitant. "May I join you or would you prefer to be alone?"

Thane shot off the sofa and went straight to Devan's side. "Please, join us." He turned his attention to Avalon. "Do you mind, Mother?"

"I'd like that." Her heart swelled at the sight of her husband strolling into the room on his own accord. He didn't even look like he'd been injured.

By then, Devan had come to her side and slowly leaned down for a kiss. "Thank you for letting me be here for this," he whispered in her ear.

As Devan carefully took the seat beside her, Avalon took a deep breath, praying she'd find the right words that wouldn't hurt or shock her son. She entwined her fingers with Devan's. He squeezed hers in return, giving her strength.

"Thane, you already have a brother," she said as gently as she could.

Her son blinked slowly, then came to sit on the other side of her on the sofa. "You mean Richard Bolen?"

Avalon sat there stunned, unable to respond.

Devan put his arm around her shoulder as if he knew the shock she felt. "How did you discover this?" he asked.

"The Wessex twins told me years ago. They knew of Richard because their father told them. They warned me not to say anything until you brought it up. They thought it might hurt your feelings if I mentioned it." Thane leaned and kissed his mother's cheek. "I'd like to meet him. That's one of the reasons I want to attend Eton." He patted her hand. "I think it's good you finally know. I love you, Mother."

A brick of disbelief landed on her chest, making it difficult to breathe. "Are you . . . upset?"

"Of course not," Thane answered. "I'm certain it was painful for you to carry that knowledge for so long without sharing it. I should have told you earlier. I have no fears or worries about meeting him." Thane grinned at her. "I think we'll get along famously. He's an only child, and I'm an only child at least for a while. Brothers bond no matter what their differences. Look at Devan and his brothers." His attention turned to her husband. "I hope you feel better. May we finish our game tomorrow instead of Latin?"

"I'm turning you into a chess fiend, I see." Devan laughed. "Perhaps a little Latin first, then we can."

"Perfect," Thane announced. "If you'll excuse me, I think I'll go upstairs and read for a while."

While Avalon mumbled her good night, Devan's gaze never left hers.

"He's known for years and never said a word." She

stared at her husband in astonishment. "I suppose meeting Mary's son won't be such a hardship then. He certainly seems ready."

"He has good judgment, just like his mother." Careful of his side, Devan slowly knelt on the floor beside her.

She blinked, clearing the daze from her thoughts. "It appears that I'm the only one left in shock."

"He'll come to you tomorrow with more questions now that you've shared it with him."

Curious by the keen interest in his gaze, she asked, "How are you feeling?"

"Perfect now." Devan cupped her cheek. "I'm pleased to announce that Mrs. Garrison delivered a healthy baby boy. Both mother and baby are doing well. I wish I could say the same for Mr. Garrison. He fainted at the news." He took her hands in his. "The food basket you sent was much appreciated."

"It's the least I can do to help support my husband and *his* parish."

He chuckled. "The reason I'm late is that I stopped by the Rowleys' after the baby was delivered. Mr. and Mrs. Rowley are happy with Penelope's betrothal to Edward Grant. They've sent word to her parents. I saw Edward there. He'd just come from London. Through Mary's connections, Harrison, Lord Renford's death has already been ruled justified."

"Thank God. I'm relieved," she said.

"As am I." He studied their clasped hands, then cleared his throat. When he finally looked at her, his eyes were brimming with tears. "Before I arrived, I heard part of your earlier conversation with Thane."

"I meant every word." Seeing such emotion on his face made her own tears fall. "You're a wonderful man, and I'm blessed to have you as my husband. You're excellent with Thane, and I can just imagine how you'd be with our baby."

He wiped away her tear, and she did the same for him. At the tenderness of his touch, she smiled, and another tear fell.

"I love you, Avalon." He pressed his lips against hers. "I think I have since the first day you walked into my study so determined."

"When I tried to run you out of the village?"

He laughed and nodded. "Indeed. I saw how passionate you were that day, and I wanted that in my life. I wanted you." He played with her fingers, then brought her hand to his mouth, where he kissed her wedding ring. "I owe you everything, including an apology."

Her unruly tears threatened to run amok. She inhaled to stop their descent. "Why?"

"Because I should have never lied about my experiences or made you think I was someone other than who I am." His earnest gaze locked with hers. "For only with you can I be the man I'm destined to be. A God-fearing man who will work every day I'm given on this earth to show you how much I love and care for you." He reached into his coat, then withdrew a box and gave it to her.

With trembling fingers, she opened it to discover a round gold locket engraved with the initials *A* and *D* entwined on the outside.

"Open it."

She pressed the latch. Her breath caught as her fingers skated over their miniature portraits that had been painted inside facing each other. A small gold chain stretched between the two portraits, connecting their hearts.

Her eyes flew to his. "It's beautiful."

"I had it made in London and planned to give it to

you at the vicarage before . . . we went to London to find Sophia and Penelope."

She pressed her fingers against her lips. "If I'd lost you, I'd never have forgiven myself for asking you to go with me."

"I will always . . . always be with you through the brightest days and the darkest hours." He took the locket from her and clasped it around her neck.

"Thank you." She kissed his cheek. "I'll wear it every day."

He turned and captured his lips with hers. Their gentle kiss turned into a troth of their commitment to each another. Through hardship and joy, they would traverse life together.

With reluctance, he broke the kiss, then cupped her head with his hands. "The end of the Song of Solomon is about faithfulness and being one with your spouse. To me, we're one, and I find absolute strength and salvation in that. You'll forever have my love, my passion, and all that I am. No matter how old or wrinkled we are, I will only see you as my heart's desire. It's my promise to you forever."

She rested her forehead against his. "Everything I am, I give to you, including my heart. You made me believe in myself. You've helped me find my own worth. Because of that, I can love you freely and without hesitation."

"I'm devoted to you," he whispered.

"And I to you," she answered.

Devan reached into his coat pocket and pulled out a piece of paper. "This is for you also."

She smiled, then glanced at the paper. It was a note made out to her in the amount of twenty thousand pounds. "Why are you giving me this? I thought this was the whole purpose of marrying an heiress."

He shrugged. "I want you to have it. Besides, it was never about the money. It was about the heiress."

Her brows drew together.

He sighed. "For a warlock, I thought you would have figured it out. I don't care about the money. I *care* about the heiress. I married the one I wanted." He stood, then took her into his arms. When his lips pressed hers, their kiss, one of awe and admiration, soon ignited into something deeper and everlasting.

It was love.

He smiled, and the affection in his eyes told her that she'd found what was truly a miracle—his love for her was never ending. He was a man who would love her without judgment.

She dashed away another tear that had fallen. "You, sir, need to rest."

"Truly?" He lifted one brow in challenge. "My warlock looks into my heart where I bare all my wants and desires, then she tells me to go to bed?"

"Why are you pouting?" she teased. "I planned on undressing you."

Carefully, he took her hand in his and led her to the door. "I should never have doubted you. You are magical. You know the exact thing to say so I'll follow your commands."

Epilogue

❦

Five months later
The vicarage

As Devan played with the loose locks of Avalon's hair that had blown free of her chignon, his gaze held a remarkable sight. Across the way in the courtyard, Thane sat at a table playing chess with Richard Bolen.

His beautiful and brilliant wife had decided that the boys needed to spend time with each other before Thane entered Eton next term. Richard already had two terms behind him. Not surprisingly, they'd delighted in meeting each other as brothers and had become fast friends.

"It's amazing that Thane is teaching Richard to play chess," Avalon said as she turned her gaze to him.

"It'll give them something to occupy their free time during the school term." He trailed a finger across her cheek, enchanted by the heat of her skin.

"What free time? You said that Thane's studies would be onerous."

He tilted his head toward her as if sharing a secret. "I may have exaggerated slightly."

"Do tell." Her eyes widened, and she laughed. "A

naughty vicar who twists the truth. Who could ever imagine?"

He humphed, then stole a kiss. When he pulled away, the sweetest smile crossed her lips. Eventually, her gaze drifted back to Thane. "He adores you, and so do I."

"I adore him. But you, Lady Warlock, have stolen my heart."

"Do you want it back?" She bit her bottom lip in an effort to keep from laughing, but the grin on her face betrayed her amusement.

"Never." He pressed a kiss to the tip of her nose as he placed his palm against the small mound of her stomach. "It's yours forever." Just then, the baby kicked against his hand.

The warmth in Avalon's eyes almost undid him. Everything he wanted in life was here in this park. His lovely wife and their children.

"Tomorrow, I'm going to help Sophia plan her wedding with Marcus. They want to marry in London," she said. "I can't believe they fell in love so quickly."

"We made an excellent example for them to follow," he said smugly. "When I took you to Mary's to find Sophia, that set their courtship on a proper course, so I take all the credit for their betrothal."

"Of course you do," she playfully argued.

He raised her hand to his lips. "There I go again telling a small tale. The truth is, darling wife, you keep me honest."

"And you keep me happy," Avalon said. She stole a glance at the two boys, then turned her beautiful head his way.

He pressed another kiss to her hand. "I still can't believe that you established a scholarship in my honor for poor third and fourth sons of peers who want to buy a commission in the military. That was the most wonderful birthday gift I've ever received."

"Only the best for my husband," she said, then leaned close. "But I hope some of the men will still seek positions in the clergy. We need more naughty vicars."

The boys stood and shook hands. Across the park at another bench, Sophia waited for them. When they reached her side, she waved to Avalon and Devan, then they all three left.

"Where are they going?" Devan looked around the courtyard. "I thought Mary was going to join us for a while before she and Richard left for London."

"We've had a change of plans so you and I could stay here alone for a bit longer." Avalon winked. "Sophia is taking them back to Warwyk Hall. Mary is picking up Richard there." Avalon stood, and Devan followed.

Together they walked back to the vicarage.

"I owe Mary everything," Avalon said.

"How so?" Devan wrapped an arm around her waist.

"For without Mary, I'd have never brought the women in need to Thistledown. Without them, Larkton would have never sent you to me."

"Hmm, I never thought of it that way. Devan tilted his head to the sky. "Perhaps it was divine providence."

"There's one undeniable fact. I'm thankful you're my husband." She leaned and kissed him on the cheek.

"I feel the same about you. By and by, I thought of a name for the baby," he said. "Morgana."

"No." She shook her head vehemently. "That's the witch from Camelot. Absolutely not."

"It's the perfect name for our baby. Since Avalon was the island where Arthur found Excalibur." He waggled his eyebrows.

She shook her head.

"I have another idea," Devan said. "Let's sneak back out here this evening. I'd like to make love to my wife under the stars while we think of more names."

Avalon shook her head again. Then she leaned in and whispered, "If we come back to the vicarage tonight, it proves what I've always thought."

"What's that, Lady Warlock?"

"Once a wild rake, always a wild rake." She pressed her lips to his. "But you're mine."

"Always and forever, my love." Devan chuckled.

"I have a better idea." The most wicked smile broke across her lips. "Let's go to your old bedroom inside the vicarage right now and read the Song of Solomon together."

He matched her wicked smile with his own. "Shall we read the parts about how he pleasured his wife?"

"Hmm, perhaps. But I wanted to read the parts where his wife pleasured him." Avalon took his hand in hers, and they walked toward the back entrance of the vicarage.

Devan's brow creased. "I don't think that's part of the poem."

"Oh ye of little faith," Avalon answered.

Author's Note

Avalon's idea of an oasis for disenfranchised prostitutes and illegitimate children would have been revolutionary and exuberantly accepted by the church and the Warwyk parish. Her charity would have lessened if not eliminated the financial responsibility of the parish under the Poor Laws.

The Poor Laws originated during the Tudor era. They were designed as a system for caring for those unable to care for themselves, particularly the elderly, sick, disabled, illegitimate and orphaned children, and unemployed—much like Annie, Jasmine, and Flora. When Devan speaks of the parish's responsibility for these illegitimate children, he's correct. The responsibility for their care fell on the individual parishes where the poor resided. By collecting funds from their residents, the parish paid for the support of the poor, but in most cases, the amount was never enough.

Throughout the Georgian and Regency periods, poverty was a concern. Not surprisingly, the majority of the victims were single women and children. It was not unusual for women who found themselves without employment and in the lower economic classes to turn to prostitution as a "stopgap" means of survival. Often they continued in the profession. Not only did they risk disease, abuse, unwanted pregnancies, but also poverty.

Many wealthy parishes were desperate to keep these "freeloaders" from giving birth while under their watch. Is it any wonder that extreme measures such as transportation by wheelbarrow as I described in the story and even public shaming were used as weapons to force pregnant women to leave so they wouldn't give birth in certain parishes? If a father could be identified, the parish made every effort to force him to pay a form of maintenance. But there was no guarantee that the father would continue payments as the child grew. Sometimes, he just disappeared, never to be heard from again. Thus, the care of the mother and child once again fell on the parish where they resided.

In 1834, the Poor Law Amendment Act took effect. The middle and upper classes had tired of taking care of the poor. Believing individuals were responsible for their own poverty, Parliament came up with a solution whereby the number of workhouses increased. The poor could pay their way by working. They were forced to work and live in harsh, inhumane conditions.

Richard Oastler, a proponent of the anti–Poor Law resistance, called these workhouses "prisons for the poor." It wasn't until after World War II that the Poor Laws were abolished completely in the United Kingdom.

About the Author

Janna MacGregor was born and raised in the boot heel of Missouri. She credits her darling mom for introducing her to the happily-ever-after world of romance novels. Janna writes stories where compelling and powerful heroines meet and fall in love with their equally matched heroes. She is the mother of triplets and lives in Kansas City with her very own dashing rogue and one smug but, not surprisingly, perfect pug. She loves to hear from readers. Visit her at www.JannaMacGregor.com.